ANNIHILATION

Holman jumped as the first torpedo exploded against the distant *Rodgers*. The nose of the destroyer disappeared in a cloud of smoke and debris, followed by three more explosions one after another along the length of the ship.

The concussion knocked Holman and his XO off their feet as a huge pall of smoke boiled upon itself where the *Rodgers* had been. Already stretching hundreds of feet in the air, a burst of flame broke through the black cloud.

Holman stared at the conflagration, still not believing his eyes as pieces of ship and debris rained down on the ocean surface and the *Stennis* flight deck. Where USS *John Rodgers* had been, it was as if nothing had existed. No ship, just a vacant expanse of ocean littered with debris where less than a minute ago over three hundred officers and sailors had manned a five-hundred-sixty-three-foot warship. Sucked into the storm of war, vanquished with honor, but gone, as if they had never existed, to become a footnote in naval history.

Don't miss the first novel in the epic combat series . . .

The Sixth Fleet
David E. Meadows

THE
SIXTH FLEET

SEAWOLF

DAVID E. MEADOWS

BERKLEY BOOKS, NEW YORK

THE SIXTH FLEET: SEAWOLF

A Berkley Book / published by arrangement with the author

PRINTING HISTORY
Berkley edition / November 2001

All rights reserved.
Copyright © 2001 by David E. Meadows.
Cover design and art by The Complete Artworks Ltd.

This book, or parts thereof, may not be reproduced in any form without permission.
For information address: The Berkley Publishing Group,
a division of Penguin Putnam Inc.,
375 Hudson Street, New York, New York 10014.

Visit our website at
www.penguinputnam.com

ISBN: 0-425-17249-X

BERKLEY®
Berkley Books are published by The Berkley Publishing Group,
a division of Penguin Putnam Inc.,
375 Hudson Street, New York, New York 10014.
BERKLEY and the "B" design
are trademarks belonging to Penguin Putnam Inc.

PRINTED IN THE UNITED STATES OF AMERICA

10 9 8 7 6 5 4 3 2 1

To the Navy-Marine Corps Team
"Forward . . . From the Sea"

Acknowledgments

My love and thanks to Felicity for her advice years ago that I should write what I know about. From her suggestion came the first manuscript for *The Sixth Fleet.*

I would like to thank Mr. Tom Colgan for his advice and encouragement. The ride for a new author in the world of publishing is exciting, and Tom took time from a most busy schedule to guide me through this new world. My thanks also to Ms. Samantha Mandor, his able assistant, for providing further insight to questions a new author has.

My gratitude to CDR Roger Herbert, U.S. Navy SEAL, and Maj. Andy Gillan, United States Marine Corps, for their expert technical advice. I would also like to acknowledge those in the Office of the Assistant Secretary of Defense for Public Affairs whose advice and encouragement were appreciated: Ms. Sharon Reinke, Mr. Art Horn, and LTCOL David "Skull" Riedel, United States Marine Corps. And a special thanks to Capt. (ret.) Frank Reifsnyder, former commanding officer of the nuclear attack submarine USS *Baltimore,* who read the manuscript and provided in-depth technical advice and encouragement. Any technical errors in this novel are strictly those of the author and should not be attributed to the individuals above, for there were times when technical advice was overridden by literary considerations.

CHAPTER 1

⚓

THE TRUCK ROLLED INTO THE DARK ALGERIAN VILLAGE, its engine off, its lights out, and the tires crunching noisily on the loose gravel. The moon had set a few hours earlier, leaving a clear sky filled with stars as the only source of light. The smell of the sea was carried on the slight wind.

"This is the village of my relatives," Bashir said softly to President Alneuf, the only freely elected president of an Algeria now in civil war, and Colonel Yosef. The overweight Bedouin's eyes nervously glanced from one side of the street to the other. "But the lights are out. They may be asleep— very unusual, very very unusual. I think I would feel better if there was some noise or something. . . ."

Bashir pulled the truck to one side, causing it to bounce several times as the left tires dropped a couple of inches when it moved off the road. Bashir pulled the hand brake. The metal-on-metal screech echoed through the silent streets. "*There's* some noise."

Yosef tightened his grip on the pistol in his lap and eased his finger onto the trigger. He shifted the barrel slightly so it pointed at the dashboard and away from President Alneuf, who sat between them. Yosef searched the shadows, expecting rebels—at any moment—to jump out and start firing. Bashir had better know what he's doing. Yosef didn't come this far to die at the hands of a bunch of smugglers. He was still wary of the overweight Bedouin, who just happened to be at the beach at the right time and who just happened to know how to get everyone to safety. But then, smugglers are supposed to know how to avoid the authorities—that is, successful smugglers.

"I think we should leave the truck here at the edge of the village until I have announced our presence, Colonel. It is possible my relatives are treating visitors with skepticism while the new government decides who are friends and who are enemies."

Bashir opened the door. The rusty hinges sounded like fingernails down a chalkboard. No interior light came on—burned out years ago and never replaced.

He leaned into the cab. "Mr. President, Colonel. My nephews and I will do a quick check. You wait here until we return. Okay?"

Colonel Yosef nodded reluctantly. "Don't be gone too long, Mr. Bashir."

Bashir motioned for his nephews. He turned to Yosef as he walked by the cab. "Colonel, if you should hear anything"— he waved his hands—"out of the ordinary, you know, like gunfire, screams, bloodcurdling yells, grenades, or mortar fire, then I would strongly recommend you take whatever actions you deem appropriate to protect the president."

Bashir touched his forehead and chin. Then he turned and, followed by his nephews, waddled off down the street. Yosef waited until the five men turned the corner and disappeared.

"Come on, President Alneuf," Colonel Yosef said as he shoved the pistol back into its holster. He opened the protesting door, reached into the cab, and half-pulled the fatigued president out.

Yosef turned to the Guardsmen in the back. Some napped among the few remaining sleeping sheep. The woman slept deeply, leaning against the cab of the truck. Her hands rested lightly on the sleeping baby curled in her lap.

"Sergeant, wake the men and get them out of the truck," Yosef whispered.

"What about the woman?"

"Leave her. She'll be safe," Yosef said. "And whatever you do, don't wake the baby." The last thing they needed was a squalling baby. Leave well enough alone. The longer Bashir was gone, the more likely it was they were being led into a trap. If so, Yosef intended to be ready.

The men jumped from the truck and formed around Colonel Yosef.

"Listen up," he said, his voice intentionally low. "Our driver and his nephews have gone into the village to find help. I don't want us trapped if it's a hostile crowd that returns."

The truck was parked near the last building in the village. It was a low, white building with no windows. A continuous, screened, twelve-inch opening ran around the top of the walls to allow air to circulate inside. Alongside the building a small ten-foot man-made hill rose, created from discarded construction residue. Desert plants had long since covered it. Across the road, in the distance, the sound of the unseen sea, rolling languidly against a beach, mixed with the sounds of the desert night.

"Corporal Omar, take one man with you and position yourself at the corner of the street to watch for their return. When you see them, I want to know how many; if the driver and his nephews are with them; if the driver and nephews appear to be with them willingly or as prisoners; and what weapons you see. Don't wait until they walk over you to get that information. As soon as you see them, make your impressions, and hurry back."

Corporal Omar saluted, touched a nearby Palace Guard on the shoulder, and the two men, with weapons at the ready, ran to the end of the block and crouched at the corner of a building where they could watch the approach from the village center.

"Sergeant Boutrous, take four others and position yourself across the street." Across from the man-made hill, a narrow ditch led downhill toward the sounds of the sea.

"The rest of you, come with me." Yosef lead President Alneuf and the others behind the low man-made hill.

One of the Guardsmen climbed to the top where he could see the two point men at the end of the street. He waved at

Sergeant Boutrous on the other side of the road, and Boutrous waved back.

Thirty minutes passed before the two point men appeared back at the truck. Yosef, who had crawled to the top with the lookout, hissed at the men. They scrambled over the top to him.

"Colonel, they're coming. Bashir is with his nephews and has three other men with them. With the exception of those Kalashnikov rifles, I saw no other weapons."

"Colonel!" shouted Bashir in his deep bass voice when the group arrived a minute later to find the truck empty, with the exception of the woman and child. "You can come out now! Everything is all right. These are my relatives! You are as safe as you can be in the new Algeria!"

The baby, awakened by Bashir's shout, started crying.

The Bedouin's ample stomach bounced as he laughed.

Yosef helped President Alneuf down the embankment. The Guardsmen followed. On the other side, Sergeant Boutrous waited motionless.

"Ah, Colonel, you did not trust Bashir? I, who have spent the last two days giving you my aid?" Bashir put his hands on his hips and roared with laughter.

"Mr. Bashir, we wanted to be prepared in the event you found a hostile reception," said Yosef. "As a great American once said, 'Trust, but verify.'"

"You are quite right, Colonel," Bashir replied seriously. Turning to President Alneuf, he said, "Mr. President, this is the elder of the village, Said Sami Abdel Yefsah, and these other two fine individuals are my cousins Memmi Baghat and Nawar Abu Nathir."

The men bowed their heads to President Alneuf, who shook each man's hand. The village elder, Said Yefsah, smiled broadly, displaying a deep cavern for a mouth devoid of teeth except for a lone horse-length tooth at the front.

"There was a visit by soldiers earlier today," said Bashir. "They searched the village, warning everyone about the consequence of harboring fugitives from the corrupt regime of Alneuf—my apologies, Mr. President—and the criminal military of the old government. Then they took eleven of the young men—who were slow to hide—for volunteer service in the new Algerian People's Army. Said Yefsah expects the young men to return soon."

"That explains the quiet when we arrived," Yosef said. It was a plausible explanation, but it seemed too plausible. The lives of the president and his men depended on him.

"Yes, Colonel, that plus the villagers expect more visits. When? They don't know," Bashir said, shrugging his shoulders.

"So," Bashir added. "Mr. President, does tea, coffee, cool water, platters of roasted lamb followed by fresh fruit sound attractive?"

President Alneuf looked at Yosef. "Colonel, should we accompany Mr. Bashir?"

"I think, Mr. President, that we have little choice."

Bashir's booming laughter broke the stillness of the night again. "Oh, Colonel, you are so precious! Come on, we don't have far to go and the truck will be all right here." He scratched under his arm and nodded at his relatives.

One of the cousin-nephews hopped up into the back of the truck to help down the woman and baby, whose cries increased with renewed vigor.

Bashir started to lead the way, stopped, turned, and cupped his hands to his mouth. "Sergeant!" Bashir shouted. "You and your four comrades should really get out of that ditch. It is where our sewage runs to the sea!"

Bashir turned to Yosef and in a confiding voice said, "It's why the grass is so much greener on that side than the hill you were hiding behind. Personally, I prefer the hill."

Bashir found this amusing. He burst into laughter, entertaining himself, as he led the group toward the center of the small village. The sergeant and his men rose, brushed themselves off, and scrambled over the ditch in their hurry to catch up with the group, Bashir's laughter guiding the way.

"Why are the lights off?" President Alneuf asked.

"The electricity is only turned on during certain times as the government repairs the damages to the grid system. The radio says any time now the electricity will be restored and we will have even better electricity than during your government, President Alneuf. Under the new government, we will receive people's electricity instead of just public electricity.

But between you and me, Mr. President, I suspect the people's electricity will cost more."

"Bashir, I detect your distrust of all governments. I know from our discussions the dissatisfaction you had for mine."

"No offense, my dear President, but governments are all alike. They are made up of people who crave power. Few politicians in today's world have the balls to do useful things with power because they're afraid they will offend someone and lose their precious position," said Bashir as they stopped in front of a two-story building. "But that is a subject requiring a long discussion, of which we lack the time. Here is where Sami Abdel Yefsah conducts the municipal business of this small community."

The village elder ran forward. Standing in front of the small, aged wooden door, Yefsah made a big production of reaching down the front of his aba to pull out a large skeleton key that hung from a leather thong around his neck. He held it up for all to see. A wide grin broke the weather-beaten wrinkles across his face, his lone tobacco-stained tooth dull in the faint starlight. Satisfied he had everyone's attention, Yefsah turned and slowly inserted the huge iron key into the ancient lock. Once it was firmly in the lock, he brushed his hands on his frock before reaching forward to turn the key. The ancient tumblers fell slowly into place, making a metallic creaking sound as they withdrew. Yefsah removed the key, dropped it down his cotton undershirt, and turned the iron handle. The door opened noisily to reveal a dark interior.

"Thank you so very very much, Said Yefsah," Bashir said respectfully as he brushed the small man aside.

Bashir squeezed through the doorway, ducking slightly to avoid the low rafter. "Wait until I have turned on a lantern!"

Rumbling sounds of the big man stumbling over things came from inside the room. A round of un-Islamic-like curses filtered through the door.

Yefsah took a deep breath, threw his hands out wide, looked at Yosef, and shook his head before he, too, disappeared into the dark.

Several seconds passed before a small light appeared in the far corner of the room. It rapidly grew brighter as Yefsah turned the wick up. Yefsah motioned Yosef and the men at the door inside. Bashir was pulling himself up from a tangle of folding chairs. Yefsah moved around the room lighting other gas lanterns.

"Ah, my friends," said Bashir as he brushed himself off. "Yefsah has once again come to our aid." He shoved the chairs aside and pulled the tail of his headdress forward to blow his nose in it. He tossed the tail over his shoulder, where it fluttered down against his back.

Bashir grabbed a few of the folding chairs and began handing them out. "As you can see, Mr. President, we lack the grandeur of the palace here."

Then realizing he was doing manual labor, Bashir shouted to his nephews-cousins, "Here, you lazy oafs! Finish setting up these chairs so the president and our friends can sit down."

The young men hastened to where Bashir stood and began to unfold chairs, placing them haphazardly around the room.

Yefsah pulled from his pocket a huge key ring, packed with an assortment of keys, at least a hundred, ranging in size from ones that looked like they were for small briefcases to giant skeleton keys that looked ancient, as if they would open a castle door. He immediately picked out a small key and opened a nearby cabinet. From the cabinet, he began throwing out cushions. Cushions of various sizes decorated with a myriad of bright crimson colors. When finished, he leaned far inside the cabinet to where only his butt stuck out and, with a lot of grunting and mumbling, pulled out a crepe-covered package. Squatting on his haunches, he undid the wrapping to reveal an ancient Turkish water pipe that, from the wear on the mouthpiece, had seen many decades of use and thousands of teeth.

"Mr. Bashir," Yosef said. "I want to put my men out to watch the roads."

"No, no, no, Colonel," Bashir objected, waving his finger back and forth. "First, there is only one road, not roads, and second, I have already sent one nephew and a cousin west for two kilometers where they will watch unobserved and see anything approaching from ten kilometers in that direction. To the east, I have sent one cousin and a relative of Yefsah to watch for patrols coming from that direction. You and your men are tired. You have an opportunity to sleep and rest while we provide protection." He slapped his chest.

"Thank you, Mr. Bashir, but I must insist."

"Fine, you may insist, but allow us to feed your men first. Yefsah's wives are, even as we speak, cooking a fine meal. Soon, you will have steaming platters of foule mudumas, humus bitahinna, and roasted lamb along with warm milk and hot bread. Maybe some feta covered with olive oil—no meal is complete without a little feta, don't you think?" Before Yosef could reply, Bashir continued. "Then, after they eat, you can send your men out. *Aiwa?*"

"Oh, Colonel, let the men rest," added President Alneuf. "We know we can't stay here long before the Algerian Liberation Front comes looking."

"Yes, sir, my President," Yosef reluctantly agreed. The thought of a hot meal caused his stomach to rumble. It had been over thirty-six hours since they had eaten. The two men were right. They needed to rest and they needed food.

"Good!" said Bashir with a quick chuckle, recognizing that he had won the argument.

In the corner, Yefsah lit tobacco he had meticulously stuffed into the bowl of the Turkish pipe. Then he stuck the flexible tip into his mouth and, with his cheeks caved inward from the effort, drew the smoke through the water. Dark aromatic bubbles rose through the slightly discolored water. How long the water had been in the bowl was something Yosef did not want to consider. Yefsah was soon passing the pipe around to those seated nearby.

Yosef sniffed the aroma, recognizing the smell of marijuana.

Bashir, watching Yosef, realized what the colonel smelled. "Ah, Colonel, tobacco is awfully expensive, while cannabis grows wild above the village," Bashir said. "Besides, alcohol is forbidden to those of the Moslem faith, and sex has been known to kill."

Yosef walked away without replying. He crossed the room and opened the door. The patch of light from the opened door, falling across the cobbled street in front of the building, was the only light visible.

Another burst of laughter filled the crowded room. Yosef didn't turn. He knew Bashir had included another Guardsman in his conversation.

Five minutes later, Yosef ducked back into the room to find several of his men already asleep. These two days had sapped even *his* energy. Some curled on the cushions. Others dozed sitting up, their heads drooping on their chests or against the walls or nodding sideways onto their shoulders. Yosef took a deep breath. Power naps during the rough trip from the west of Algiers, through the wadi south of the capital to avoid pursuing rebels, to this small seaside village east of Algiers had kept him going. The thought of a few hours of uninterrupted sleep drew him like a moth to a flame. It might be days before an opportunity like this arose again, he explained to his military skepticism.

Bashir waddled over to Yosef. President Alneuf squatted beside the village elder and the two were soon sharing the pipe. Yosef doubted that Alneuf even knew what he was smoking. The colonel didn't say anything. There were more important issues to worry about than the deposed president of Algeria sharing a toke.

Bashir touched Yosef's arm slightly. "Colonel, we know you can only stay for a short time. I am going to go check on the food, and then we need to discuss how we are going to get President Alneuf out of the country. Okay?" he asked. His thick eyebrows arched as he waited for Yosef to reply.

Several seconds passed before Yosef nodded. "Mr. Bashir," he began.

"Please, Colonel, call me Bashir. The *mister* makes me think you are talking to my father, Allah rest his soul." He looked up and threw his hands skyward for a second as if his father was watching from above.

"Bashir, I owe you an apology. I have not meant to be rude or anything. My job is to protect the president and with Algeria in chaos, it's hard to know who to trust. You are doing a great service to everyone in this room and, eventually, to Algeria itself. For that I thank you."

Bashir waved the compliment away. "No, Colonel. I am doing what any patriot would do. You too are very patriotic, and I have to admit I have wondered why." Then, in a whisper, he asked, "You are Jewish, are you not?"

Yosef failed to mask his surprise. He gave the question several seconds of serious thought before he replied defensively,

"Yes, but every Arab country has Jews living, working, worshipping alongside their Islamic brothers. Algeria is no different, except here we are allowed to join the military service."

"Yes, they do live in Arab countries, but with the rebels at the helm of state, your fellow Jews will suffer."

"I am Algerian first, Jewish second," Yosef replied, hoping the lie was not transparent. If they knew the truth, he doubted he would leave here alive. He touched the transmitter in his pocket. All in good time, he thought.

Bashir squeezed Yosef's arm. "And I thought I had problems being a member of a Libyan Bedouin tribe. Good luck, my friend. Some of my best friends are Jews . . . unfortunately, I can't remember any of their names." Bashir laughed at his joke.

Continuing to laugh, Bashir pushed the door further open before he turned. "Colonel, we will talk later. While I am gone, see if you can come up with some ideas how to get President Alneuf out of the country." Bashir squeezed through the doorway and, with rusty hinges grinding, pushed the door shut behind him.

Only a few Guardsmen remained awake. One was near a boarded-up window, a second sat on the floor with his back resting against the wall, a third sat in a folding chair—his weapon on the floor—watching other soldiers share the pipe with the president and the village elder.

President Alneuf passed the pipe to a Guardsman, stood, and motioned Yosef to him. The colonel strolled over to where the president stood.

"Colonel Yosef," said President Alneuf. "I need a telephone. See if you can find me one." Alneuf hiccuped. "Excuse me."

"Mr. President, if I may ask, why do you need a telephone? There is no one to call and the lines are probably being monitored even if you do call." Yosef suspected the strong marijuana was affecting Alneuf's faculties. The man's eyes looked slightly glazed.

"Colonel Yosef, I would be surprised if this village has a landline telephone, but I would be equally surprised if Bashir does not have a crate or two of mobile phones with forged cards and PIN numbers." He reached up and patted Yosef on the shoulder, then giggled. Alneuf put his hand over his mouth. "Sorry, Colonel. I don't know what caused me to do that."

President Alneuf shook his head, cleared his throat, and ran his hands down his wrinkled, torn suit coat in a failed attempt to restore it to some semblance of neatness. "As to whom I am going to call, there are some things that even a colonel in the Palace Guards does not need to know, and this is one of them. The telephone is necessary to arrange our way out of Algeria."

"Are you sure, Mr. President?"

"I am, Colonel. That is why I am the president and you are the colonel." He laughed softly. "Sorry, don't know why I said that. I am going to the bathroom. Said Yefsah says that through there"—he pointed to a curtain-covered doorway—"is a small one down the hallway and to the left." President Alneuf stumbled, and put his hand on the back of a chair to steady himself. "I am more tired than I thought."

Yosef watched Alneuf weave out of the room. And he watched him a few minutes later return white-faced, wringing his hands, water dripping on the carpet. Yosef ran his hand through his hair. He'd have a hell of a time getting Alneuf out of here if anything happened.

The front door opened and Bashir entered. Behind him, men poured into the room, scurrying and tripping over each other as they took shoulder-to-shoulder positions along the walls, stepping over a waking Guardsman, who looked up in shock at the armed group. Each man carried a weapon. Three had AK-47s, several carried shotguns, but the majority held ancient Kalashnikov rifles like the ones Bashir's nephews carried. The guns pointed inward at Yosef, President Alneuf, and the unprepared Guardsmen.

Yosef started to reach for his pistol, but Bashir waved his finger at him. "No, no, Colonel. There are more of us than you."

Yosef felt a sinking sensation in his stomach. To come so far and to be captured like this.

"What is the meaning of this, Bashir?" President Alneuf asked, taking a handkerchief from his inside coat pocket to dab sweat from his forehead.

"Ah, Mr. President. There is no meaning. None whatsoever. These young men from the village are loyal to you. They want to join your anti-revolution movement and hereby swear to protect you until we can get you out of the country. It is not as the colonel first thought. Right, Colonel?" Bashir winked at Yosef and laughed. "No, we are not here to capture, but to cooperate. I don't think I have had this much fun since my younger brother fell off the rocks into the sea. Took twenty-two stitches to sew his head up. You should have seen the expression on his face . . . much like yours, Colonel Yosef.

"But on a serious note, Colonel, I present you with more patriots for your small force." He executed a mock salute, drawing smiles from the villagers. "These are the young men whom the New Algerian Army drafted earlier today. See— they have returned."

The village men fell out of the encircling formation and eagerly moved forward to touch Alneuf and shake his hand. Several bent to kiss his hand, even as he shook his head trying to stop them. Some were as young as fourteen, with sparse facial hair. Most were in their twenties or older, sporting mustaches of varying degrees of black and gray. Alneuf patiently shook hands with each as they mobbed the charismatic Algerian leader.

Yosef stalked over to Bashir and whispered angrily, "Don't do that again, Bashir. We could have had an unfortunate incident." If he had given the word, his men would have fought, even if death had been the outcome.

Most who were asleep when the village force entered remained asleep.

Bashir grinned. "Yes, Colonel, once again you are correct. We could have, if your men had been awake. But the purpose of this exhibition was to show you that we are trustworthy, and what better way to prove it. But," he added as he laughed, "why give up what freedoms we had for the yokes the new government will place on us? You know the American saying, 'Better the devil you know'?"

Before Yosef could respond, the front door opened and several women dressed in the traditional chukkas and veils entered, carrying bowls of steaming rice, beans, and fresh-broiled lamb balanced precariously in their hands and along their arms. Pita bread lay haphazardly around the edges, instead of eating utensils. The aroma did what Bashir and the villagers had failed to do. It woke the remaining bone-weary Guardsmen, who anxiously edged forward.

The women shooed them away while two young girls, about sixteen, cleared a spot in the center of the room. One girl shook out a carpet she carried, and spread it on the cleared area, while others arranged the dishes and bowls of food on it. The sound of female tittering, incomprehensible to the men, accompanied the activity. As the older women moved away, more young girls entered bringing tea, juice, and water for the famished group. Several brought bowls of fresh fruit.

Everyone gradually stood, their eyes feasting on the banquet in front of them. They looked at Yosef, waiting for permission to begin. Bashir placed his hands over his stomach as his booming laughter echoed through the room. If he had to put up with this incessant laughter long, he could learn to hate their benefactor, thought Yosef.

An older woman, standing near Bashir, slapped his arm, causing the laughter to abruptly stop, and said something in a Berber dialect that Yosef failed to understand. Bashir blushed. Saliva filled Yosef's mouth. Hunger was a relentless foe.

"Gentlemen," Bashir announced. "The number-one wife of Said Yefsah, village elder, leader of this small village, and renowned for his choice of tobacco, welcomes you to her table and says that while you stare the food grows cold. Please eat." Then rolling his eyes, he said in a lower voice, "And, for the love of Allah, keep your hands away from the young women."

Like hungry wolves on unprotected sheep, the men dove into the food, bumping each other as they filled the pita bread, dipping it in the strong garlic humus before shoving the tangy mixture into their mouths. Olive oil and bits of humus trickled down their cheeks to be wiped away by dirty hands.

Bashir said something to the number-one wife. She hurried over, shoved the men apart, and hastily prepared two plates with a small helping from each dish—a *mizi* of everything. She carried the plates to President Alneuf and Yosef. Both men thanked her. She bowed her head and silently backed away.

Then, turning abruptly, she clapped her hands and the women silently departed, herding the young girls, reluctant to leave, ahead of them. The number-one wife was the last to depart. She held her head high with pride, knowing true men were massacring the food prepared under her supervision.

Bashir waited until she disappeared. He grabbed some pita bread, made a thick sandwich, and moved to where President Alneuf and Yosef sat eating.

"So, Colonel, have you given thought to what we do next?" Bashir asked as he took a huge bite of the soft bread. Grease dripped onto his aba. He pulled the tail of his headdress forward and wiped his mouth and chin. Then he blew his nose on it again before tossing it over his shoulder.

President Alneuf looked up. "Said Bashir, do you have a telephone that I may use?" Alneuf broke off a small bit of pita bread to go with his chicken.

Bashir's eyes opened in amazement. "A telephone, Mr. President? You do realize, sir, that I would suspect the new government is monitoring telephone calls to anywhere you may call? It would not surprise me if your voice would set off alarms."

"I understand, Said Bashir, but I would also suspect that you have a cellular telephone that will be hard to locate?"

"Yes, that is true. I do have a telephone, but as to whether they can locate it or not, that remains to be seen." Bashir looked at Yosef, who nodded.

"Mr. President, maybe it would be better to wait to use the phone until morning. Then, if they are able to find us, we will at least have had a night's rest before running again," Yosef added. "Plus, we do not want to endanger the village by calling from here."

Bashir searched his pockets. "I know I have one here somewhere."

"I thank both of you for your concern, but I need to call if we are to get out of the country safely. I appreciate your concern, Colonel, but I hardly think that one phone call from a mobile phone is going to endanger this village."

"Can I ask who you intend to call?" Yosef asked.

"No, I think not, Colonel. The less you know about this phone call, the less you have to worry."

"Okay, Mr. President," Bashir replied. He pulled out a small GSM cellular phone with the word *Motorola* embossed in silver lettering across the top. He flipped open the mouthpiece and punched in the PIN number. "Here you are, Mr. President. Behind the curtains there"—he pointed to the back wall—"is a small stage. If you stand near the boarded window you will have better reception."

The president stood, brushed his pants off, and took the phone. "I thank you both for all you have done. I have debated this, but I feel I am endangering you and every loyal Algerian fighting on my behalf. Let's hope this works," he said, holding up the cellular telephone.

President Alneuf strolled to the curtains, lifted them slightly, and disappeared behind them.

"Colonel, a debate with oneself lacks a dissenting opinion," Bashir said, noticing the concern in Yosef's face.

PRESIDENT ALNEUF PUNCHED IN THE MEMORIZED NUM-ber. When the American ambassador had given him the number months ago, he had nearly thrown it away. While he had accepted it with grace, his initial reaction had been anger and disgust that America believed it had the right to offer protection to the leader of another sovereign country. The audacity! He had placed the number in his suit coat and forgotten about it until a couple of days later when he went to wear the coat again and rediscovered the number. For some reason, he never quite fathomed why, he had periodically pulled the number out, staring at it, until eventually he had committed it to memory. However reluctant he might feel, the future of his country might well be in the hands of America.

The numbers punched by Alneuf routed his call to a nondescript, unoccupied apartment in a southern suburb of Algiers. The electronic communications system, hidden in the walls behind the telephone receptacle, took the incoming call, changed its sequence, and returned it to the telephone system. There, the PKI (Public Key Infrastructure) coded program added to a fake number caused the Algerian telephone system to identify it as originating from Cairo and going to a little-known Algiers travel bureau. The system directed the call to the telephone at that address, where a slave wire, expertly melded into the lines, piped the call to a small electronic device located on top of a nearby telephone pole. The call then went covertly into the line leading to the American Embassy.

President Alneuf waited as the phone rang several times.

PAUL MCMILLAN, THE DUTY OFFICER FOR THE CHIEF OF station at the American Embassy, heard the telephone ring, but finished slamming the top slice of bread on his peanut-butter-and-jelly sandwich before reaching over and answering. Twenty years doing this job and, for the first time in his career, he wished he was back at Falls Church pushing papers.

"Hello," he said, taking a large bite of the sandwich at the same time, believing the phone call originated inside the embassy. He pushed a wisp of gray hair, matted to his forehead from the heat, back across the top of his head, leaving a few crumbs of bread in its place.

"Hello, my friend. I was given this number to call in the event that I wanted to take a trip for my health. I understand that travel arrangements can be made through your excellent services?"

Paul coughed as the peanut butter and jelly clung to the roof of his mouth. He moved the phone away momentarily to spit the unchewed mess onto the plate, and ran his finger inside to free what was stuck to the roof of his mouth.

"Yes," he said, coughing twice, as he flipped on the nearby recorder. "We have many nice packages that may be of use to you, sir. May I ask which one you are interested in?"

"I am interested in the 'Big Apple,'" Alneuf replied.

Paul ran his finger down the list of code words taped to the desk beside the phone. He found "Big Apple."

"Jesus Christ!" he said aloud to himself.

"No, just a humble traveler who would enjoy a short tour to the Big Apple."

"Yes, sir. New York is available at this time of the year. The heat is extremely high right now, but I am certain that we can arrange the flight, hotel reservations, and follow-on transportation that you require. I will need to know how we can contact you."

"Ah, yes, my friend. Your friend Mark contacted acquaintances of my father years ago. I will visit that same chalet tomorrow night. I can give you a call at that time. I would give you this number, but I doubt that I will be here much longer. My travel plans are slightly erratic at this time, you understand?"

"I understand, sir. My name is Paul McMillan and I will be your representative until travel is arranged and delivered."

"Thank you, sir, and when may I expect confirmation?"

"I will be expecting your call tomorrow night. I am very familiar with Mark's visit and, if we are unable to talk further about your plans, you can expect our travel representative to arrive the same way my friend Mark did."

"Thank you. I look forward to meeting with your representatives tomorrow night. I am booking this with the understanding that there are no strings attached for me using your company. In other words, I am not obliged to use you in the future or to stay with your travel agency after I arrive? Right now, I find no other travel bureau available with the same offers as yours," Alneuf said.

"No, sir. Our policy is quite clear, as our representative told you. We are a respectable company whose only desire is to see our customers have the degree of freedom to choose their own holidays."

"Thank you. I look forward to meeting you, Mr. McMillan."

The agent waited until the phone clicked on the other end. Damn! The whole country and world was looking for President Alneuf, and he'd just gotten off the phone with him. The rebels hadn't captured the deposed president as their radio broadcasts had reported.

He hurriedly scribbled the appropriate log notations, and checked to see that the voice-actuated recorder was reset to the intercept-and-record position. He tossed the digitized tape of their conversation onto the table.

Thirty seconds later, Paul was out of the windowless, steel-lined compartment. CIA work was never as glamorous as novels made it, but instances like this made it rewarding. Stepping into the corridor, the agent hurried down a flight of stairs, two steps at a time, to the second floor and onto the bal-

cony. A Marine sentry watched the crowd below in the courtyard.

"Lots of people?" Paul asked as he approached.

"They're still delivering them," the Marine replied.

Another truck pulled in front of the embassy. About twenty
people, some with families, crawled out of the military vehicle and were escorted by unsmiling rebel sentries to the entrance.

"How many now?" Paul asked.

"Over six hundred as of this morning."

Paul shook his head. "Well, we should be all right as long
as they leave the electricity and water alone."

The Marine looked at him. "Haven't you heard? They
turned the water off an hour ago."

The truck pulled away. Combat-garbed Marines opened the
gate to allow the refugees inside the compound.

"The *Nassau* amphibious readiness group is closing the
coast," the young Marine offered. "Then we'll show those
assholes who the hell they're messing with."

"Can't get here soon enough for my taste," Paul said as he
eased past the sentry. "Good luck, Marine. See you later."

The Marine waved. From the distance, sporadic gunfire
echoed through the night. Lights in the building had been
turned off to reduce targets for the snipers, who periodically
peppered the embassy. The number of sniper incidents had increased today. Since 1800 hours, two Marines and two
refugees had been wounded. The wounded Marines were already back on the perimeter.

Paul reached the ambassador's offices and entered without
knocking.

Thirty minutes later the message left the embassy, released
by the chief of station, to the duty officer at Falls Church, Virginia.

THE CIA DUTY OFFICER PRINTED THE MESSAGE AS SOON
as it appeared on her console. She ripped it from the printer
and hurried upstairs to the deputy director's office. The secretary said the deputy director was out jogging, but was due
back soon. She offered to wait for the former Marine Corps

colonel's return, but the secretary said she'd see that he got it. Okay, the duty officer said reluctantly, and then left. But she'd return later, she said to herself. She'd return for two reasons. One, professionally, she wanted to ensure that the deputy director received the message. Two, he was single and so was she; he was much older, but she preferred them that way.

An hour later the deputy director strolled through the door as his secretary locked the safes and turned off her computer.

"Going home?" he asked as he rubbed his short salt-and-pepper hair with a small towel that he always took with him when he ran.

"Yes, sir," she replied. "I put the phone calls and messages on your desk that came in while you were out scaring the natives, running around the park at this time of night."

"Still daylight, Sheila. Got to run sometime or all that beer and pasta I love will go right to the tummy."

"It's disgusting anyway, a man your age without a beer gut. Not to mention without a wife. What do you think you're doing to the world's image of the American couch-potato male?"

He chuckled as he moved to the inner door. "Good night, Sheila."

"Good night, sir," the elderly secretary replied as she pulled the door shut behind her.

He saw the stack of work on his desk that had piled up during his two hours away, nearly started to go through it, but decided at the last minute that a quick shower was more attractive. If he started through the stack, he'd find himself sitting there an hour later, his wet gym shorts stuck to the leather upholstery with the air-conditioning behind him aggravating his sports arthritis.

Thirty minutes later, dressed in Docksider slacks and an open-necked Gucci navy-blue shirt, the deputy director turned the air-conditioning down before he sat down and began methodically going through the stack of messages and phone calls. He shuffled them periodically to keep the stack as neat as possible as he worked through the pile. Being single allowed him to stay as late as he wanted; sometimes he slept on the couch rather than go home.

Meticulously he read each note, one at a time. Several re-

quired phone calls, and he made them. Some he put back in
his in box for tomorrow. Others, he read, crumpled, and
tossed into the nearby burn bag for the night staff to shred.
Around nine o'clock he reached the message the duty officer
had brought earlier; at the same time she appeared in the
doorway.

"Yes?" he said, his eyebrows raising in question as he
looked at her.

"Sir, I was just checking on the message I brought up from
the chief of station in Algiers about President Alneuf."

"What message?" he asked as he glanced down at the one
in his hand. "Wait a minute, here it is."

He read it, slowly lifting the phone as his eyes moved down
the message. "Go tell the chief of station to expect instructions within the next four hours and tell him that, yes, we will
arrange President Alneuf's evacuation." He punched the programmed telephone number on the STE-II secure telephone.
Looking up, he saw her still standing there.

"Go!" he said. "Go and relay my instructions to him immediately!" He waved her away.

"Do you want to chop it before it goes?" she asked as she
backed away.

"No, just tell him we're working the issue, we agree and
will be back to him ASAP!" he replied sharply. "Now get
down there and get that reply out. When they've acknowledged, come tell me."

She ran out of the room. At least he'd invited her back, she
thought. There was something about Italian men that . . .
Well, later. First things first. She ran down the stairs, not bothering to wait for the elevator.

The director answered the phone. "Mr. Digby-Jones," the
deputy director said, "we need to go secure." Then he relayed
the information and tactfully guided the political appointee
through the maze of what they had to do.

CHAPTER 2

⚓

"WHERE IS MR. DIGBY-JONES?" THE PRESIDENT SCANNED the security council members seated around the table, and they shook their heads and shrugged their shoulders.

After several seconds when no one answered, President Crawford continued impatiently. "Here I am late for a meeting and he still can't be here when I arrive." He threw his pencil down on the table. "And, this is a meeting where the *advice* of the director of Central Intelligence would be appreciated, and what do we have? No DCI is what we have!"

President Crawford shook his head, started to say something, thought better of it, and instead, looked at the secretary of defense. "Roger, bring me up to date on what we're doing militarily."

"Mr. President, the USS *Stennis* is off the coast of Norfolk, conducting routine sea trials and carrier qualifications for a bunch of F-14s and F-18s out of Oceana. She's been ordered to return to Norfolk to outfit for an immediate deployment to the Mediterranean. After turnaround, two F-14 fighter squadrons from Oceana, will bingo aboard as soon as she clears the Norfolk channel. Two F-18 squadrons—one of them the Marine Moonlighters from Cherry Point, a couple of

S-3A antisubmarine birds from Jacksonville and an E-2C early-warning aircraft out of Norfolk. Estimated time for the *Stennis* battle group to deploy is three to four days after return."

Roger Maddock paused to take a sip of water. "I'd estimate nearer five days for the carrier battle group to get organized, outfitted, and turned around. At max speed, she can be at the Strait of Gibraltar eight days later. Commander in chief, U.S. Atlantic Fleet, is in the process of identifying the escorts for the battle group and will have that done today."

"Escorts?"

"Yes, sir. The cruisers, destroyers, auxiliary ships needed to round out protection for the carrier and provide the logistic support to keep the group steaming."

"So, the United States is going to have to wait nearly two weeks before a carrier battle group is in the Med?" Crawford asked, leaning forward, his hands spread out on the table.

"Yes, sir, Mr. President," the secretary of defense replied sheepishly. "We only have eight carriers. In the meantime, European Command has ordered two squadrons of Air Force F-16s from our northern Italian base at Aviano to Brindisi near the tip of Italy's boot. They arrive today to augment the four other F-16s that landed yesterday. Those four, already in Brindisi, are flying air protection for the RC-135 reconnaissance missions. An Air National Guard C-130 transport aircraft, carrying additional Air Force F-16 ground-crew personnel, arrived a few hours ago. We are moving airborne tankers from the States to Brindisi. I have given approval to recall the RC-135 involved in drug-interdiction operations in South America, and the Air Force will turn it around to the Med within the next forty-eight hours."

"Will those F-16s help if I order the evacuation of citizens from Algeria?"

"Sir, the F-16s won't have the range to reach Algeria from Brindisi until the tankers arrive, but they will be able to provide combat air protection over Sigonella and Souda Bay in the event Libya initiates another attack. They are already providing air protection over the survivors of the USS *Gearing*."

"Roger, we needed the air protection and the carrier in the Mediterranean before the attack. Why didn't we have those?

Doesn't seem to me we had much in the Med when this Libyan attack occurred."

"Mr. President, we don't have the maritime forces to patrol everywhere, sir. We made a conscious decision, years ago, to deploy a carrier in the Med for only a few months a year. It seemed acceptable at the time. It gave us our show of force and kept our presence evident, while giving us the flexibility to show the flag elsewhere. We just do not have enough carriers to keep one in the Mediterranean permanently."

"Seems pointless to me, Roger. We didn't have a carrier this time, which brings another question. Why so many aircraft parked so close together in Sigonella?" President Crawford picked up a photograph in front of him and tossed it to the secretary of defense, who was sitting to his left. It nearly slid off the end of the brightly polished conference table. "Why? I want to know why! Look at this photo taken before the attack. What the hell was the admiral thinking?"

Roger Maddock peered over his bifocals at the satellite photograph of Sigonella Air Base, and decided it would be pointless to point out to the president that the commanding officer of Sigonella is a Navy captain, not an admiral.

"It's our only major base remaining in the Mediterranean, Mr. President. It's a logistics base, not a fighter base. It's not as big as Rota, Spain, so the aircraft have to be parked closer together."

"And I guess we think Libya didn't know this? Didn't the Navy do any thinking before they crowded this base?" President Crawford asked sarcastically.

"No one expected the Libyans to do something like this," Roger replied meekly. "Besides, the Italians are responsible for the air defense of Sigonella. It is a NATO base."

General Eaglefield, sitting beside the secretary of defense, wiggled uncomfortably in his seat and bit his lower lip in an attempt to keep his comments to himself. Rebutting the president of the United States—his commander in chief—was not a good career move. What he wanted to say was that the crowded situation in Sigonella was caused by the administration, not the military. Crawford and his two predecessors had closed most overseas bases, but had never reduced operational commitments, and had never ever closed a base stateside even when the military had no use of it. The American military was a political pull-toy for the president and Congress. Policing the world was good politically, and when the political heat got hot, then a little military action overseas took the American public's mind off it. Look at that aspirin factory in Sudan.

To meet the never-changing operational tempo, the military overloaded the remaining overseas bases. Sigonella and Souda Bay were two of them. If Rota had remained open, the scale of the catastrophe in Sigonella would never have occurred. But he didn't say it. He probably should have, but what would it have accomplished? If he ever wrote his memoirs he'd say it then. General Eaglefield looked around the room. With the exception of him and General Stanhope, not a soul around the table had one day of genuine military experience.

"Yeah, and no one expected the Japanese to sail halfway across the Pacific Ocean and sink the United States Pacific Fleet in 1942 either. You'd think our Navy would remember Pearl Harbor." President Crawford rubbed his temples, and then in a softer voice continued. "Roger, update me when this has been worked out. I want to read the reports on the Gaeta attacks and on the USS *Gearing*."

"Sir, it was 1941."

"1941?"

"Yes, sir, the attack on Pearl Harbor was in 1941 and the Navy does remember."

"Okay, Roger. Point taken. What is the status on rescuing the survivors of the USS *Gearing*?"

"USS *Miami* is headed into the Gulf of Sidra to rescue the survivors. We have no helicopters in the Med with the legs to reach that far, and the Italians and Greeks refuse to commit their own that close to the Libyan mainland. The *Nassau* battle group is moving into position off the coast of Algiers to conduct what is beginning to look like an opposed evacuation."

"Roger, Algeria is very important, but I want those sailors rescued. I want them out of the water, and if I have to, I'll send the entire damn Army into Libya. I swear I will. But I want those Americans out of the water first! Have you been reading the papers? They're coming home!" He slammed his fist down on the table.

"The American public is firmly behind you, sir, on the decision to retaliate against Libya," Franco Donelli offered. "The polls show—"

"According to the battle-damage assessment provided by that Defense Intelligence Agency, those Tomahawks wiped out most of the Libyan senior military leadership," Bob Gilfort said, interrupting. "The question this will pose is: Who now is in charge of the Libyan military? The junta has only retained its power through the support of the Libyan military."

The president nodded his head. "Bob, Roger; it is a disgrace to America for our young men and women to still be out there, floating in the middle of the Mediterranean. How long has it been?"

"About thirty hours, Mr. President. As I said, sir, Sixth Fleet has detached the USS *Miami* from the *Nassau* battle group. It'll take her twenty-four hours to get there."

"Miami?"

"Yes, sir. She's the fast-attack submarine that launched the Tomahawk retaliatory strike."

The secretary of state, Robert Gilfort, raised his hand and interjected, "Mr. President, if I may, those sailors are important, but so is our situation in Algiers." He unfolded a sheet of paper in front of him. "I have an update from our ambassador to Algeria, Mrs. Becroft. She says refugees are continuing to be trucked into the compound. Three hours ago over five hundred refugees were crammed into it. The portable toilets are kaput and unless we do something soon—she estimates within the next forty-eight hours—the embassy will have a major health crisis on their hands. She wants to know how much longer before the Marines show up. And she wants more Marines on the ground at the embassy.

"Options? Do we have any, or are we being backed into a corner where we don't?" President Crawford asked, his chin cradled in his hands. "What is going on in North Africa?" he asked quietly.

"No, sir, I don't think we're in the proverbial corner yet," replied Gilfort. "The British have asked to coordinate the evacuation of their citizens in the event they are unable to dispatch their rescue force down there in time. His Majesty's Government says that it will take seven days for their forces to arrive."

"Seven for them, twelve for us, and they're asking us for help? We should have had a stronger presence in the Med than what we have."

"Yes, sir," Roger Maddock added. "I believe the British think *we* already have sufficient forces in the Med and *they* don't. The British are outfitting a carrier task force around the HMS *Invincible*—their remaining Harrier aircraft carrier. We are discussing combined operations with their forces and ours once they arrive in the area. We should have an answer shortly."

"Good," the president said, nodding his head. "About time some of our allies showed up." He paused a moment. "Sorry about that. If I depend on anyone in Europe, it's the British. It's unfortunate that our relationship is so low-key nowadays. We should have been more attuned on how a common European currency and the growing European Community was going to affect American influence. I sometimes wonder how the common British citizen feels about being ruled from the Continent."

"Sir?"

"Nothing, Bob. Just thinking out loud. Back to the subject at hand. CNN had a news bulletin just before this morning's earlier, disastrous press conference; a bulletin that a reporter from the *Washington Times*—Franco, I want him out of the White House Press Corps; I told you once and I mean it. He never sticks to the script. According to CNN, the Libyans say they acted in self-defense after the USS *Gearing* fired on their aircraft and ships while violating Libyan territorial waters."

"Yes, sir. I received a short communiqué from Ambassador Cannets about that. Alex says the Libyans are displaying radar images and photographs to anyone who will listen at the United Nations, hoping to prove that the *Gearing* was less than nine nautical miles off their coast."

"What does that tell me, Bob?"

"Sir, international convention recognizes twelve nautical miles as the legal limit of territorial waters."

"And, Mr. President, if I may add," Roger Maddock said,

drawing the president's attention. "The *Gearing* was directed to remain outside fifteen nautical miles for the Freedom of Navigation operation. She had GPS' and her normal complement of navigational equipment and personnel. There is nothing to suggest she was closer."

"Mr. President," General Stanhope said. "My apologies to the secretary of defense, whom I have not had an opportunity to brief on this bit of information, but we may have a problem concerning that."

"Go ahead, General."

"Late yesterday, our analysts discovered the geopositional readings coming from four GPS satellites that provide most of the navigational data for the Mediterranean are incorrect."

"Incorrect?"

"Yes, sir. It seems that anyone using GPS in the Mediterranean will discover they are five nautical miles further south than what their displays show."

"Are you saying the USS *Gearing* could have been inside Libyan territorial waters?" Bob Gilfort asked, leaning forward to look around Franco Donelli at General Stanhope.

"Yes, sir. I guess what I am saying is that we could have been as close as ten nautical miles, if the USS *Gearing* was using GPS for its navigation."

"Mr. President, I recommend we keep that information within this room. I submit we remain firm in that the USS *Gearing* was outside of Libyan territorial waters . . . that's our story and that should be our Bible. Deny, deny, deny," Roger Maddock added, slamming his hand down on the table. "Screw the Libyans."

Crawford ignored the SecDef. "General Stanhope, as director of the National Security Agency, you must have some reason or facts to support this. Why do you think the satellite readings were off? Was there a malfunction or something?"

"Mr. President, we are investigating, but we cannot discount tampering, either by a cyber attack against the satellites or technical malfunction in the GPS software. We are passing this information to the Joint Chiefs of Staff. They will notify European Command. By this afternoon, our forces will be using conventional navigational techniques until the GPS error is corrected."

"Thank you, General. Roger, keep me notified." The president turned to the secretary of state. "Bob, before we start discussions on Algeria, I need State Department to develop a position paper in the event we have to admit that the *Gearing* was in Libyan waters. But make sure our position reflects that I don't care if the *Gearing* was skirting the beaches from a hundred yards out; they attacked our warship without provocation and then launched a dastardly, unforgivable attack against our bases in Italy and Crete.

"Now, quickly to Algeria, do we have any contact with the new government?"

"No, sir. Not at this time. Attempts to contact government offices result in either constant ringing of the phones with no answer, or a continuous busy signal. And for obvious reasons, we can't send someone around from the embassy. They refuse to allow anyone to leave. We have told the insurgents surrounding our embassy that we want to discuss the situation with their authorities. They promised to relay the message, but no reply has been received.

"We have several rambling press releases from the rebel government. None of which make much sense. One warns the United States that the Mediterranean is a North African sea, that we are intruders who are not welcome, and that the new Algerian government intends to keep us from ever returning again. A radio broadcast later in the day said basically the same thing: that Satanic American forces had been wiped from the face of the Mediterranean and that our Navy would never enter it again. The Mediterranean is closed to America."

"No one is going to tell America where its Naval forces can go or not go!"

"Mr. President," Roger Maddock said. "We still have forces in the Med. In fact, the *Nassau* battle group has recovered its Harriers from Sigonella and is heading toward its station off Algiers. We expect them in range of the Algerian capital within the next twelve hours. Then, they'll be in position to commence evacuation of the embassy. From Norfolk and Little Creek we are preparing another amphibious task force around the amphibious carrier *Kearsarge* and the *Ponce*—an older, but quite capable LPD. They will embark a full Marine air-ground task force, called a MAGTF, with tanks, aircraft, and two battalion landing teams, totaling about two thousand troops on the two ships. The *Nassau* has a smaller MAGTF embarked, centered around a smaller team of approximately one thousand Marines. That being said, the *Nassau* is capable of bringing out the refugees, if we have to go ahead with the evacuation prior to the arrival of the *Kearsarge* amphibious task force. The *Kearsarge* and *Ponce* will arrive at Morehead City tomorrow to start embarking the Marines. It will take three days to completely embark the Marines and their equipment. We expect them to enter the Med a few days behind the *Stennis* battle group."

"Roger," Bob Gilfort said. "I don't think we can wait for their arrival. The ambassador demands that we pull them out now!"

"Bob, I understand that," Maddock replied, an edge of impatience in his voice. "The *Nassau* is capable of doing the job under emergency circumstances. If I remember correctly, the ambassador cried wolf about sending in the Marines last year during the food riots."

"I think that's uncalled for, Roger," Gilfort replied sharply. "She provided an honest assessment from her viewpoint at the time."

"Let's hope she's reasoning more calmly this time," Maddock replied.

Gilfort opened his mouth to reply, but Maddock continued, cutting him off. "Sixth Fleet is on board the submarine *Albany,* en route to the *Nassau* to personally take charge of the evacuation, but if we go in and the Algerians heavily oppose the operation, we lack the airpower to counter it!"

"But we'll have the Marines," President Crawford added.

"Yes, sir, Mr. President. We have the Marines, but even Marines are not invincible. If we send them in, they will be taking on an entire country by themselves. Our problem is we have abandoned the Mediterranean—"

"That's not exactly accurate!" Bob Gilfort interrupted.

"We have sent the wrong message to an area known for its instability. Today, we are seeing the results!" Roger Maddock finished, ignoring the secretary of state's outburst. Then he looked at Gilfort. "It's just what I told you two years ago, Bob."

"You're overreacting, Roger," Bob Gilfort said. "We are not the world's policeman! Let them sort out their own mess."

"If we're not the world's policeman, then why in the hell—"

"Roger," President Crawford interrupted, patting the air in front of the two men to stop the confrontation. "Do we have sufficient forces in the Mediterranean to evacuate the embassy if necessary?"

Maddock took a deep breath. "Yes, sir, Mr. President. But Defense Intelligence Agency estimates, if we put the Marines in the *Nassau* amphibious task force ashore, they will be outnumbered anywhere from ten to twenty to one."

"Could the Marines win against such odds?"

"Mr. President, they would fight until either the Algerians retreated or every one of those brave American souls were dead. And there would be a lot of brave American souls dead. We need the *Stennis* battle group. With the carrier, we can project our power as far inland as we need; without it, we're limited to coastal operations."

"The newspapers would murder the administration, Mr. President," Franco Donelli added.

Silence greeted the secretary of defense's prognosis, with the exception of Bob Gilfort, who muttered, "Still overreacting, I think."

President Crawford cleared his throat. "Okay, Roger, I have the picture. The last thing I want are more dead Americans. Here's what I want you to do," the President said. "I want the *Stennis* deployment speeded up." He waved his hand at Maddock as Roger opened his mouth to speak. "No, hear me out. I don't know how you're going to speed up the deployment, that's your problem. Just do it. How about our carrier in the Persian Gulf?"

"Mr. President, we have moved the USS *Roosevelt* from the Persian Gulf into the Gulf of Oman. I am reluctant to move it further because of the lack of counterbalance to the Iranian Navy."

"Roger, move the carrier. I want it in the Mediterranean along with its escorts ASAP. Okay? Tell the Air Force to provide that counterbalance. They've been arguing for years they can be as effective as a carrier; the Persian Gulf is a great place for them to prove it."

"Yes, sir, Mr. President," he replied, his eyebrows arching as he considered the consequences. He turned to his military aide and whispered the necessary instructions to redeploy the *Roosevelt* from Fifth Fleet to Sixth Fleet.

"Roger, how long will it take the Persian Gulf carrier to arrive in the Med?" the president asked.

Roger looked at his military aide, a surface warfare Navy captain, who responded for the secretary. "Mr. President, four days at full speed to the Suez Canal, allow one-day transit time. I estimate five days for the carrier battle group to enter the Med and another two to two and a half days transit to the Algiers area."

"Thanks, Captain," the president replied. "It's not off Algiers I want that carrier. Roger, I want to bomb Libya. I want to eliminate her entire Air Force and Navy. I want to send a message to Libya, and any other nation that contemplates attacking the United States, a very visible lesson. Six Tomahawks cannot balance what the Libyans did to us."

"Yes, sir, Mr. President." Behind the secretary of defense the military aide took copious notes. "We'll use the Air Force—"

"I would hope so, Roger," the president interrupted. "But the Navy took the brunt of the Libyan attack. I want the Navy to lead the action. They have a score to settle and let's give them the opportunity to settle it."

Franco nodded. "Navy Avenges *Gearing*." He could see the sympathetic headlines now. The polls would swing even further to the right. The administration was going to look good in the eyes of the public. He caught himself as he nearly laughed out loud.

"And," the president continued, "I want the world to know we are ramping up for retribution. I want the Libyans to sit in their box and watch the American might build up. I want them sweating, worrying, wondering about when we will strike. Emotions are at fever pitch throughout the United States. I was watching CNN earlier. Did any of you see the over ten thousand American demonstrators surrounding the United Nations building? Do you know what that says? It's a hundred degrees in New York and we actually have New Yorkers— New Yorkers, I'm telling you—leaving their air-conditioned offices, turning off their television sets, and showing their anger over something that has happened to their fellow Americans over half a world away. New Yorkers! Can you believe that?"

He paused and took a sip of water. "The average American doesn't even watch the evening national news, much less understand what is happening on the international scene. Today, we have the entire country more mobilized, more together than since Desert Storm. For that alone, I will move forces into the area to show American resolve."

He paused, then added, "Don't be shocked. I know I'm viewed as a dove in world politics, but the American people demand action and I want to show them that the Crawford administration is taking steps to protect American lives and interests. That unprovoked attacks on Americans will receive appropriate responses. We are going into the Med and we're going in force. No one is going to keep us out. Let no nation doubt the willpower of America to use its military force. American maritime might is far from dead." He suddenly realized that he had found the key to the legacy for his administration. This crisis would carry his name into the history books.

"Let's move on. Bob, have we located President Alneuf yet? Do we know what happened to him?"

The secretary of state shook his head.

"Mr. President," General Stanhope, the director of the National Security Agency, said from the other end of the table. "We have a report from the Air Force RC-135 Rivet Joint that flew a West Mediterrean mission yesterday about an Algerian MiG attacking a fishing trawler east of Algiers. The trawler subsequently beached itself. No final analysis on the attack yet, but a large-scale search of the area is being conducted by Islamic forces. Considering the fighting, and the chaotic situation in Algeria, the number of troops involved in the search convinces us that it is out of proportion for a fishing crew. We believe President Hawali Alneuf may have been aboard the fishing trawler and is somewhere east of Algiers, either fleeing for the border, or gone to ground."

The door burst open and the bespectacled former bookkeeper who was now the director of Central Intelligence ran into the room amidst a flurry of stammering apologies. Papers fluttered from the binder he carried under his right arm. He snatched for them, knocking his bow tie askew.

"Farbros," growled the president. "If you're late again to one of my meetings, just continue home. I think my time is more valuable than yours."

Farbros bent over behind his chair to pick up the papers. Pens and notes fell out of his shirt pocket. He made a mad grab for them as more tumbled out.

"Yes, sir, Mr. President! Yes, sir. There was something I wanted to make sure was accurate before I came. It's just that—" Farbros stammered.

"Farbros, next time just come. I'll decide whether a piece of information is important enough for you to go back for it. Sit down and catch up."

Farbros Digby-Jones pulled the heavy chair out, unbuttoned his blue business suit coat, and sat down. His small frame had a childlike appearance in the massive leather chair. He licked his thumb and flipped through his papers as he attempted to return them to proper order. His thick coffee-colored hair lay jumbled on his head.

"Mr. President, General Eaglefield has additional information on our preparations to respond to the Libyan attack," Roger Maddock offered.

The president nodded to the chairman of the Joint Chiefs of Staff, who sat reluctantly, quietly to the left of the secretary of defense.

"Mr. President," General Jeff Eaglefield began. "This is a preliminary status, and as we firm up the timetables, we will have a better picture on response time and the forces we can bring into play.

"The Air Force is prestaging five C-5s to Fort Bragg to transport the 82nd Airborne. We are waiting for Italian permission to move the first elements of the 82nd Airborne to Sicily. We expect to receive that permission today. The Seabees estimate they'll have Sigonella Airfield operational within the next twenty-four hours. The Army will deploy a Patriot air-defense system to protect themselves and provide base protection against further air attacks.

"The light mechanized infantry at Fort Steward is mobilizing, and the Navy is working out transportation arrangements to move them. Depending on the scope of response and the concept of operations, we can move an entire division by air in four days."

"What can we do with them in Italy?"

"Mr. President, they increase your options, ranging from invading Libya to conducting an opposed evacuation of Algiers. Either way, the forces will be forward-deployed and in position to respond. C-141s and additional C-5s will back-fill the five C-5s at Bragg to embark the remainder of the 82nd Airborne. The 101st Airborne is on ninety-hour alert to follow, if so ordered."

The president rested his left hand on his chin with his index finger tapping his cheek. "Damn," he said. "This must have been what Roosevelt felt like in '42."

"Yes, sir," General Eaglefield replied, thinking, "'41,'" wondering about the president's grasp of history and worrying over the commander in chief's lack of military experience.

"Thank you, General. Roger, come see me later."

President Crawford peered over his bifocals at the DCI. "Farbros, quit wiggling in your seat. I know you want to tell me what caused you to be late. So go ahead."

There was a knock on the door before the DCI could respond. Without waiting for an invitation to enter, an Army colonel opened the door. He seemed surprised to see the president sitting at the head of the conference table. "Sorry, Mr. President," he muttered, and then nearly ran to where General Eaglefield sat. He bent to whisper in the ear of the CJCS.

"Wait a minute, Colonel," the president said, waving his hand. "If it's important enough to interrupt my meeting, then it's important enough to let me hear what you have to say."

The colonel looked at General Eaglefield, who nodded for him to go ahead.

He stood at attention and looked at the president. "Mr. President, thirty minutes ago forces of North Korea began shelling across the DMZ; followed by large-scale air attacks of the immediate area. Intelligence shows North Korean armored forces moving toward the border. When I left the situation room two minutes ago to come up, North Korea had commenced a call-up of its reserves."

The president peered over his glasses at the secretary of state. "What's going on, Bob? I thought we had North Korea in its box."

"I don't know, Mr. President. They're not suffering the famine of several years ago. We've been shipping them food. Of course, they've been protesting for two days about a perceived South Korean violation of their territorial waters, but that's normal. I'm sure it's just posturing."

"Sorry, sir," the colonel said. "But they've already attacked across the DMZ." The colonel stopped and started to lean down to talk with General Eaglefield, but saw President Crawford looking at him. "That's not normal. Mr. President, two formations of North Korean jets bombed Seoul about thirty minutes ago. No major damage and no additional raids since. They flew low-level, dropped approximately eight iron bombs, and then scurried back across the border. Air defense did pick them up, but thought they were South Korean Air Force jets completing routine flight operations."

"Bob, the colonel's right," Roger said, a touch of sarcasm in his voice. "Doesn't sound as if the North Koreans are posturing."

General Eaglefield pushed his chair back and rose. "Mr. President, with your permission, I would like to return to the Pentagon. These new developments influence our plans for the Mediterranean."

"What do you mean, General?" the president asked, concern in his voice.

"Mr. President, we have about twenty thousand troops on the ground in South Korea. Most of them are light infantry supported with a couple of Air Force fighter squadrons. The United States purposely left those forces behind, during the drawdown, to support the South Korean government and act as a trip wire for American intervention. They can fight, but only for a limited time." He took a deep breath. "Our forces lack the firepower, numbers, or logistics to stop a determined North Korean push into South Korea. Plus, they are on the front lines at the DMZ intermingled with the South Koreans.

We would sustain significant casualties during the early hours of a major assault."

"General, we have forces in Japan. We can move them into South Korea. If we build up South Korea, then the North Koreans will see the resolve, settle down, and return to their normal seething turmoil within their own borders," President Crawford said hopefully. "Where's the nearest carrier?"

"The nearest carrier is stationed in Yokoto, Japan. Depending on where she is, we can move her off the coast of the Korean Peninsula. As for the option of moving forces from Japan, like the Mediterranean, over the years, we have recalled our overseas forces from the Pacific. We have no ground troops in Japan or Okinawa. The nearest ones are in California."

"Of course, with the North Koreans, you never know what they'll do," Roger Maddock added. "Sensible nations do rational things. With the North Koreans, they tend to act irrational and never worry about why the world reacts as it does. It's like dealing with an obstinate, surly teenager."

"Unfortunately, in this case, the obstinate, surly teenager is psychotic and has long-range missiles," General Eaglefield added.

"Let's hope that a show of force will temper any ill-conceived plans they may have," the president replied. "Roger, we should be able to continue with our response in the Mediterranean. Right?"

The secretary of defense looked to the chairman of the Joint Chiefs of Staff to reply.

"Yes, sir, but the 82nd Airborne, 101st Airborne, and mechanized infantry at Fort Stewart are also the contingency forces for a Korean conflict. We lack the active-duty forces to meet both. Our Major Regional Conflict—MRC—plans place a Korean crisis above events in the Mediterranean."

"Why?"

"Sir?" General Eaglefield asked, unsure as to what the president meant.

"Mr. President," Bob Gilfort interjected. "In the Korean Peninsula, we are talking about direct conflict on territory occupied by an ally and, by treaty, under the defensive umbrella of America."

"The Med can be held with forces already in theater until the *Stennis* arrives," General Eaglefield added.

"Let me make sure I understand," the president said. He pointed his pen at the secretary of state. "Bob, you're telling me regardless of the fact that U.S. forces have been attacked, an American warship has been sunk, and there are American dead in Europe, that the saber-rattling by North Korea takes precedence?" He then looked at the general. "And General Eaglefield, you're telling me that the forces we intended to send to Europe in response to Libya's attack are the forces that we must send to Korea if we have a war there?"

Both the secretary of state and the chairman of the Joint Chiefs of Staff nodded, as did the secretary of defense, who was drumming his pencil on the table.

"Okay. This has the potential of a quagmire where we find ourselves doing nothing. I don't want to do nothing. I want to do something that sends the right message to both Libya and North Korea. So, tell me what that something is going to be." The president looked at Bob Gilfort. "Bob, what can we do politically to resolve both these crises?"

"Mr. President, I would like to consult with my staff before offering advice. I want to ensure that every option is considered and fully vetted."

President Crawford looked over his bifocals at General Eaglefield.

"Sir, I, too, need to sit down with the other chiefs and determine how we can best employ our forces. We need to send the right message to both sides of the world and at the same time make sure that those forces are capable of exercising whatever option they are called upon to do."

"Okay, I need results." The president stood. This was definitely going to be a legacy-making event. Everyone rose. "I think we'll adjourn to give everyone an opportunity to weigh the situations and come back with some ideas. I expect everyone back here by six P.M." He looked down at the DCI. "You hear the time, Farbros?"

"Yes, sir. I'll be on time. Mr. President, I do have something. We believe that the North Koreans are being manipulated by the Chinese."

The president sat back down. "How and why?" His voice

betrayed disbelief. "The Chinese enjoy favored-nation trade status with us. We are their largest market for the cheap goods they make. They wouldn't dare jeopardize that." Crawford shook his head. "No, I don't think they'd jeopardize that."

"We don't know the why, but several events have occurred to indicate the actions by North Korea are in response to a guarantee of increased food aid and unknown economic and military considerations by China."

"Why would China stir up a crisis near her own borders? It doesn't make sense, Farbros. China is having near-record economic growth, and for the past few years has begun to exert some positive world influence."

"It's still a Communist country, Mr. President, and its goal of driving Western influence from Asia and becoming a world superpower has never wavered."

"So? What does that mean, Farbros?"

"Mr. President, the North Korean action is a ruse. They will not cross the DMZ in force nor will they push the envelope to the point that we'll be compelled to counterattack."

"Well, they've already done something to encourage a counterattack. Regardless of what they intended, we have to respond. They crossed the DMZ when they bombed Seoul."

"We have a commitment to the people of South Korea," added the secretary of state. "If we don't respond, and Farbros is right that it is a ruse, then they could easily change their plans and turn a ruse into an actual invasion of South Korea."

"Yes, and we have nearly twenty thousand military men and women based in South Korea who would be in danger if the North Koreans invade," added the secretary of defense.

"I know. I know all that," whined the DCI. "Even so, the Chinese military has increased its meetings with their North Korean counterparts. North Korean military observers were recently invited to the annual Chinese exercise near the Chinese-Russian border—first time in ten years. Following the exercise, the North Korean generals and their Chinese counterparts spent a week in Hong Kong in secret, closed-door meetings. We believe that a Chinese sale of advanced Information Technology, along with replacement fighter aircraft for the North Koreans, have been offered in return for some yet-to-be-identified service. We believe this ruse is part of the agreement."

A cough at the other end of the table drew the president's attention to the director of the National Security Agency. "General Stanhope, you have something to add?"

"Yes, sir. We are still putting all the factors together, but we have some disjointed facts that may support Mr. Digby-Jones. They also relate to the sinking of the USS *Gearing* and the air attacks against Souda Bay and Sigonella. Mr. President, I need to caution, sir, that this is unevaluated raw intelligence and we are still analyzing the data."

"Well, go ahead, General, and let me be the judge."

"Yes, sir. We detected unusual data activity between Libya and the People's Republic of China earlier this week. Within forty-eight hours after detecting this anomaly, Libya attacked the *Gearing*. Another item of interest is that the unit in China that received the data was their Information Warfare unit. Two hours after the data was sent from Libya, this Chinese unit passed unknown instructions to the North Koreans. While we have yet to correlate the satellite screwups, the fact that their readings are erroneous suggests an attack against their computer algorithms—an Information Warfare unit would have that capability."

"You're right, General. I think we are seeing ghosts in the pantry."

"But, Mr. President—" Farbros started.

"Yes, sir, you may be right," General Stanhope agreed. "But before I departed Fort Meade, we were seeing unexplained activity between the North Korean military headquarters and subordinate military units."

"Thanks, General," President Crawford said curtly. Then he added, "And to you also, Farbros. You're the DCI. You and General Stanhope figure out what this means. I have enough information for a major headache. I intend to go upstairs to see Mrs. Crawford and have her rub my temples. When I see you next, I want answers. We need to move fast. If we don't, events will continue to dictate our actions. We've got a runaway stagecoach heading downhill, with no one driving. I want to grab those reins before it's too far gone for us to steer."

Everyone stood again in response to the president standing.

There was a knock on the door, immediately followed by the entry of the chairman of the Joint Chief of Staff's executive assistant. Heads turned as the Air Force colonel hurried to General Eaglefield and handed him a message.

General Eaglefield read the message before looking at the president.

"What is it, General?" the president asked, raising his bushy eyebrows.

"It's a message from the USS *Stennis,* Mr. President."

"What does it say?" Roger Maddock asked.

"The *Stennis* acknowledges the order to return to Norfolk in paragraph one of the message. In paragraph two he says—" The General looked down at the message. "It might be better if I read it, sir."

He cleared his throat and began to read. "'Unless otherwise directed, *Stennis* will not return to Norfolk. Ready for deployment now. I have twenty-eight fighters on board, am escorted by the destroyers USS *John Rodgers* and *Ramage* and the cruiser USS *Hue City,* along with the auxiliary ship *Concord.* Our sterns are to the west, our weapons point east, and our hearts and souls are with the officers and sailors of USS *Gearing.* I estimate Gibraltar in four days at flank speed. If additional fighter/bombers available, am prepared to embark them. Otherwise I go to join the Mediterranean Fleet as armed and to avenge the *Gearing.*' Signed, Richard A. Holman, Commanding Officer, USS *Stennis.*"

General Eaglefield handed the message back to the colonel. "Mr. President, Mr. Secretary, with your permission, I request to be excused."

"Where are you going?" the president asked.

"I'm going to find some aircraft, sir, for Captain Holman. As you directed, we are returning to the Med. And I think America has just found one of the warriors to do it."

CHAPTER 3

⚓

"**WHAT THE HELL DOES HE WANTS THIS TIME, DUNCAN?**" Beau asked, pointing to the closed door. He stood with his feet slightly apart and bounced his body back and forth off the bulkhead of the passageway.

"I have no idea, unless it's to provide more advice."

"I hope not," Beau said, shaking his head. "He's a master of taking thirty minutes to pass three minutes' worth of information. I hope he realizes we have things to do."

Duncan touched the folded paper in his pocket, his thoughts turning to its contents as Beau's conversation turned to the members of the team. He heard H.J.'s name a couple of times. Duncan had read and reread what his buddy Bill Hodges had sent. He needed to write a reply, but what do you say? There was little the admiral who'd shanghaied him for this job could do, even if Duncan had confidence in the two-star to do it. It was his headache, and a civil matter to boot.

Beau punched him on the shoulder. "Captain, you listening to me? I said, did you know she boxed during college?" He reached up and ran his hand through his unruly blond hair.

"Of course, I'm listening. Who boxed during college?"

"Who do you think we've been talking about? H.J., that's who."

Duncan shook his head. "Against other women?" he asked, though his thoughts wandered to Reston. He wondered if his wife had found the dog's body. He wished he'd had time to bury it rather than leave it in the garage stuffed in an old trunk.

"No! In the male smokers. Said she actually won a couple because the men were hesitant to hit her, so she beat the shit out of them for being male chauvinists." He grinned. His neon-blue eyes sparkled. "I bet there's a red hourglass tattooed on her stomach just above the number-two barbwire pierced through her navel."

"Beau, I've got other things on my mind than your sex life. So don't put me in an awkward position where I have to think of my pension. I'm too short, with too many things going on, to be dumping pails of cold water on you. Besides, for some ungodly reason, I like you. You're like a pet to me, so don't make me rub your nose in your mess. You see, I won't endanger my pension for you—though, the way my luck's going, my soon-to-be ex-wife will take most of it to spend on that boy toy of hers."

Beau touched his heart. "Duncan, how can you ever think that I would do something so outrageous; especially on a U.S. Navy ship of war. Why, it's—it's unthinkable! It's pure nonsense. Besides, we haven't been able to find an appropriate place to even discuss weapons, much less sex." He wondered if H.J.'s nipples were pink or brown.

"Good, then don't. Stay on the professional level," Duncan replied. He rubbed the hard features of his face. His index finger lightly stroked the three-inch shrapnel scar on his left cheek courtesy of Desert Storm. He needed another shave. There was no reason for Hodges to have sent him on this trip. The admiral must have a hidden agenda. Two sailors hurried past, causing the two men to step back to make way.

"But we both know that strict professional relationships have never built the camaraderie needed for war," Beau added after the two sailors passed.

"True, but sex hasn't either."

The door opened. Commander Mulligan, the short pudgy

intelligence officer, and Commander Peter Naismith, the tall, lean, Task Force 61 operations officer, stood just inside, reminding Duncan of the old comedy team of Laurel and Hardy.

"Come in," said the commodore, blocking the door. He moved aside. "Sorry to keep you waiting, but we were going over the rescue operation for those poor souls on the *Gearing*. The *Miami* continues en route and should arrive sometime tomorrow. Meanwhile, we have the problem of the Libyans. We don't want them rescuing our sailors. The last thing we need is another Kodak film moment of our people being marched through the streets of Tripoli like our prisoners of war during Vietnam."

The intelligence officer's eyes were red and bloodshot, making Duncan think of a road map of New Jersey. An intelligence officer's job like Commander Mulligan's would have been boring as hell for Duncan. Lots of work, little appreciation, and if you're wrong once, off the ship, off the staff, and out of the service. He thought of them as public affairs officers with a top-secret clearance.

The inevitable chart was taped to the table with red lines and black overlays displaying various options for an evacuation of Algiers.

"Duncan, something important has come up and you're the only game in town to do it. You and your teams," Commodore Ellison said as he moved to the other side of the table so he could face the two Navy SEALs.

"This is top secret, eyes only. Joint Chiefs of Staff called this morning. Apparently, President Alneuf had a secret agreement with the CIA to get him out of Algeria if he ever needed to leave in a hurry. Last night he apparently contacted them and called in the marker. We've been tasked to go in and get him. Sorry, Duncan, but as this shit job rolls downhill, you're the one stuck with it. You're going to have to go into Algeria and bring out President Alneuf." He shook his head. "It ain't enough we don't have the forces to rescue our own citizens; we've got to go rescue a foreigner who spent most of his time giving America the finger."

"President Alneuf? I take it then, Commodore, we know where he is?"

The door opened and the communications officer, Lieutenant Junior Grade Smith, apologized for interrupting and handed the commodore a sealed message.

"What's this?" Commodore Ellison asked, not expecting an answer and not receiving one. He tore the envelope open and removed the message.

"Well, well, well," he said, looking up and smiling. "Seems the old warrior spirit is still alive and kicking in some of us old veterans. Dick Holman, commanding officer of the USS *Stennis,* has turned his carrier battle group east and is heading this way. He estimates four days until he inchops the Med."

"That's good news, Commodore," the IO added.

Duncan nodded. "Nothing like Naval airpower to shore up a NEO."

"Good news? It's great news! Means that in three days, with tankers, the *Stennis* can be in range to provide us air support. Nothing against the Marines and their Harriers, but Harriers can't provide the air superiority we need to control the skies."

"I bet you they're scrambling back on the East Coast now to identify fighters for Holman. Do you know him, Commodore?" Pete Naismith asked.

"Yeah, I know Dick Holman. He got passed over for flag last year." Ellison patted his stomach. "Failed the body-fat measurements. The man has a reputation for speaking his mind. Rumor has it, he has something in a fitrep when he was a junior officer about being a gregarious individual with great professional potential, but prefers to resolve personal differences with physical means. He's probably lucky to still be in the Navy, and it's a miracle he even made captain, much less commanding officer of a carrier. That being said, I'll light a candle tonight for Dick Holman.

"Duncan, back to you and your question. No, we don't know where President Alneuf is, but we know where he's going to be. Have you ever heard about General Mark Clark's covert trip to French Algeria during World War II?" the Commodore asked, and before Duncan or Beau could answer, he continued. "Prior to Operation Thunder—the American invasion of North Africa—a British submarine sneaked General Mark Clark, who was Eisenhower's right-hand man, onto a beach near the French villa of a man

named Tessler, located west of Algiers. The general met
with the Vichy French military leaders in an attempt to convince them to allow the upcoming Allied invasion of Algeria to go unopposed. Wasn't too successful. The Vichy
French fought the invasion, killing a bunch of Americans
before they finally surrendered." The commodore took his
glasses off and waved them at Duncan as he shouted, "They
opposed the landing so they could say they fought with
honor! That bullshit cost American lives. Should have shot
the lot of them." He put his bifocals back on.

"Anyway, Duncan, President Alneuf is going to meet you
at the same villa."

The commodore picked up a pencil and placed the tip on
the coastline west of Algiers. "Right here is where President
Alneuf and his party will meet you."

"How many are in his party?"

"Don't know. Could be just him or could be a slew of
them." Ellison waved the message in front of them. "This
damn thing doesn't tell us anything other than where and
when to meet him. So, all we know is that President Alneuf
will be waiting there, beginning tonight."

"Transport, sir?" Duncan asked as he scrutinized the chart.

"Submarine."

Duncan looked up at the commodore. "I thought you said
the *Miami* had been dispatched to rescue the survivors of the
USS *Gearing*?"

"It has been, but the USS *Albany* arrives within the next
six hours to transfer Admiral Cameron and his staff to the
Nassau. At that time, you and your crew will embark. I have
already discussed this with the Sixth Fleet chief of staff,
Captain Clive Bowen. We both agree. We need the SEALs
to bring him out, and because it's President Alneuf, they
want a senior officer to represent the United States. You fit
both criteria, Duncan. Therefore, the *Albany* will transport
you and your team to the rendezvous." He pointed to the operations officer. "Commander Naismith has the details
you'll need to work out your CONOP. How you will contact
President Alneuf and his party is anyone's guess. Commander Mulligan will provide the latest imagery of the area
and an intelligence brief on what you can expect. Work with

Pete on getting you and your team out after you locate President Alneuf."

"That's seems simple, Commodore. We'll come out like we go in," Duncan said, thinking out loud.

"Captain James, that's easy to say, but I'm sure we've both seen enough operations to know that nothing goes as smooth as planned. Let's have some backup in the event, like Clark, you find yourself stranded for a couple of days. We need alternatives to other than just the *Albany*."

"Clark was stranded?" Beau whispered.

Commander Naismith handed Duncan a thick brown envelope.

"There are some additional factors to consider, Captain James," said Commander Mulligan, stepping into the faint light over the table. "The two Algerian Kilo submarines are still unaccounted for. The primary threat to the *Albany* during this mission will be those two submarines. That is, if they have, like most of the Algerian Navy, gone over to the insurgents. When the *Albany* surfaces to disembark you and your teams is when she'll be most vulnerable. The commanding officer of the USS *Albany* has already expressed reservations on taking you in close, and is less than enthusiastic about waiting in shallow water for you. You'll need to disembark fast, complete the rescue, and get back on board as soon as possible."

"Thanks, Intell. As for the *Albany*, submariners are as congenial and sociable as we SEALs are. If he has to stay, he will. He'll be like the rest of us. He'll bitch and moan, but he and his crew will be there. I'd trust my life to any submariner."

"Well, good, because we're going to have to," Beau mumbled.

"I agree, Duncan. Now about the CONOP."

"Commodore," Duncan interrupted. "What we need is more information. I need to know how many we are going to bring out, the shoreline terrain, what is the population in the area, the weather, and what kind of opposition we can expect."

"My orders to the *Albany* are to be careful and avoid contact with Algerian forces. We don't want another *Gearing*," Commodore Ellison emphasized. He looked at the intelligence officer. "Commander Mulligan, what are the chances of the *Albany* encountering those two Algerian Kilos, the *Al Solomon* and the *Al Nasser*?"

Commander Mulligan shrugged his shoulders. "Without locating data, we are unable to give any reliable estimates, sir."

Commander Naismith added, "If the *Albany* detects them before they detect her, then the Algerians won't stand a snowball's chance in hell. Knowing your enemy's location is sufficient to turn the tide of battle."

"Most times, Commander," Duncan corrected. "Sometimes it just allows you to avoid them."

Commander Mulligan stepped in. "Captain James, the Algerians are conducting helicopter patrols during the daytime along the coast. If you should be there when the sun comes up, keep an eye on the sky."

The commodore grunted. "There is a lot we still don't know, Duncan. Unfortunately, we never know enough. Commander Mulligan will brief your team in an hour in Intell. By then, I expect you to have a rough CONOP to my staff for my review."

"Commodore, I won't be doing a written CONOP," said Duncan, his voice low but firm. He looked directly at Ellison and paused, for he wanted no misunderstanding. It wasn't that Duncan objected to a Concept of Operations; it was just that with only six hours to prepare, he didn't have the time to sit down and do the bullshit, tedious administrative paperwork Ellison wanted. "A rescue mission is just that, a rescue; and a rescue mission in hostile territory is a time-sensitive operation with a lot of danger. What we need is more than six hours to properly plan, but we don't have it. When we leave the submarine, there is a good chance that events ashore will determine our actions. About all we can do is coordinate with the *Albany* for pickup and with your communications people for comms. After that . . . Well, let's hope we find Alneuf waiting on the beach."

Surprised when Commodore Ellison failed to object, Duncan continued. "What you need to know, Commodore, is when to pick us up. What I need to know is what I've already asked."

"But, Duncan," the Commodore argued. "Without a

CONOP I won't know the sequence of events or be able to plan effectively if something happens to you and we have to come in."

"Yes, sir. I understand the battle staff concerns. When we have all the information together, I'll pass it to your staff. Have them write the CONOP, Commodore, and pass me a copy, if you would. We have too much to do in the next six hours to burden ourselves with a lot of administrative crap," Duncan replied, and then added politely. "Sir."

Commodore Ellison's eyes widened and he opened his mouth to say something, thought better of it, and instead turned to Commander Naismith. "Pete, have one of your junior officers start a CONOP for Captain James. Duncan's right. They have too much to do in too short of a time to write a CONOP."

"Yes, sir," replied the Operations Officer.

"Commodore," Duncan said. "I appreciate your concerns about us while we're in-country, but we both know you don't have the forces to rescue us if something does go wrong. You're going to be hard-pressed to evacuate our citizens at the embassy. Especially if it's opposed. That being said, Commodore, if you should have to come in to get us, I recommend you come in shooting because we'll either be fighting or dead."

Beau cocked his head toward Duncan. "Fighting is my preference," he said. He pursed his lips together. Usually Duncan agreed with orders and then went on and did it his way anyway. Beau put his hand over his mouth, as if to stifle a yawn, but mainly to stop himself from saying anything else.

Duncan turned toward the door. "Come on, Pettigrew. We've got lots to do before *Albany* shows up. Commodore, we'll be in the SpecWar spaces if you need us; otherwise we'll be at the gangway when the *Albany* arrives."

"Lieutenant Commander," Beau said once outside the compartment.

"Lieutenant Commander what?"

"Lieutenant Commander Pettigrew. You called me Pettigrew. I don't like being called by my last name without a

Lieutenant Commander or Commander in front of it. Especially in front of others."

"How about a Lieutenant in front of it?"

"How about remembering that I'm always behind you?"

They both laughed as they hurried down the passageway, ducking through the hatches and turning sideways when they encountered others, acting more like two high school boys who had pulled a fast one on their teacher or gotten a glimpse of the head cheerleader's panties than two deadly Navy SEALs.

"Damn, Duncan, kind of proud of you," Beau said as they slowed their gait near the SEAL spaces. "Surprised, but proud. Now, if you'll listen to me, I'll teach you some nice words to sprinkle your speech with the next time you want to tell a commodore to 'go to hell' or 'go fuck yourself.' You'll find it'll save you a lot of time as you ruin your career. Personally, I prefer to ruin mind gradually, without a heartrending race to a cliff, only to tumble off it without a line or parachute."

"Shut up, Beau," Duncan said good-naturedly, rubbing the stubble he called hair on the top of his head. "You tell me how a Navy captain, who has been ordered to retire in less than sixty days, is going to ruin his career? Or a Navy captain, who has . . ." He stopped.

"There is always a chance that they may change their mind, Duncan."

"When pigs fly. Besides, look at this!" He opened his pocket and handed the "personal for" message to Beau. "You tell me why I should be grateful to Admiral Hodges for sending us on this vacation."

"Hey! Slow up! You're walking too fast."

Beau read the message as he tried to keep up with Duncan. Duncan slid down the ladder that ended at the door to the SEAL spaces. Beau tripped on the bottom step.

"Took everything?" Beau asked, slapping the paper. "She took everything in the house while you're over here in the middle of a war? What type of bitch is she?"

Duncan stopped at the door leading into the NSW spaces, his hand on the metal doorknob.

"She's a former-wife bitch. That's the type she is. She not

only has a battery-less dildo, but now she has everything we ever bought, collected or kept. God knows where she took it. I mean, Beau, she took everything, including the car and the mantelpiece that we bought at an auction in Frederick, Maryland! I mean, what type of woman goes into a house and rips out the mantelpiece?"

"But how do you get into a house without anyone knowing and load up all the furniture, take down overhead fans and mantelpieces, and no one calls the police?"

Duncan's shoulders slumped. He leaned his head on the door. "Beau, she lived there for six years," he said softly. "Neighbors know her. You don't call the police when someone who lives in the place decides to move everything out." He looked up and grinned at Beau. "If she took the old steamer trunk in the garage, she's going to get one hell of a surprise when she opens it."

"How's that?"

"That's where I stuck the bag with Sammy's body. I forgot to bury the damn dog before we left. Shit, Beau, there may be justice in this world after all."

"And don't forget, Duncan. Your car don't work, so if she took it, she towed it."

Duncan shook Beau by the neck. "Screw you, shipmate." He laughed.

Duncan opened the door to the SEAL offices and walked in. The arguing between Lieutenant H.J. McDaniels and Ensign Helliwell spilled out into the passageway before it ceased abruptly at the sight of Captain James.

"OK, what the hell is going on?" Duncan asked. Hell hath no fury like a woman scorned, but storms had no tempest like a wronged man's frustration.

Lieutenant Sunney appeared behind Duncan and Beau and followed them into the room.

Beau folded the message and handed it to Duncan, who slipped it into his left shirt pocket. Duncan rubbed his temples. *Damn, a headache! Just what I need on top of everything else.*

"Listen up," he said, ignoring the fact that neither of the two had answered his question. "There has been a change of plans. Beau and I are taking the two four-man teams organized to go on the CH-46 and are embarking with them on the *Albany* in six hours. Mike, we'll need to change the load-out from a force-protection operation to a hostile rescue."

"I'll be going, right?" H.J. asked.

"With all due respect, sir," Ensign Helliwell interrupted. "This is her first SEAL operation and we don't need to endanger our situation with a rookie. Nothing against her being a woman, Captain, even though she thinks it is, but the other team members have at least some experience."

"Screw you, Ensign," said H.J., with her finger poking him in the chest. She leaned over him from her full six-foot height and brought her face six inches from his. "How the hell did you get experience? Did it come in some midnight wet dream where you woke and lo and behold"—she waved her hands above her head—"Ensign Helliwell is blessed with experience? No, you went and earned your battle scars, and I'm not, I repeat, not going to be kept back because you're afraid that the big man"—she patted him on the head—"is going to have to rescue the fair maiden. Well, for your information I'm anything but a fair maiden. And—"

"Cut it out, you two. We're going into a combat, so can the crap. Lieutenant McDaniels goes. She's a SEAL and already assigned by the Navy to my team. Ensign Helliwell, you're coming, too. I need your experience and your expertise. Forget she's a woman. Hell, forget that you're a man. You're both SEALs and I expect both of you to act like Navy SEALs. If either of you get shot, we'll treat you just like any other wounded SEAL."

"How's that?" H.J. asked, standing back from Bud Helliwell, her voice curious and her eyes questioning.

"We shoot them in the head," replied Beau, cocking his finger and putting it against his head. "And bang, don't have to worry about them spilling their guts to the enemy about the mission or the team. I don't mind telling you that the first time I had—"

"Stow it," Duncan said. "Get your kits together and be prepared to embark on *Albany* when she arrives." Duncan went on to explain the purpose of the mission and the specifics he expected.

"Sir, request permission to accompany the operation?" Mike Sunney asked.

"Sorry, Mike. You know the only reason I am here was Washington sending me out to lead that combined exercise with Spanish special forces. Too bad the events in North Africa caused the exercise to fall apart. If not for them sending me, then you would be the one going in. But I need you here for backup and to support the Marines on what is looking more and more like an oppose evacuation by hostile forces. If we have to pull a 'John Wayne' and go into Algiers, with guns blazing, to bring out the American citizens, then the battle group is going to need the remainder of the SEALs to support that effort."

"Yes, sir. I realize that, but you're a captain and, with all due respect, sir, captains don't usually go on SEAL operations."

"This particular SEAL operation the captain does go on," Duncan replied. "Our mission is to bring out the Algerian President, Hawali Alneuf, who is hiding from the insurgents. Since he's a bigwig, they figure a captain should meet him."

"Yeah, meet him, greet him, do some high-fives, maybe dance a few steps with him, and when we've amused him sufficiently, scurry him out of his gone-to-shit country," Beau added.

Duncan held up his hand to stop the laughter, and added, "Commander Mulligan will brief everyone in about an hour in the Intell spaces. Mike, have the teams assembled and there on time."

"Yes, sir," Mike Sunney responded dejectedly.

"H.J., hand me the chart you keep in your shirt," said Duncan.

She unbuttoned the top two buttons and reached inside to extract the chart, which she passed to Beau, who stood between her and Duncan.

"Nice chart," said Beau. "Lucky chart," he whispered to himself.

H.J.'s eyes narrowed as she stared at Beau. "You were saying something, Commander?"

"Sorry," he mumbled. "Just thinking out loud."

Duncan took the papers from the envelope Pete Naismith

had given him, and scanned them rapidly as he looked for how they were to make contact with President Alneuf. Satisfied they had nothing to offer other than telling him to go to the location of the villa, he laid them on top of the chart Beau was unfolding on the table.

Duncan pulled a stool up and sat down. He picked up a pencil and leaned forward across the chart. "Here is our destination," he said, indicating a point along the coast near a small fishing village about twenty kilometers west of Algiers. "We will conduct a submarine debarkation around midnight. Mike, we'll need two rafts for the *Albany,* and make sure we have pressure bottles to inflate them. Don't want to get aboard and discover they lack the capability to inflate them except inside the submarine. Won't do us much good if we can't get them outside of the submarine.

"We won't do the normal approach to shore operations. We'll still form a boat pool about five hundred yards from shore, but instead of sending in swimmers, we'll take a boat all the way to the beach. Beau," he said, "I want you in that boat. If Alneuf is there, put him in the raft and return. If not, then conduct a normal recon when you hit and be prepared to fight a retreat if necessary. When the recon team completes its search, we'll join them ashore. I would prefer to do a normal op, keep the boat pool off shore and swim them out, but President Alneuf is in his late sixties, early seventies, and I doubt he can swim five hundred yards. My intentions are to load him immediately and return to the submarine. If everything goes right, entire operation will be completed within three hours. Any questions?"

Every hand went up. He paused before replying, "Well, write them down for the commodore to answer in the CONOP. I have questions, too, and since we don't know the answers, let's busy ourselves getting ready and we'll answer the questions the way Navy SEALs answer them best: with bullets and brawn. Mike, scrub the snipers, but I want those mini-MGs included—at least two. Have the team outfit themselves with their weapons of choice for close-in combat, and I want stun grenades used. We don't want to kill anyone unless we have to. I also want sufficient rations for two days in the bush if we have problems."

"Ain't no bush to survive in," commented Ensign Helliwell. "And ain't no private heads either," he added petulantly.

"I doubt seriously that you have anything I haven't already seen, except maybe in a smaller package," H.J. replied.

Just what I need, thought Duncan. He reached up and squeezed his nose a couple of times. A professional team had to have confidence and trust each other. Their lives depended on it. It was bad enough he, Beau, and H.J. were newcomers to the SEAL detachment aboard the *Nassau,* but it was going to be worse if he had to referee a running feud between Helliwell and McDaniels during this mission. And he had no intention of leaving McDaniels behind. Not only because she was part of the team, but because maybe that was what Admiral Bill Hodges wanted. Helliwell he needed because the man had combat experience. Mandatory retirement in August was beginning to look brighter, but further away.

"Okay, that's it. If I hear another word out of you two, I'll put you across my lap and spank you both. Straighten up and act like the SEALs you are and not arrogant teenagers. You two shake and get on with your assignments."

"Yes, sir," H.J. and Bud replied in unison.

The two reluctantly grinned at each other like two kids forced to make up. H.J. stuck out her hand toward Bud, who nodded and gripped it in return.

"That's better. Mike, you're in charge of organizing the mission. Report to Beau when ready. Commander Pettigrew, I want you to inspect the team in two hours. Two hours is when I expect everyone to be ready to embark. Two hours is the time we have to outfit the team, Mike, and to throw the right weapon kits together. Report back to me when you're ready. I'll be in Intell trying to find out a little more on events in Algeria and what we may face when we hit the beach. I expect to see everyone in the conference room in the Intell spaces in"—he looked at his watch—"forty-five minutes."

Mike Sunney, Heather J. McDaniels, and Bud Helliwell left the compartment.

"Well, Duncan, belay my last," said Beau. "I don't think you have to worry about me and H.J."

"Why's that?" he asked as he folded the chart from the table.

"Because I've just had a vision of her in a rocking chair, telling her grandchildren about how she came to have a pair of large balls in a quart jar sitting on her mantelpiece."

"I wish you hadn't said mantel," Duncan replied. "I'm going to Intell if you need me," he said as he walked out the door. Less than six weeks until August. Retirement was going to be great. He kept repeating the refrain as he walked down the passageway, hoping that if he kept repeating and repeating it, he'd convince himself it was true. Retirement was going to be great. Yeah, great. *Just keep telling myself that,* he thought.

CHAPTER 4

⚓

As Duncan, Beau, and H.J. boarded the USS Albany with five other SEALs, events were occurring in Libya that would impact their rescue of President Alneuf.

"Hand me those photographs," Colonel Alqahiray said, pointing to a stack of large colored prints on the briefing table.

Colonel Walid scooped the stack up and handed them to his impatient boss.

Colonel Alqahiray laid his cigarette in a nearby ashtray as he flipped through the photos. "You know, Walid? The best photos are the ones that show the stern of the American warship sticking out of the ocean surrounded by the petty war criminals, weeping in their puny life rafts. It is moments like this that makes one proud to be a Libyan."

"*Aiwa,* Colonel. I also like the ones recovered from the bomber that was destroyed on Tripoli Airfield. It is sad that it cost the lives of some of our finest pilots."

Colonel Alqahiray gave Walid a hard look. "Walid, a commander unprepared to accept deaths never achieves victory. Look at Napoleon. He never went into battle without knowing how many casualties were acceptable for victory, and when that number was reached and victory was questionable, he would magnificently retreat to wait for another opportunity. We will have more deaths before Jihad Wahid—our Holy War One—reaches its goal, but those will rock the world on behalf of the faith of Islam, more than any other thing could hope to accomplish. Victory is never achieved without death, and ultimately, it belongs to the leader who is willing to sacrifice his troops."

"Yes, Colonel," Walid replied, looking down to break eye contact with the skull-like apparition that Alqahiray presented.

Colonel Alqahiray shuffled through the large photographs, humming as he put most of them into a large brown envelope, silently thanking the Americans for killing most of the senior Libyan military leaders with their Tomahawk strike. "That should do it, Walid." He picked up his cigarette, which had rolled out of the ashtray and burned a small spot on the polished table, flicked the long ash off, and took a deep drag, letting the smoke filter slowly out through his nostrils.

Walid pinched his nose.

The two walked out of the operations briefing room into the blue-lighted operations spaces. Walid flipped off the lights as he pulled the door shut behind them. He returned to the supervisor's console while Alqahiray hoisted himself onto his chair above the operators.

The three Libyan Intelligence Officers waited stoically for the colonel to acknowledge their presence. He finished his cigarette and ripped open another pack of Greek Old Navy, knocked out a new fag, and lit it. He placed the cold cup of tea to one side, deliberately keeping them waiting. Colonel Alqahiray motioned for the steward to bring him another cup.

Then he turned to the three officers. "Go ahead, Major Samir."

The major pulled several file cards from his pockets, glanced at them, and directed the colonel's attention to the intelligence screen in front of them. On the screen a colored map of the North African coast, stretching from Egypt to Morocco, appeared. Egypt, Libya, and Algeria were highlighted in green, the color of the Libyan flag and the color associated with the Islamic religion. The outlines of Tunisia and Morocco were filled with diagonal lines of alternating red and green, while the Sudan, along with Chad and Somalia, were shaded a light brown.

"Colonel, the Algerian operation is near completion," said Samir. "Sporadic fighting continues in several isolated pockets centered around Oran, Mers El Kebir, and other portions of western Algeria. We expect those pockets to collapse or surrender by tomorrow evening. Search operations east of Algiers continue for the war criminal Hawali Alneuf."

The colonel leaned forward. "When do they expect to capture him? I hope they understand that they need him to consolidate their hold over the country."

"Yes, sir," Major Samir replied. "They realize that the capture, or death, of Alneuf brings solidarity to the government. It removes a figurehead for loyalists to rally around. They continue to broadcast that Alneuf has surrendered, but they have yet to capture him—at least that is the last thing we heard. As the colonel is aware, we lost communications early this morning for six hours with our comrades in Algeria. Those links have been restored, and we have maintained continuous communication since discovering the break was deliberately done at the Tunis microwave relay center. We rerouted communications via landline to southern Algeria and then across our border."

The colonel nodded. A steward approached with a tray. A cup full of strong Bedouin tea rattled on its dish. The colonel accepted the cup without comment and leaned back to sip the tea. He motioned for Major Samir to continue.

"Our friends in the east have kept their promise, Colonel. Earlier today North Korea staged an air attack against Seoul, and they have commenced massing their forces for an attack along the DMZ."

"An attack that will never come," the colonel added softly.

"Yes, sir, an attack that will never come. The Americans are confused. Because of the North Koreans, the Americans are reviewing their options. Forces that could have been threatening our shores are still in America, waiting for a decision. The North Korean deception has worked as we expected."

"Don't forget, Major," the colonel said, leaning forward to emphasize his statement. "The American warship violated our territorial waters and fired on our peaceful forces when we asked them to leave. Because of the war crimes of the USS *Gearing*, many wives weep and orphans cry in Libya."

"Yes, sir," the major answered, covering a cough with his hand. "Our agents monitoring the base at Fort Bragg in North Carolina will report if the supertransports that have arrived take off."

"How are their reports being transmitted, Major?" the colonel asked. "How can we maintain communications with someone in America without being caught?"

"The Internet, Colonel. The Internet transcends all borders. No one watches it. We put a covert web site on the line and then, regardless of where our agents are, all they need is a laptop computer, a place to plug it in, and a search engine to find our home page. Once there, they can download their report, ask questions or receive instructions. Granted, there is little security, and we get e-mails and orders from ordinary people who believe they have found a source for inexpensive vitamins. For those, we honor their business. For our agents, they provide the information we need, and once downloaded, we erase it from the web. So, a hacker, venturing into our web site, would have a very hard time discovering the true nature of the home page."

"This is confusing, Major. I'll take your word. Who else do we communicate with in this matter?"

"Colonel, every agent wherever they may be."

"Enough! You've given me, once again, more information than I really need, Major."

The major coughed slightly as he nervously played with the file cards containing his cues for the brief. He motioned to the computer operator managing the slide show. A second Power Point briefing slide faded onto the screen, replacing the previous map of North Africa with a map of Tunisia and the surrounding border areas of Algeria and Libya.

"Colonel, Algeria has moved several battalions of its revolutionary volunteers to the border with Tunisia, including two companies of tanks backed by two mechanized infantry units. The Algerian Liberation Front government has grounded its Air Force for the past twelve hours to prepare for the attack; with the exception of certain helicopters involved in the search for Alneuf. Two hours ago they reported their Air Force ready for event zero two zero."

The major took a swallow from a nearby water bottle. "Our side of the border with Tunisia is not accurately represented here, Colonel. We have moved a tank battalion and two mechanized infantry companies to the Tunisian border. They are in place. The map reflects only one mechanized infantry unit. Two SU-20 ground-attack squadrons are fueled and armed. Air protection is to be provided by MiG-25s out of Tripoli. Helicopters with Army Special Forces landed inside Tunisia late last night and await our signal."

The major cleared his dry throat, but before he could continue the colonel asked, "How is Tripoli Airfield? Is it operational? Tell me again."

"Sir, we lost the TU-20 and three MiG-25s to the Italian F-16s, but airfield damage was minuscule and easily repaired. The repair by our engineers took less than two hours."

"Good."

"Yes, sir, SU-20s were approaching the landing pattern when the Italian fighters attacked, but were safely vectored south."

The colonel leaned forward and stared directly into the intelligence officer's eyes. "Tell me, Major. I seem to remember you telling me that it would take the Italians, and the Greeks, a minimum of forty-eight hours to respond to our attacks. Forty-eight hours to prepare for any retaliatory strikes. Instead, we have four Italian fighters attacking our air base immediately after we attacked Sigonella, Sicily, and we have Greek aircraft shooting our aircraft down even as they bombed Souda Bay, Crete! Where was this incompetence that I was promised?"

"Yes, sir, I understand. We did not expect the Italians to pursue our force, nor for the Greeks to be this prepared. It is not in their natures to go on the offensive. Our analysis indicated that if our aircraft encountered any resistance, it would be against the vintage Italian Tornado fighters. We were amazed when the Italians committed their new F-16 fighters to an attack over Libyan soil."

"Amazed? You think we were amazed? No, Major, we weren't amazed; we were surprised! We were caught with our pants down. We looked stupid. Because of *intelligence,* because of *you,* we failed to have interceptors up or air-defense units at maximum readiness. Well, scratch another one for the intelligence community, Major."

"I apologize, Colonel," Major Samir replied, his face burning. "We know the aircraft did not have sufficient fuel to return to Italy. The destruction of Sigonella destroyed the air tankers necessary to refuel them. As for the estimate . . ." Major Samir stopped abruptly. He had nearly slipped and reminded the colonel that it was the colonel's idea not to have combat air patrols over the airfields or to raise air-defense readiness because of the risk that the actions would be detected and alert the West. An alerted West could have destroyed the surprise of the Libyan offensive. But Colonel Alqahiray was not one to accept blame for failure, especially when it was his own.

"So, what happened to the F-16s?" the colonel asked.

"Two made it to Lampedusa and glided in on fumes to the small airfield there. Two pilots ejected twenty-five miles southeast of the airfield, and were immediately picked up by Italian fishing boats."

"So, for our three Foxbats and one Tupelov Twenty, we can subtract two F-16s, but not one Italian pilot. That means those four pilots can be given new aircraft and returned to the fight. We, on the other hand, lost not only our aircraft, but more important, we lost pilots we can't replace." He snubbed his cigarette out, grinding it fiercely into the side of the chair.

"Go ahead, Major, and finish this. I have more important things to do."

The major motioned to the operator, who projected the next slide.

"Here is a photograph, downloaded from an agent in Gaeta, showing the damage to the USS *La Salle* and the USS *Simon Lake.* The submarine alongside the USS *La Salle* departed soon after our attacks on Souda Bay and Sigonella. Of note is that the admiral's flag, three white stars on a field of blue, was hauled down shortly before the submarine cast off and left Gaeta."

The colonel leaned forward to scrutinize the computer-enhanced photograph. He bit his lower lip and then, apparently satisfied, he grinned. "If the USS *Gearing* didn't show the world, these daily reminders, sitting in Italy, demonstrate that Americans are not invincible." He leaned back, a freshly lit cigarette dangling from his lips.

"What do we think about the submarine?" he asked. Ashes fell on his shirt.

"Sir, we believe the American admiral, Gordon Cameron, is on board."

"Why didn't they kill him? They killed nearly everyone else but the one they were sent to kill. They killed his wife, and she was sitting beside him. In fact, they killed a lot of wives, but the one person they needed to kill, they missed." He shook his head. He was surrounded by incompetence.

The three officers exchanged nervous looks, but none answered.

"On board the submarine, is he?"

The colonel held his hand up to stop the major from answering as he pondered this information. Finally, he asked Major Samir, "And where do we think he is heading?"

"Colonel, there is only one place for him to go and that is to the American ships heading toward Algiers."

"Why would he go there?"

Major Samir swallowed. He wiped his forehead. "We think, Colonel, that he will take charge of the American battle force and, depending on the situation, rescue either the Americans in Algiers or the American survivors of the USS *Gearing*." He deliberately neglected to mention the other alternative: that Admiral Cameron could be moving to avenge the USS *Gearing,* Sigonella, and Souda Bay.

"What is the status of those war criminals?"

"War criminals?"

"Yes, you fool! Those war criminals floating off our shores—those war criminals that survived the fate of their ship! Those war criminals that we are going to bring back here and execute! Yes, those war criminals, *Major Samir.* Who the hell did you think I was talking about?"

"Yes, sir, Colonel. Those war criminals," Major Samir said. He pressed the projector button. "A helicopter took these photos late yesterday. At that time the survivors were about thirty-five miles northwest of our coast, floating in the Gulf of Sidra.

They have tethered their life rafts together. The helicopter crew counted eight small life rafts and one large one." Major Samir motioned to the operator.

The next slide showed photographs of the life rafts with the Americans in it. There was no sign of the USS *Gearing*.

"Where's the ship?"

"It finally sank, Colonel, sometime yesterday between ten hundred and twenty hundred hours when this helicopter made its reconnaissance run."

"Walid!" the colonel shouted, and was rewarded with the man running to him.

The officer saluted. "Yes, sir."

"How long have the American war criminals been in the water?"

"Over two days, Colonel."

"Good. Time enough for them to welcome any rescue. Call Benghazi Airfield and tell them to prepare to rescue the Americans. It is time we show the world that we are not barbarians. Of course, they will have to stand trial for war crimes committed against the Libyan nation before we execute most of them. Then, depending on the actions of the Americans, we may allow a few to go home in disgrace. On the other hand, the Libyan people may demand their execution. You never know how the winds of the Sahara blow the dune."

"Yes, sir," Walid answered, and rushed to a nearby phone to pass the order.

Colonel Alqahiray returned his attention to Major Samir. "And now, Major, tell me about Morocco."

"Yes, sir," he answered, nodding to the operator, who sent the next slide to the overhead screen. A map of Morocco appeared.

"Colonel, Algerian units are poised along the Algerian-Moroccan border, but only as a defensive measure. Rebel commandos, who have been in Morocco for the past thirty days, have linked up with their Moroccan counterparts. They are in position for their part in Jihad Wahid and await your orders."

"How many units are we talking about, Samir?"

"Twelve commando units, but that fails to count the Moroccan military units who are sympathetic to the cause. We expect those units to rise to our side when the event commences."

"Do we have communications with our people in Morocco?"

"Yes, Colonel, we do. The same way we have with our agents, but using a French web site."

The colonel nodded.

Walid returned. "They are ready at Benghazi, sir. They have four stripped-down MI-14s on standby to rescue the American war criminals at your command."

"Good, tell them to expect to execute the rescue operation sometime tomorrow morning. Let the Americans drift at sea for another night. When they see the helicopters, they'll come aboard with no problem. Three nights without food and water should temper any resistance."

The three intelligence officers looked at each other, but none volunteered that American patrol aircraft had been steadily dropping supplies. The colonel hated to be wrong, and Major Samir was not going to be the one to tell him. He would bide his time. His moment would come later.

Walid saluted. Samir locked eyes with Walid momentarily before Walid looked away and returned to the telephone.

Colonel Alqahiray discovered early in his military career that issuing one order at a time and seeing it properly carried out worked better than expecting his lesser-educated force to perform numerous orders perfectly. He vaingloriously believed that there were few such as him who were capable of the intellect to balance a multiple-tier operation such as Jihad Wahid.

"Very well, Major, tell me about the Italians and Greeks. Do we have to worry about them conducting another strike against us?"

"No, sir. NATO has ordered everyone to stay at least two hundred kilometers north of our coast while they debate an appropriate response to our attacks."

He laughed. "Stupid Westerners. I presume the French are leading this effort?"

"The new French general who replaced the dead American admiral has so ordered it."

"What are the French doing?"

"A French battle group sailed this morning toward Algeria, and has issued a warning to the new government there, and to us, that they will hold us responsible for the safety of their citizens. Further—"

The colonel tossed his cigarette down and gripped both arms of his chair as he leaned forward.

"Wait a minute! What do you mean, hold us responsible for the safety of their citizens? Why would they warn us about the situation in Algeria?"

The major glanced at the other two officers, who shook their heads. "I don't know, sir." He looked to Walid for support, but the officer was deep in conversation on the phone.

The colonel thought a minute. "The only reason they would issue such a démarche to both us and Algeria is that they know something about our plans."

"It could be, Colonel. It could also be that after the attacks on the American bases, they are concerned about their citizens in Libya."

"Could be, but we have never done anything to antagonize the French."

"No, sir," one of the two officers with Major Samir volunteered. "The French specifically identified their citizens in Algeria as being the ones that they would hold us responsible for."

"You sure?"

"Yes, sir. I'm sure," he said. Sweat broke out on his forehead. In the future, he would not pass up an opportunity to keep quiet.

The colonel leaned back to ponder this development.

Walid appeared beside Colonel Alqahiray and reported the relay of the rescue order.

"Walid, have we seen any indications that the French are aware of Jihad Wahid?"

Walid shook his head.

The other intelligence officer with Major Samir spoke up. "Colonel, the merchant vessel *Shanghai* reported an overflight by a French Atlantique in the Gulf of Aden, following their delivery of the program for event zero zero one."

"I don't like this. It makes me nervous and uncomfortable when I don't fully understand something. Find out more, but say nothing to our friends in the east or to our comrades in Algeria."

The three officers acknowledged the colonel's directions. The intelligence briefing slide faded, to be replaced by a map showing the location of Algerian and Libyan Army units along the border of Tunisia.

"Walid, it's time. Regardless of what the French may know, or suspect, we have no choice but to move forward. We are too committed to turn back now. Tell our comrades to execute event zero two zero in"—he looked at his watch and compared it with the digital clock over the intelligence screen in front—"forty-seven minutes."

He stood and followed Walid to the command, control, and communications (C3) console to observe his order being transmitted. When they received the acknowledgment seconds later, he pulled another cigarette from his pocket and lit it.

Forty-seven minutes later, Algerian and Libyan Army units crossed the Tunisian border, meeting light resistance as the surprised blitzkrieg advanced rapidly toward Tunis. Algerian and Libyan aircraft, flying low-level, attacked the Tunisian airfields, destroying most of the small nation's aircraft before they had an opportunity to get airborne. At midnight Algerian and Libyan forces met on the outskirts of Tunis, the last holdout against the invasion. They waited there through the night, poised to enter the Tunisian capital.

When the morning sun cast its early haze across the Tunisian countryside, Algerian and Libyan infantry began a house-to-house fight for possession of the capital, encountering fierce opposition from the betrayed patriots of pro-West Tunisia.

In Morocco, another scenario unfolded simultaneously with the invasion of Tunisia. Twelve terrorist and rebel commando units initiated a series of coordinated attacks in Rabat. A Moroccan military unit, led by a zealous Islamic major, stormed the king's palace through a massive breach in the walls caused by a suicide bomber. Brutal fighting inside the palace sparked enormous losses for both sides. Two hours later, the rebellious major and four others, all that remained of the original twenty-five attackers, reached the monarch and fired several shots into the king's chest before being riddled by bullets from counterattacking Moroccan commandos.

Moroccan Islamic cells captured the more popular radio and television transmission sites throughout the country. Other units destroyed stations they were unable or unwilling to use. By morning, the country was in full rebellion, with loyal Army units converging on the capital to fight the rebels. The Air Force quickly sealed its bases and refused to choose sides, preferring to wait until the victor was more clearly defined. Crew rest was the term of the day.

Fez, the historic mountain city notorious for ferocious barbarian warriors who were renowned for their love of the lance and the feel of the wind across their faces as they charged into battle, failed to live up to its reputation. Fez fell within two hours to sun-hardened Bedouins who quickly overran the city before turning their camels toward Marrakech to join rebellious Army units marching against loyal forces fleeing toward Rabat.

The Moroccan military units at Fez joined the rebellion, and along its march to support the uprising, picked up peasants, farmers, and other disenchanted citizens. Overnight a people's crusade, like those of the eleventh century by Europeans to free the Holy Land, converged toward Tangier, intent on seizing this important seaport for the revolution. It was strictly the decision of the colonel leading the former loyal troops as to the destination. He chose Tangier because a senior Moroccan Army general, whom he hated with a religious fever, lived there. That, he kept to himself. He promised the wealth of the city to those following. The anticipation of achieving some modicum of wealth added to the zealotry of the crusaders as they moved forward like locusts, pillaging everything in their path.

In Tangier, the military units remained evenly balanced between those loyal to the Crown, those who were fervent Islamic supporters and the undecided Army units who waited anxiously to see which side appeared to be winning before they decided their course of action. Eight hours later, the Islamic crusaders from Fez reached Tangier. At that time the undecided Army units threw their support to the Islamic revolution.

The battle for Morocco was under way. Frightened tourists streamed to the airports to discover them closed and themselves stranded as gunfire, mortars, and hand-to-hand combat flowed around various refugee pockets like streams around boulders.

WALID TOUCHED THE COLONEL ON THE ARM AND LIGHTLY shook him. Colonel Alqahiray slept heavily. Sweat stuck his shirt to the plastic upholstery of the chair. An occasional throaty snore escaped to disturb the professional quiet of the command post. Walid, reluctantly, shook the colonel harder.

The colonel grunted and straightened himself upright. He pushed himself out of the chair, stretched, and rubbed his face. "It's been a long night, Walid. What is the situation?"

"Colonel, Tunis is nearly ours. The president fled by helicopter to the Italian island of Pantelleria about an hour ago. Thirty minutes after he fled, the Tunisian General Alasousse requested a truce to meet with our combined forces leader, General Abouimin. We have this proposal from Alasousse." Walid attempted to hand it to the colonel, who waved it away.

"Just tell me what it says."

"He proposes to surrender the country, if we promise no reprisals and that he and his soldiers be permitted to lay down their arms and return to their homes and families. In return, he pledges, on behalf of his officers, their professional honor not to take up arms against our forces nor oppose our occupation."

The colonel shook his head. "Not enough. Tell Abouimin to present my compliments to General Alasousse for his patriotism. Tell him that I honor his concern for his men, but we do not want their weapons, nor do we want them to go home. What we want is for him to swear allegiance to the revolution and integrate the Tunisian military into our combined forces. If he will do this, he will retain his rank and control over the former Tunisian forces during integration. If he refuses, then obviously we cannot have traitors in our midst." He lit the morning cigarette and took a deep breath. A dry hacking cough followed. "Sound fair, Walid?" he asked.

"Sir, it is very compassionate. Such an honorable solution will show Arab solidarity."

"You are right. But, Colonel Walid, be careful with General Alasousse. Tell General Abouimin to ensure that Alasousse understands that failure to agree to these terms will result in renewed fighting until no one is left in Tunisia with the skills to ferment rebellion. Make sure General Abouimin knows that I want the threat portion of our reply delivered very tactfully. Do not put General Alasousse in a position where he feels honor-bound to fight. Damn Sandhurst graduate would fight just for the footnote he'd make in history and a misguided sense of honor."

"Yes, sir." Walid hurried to the C3 console. Twenty minutes later the reply to General Alasousse's surrender proposal was transmitted to the Algeria-Libyan Army headquarters located on the outskirts of Tunis.

Colonel Alqahiray looked at the digital clock as it changed to 0800. Not bad for a night's work, he thought. The steward hurried over with several croissants and the inevitable cup of tea. The colonel motioned for the tray to be set on the small folding table beside his chair. He stood and grabbed a croissant. Then, chewing on the fresh pastry, flakes falling down his gray tunic and onto the recently swept tiles, he walked to where Walid waited for a reply.

"Walid, tell Benghazi to initiate the rescue of the American sailors at ten hundred hours."

Walid acknowledged the colonel's order. He turned to the console and dialed the number for Benghazi Airfield.

Colonel Alqahiray strolled across the room, leaving Walid to execute his orders. He patted the operators on their shoulders congratulating them on the night's success. He basked in the admiration, bordering on worship. As it should be, he thought, making the mistake that charismatic leaders throughout history had made. He believed in his own omnipotence. He wiped the pastry flakes from his heavy, black mustache, and tweaked the ends to make them stand up. Self-worship surpassed strong self-confidence. He had reached that righteous level where disagreement meant disloyalty. Conflicting advice, even if good, would be considered traitorous. Hidden in the dark recesses of abnormally deep sockets, his dark eyes twinkled with the realization that he was the new Nasser of the Arab world!

He stopped at Walid's supervisory console and sat down. He called up the file marked "Jihad Wahid," and downloaded it to a duplicate file. He displayed the original and read it thoroughly, deleting some of the information and pasting a large segment from the center of the file to the beginning. By the time he finished, thirty minutes had passed. He saved the file, called forward an e-mail format, attached the file to it, and transmitted it. Fifteen minutes later it arrived in a nondescript building on the former British Naval base at Hong Kong.

Walid, silently observing the Libyan leader at the console, confirmed his suspicions that the colonel knew more about computer technology than he let on.

THE CHINESE GENERAL, STANDING AT THE CONSOLE, SAW the file arrive and impatiently demanded for it to be printed. He grabbed it, departed the room, and read the file as he walked to his office. There, he laid the file on his desk. From the full-length window across one side of the room, he looked out over the floor below, where numerous operators manned individual PCs. Wisdom came from the ways of the ancients, but a little luck, such as the computer technology left behind when the British returned Hong Kong and that purchased yearly from American commercial firms, helped also. The success of the Libyan adventure depended on the support of the People's Republic of China. His recommendation would mean the difference between success and failure of the North African quest.

He drummed his fingers on the desk as he weighed the pros and cons on whether to recommend they continue covert support or remove China from participation. So far, little linked the actions in the Mediterranean with the People's Republic of China, but like all secrets, the more who knew and the longer it continued, the more likely it would be discovered. He nodded once as he reached his decision, grabbed the piece of paper, and departed his office with it. Any accusations against the PRC could be adequately explained. Plausible denial was something the Chinese invented long before the American presidents put a term to it.

COLONEL ALQAHIRAY FINISHED HIS TEA AND HIS THIRD cigarette before popping the last bite of that first croissant into his mouth.

"Walid, you're in charge while I am gone," he said as he chewed. "I expect I will be away—maybe two hours." He swallowed, and then leaned forward until an inch away from Walid's face. "Remember, Walid. I trust you."

Walid straightened. "You can trust me, Colonel."

"Trust you, Walid? Of course I do. If I didn't, do you think you'd be here now?" he asked, watching Walid's face intently.

"Yes, sir. I mean, no, sir."

"Relax, Walid. Two more days and this will be over. Just two more days, praise be to Allah."

Walid stood nervously while the colonel picked up the photographs and slid them into the envelope. "I'll be back soon, Walid."

He patted Walid on the shoulder and walked swiftly through the operations room to exit through the double steel doors. He walked past the elevator to the second door on the right. Walid was hiding something, and he'd find out what it was eventually, but right now, he had to execute his own event.

WALID WAITED A COUPLE OF MINUTES AFTER THE DOOR closed. He glanced around to make sure no one was looking, got up, and left the operations room for the nearby lavatory. He latched the door and tugged it a couple of times to make sure it was secure. Then he pulled a small cellular telephone from the inside of his jacket. He plugged a connection into a wall socket, giving the telephone the means to communicate from three hundred feet beneath the surface by using the electrical lines as a makeshift antenna. When the connection was made, Walid whispered in French, "Two days," to the person on the other end, and then disconnected.

COLONEL ALQAHIRAY ENTERED WITHOUT KNOCKING, pleased to see the men inside the anteroom snap to attention. He nodded approvingly.

"Good morning, Captain," the colonel said. He inspected the ten soldiers. Each of them stood ramrod-straight. Each were within one inch of six feet. Only the captain was shorter, at five feet seven. Each man held an AK-47 tucked neatly under his right arm. The starched gray uniforms displayed razor-sharp military creases that accented the shirts. Every trouser leg was identical: pants wrapped tightly toward the inside of the legs and tucked into leather, spit-shined combat boots. It was enough to bring a tear to the eyes of a career soldier.

"I see your men are as impressive as always."

"Yes, Colonel. Each man was personally selected by me for this, and all are prepared to give their lives if necessary."

"Let's hope that it does not come to that, Captain, but I would expect nothing less from you and the men of your command," Colonel Alqahiray said. A slight smile escaped. The secret the two officers shared was that the captain was the colonel's blood cousin. Nothing was stronger in the Arab world than blood kin, not religion, not patriotism, not money—nothing.

"And the photographer?" the colonel asked.

One of the soldiers stepped forward. "I am the photographer, Colonel."

"Where's your camera?"

The soldier pointed to three black fabric suitcases stacked in the corner. "There, Colonel. All I have to do is unpack and set up."

"Are you any good with this stuff, Sergeant?" he asked.

"Yes, sir! I am very good."

"Come then," the colonel ordered. "And let's give you an opportunity to prove it." He stepped out of the door, without looking back, knowing the cousin-captain and the soldiers followed. The photographer carried his equipment, while another soldier carried his AK-47.

The elevator waited. They squeezed into the large elevator. Two guards waited at the top when the doors opened. Two

AK-47's, quickly pressed against their throats, disarmed the two guards.

The colonel briskly led the armed men down the hallway to the room where the junta waited. He told the captain to wait outside until called, and that no one was to enter or leave while he was inside.

He opened the door; the photographer followed.

"Colonel Mumtaz Mohammed Alqahiray," said the man at the head of the table. They all stood. "You honor us."

"My masters," the colonel replied. "I bring great news for the leaders of Libya," he said as he opened the envelope and spread the photographs on the table in front of the members of the junta. "Pictures to show that Libya has tweaked the tail of the tiger and found it toothless."

The seven men remained silent as the photographs were eagerly passed around the table. Photographs showing the USS *Gearing* and its sailors were mixed haphazardly with those showing the destruction and carnage of the Sigonella and Souda Bay air attacks. As they clicked their tongues in admiration, Colonel Alqahiray began a detailed briefing on every event that had occurred, the events ongoing at that moment, and the events expected in the next two days. At the farther end of the table, oblivious to the conversation, the photographer opened his suitcases and began assembling his cameras, tripods, and lights. The far end of the room began to look like a professional studio.

"This is very good, Colonel," the elderly Libyan statesman said. "But we question the use of the word 'toothless.' The American Tomahawk attack has killed many senior military officers in Tripoli and Benghazi. We are concerned that this attack was only a prelude to further action. Qaddafi learned his lesson in '86 when a bomb from an American aircraft nearly killed him. Also, we have already had the Italians and Greeks attack and kill some of our warriors."

Several members of the junta nodded in agreement.

"Yes, sir, I understand."

"Whatever happens, Colonel, you have done well." He nodded to the other junta members. "We must discuss how we defuse the situation without further losses." He grinned at Alqahiray. "Now, tell me, why is the photographer here?"

"For you, gentlemen. Our people and the Arab world must know how Libya has avenged itself. If you will do me the honor of assembling in front of the cameras, we will take photographs for the newspapers. Let the world know who controls Libya at this momentous time in our history. Let the world know that we have passed the legendary era of Colonel Qaddafi and are ushering in a new, vibrant era of Libyan pride." He shook his clenched fist.

The men rose, smiling and shaking each other's hands as they moved gradually to the area where the photographer stood welcoming them. The colonel nodded at the soldier-photographer, who guided the men forward and aligned them side by side. The leader of the junta stood in the center, with the next two most powerful men on each side of him. These three wore traditional Arab dress, while the other four were attired in Western business suits.

The leader waved. "Colonel, you come stand with us."

"Thank you for the honor, sir, but this moment is for the leaders of Libya. We in the military are here to serve. With your permission, I will stand with you for the next photograph—the one for the Western press."

They nodded among themselves, aware of the colonel's hatred for the West as well as the reason for it. The colonel had never forgiven America and its allies for that night in 1986 when, as a small boy, bombs rained down upon Tripoli and killed his mother and father. A hatred burned within him that they could only imagine.

The colonel walked down the line, handing each man a single large photograph from the table.

"Please, hold the photographs at chest level," the photographer directed. "Smile, now."

"Yes, smile, please," echoed the colonel. "Show the Arab world what you have done. Let them share in the glory of your power." He nodded eagerly. This was easier than expected.

They smiled more in reaction to the colonel's theatrics than the request. Lights flashed as the photographer began. Ten minutes and numerous photographs later, the soldier-photographer signaled that he was done.

The junta leader appeared tired. "Colonel, don't you think these will be sufficient?"

"Sir, if you will allow me. We need photographs of everyone in proper Bedouin clothes. My apologies, sirs. I know this is tiring business, but once done, we can use these photographs for weeks without worrying you again."

The leader sighed audibly. "Once again, you are right, Colonel." He motioned the four in business clothes to the nearby closet, where they pulled white abas over their suits and put on the red squared headdress preferred by men of statute and power. When finished, they looked more like the Saudi royal family than junta leaders of a new Mediterranean power.

"Tell me, Colonel," the leader asked. "How do we deflect further retaliation against our government? We know the Americans will return, and when they do, they will return in sufficient force that we will be unable to oppose them. As much as I appreciate your loyalty and the dedication of our military forces, we are quite unable to meet Americans on equal terms. This gives us cause for concern."

He wanted to strike the man. Cowards. That was what had brought Libya to where it was today. Cowards! And Qaddafi had been the biggest one of them. Scared to stand up to the Americans. Relying on terrorism and sly methods to deflect any trace back to the country responsible. It goaded him that the junta leader was right! True heroes met the enemy head-on. When he wielded sufficient power to oppose the great Satan, that was how he would respond—head-on. But now was the time for guile and stealth. Time to build toward that moment when the truth could be told.

The photographer moved behind the men and began removing the patriotic portraits that decorated the white wall.

"Sir," the colonel replied after a few seconds. "We are going to mount a massive press campaign, telling everyone what we did. We are going to convince the world that the Libyan people were not responsible for the military attacks against the Americans, the Italians, or the Greeks. We will announce that a rogue element within our government planned and executed the attacks. That we captured them, tried them, and executed them. We will broadcast photographs of the execution to the world. There will be no reason for them to disbelieve us."

Colonel Alqahiray continued. "The West grasps for anything believable to avoid conflict. Look at Kosovo in 1998. By the time they decided that the Yugoslavian government was lying to them, a half-million ethnic Albanians were homeless and many were dead. So, what we do is to give them something to believe. Something that makes sense of what to them appears to be an act of lunacy on the part of Libya."

The leader nodded as the other members of the junta returned to the photography area in their new outfits. "That sounds very ingenious, Colonel. I am presuming that you already have the details of such a ruse figured out?"

"That is correct, sir," the colonel replied. He walked to the door and opened it. "We need a set of photographs showing the rogue elements dead. And the rogue elements have to be people high enough in our government for the West to truly believe the story."

The cousin-captain and the other nine soldiers rushed in with their AK-47s trained on the men who were lined up along the wall.

"What is the meaning of this, Colonel?" said the outraged leader, stepping forward.

The clicks of the AK-47s caused him to step back.

"Who are these men? What is going on? Speak up, Colonel!" he demanded angrily.

"As you said, sir, placing the blame on a group of Libyans who acted without the blessings of the Libyan people would be an acceptable ruse. For that ruse to work, we have to ensure that those executed are of sufficient stature that the world will little doubt our story."

"Not me!" one of the men shouted, and ran toward the door. "I wasn't in favor of attacking the Americans!"

The cousin-captain pumped two bullets from the pistol in his hand into the junta member's back. The sounds of the gunfire echoed, and the smell of burnt gunpowder quickly filled the small conference room.

"I hate cowards," said the colonel, spitting at the body. "Now stand tall, please. Think of yourselves as patriots dying for your country."

Frightened, two more tried to run for safety. Two soldiers opened fire before the elderly men managed more than a few steps, causing their comrades to open fire at the others too frightened to move. Bullets peppered the wall. Pieces of plaster mixed with blood and flesh. Blood splattered on the white wall and the marble tiles. The impact of the bullets, fired from less than ten feet away, sent two of the junta slamming against the wall, where they slid to a sitting position, leaving a bloody trail down the wall.

"Not the faces!" shouted the colonel. The shooting stopped. "Not the faces."

The cousin-captain moved among the dead, kicking each one, his pistol at his side. One moaned when the steel-toed boot broke his rib. The captain stopped, put the pistol directly over the heart, and fired. The body jerked as the bullet went through the body and ricocheted off the floor back into the chest. Satisfied, the captain turned to the colonel and announced, "All dead."

"Take their photographs individually," he said to the photographer. "Then line them up along the wall in the same order they were in for the earlier photographs, along with the photographs they were holding, and take them as a group. When finished, have all the photographs developed immediately. I want several copies of each, and you will personally deliver them to me."

"*Aiwa, ya Madi,*" the captain said.

Madi, the chosen one. Mohammed returned to earth—better than being the new Nasser. Just as Christians believed Christ would return someday, so Moslems believed that Mohammed reincarnated would return to restore Islamic greatness.

The colonel bowed his head. When he raised it, he smiled so that everyone saw the prominent gap between his two front teeth—a gap that the prophecies foretold as a sign of the chosen one. The last to assume the mantle of Madi had defeated and beheaded the great British General Gordon in the nineteenth century at Khartoum. Alqahiray had no intention of losing his head to anyone.

Several of the soldiers bowed. The cousin-captain bent and kissed the gold band on the colonel's right hand.

"I will be in the operations room," Colonel Alqahiray said. "Call the others, Major, and quietly assume control of this building. Let me know if anything happens."

"Major?"

"Yes, Major. In the new Barbary Army, the loyal are righteously rewarded."

The new cousin-major saluted as the colonel departed. The door shut behind the colonel, but not before the slow chant of "Al Madi" reached his ears. Best thousand pounds he'd ever spent was in London at the dental clinic on Wigmore Street, having a dentist widen the natural gap in his upper teeth.

Five minutes later, the colonel strolled into the operations room. Walid ran across to him. "Oh, Colonel, I am so glad you are here!"

"Walid, calm down. What possibly could have gone wrong in an hour?" the colonel asked as he continued to bask in the knowledge that now he was the absolute ruler of Libya, like his predecessor Qaddafi. The difference, though, was that he planned to rule a much larger empire—an empire that the world had not seen since the eleventh century; an empire that would influence every country in the world and give control of the Mediterranean to him.

"Sir, a battalion of Islamic Moroccan Army units have crossed the border into Cueta. They are fighting—"

"Cueta? What is a Cueta?"

"Cueta, sir, is the small Spanish colony on the Moroccan side near the Strait of Gibraltar."

"Spain? Why in the hell would they want to do that? Our plans do not call for us to antagonize the Spanish."

"Morocco has always claimed the city, much like Spain claimed Gibraltar. While Spain and Britain worked out a mutual agreement on Gibraltar, the Spanish have always refused to discuss the sovereignty issue of Cueta with Morocco. The Moroccans have always viewed Cueta as an issue of national honor."

The success of Jihad Wahid depended on everyone doing what they were ordered to do. Events had to dovetail as planned. Cueta could jeopardize Jihad Wahid.

"Tell them to return to their soil. To leave Cueta immediately," ordered the colonel, his voice rising.

"Yes, sir, I know, and we have contacted the leaders of the rebel commandos. They profess to have no control over this Moroccan military unit. The unit that has invaded Cueta is operating independently, but flying our banner."

"What is Spain doing?"

"They have a small military garrison in the city and are fighting. Some of the reports indicate they may be winning the battle. If we are defeated by the small outnumbered Spanish—"

"We neither want to defeat the Spanish, nor do we want them to defeat us. Get me the leader we sent to Morocco to orchestrate this coup. Let me think, Walid." After nearly a minute, the colonel said, "We have to get the Moroccans out of Cueta and we need them out now. You work on it, but by tomorrow they must be out!" When in doubt give the hard problems to a subordinate. They'll either figure out something, or can be blamed for the failure.

He left Walid standing beside the C3 console, and went to his chair. Innovative leaders whirled off on their own agenda too many times. That had been the reason for lack of unity in the Arab world for the past six hundred years. This was a critical time in the operation, and Cueta could ruin it all. He picked up the phone and dialed.

The soldier-photographer arrived two hours later and proudly presented a brown envelope with the photographs in it. The colonel looked through the expertly done photos, scrutinizing each one.

The soldier-photographer was still smiling when he departed an hour later, meritoriously promoted to master sergeant. What a great day to be an Arab! How great it was to serve the true Madi!

CHAPTER 5

⚓

"NOBLE TWENTY-TWO, TIGHTEN UP YOUR POSITION ON Wizard," Noble Sixteen, the lead F-16 pilot, broadcast to his wingman. Noble Sixteen was the call-sign for Howard "the Bird" Webster, twenty-six years old, lean, cocky, and already a captain in the United States Air Force. He hated Howard, but *loved* to be called "The Bird." He was so called because of his thin craggy facial features and a nose that his flight training instructors swore reminded them of a "goddamn chicken beak." He considered himself lucky they didn't call him "Chicken." "Rooster" would have been all right, but "The Bird" was best. If anyone ten years ago had told this son of a cotton-mill family that he would be a fighter pilot one day, he would have called him a liar. Sometimes he lay in bed in his two-bedroom bachelor apartment, or sat on the barbecue deck, smoking a stogie and pretending to be Will Smith in *Independence Day,* and amazed himself over how he'd gotten there. A poor boy from the wrong side of the tracks who'd lucked out on a math scholarship, followed by a commission in the world's greatest Air Force. Someday he'd have to leave the Air Force and get a real job, as everyone joked.

The four United States Air Force F-16 fighters flew a tight

tandem pair formation alongside the huge four-engine RC-135. The Bird's pair, high and tight, were on the left and in front, while the other two took a low rear and right position. Their primary mission: to provide immediate protection for the Air Force reconnaissance aircraft as it relieved the EP-3E on station seventy-five miles north of the survivors of the USS *Gearing*. Today, they would leave the RC-135 for a while and escort a Navy P-3C on a supply drop for the survivors. The Bird hated to fly protection for turboprops. Not because they weren't jets, but because they were so slow he had to watch his console constantly to make sure the F-16 didn't stall.

Since the sinking of the American warship and the surprise attacks against Sigonella and Souda Bay, the United States Air Force had been flying round-the-clock air-defense patrols out of Brindisi Airfield. Dual purposes drove the defensive actions. One was to ensure the Libyans didn't get froggy again and mount another attack; the other was to provide overhead protection for the survivors of the USS *Gearing* until rescue arrived.

"Noble Sixteen, this is Wizard One. Hunter Six Zero entering our zone in ten minutes."

Hunter Six Zero was one of four P3C Orion maritime-patrol and antisubmarine-warfare aircraft that had escaped the destruction at Sigonella. This one had been conducting a maritime patrol in the west Med when the attack occurred. Unarmed normally, the P3Cs were capable of carrying air-launched Tomahawk and Harpoon missiles. Unfortunately, the missiles were at Sigonella and the aircraft were operating out of Brindisi. It would be tomorrow before Harpoons arrived at the recently reopened airfield at Brindisi.

This morning the P-3C mission was to airdrop additional water and food to the survivors of the USS *Gearing*. Along with the supplies would be a note telling them that the attack submarine USS *Miami* was en route and expected to pick them up sometime today.

"Wizard One, this is Hunter Six Zero. Do you have me?"

A digital beep alerted the radar operator on the RC-135. He clicked on his internal communications system to alert the tactical officer to the video return appearing on the radarscope from the northeast. The tactical officer gave the young airman a thumbs-up.

"That's an affirmative," the tactical officer on board the modified Boeing 707 answered. "Stand by, Hunter Six Zero, we have a four-aircraft formation of Foxtrot One Sixes under my belly to keep you company. Expect rendezvous in five minutes."

"Roger, request they form up behind me, one-thousand-foot separation overhead. My intentions are to continue to last contact point and commence a circular search until we locate them. Expect to be in VHF range of their survival radio within fifteen minutes."

Two clicks acknowledged the P-3C Orion aircraft.

"Let's go, Noble," The Bird said.

Noble Formation broke off the Rivet Joint aircraft as the RC-135 air-traffic controller vectored the F-16 formation to the P-3C.

The Bird knew from the premission briefing that during the P-3C insertion, Wizard One would orbit at 36,000 feet. The sensitive RC-135 Rivet Joint reconnaissance systems would monitor the P-3C's and four F-16s' approach toward Libya, while simultaneously watching for any reaction to the five aircraft. If its sensors detected anything resembling a hostile reaction, Wizard One would take control of the aircraft and vector them out of harm's way.

Ten minutes later the F-16 formation zoomed by the P-3C; The Bird and his wingman, Noble Two Two, passed down each side, while Noble Four Eight rolled by overhead. Noble Three One flew beneath the Orion, and pulled up a half mile ahead in front of the turboprop aircraft. The turbulence in their wake shook the P-3C.

"Okay, hotshots," said the P-3C pilot. "You want to blow us out of the air before you get a shot at the Libyans?"

"Hey, Noble One Six," called Noble Two Two. "Can we paint a P-3 on the side of our aircraft and put a red cross through it?"

"Noble Two Two, cut the chatter," Noble One Six replied. Getting chewed out by a swabbie pissed him off.

"Hunter Six Zero, this is Noble One Six. Sorry about that, we'll watch our flight pattern. We're coming right, and will set up a racetrack orbit overhead at six thousand feet. We will maintain this frequency. In the event of encounter, hit the deck and head north; we'll provide the surprise."

"Roger, Noble One Six. Welcome aboard," the P-3C pilot said in a more mellow tone. "Watch your passes by our aircraft. We're not as sturdy as your other companion, and that last pass caused several of our crewmen to drop their breakfast trays. Lucky for us, the candles were unlit and the champagne still corked."

"Roger, Hunter Six Zero. Last thing we want is to disrupt breakfast." A chuckle followed over the radio.

On board the P-3C, the radio operator continued to call the survivors of the USS *Gearing,* trying to raise them on the emergency radio dropped by the EP-3E, Ranger Two Niner, three days ago. Five minutes later a weak, barely audible transmission came across the circuit. The radioman pushed his headset tighter against his ears.

"Hunter, this is *Gearing.* We read you fivers, how me, over?"

"*Gearing,* you are weak, but readable. We are heading your way. Activate your emergency beacon at this time."

A few seconds later a steady beeping sound from the speaker drew the radio operator's attention. On the small scope in front of him a pulsing green line, synchronized with the beeps, indicated the relative bearing to the signal.

"Pilot, Radio; I have the *Gearing,* sir," the radio operator reported over the internal communications system to the cockpit. "The emergency beacon bears zero one zero relative."

The strobe drifted to the left as the plane changed direction slightly to align its nose to the beacon.

"Mark!" the radio operator said on the ICS.

The plane leveled off. The green strobe pointed straight up. "Beacon zero zero zero relative, one seven five true," he reported.

"Roger, that."

"Noble Formation, Hunter Six Zero; on course one seven five direct to *Gearing.* Am descending to five hundred feet."

"Noble Three One and Noble Four Eight, take air-defensive position three miles west of Hunter. Noble One Six and Noble Two Two will take eastern sector."

The four-fighter formation broke apart into two pairs. The clear skies over the Gulf of Sidra enabled the four F-16 Fighting Falcons to maintain visual contact even at six miles separation.

"There they are, sir," the P-3C flight engineer said, tapping the pilot on the shoulder and pointing to the sea slightly to the right of the nose of the aircraft.

"Yeah, I see them." The pilot nosed the Orion lower, dropping to one hundred feet before he leveled off.

"Hunter Six Zero, this is Noble Three One. We see the life rafts to our left about one five zero relative."

"Roger, Noble Formation, we have contact."

Two clicks answered in the headset.

"Hunter Six Zero, this is Wizard One. What do you see?"

"Wizard One, I count eight life rafts tethered to the larger number-three raft dropped by Ranger Two Nine."

"*Gearing,* this is Hunter Six Zero. That's me overhead. We are going to commence a food-and-water run. How are conditions?"

"Hunter Six Zero, this is the Charlie Oscar. We lost six last night. We are sixty-two souls on board with four in critical condition—fuel inhalation, internal injuries. Water is low and no food. The whole world, which is right now nine life rafts, wants to know when in the hell are we getting out of here?"

"Skipper, attached to the first drop is a sealed watertight envelope with the details. Be prepared to execute its directions. Hopefully you won't be spending another night out here."

"Roger, you guys don't know what this means to see you. But we would prefer to be able to shake your hands. I think three days and four nights are enough! I've got sailors dying out here and I want to know what the Navy is doing to rescue us."

"I understand, Skipper. We are doing everything we can with what's available. Read the enclosed message. Meanwhile, you're going to continue to see us until you're rescued. We are maintaining a continuous watch north of here over your position. When you leave those rafts, it will be back into the arms of Mother Navy. Rest assured that help is on the way and we have no intention of leaving you out here any longer than necessary."

"We have already been out here longer than necessary. Rescue would be appreciated. If you have pencil and paper, I will turn this over to Warrant Officer Robertson to update the names of the survivors. I think we have everyone who survived the sinking, but I can't be sure. There are many unaccounted for. Here's the warrant, she'll provide the names."

"Roger, am prepared to copy and we'll make a wide circle of your position after the drop and commence an expanding search pattern to see if we can locate any other survivors."

"Thanks. Let us know if you find anyone," Captain Heath Cafferty replied. He handed the radio to Warrant Officer Robertson sitting beside him. This was ridiculous. The United States Navy was the most powerful Navy in the world, bar none, and here they had been drifting at sea for nearly four days. Something was wrong when your own Navy couldn't rescue you.

"Hunter, the following officers, chiefs, and sailors are accounted for." And the warrant officer began a monotonous reading of names followed by Social Security numbers. The list also identified the six who'd died during the night.

The P-3C radioman scribbled the names on yellow lined legal paper, while a nearby voice recorder backed up his effort.

The P-3C pilot brought the aircraft out of its bank and aligned the Orion with the rafts four hundred yards ahead. The plane descended to fifty feet as it began its approach. One hundred yards from the rafts, the pilot ordered the back-door crew to push the containers out. Bright orange and buoyant, the waterproof containers of water and food fell from the sky, landing within fifty feet of the rafts and the occupants. The survivors paddled the rafts to the orange floats, and as the Orion turned, four hundred yards later, the pilot observed them hoisting the supplies aboard.

"Warrant, can you repeat that last name? I missed it when we turned."

"Roger, Hunter. Williams, Josephine A. CTR1. Did you get her Social Security number?"

"Affirmative, Warrant. I got the number, it was the name that was garbled."

A different voice came over the USS *Gearing* survival radio. "Hunter, this is the Charlie Oscar again. Have reviewed the package. Finally, great news. We'll be ready. Do you have a more exact time for this to happen?"

"Regrettably, I don't," the pilot replied. "I wish I did. I wish it was right now, and I further wish that there was more we could do for you than just orbit overhead and drop supplies."

"Not to worry, Hunter. Kind of make you wish the Navy had kept seaplanes in its inventory. A night under the stars in a life raft, out of sight of land, is not something sailors want to go through," said Cafferty, his voice sad and soft. "Much less a fifth one, but knowing our shipmates are nearby boosts our morale and strengthens our courage and resolve."

"Roger, Captain. Your plight is known throughout America. The hopes and prayers of the nation and the Navy are with you even as we speak."

"Roger, Hunter. Sigonella will even seem good after this. The sooner we get there, the better. Even those who with no injuries need medical attention from the sun and sea exposure they're suffering."

"Sigonella?"

"Roger, I am assuming that will be our initial destination. It has the hospital facilities my crew needs, and is one day closer than Naples."

The pilot and copilot looked at each other. "That's right," the copilot whispered. "They don't know about Sigonella and Souda Bay."

The pilot switched off the radio. "Should we tell them?"

The copilot thought a moment, and then shook her head. "No, sir. I wouldn't recommend it. Libya may be listening, and they don't need to know the full extent of the damage we suffered."

"You're right. And the *Gearing* doesn't need to know that the hospital was destroyed in the raid. They'll find out the details soon enough when the sub arrives." He flipped the radio back on.

"Wait a minute!" the copilot said. She unzipped the pocket

on the left leg of her flight suit and pulled two newspapers out. "We can slip these in the next drop."

The pilot smiled. "Go to it! And throw in any paperbacks or other magazines we have on board. They're sailors; they'll want something to read. They deserve more for the heroes they are: sinking a Nanuchka missile patrol boat, possibly a Foxtrot submarine, and two aircraft before they were sunk. They fought a battle that will go down in Naval history."

She touched him on the shoulder. "I'll be right back, Commander." She shook her head as she walked back to where the aircrew were stacking the next drop. Naval history usually had the ship surviving, she thought.

The pilot nodded and clicked the transmit button. "*Gearing,* sorry about the delay. We were checking on something. Don't know where your destination will be, but it will be American-controlled."

"The sooner the better," Cafferty responded.

Five minutes later, the P-3C made its fourth bank for another pass. The copilot slid back into her seat and strapped her seat harness around her.

"TCO'd," she said, giving the pilot the "okay" sign.

The pilot winked and nodded.

"*Gearing,* here we come again. Mainly food this time, but you'll find a *Stars and Stripes* along with the *International Herald-Tribune* newspaper and several magazines and books. You can figure from the stories some of the things going on now."

The *Stars and Stripes* was the military newspaper published out of Germany. Distributed daily throughout the world to the military, it focused on news of specific interest to the United States military overseas. Both it and the *International Herald-Tribune* had headline stories on the plight of the *Gearing* survivors as well as the air attacks against Sigonella and Souda Bay. The photograph of the stern of the USS *Gearing* sticking out of the water, surrounded by tiny life rafts and the survivors in the water, filled the first page of the *Stars and Stripes* under a bold-lettered banner headline reading, "America Suffers Second Pearl Harbor." It was a terrible way for the survivors to relive the sinking, but the support from home would raise their morale.

More orange containers fell from the Orion, landing a little further from the life rafts than the last drop, but still within reach.

"That's all of it, Captain," the pilot apologized. "Another aircraft will return later this afternoon for another drop. Recommend rationing your supplies in the event circumstances delay the drop."

"Hunter Six Zero, this is Wizard One! We have slow-flying bogeys breaking feet-wet northwest out of Benghazi, heading your way. Break left to course zero double zero."

"*Gearing,* this is Hunter Six Zero. We are departing the area. Our prayers are with you. Captain, as hard as it may be, keep your spirits up. The whole world watches. You've replaced the Alamo."

"The Alamo?"

"Yeah, it's now 'Remember the *Gearing.*' "

"Hunter Six Zero, break off now!" interrupted the tactical controller on board the RC-135.

The Orion turned north, wiggled its wings as a salute to the *Gearing* survivors, and departed. It maintained fifty-feet altitude to avoid radar detection from the inbound aircraft.

"Hunter Six Zero, Noble Formation, this is Wizard One. Bandits' course is direct toward *Gearing* survivors. Hunter Six Zero, continue on course zero double zero. Noble One Six, you are free to execute defensive attack. Weapons free."

"Hunter Six Zero, this is Noble Formation. You should be safe. We're breaking off now. See you at the club tonight. First round's on you. Noble Formation, we have company. Let's show them some Air Force hospitality."

"Roger," replied Hunter Six Zero. "Good hunting. Kick ass for us and we'll buy the second and third round, too!"

"You Navy guys aren't as dumb as the Air Force manual says. You just read our minds."

"Hunter Six Zero, this is Wizard One. Stay low! Change to channel one eight for vectoring home. Maintain radio discipline. In other words, cut the chatter."

Two clicks acknowledged the command.

"Noble Formation, reform line abreast," ordered Howard "The Bird" Webster. He felt the sweat on his hands inside his flight gloves. This was his first air combat, but it was also the first for the rest of the formation. He took a deep, slow breath.

The four aircraft merged ten miles northwest of the USS *Gearing* survivors. A minute later they blasted over the life rafts at three thousand feet, descending as the Rivet Joint vectored them toward the bogeys. On the life rafts the sailors covered their ears even as they cheered when they recognized the American insignia on the bottom of the wings.

"Noble One Six," the ATC on the Rivet Joint said. "I confirm six bandits still on course directly toward the *Gearing*. Speed and altitude indicates they're probably helicopters. No ELINT picture available."

"Roger, we copy."

"Noble Formation, turn to course one one zero. Bandits are twenty miles at five hundred feet on course two niner zero, speed one zero zero."

"Why the hell would helicopters be heading out this way?" The Bird asked.

"Noble One Six, we speculate that they intend to take the *Gearing* survivors as prisoners."

"Roger, Wizard."

Noble Formation," said The Bird, a hint of anger in his voice. "Weapon systems on." He leaned forward and activated the fire-control system of the fighter-bomber aircraft. "We will blaze a path through them with cannon if they're helicopters. Save the missiles, unless they turn out to be fighters. If they want to take prisoners, then try to take us."

The three other F-16 fighters roger'd the order.

The Bird's eyes flashed across the heads-up display, checking the aircraft's instruments.

"Noble Formation," said the ATC. "You are ten miles and closing fast. Should be able to see them. Be careful or you'll overshoot."

The Bird looked at where his radar reflected the bogeys. The sunlight reflected off the fuselage and revolving blades of the aged helicopters. "Roger, we have them in sight. I count six transport helicopters."

"What type are they, Noble One Six?"

"I don't know," he replied testily. "They look like old Rus-

sian helicopters. We don't train on recognizing them any-
more."

The Libyan MI-14 helicopters sent from Benghazi Airfield
with instructions to pick up the survivors of the USS *Gearing*
flew on a steady course and altitude, unaware of the four
American F-16 fighters bearing down, bringing death to them.
And even if they were aware, their only defense over an open
sea, other than low altitude, was slow speed and a lot of luck.

"Noble Formation, weapons free," The Bird repeated.
"Two miles to target. Tallyho, boys!"

"How about me!" yelled Noble Three One.

"Tallyho, boys and girl!"

Twenty-millimeter cannon fire shook the F-16s as the pilots
fired into the MI-14 formation, creating a two-hundred-yard
wide swathe of death for the Libyan helicopters. Four of the
behemoth clunkers exploded, their blades still turning as the
helicopters fell. A trail of black smoke stretched from their
positions in the sky to their crashes into the sea. The other two
MI-14s hit the deck, splitting apart as they turned back toward
the coast.

The F-16s pulled up as they passed the burning inferno behind them.

"Noble Three One, take the helo on the left. We've got the
helo on the right."

The F-16 formation banked apart into two pairs as they
chased their targets, closing the coast in their desire to splash
the enemy. The Libyans weaved from side to side in a futile
attempt to avoid the cannon fire erupting around them.

Noble Two Two sent bullets through the fuselage of the
lead helicopter, killing a crew member and two soldiers cowering in the back. An electrical fire blazed up on the MI-14,
sending white smoke pouring out of the back door. But the
MI-14 managed to turn, go lower, and head back toward
Benghazi, trailing smoke from its interior. Cannon fire from
Noble Three One and Noble Four Eight blasted the trailing
helicopter, blowing its forward blades off and sending it
crashing into the sea.

Noble Three One pulled up, the lead helo, trailing white
smoke, framed in her fire-control box. Automatically she fired
an air-to-air missile that hit the turbos behind the turning

blades. The helicopter exploded in midair. Only the blade remained visible to hit the sea. Funny thing about aircraft hit by missiles. Metal cascaded through the sky, but human bodies seldom survived intact. Vaporized, torn apart, and spiraling outward, the crews disappeared forever. *Ah, the moral dilemma,* Noble Three One thought as she smiled.

"Good shooting, everyone. Form up on me," said Noble One Six.

From overhead a missile blasted by the front of Noble One Six, narrowly missing the F-16 before exploding harmlessly in the sea.

"We've got company overhead, guys," said Noble One Six. "Afterburners on! Climb! Climb! Break apart and reform at twelve thousand. Wizard One, what's going on?" he shouted into his face-mask microphone. "Where the fuck are you?"

"Noble, this is Wizard One. We have four MiG-25s in your vicinity. Don't know where they came from, but they have you sighted! Must have been in radio silence with their radars focused until they attacked. Do you see them?"

"Negative, Wizard One, we don't see them. Narrowly missed joining the *Gearing*. Scratch one enemy missile. We need information! Vectors, we need vectors! Wizard One, talk to us! Where the hell are they? Reform us at twelve thousand feet. Do you have us?"

"We have you, Noble One Six. Okay, we have them now," a calm voice announced. "They're at your five o'clock and descending. Roll left, come out on course two seven zero. Bandits are at altitude eight zero, distance seven miles. They should be straight ahead. They're coming right toward you! You're lucky, there's only four of them."

"I see them! On the left! On the left!" shouted Noble Four Eight as the Libyan and American formations passed each other, neither firing.

"Lead the way, Four Eight. Ain't no fucking MiG-25 going to ruin my day," said Noble Three One.

Ahead of Noble One Six and Two Two, two MiG-25 aircraft rolled back toward them in tandem formation. The two opposing formations saw each other about the same time. The fire-control radars on the F-16s locked on the oncoming Libyans.

"I have lock-on!" shouted Noble Two Two.

"Noble Formation, tallyho! Remember the *Gearing!*" shouted Noble One Six as he banked left, bringing his nose head-on to an attacking MiG-25. The Bird rocked his F-16 left as bright flashes of cannon fire erupted from the Libyan MiG-25. The shots went down his right side, narrowly missing the F-16. He swung the F-16 back in attack position as the Libyan maneuvered for another firing solution.

The four F-16s engaged the MiG-25s. The air battle raged directly overhead above the *Gearing* survivors, who watched the aerial combat as the aircraft dodged and weaved for position. Another missile impacted the sea half a mile from the rafts of the USS *Gearing*.

Noble One Six and Noble Two Two fired two Sidewinder missiles as two AA-7 missiles left the pylons beneath the wings of two MiG-25s.

"Flares, chaff!" screamed Howard "The Bird" Webster as he jerked back hard on the throttle, sending the F-16 in a near-vertical climb.

From the rear of the two F-16s, four flares shot out at one-second intervals, their burning magnesium temperature drawing the IR sensors of the MiG's missiles off target. Chaff clouds confused the semiactive homer on the older Soviet missile, decoying it away from Noble One Six and his wingman.

The Bird raised his eyebrows in surprise when no ECM erupted from the MiGs. The two Sidewinders blasted into the Libyan fighters. Damn, just like an arcade game.

"Scratch two MiGs!" shouted Webster. "Two Two, right turn, reform. Do you see Three One and Four Eight."

"Noble One Six, this is Wizard One. Three One and Four Eight are to your right ten miles. Steady on course two eight seven for intercept. Altitude ranging between eight and twelve thousand feet. They are engaged."

"Let's go, Noble Two Two!"

"Noble Three One and Four Eight, we are on our way!"

The Bird and his wingman pressed the throttles of the F-16s forward to maximum speed, and roared past the *Gearing* survivors in a headlong dash toward the other two Air Force fighters.

Ten miles from where The Bird and his wingman, Noble Two Two, shot down their two opponents, Noble Three One and Four Eight flipped, rolled, and fired in the continuous ballet of a close-air-combat duel. So far, four missiles had been expended by both sides with no hits.

Noble Three One rolled to the right as the MiG-25 banked left. She pulled the F-16 up, executed a half loop, and came out behind the MiG-25. The locked-on alarm sent a steady tone to her earphones. She squeezed the trigger. Her third Sidewinder ignited and shook the F-16 slightly as it blasted away at Mach Two toward its target. Flares shot out from the MiG-25.

Noble Four Eight, two miles further west, had the remaining MiG-25 on the run. The Libyan pilot was on the deck, rocking back and forth in a frantic effort to avoid the American fire-control radar.

A minute passed without the MiG-25 pilot hearing the warning tone from his sensors. The fleeing Libyan grinned as he congratulated himself on evading the American fighter. He eased his aircraft up to three thousand feet. As he keyed his microphone to call Tripoli military airfield, Noble Four Eight fired his missile. Inside the MiG-25 cockpit the beeping alarm of an inbound missile disrupted the call for eight seconds before the Sidewinder hit the engine exhaust. The MiG-25 wheeled over and began an out-of-control spiral toward the sea. It exploded when it hit, sending debris a hundred feet into the air, enveloped by a dark cloud of smoke. Noble Four Eight looked for the Libyan pilot's parachute, but didn't see one.

"Scratch another MiG!" shouted Noble Four Eight gleefully.

"He's on my tail!" shouted Noble Three One. "He has lock-on."

From the tail of Noble Three One, four flares and a cascade of chaff shot out. The missile from the MiG-25 hit the number-two flare and passed harmlessly under the F-16 to explode fifty feet in front of it. Noble Three One faked a left roll, and pulled up on the throttle as the MiG-25 flew by her to the left. She banked a hard-left diving turn, coming out behind the MiG and "luck firing" her cannon as her missile system searched for a lock-on. Hitting an aircraft with cannon fire when the target is evasive-maneuvering is hard. Most pilots believe it is just plain bad luck if you get shot down with cannon fire. Missiles were the weapons of choice for aerial combat. They required little thought, and electronics did the work. One of the twenty-millimeter shells penetrated the hydraulic system of the complex MiG-25 avionics, causing the Libyan pilot to lose control.

The Foxbat jerked, swinging from right to left and back again, as the pilot strained with muscle power to compensate for the loss of hydraulics. Without the critical hydraulic systems to move the ailerons and flaps, the aircraft was barely manageable.

Noble Three One lined up behind the Foxbat and laced the aircraft with a burst of twenty-millimeter cannon shells. The left engine of the MiG-25 burst into flames.

Without hydraulics and with only the starboard engine, the Libyan pilot lost all control of the MiG-25. The heavy Foxbat began to spin in a left-hand roll on a downward spiral to the sea.

An ejection seat blasted out from the MiG as the Libyan pilot abandoned his fighter.

"Noble Formation, reform on me," The Bird said as he began a right-turn circuit, waiting for the other three to show. "Wizard One, how does it look out here?"

"Noble One Six, Wizard One; clear skies. Well done. Time to go home now."

"Roger, Noble One Six," said Noble Three One. "Scratch another Foxbat. One pilot in the drink about five miles from *Gearing* survivors. And not one nail damaged, not one hair out of place, and—dry knickers! How's that for calm?"

"Was that why you were crying, 'He's on my tail,' 'He's on my tail'?" Noble Four Eight laughed.

"Hey, you twit! That wasn't a cry. It was just me stating a mere fact that all women understand; there's always some man somewhere on your tail."

"Good job, Noble Formation," The Bird said.

"Noble Formation, this is Wizard One. Congratulations! We watched everything from here."

"Roger, Wizard, we be ready to go home. Want to make one

pass by the *Gearing* as we exit area. They were the only audience for this little air show and they deserve the finale."

"Wizard, this is Hunter Six Zero," the P-3C interrupted. "We are north of thirty-sixth parallel and heading home. Noble Formation, well done. Thanks for doing what we would have loved to have done."

The four F-16s reformed into a diamond formation. At one thousand feet the Air Force fighters roared over the *Gearing* survivors, who waved their hats. Noble Formation executed a formation victory roll as they departed the area.

"Wizard One, this is Noble One Six. Scratch six helicopters and four MiG-25s. Request two more Foxtrot Sixteens and we'll take on their entire damn Air Force."

"I think you just did, Noble Formation!" yelled the Navy P-3C pilot.

"Noble One Six, fuel state?" the ATC asked.

"Roger, fuel low. Request tanker."

"Roger, turn to course three five zero for tanker support. Kilo Charlie One Three Five standing by," the ATC said, informing the F-16 formation that a KC-135 tanker was orbiting in the assigned refueling zone. "Turn to channel sixteen and contact tanker. Upon refueling, check back in on channel fourteen and contact Wizard One. Noble Formation, Admiral Cameron, Commander U.S. Sixth Fleet, sends 'Well Done.'"

"Noble Formation, this is Hunter Six Zero. The pitchers will be waiting at the club."

"Just make sure they're full, Hunter."

"You can be sure of that, but a full pitcher of beer in front of a lot of thirsty sailors doesn't stay full long."

CHAPTER 6

⚓

SHORTLY BEFORE MIDNIGHT THE SUBMARINE SURFACED.
Silently and quickly, sailors spilled out of the black monster
as they ran to their positions. Each was acutely aware of the
vulnerability of the USS *Albany* while surfaced. They hurried
about their tasks, conversations low as they rushed to disembark their riders. Groaning from exertion, several sailors
helped the SEALs pull the awkward rubber boats topside.
Faint red light from the interior illuminated the nighttime
task.

Belowdecks, Duncan stood with the remaining SEALs, waiting for the "all clear topside" before heading up the ladder to
what Duncan termed freedom. Cooped up inside a steel coffin
for the past thirty hours had made him feel like he was trapped
in a stalled elevator; only this elevator was surrounded by tons
of water. On top of that, they were twenty-four hours late for
their rendezvous. They had no idea whether Alneuf was there or
not, and wouldn't until they hit the shore. What a waste of time
if they got ashore and found they'd missed him. Then, Duncan
would have endangered his SEALs for nothing.

"Damn, what a time to get a headache," Duncan whispered
to Beau, who stood inches behind him.

"Drink water and take plenty of aspirins. If you still have it in the morning, call me," Beau replied.

Duncan rubbed his temples, feeling the cammie paint rub off on his fingers.

He pulled a stick of camouflage paint from his pocket. Squeezing a small portion on his fingers, he smeared the black-and-green makeup over his face.

A head stuck itself in from above. "Pssst! Captain, y'all come on."

"Damn, I'm surrounded by you Southerners."

"Wasn't he supposed to say, 'All clear topside'?" asked Beau.

"Well, Beau, I guess this is it. Good luck."

"You, too, Duncan."

Duncan turned to the squads. "Okay, let's go," he said softly. "You know what to do. Do it quietly and do it fast." He slung his carbine over his shoulder and scrambled up the ladder. Faster than he thought he could. His sports arthritis bothered him more as he got older. He recalled fleetingly, as he pulled himself through the hatch, when he could break a six-minute mile with a hangover. Now, it took eight on a good day. Here he was doing something a younger officer should be doing, and the migraine wasn't helping. He should have let Mike Sunney take this mission. To hell with whether President Alneuf of Algeria would have been offended or not if a junior officer rescued him. Duncan could have always stayed behind. Plus, there was always Beau. Beau was more than capable of leading this expedition. But in the end, Duncan knew he would never throw in the towel or stay behind or give the mission to Beau. In spite of misgivings, in spite of what the Navy had done to him, this was his mission. And as he had done countless times during his Navy career, he would execute as ordered. A stab of migraine pain zapped him. Slight migraines had plagued Duncan periodically ever since a blow to the head years ago in a brawl outside a merchant marine bar near the piers in Marseilles. He hoped it would go away before they hit the beach.

"Captain James," a voice called from above.

Looking up, Duncan recognized the silhouette as the captain of the submarine, Commander Pete Jewell, leaning over the rail.

"Yes, Captain," Duncan answered, using the title that all commanding officers of Navy vessels earned, regardless of their true rank.

"We're at the launch point. The landing site is two miles away at one eight zero. I must really love you guys!" Jewell sighed audibly. "I never bring my boat this close to the beach unless I'm going on liberty. Captain, we show no signs of aircraft or ships in the area, though EW has picked up a Marconi radar west of us. They think it's a merchant. We have no lights from shore other than those off Algiers." He pointed over the horizon to the east, where a slight glow reflected off the clouds overhead the port city.

"I want to stay surfaced as little as possible, so when you and your teams disembark, the *Albany* will submerge and turn seaward. We'll be back, as agreed, in three hours, no sooner. What time do you have?"

Duncan looked at his luminescent wristwatch. "I show zero zero twelve."

Jewell tilted his watch under a red-lens flashlight. He twisted the setting hand slightly. "There, I show the same, zero zero twelve hours. Sunrise is zero six fifteen. False dawn is zero five hundred. We'll be back here at zero three hundred. At zero three-thirty, if we haven't heard from you, *Albany* will depart and return at midnight tonight to effect a second rendezvous. If you're not there then . . ."

The two reviewed once again the particulars of the pickup arrangement, with Duncan warning Jewell that if the SEALs failed to keep the rendezvous, Jewell was to forget about the pickup and rejoin the battle group. Jewell listened and told himself that he would make the decision when to abandon the prearranged pickup. After all, he was the commanding officer of the USS *Albany* and operational plans only follow the script until the first bullet is fired.

"Good luck, Captain," Duncan said, shaking hands with the submarine skipper.

"Good luck to yourself, Captain. I don't envy your job. I feel safer here, knowing I've got two Kilos out there somewhere who would love nothing better than to sink an American submarine, than going where you're going."

"Funny thing, Skipper. I feel the same way about being topside."

Two SEALs crouched on their knees as they busily inflated the two rubber boats with the help of two *Albany* sailors. Meanwhile, other team members passed two thirty-five-horsepower outboard motors up through the hatch and onto the deck. The other SEALs squatted patiently on the rocking deck, waiting to shove off. Their weapons rested across their laps.

"See you, Skipper," Duncan said.

He hurried aft. The hissing sound of the boats inflating filled the air over the light slap of the waves against the side of the submarine. Clouds passing overhead periodically obscured the slight starlight.

"Beau, you launch your swimmer scouts when we're three hundred meters from the beach, then follow them in slowly."

"Aye, aye, Captain," Beau responded with a smile. "You mean like the way we've been briefing and rehearsing for the last twenty-four hours?"

Okay, so he was a little nervous.

"Ready, sir," Ensign Bud Helliwell said, looking up from where he squatted beside one of the boats. He patted the outboard motor he had just finished latching to the transom. "All ready, Captain."

Duncan had consciously planned the infil for five knots. On a calm sea like tonight, they'd make that easy. Four paddles per boat backed up the motors. It would take less than a half hour before they'd be in position for Beau's swimmer scouts to break off.

"Launch them," Duncan commanded.

The boats eased over the side, tether lines held by sailors on the *Albany*. The SEALs crawled over the side of the submarine, four to each boat. Duncan was the last to go. His knees creaked when he hit bottom and more fell into than boarded the rubber boat. He rubbed his knee. Can't be pulling stunts like that. Be a fine thing for the SEAL captain to pull a tendon before they even got ashore, or worse, break a leg.

Damn, I hope this migraine goes away before we land. He

sat down and surreptitiously bent his right knee a couple of times, feeling the cartilage grate against the kneecap. He glanced around, but it seemed he was the only one to hear the kneecap grinding and popping.

The SEALs took an oar each and pushed the boats away from the submarine. Looking up, Duncan saw Jewell against the backdrop of starlight, waving slowly at the departing SEALs. Then the silhouette vanished as Jewell followed the last sailor on deck into the submarine.

The outboard motors caught and the rafts began to move slowly toward the beach. A few minutes later Duncan looked back. Nothing. The USS *Albany* had disappeared beneath the surface without a sound. The SEALs were alone with slightly under two miles of Mediterranean separating them from Algeria. Duncan looked at the dark coastline and wondered briefly what would greet them on this hostile shore when they landed.

H.J. sat quietly beside Duncan. Her CAR-15 was cradled in her arm. A prophylactic that was stretched over the barrel kept the seawater out.

Duncan leaned forward. "H.J., why have you got a rubber over your piece?"

"To keep the sand out," she whispered.

"We quit doing that years ago," he replied. "The Navy issues plastic sleeves because of the negative press about using rubbers."

"I know, Captain, but I couldn't find mine so I used some rubbers I had."

"Why would you— Oh," he said, his voice trailing off. Yeah, he was too old for the new Navy.

The boats stayed within ten meters of each other as they headed toward the beach. The wind from landward stirred few waves against the incoming tide. Monkey kept switching his looks from the compass, mounted on the port side of the boat, to a shore point he had picked out. He was the only one who sat up, providing the only discernible silhouette. The other SEALs remained tense and prone against the spray tubes, their weapons pointed toward shore. Their eyes swept the beach for signs of activity, and scanned the surrounding wa-

ters for any fishing boat or patrol craft that might have gone
undetected.

Duncan glanced again to where the submarine had been.
Starlight revealed a great expanse of sea lightly rolling upon
itself. A nuclear submarine on your six is remarkably com-
forting. With *Albany* gone, Duncan felt damn lonely.

IF DUNCAN HAD BEEN LUCKY AND CONCENTRATED HARD,
he would have seen the periscope Commander Jewell raised
as soon as *Albany* submerged. Jewell mumbled to himself as
he moved the periscope back and forth in an attempt to spot
the SEALs, but the boats blended with the dark coastline, ren-
dering them invisible to the casual observer. He switched to
infrared, but the heat from the land mass obscured the sensors. After several minutes with no joy, Jewell lowered the
periscope and ordered the *Albany* out to deeper water. Now,
Duncan and his crew really were alone.

TIME, SPEED, AND A GOOD MARINER'S EYE TOLD DUNCAN
when he was five hundred meters from the beach. Using his
red-lens flashlight, he flashed three dots to Beau's boat. Beau
acknowledged the signal.

Duncan turned to the men in back. "Stop the engine."

Here, his squad would wait for Beau and his team to reconnoiter the landing site.

"H.J., you keep your eyes on the right flank of the beach.
Gibbons, you take the left. Monkey," he said to his coxswain,
calling him by his nickname. "You watch our drift. Keep us
pointed toward that sharp rock above the beach. You see it?"

"Aye, Captain, I see the precipice," Monkey answered, se-
cretly glad that the captain had identified the same shore
marker he had been using for navigation.

"It's a hill, you big asshole," whispered Gibbons. "Why
you gotta use words like precipice?"

"I'm reading a new book," Monkey replied softly.

"What book?"

"Roget's Thesaurus. Has to do with a man named Roget
who could never decide what word was best when he was

talking, so he wrote down all the choices," Monkey teased. The petty officer's huge hairy hands eased an oar into the water and with two soundless paddles corrected their head.

"Captain, what is this place? I heard that this is where an Army general named Clark landed during World War II," H.J. said in a whisper.

He felt the wind in his face. Their voices were being carried out to sea.

Satisfied they could talk and with his voice low, Duncan replied, "Yeah. On the hill up there"—he pointed at the sharp rock that Monkey and Gibbons were discussing—"is an old villa owned by a Frenchman who during World War II offered it to the OSS for a meeting between American and Vichy French officers. I saw some photographs that Navy Intelligence took before we left the *Nassau*. Library pictures of the place showed a beautiful garden surrounding a white villa with a red roof. Today, it's a dilapidated wreck. The roof is caved in. The garden is overgrown and the windows appear to be a memory. The intelligence specialist who explained the photographs said the green that was covering the house was ivy gone wild."

"Why did you go through that much trouble, Captain?"

"It helps to know the layout if you have to fight. The overgrown garden will make a fight inside the compound hard in comparison to the relatively clear countryside surrounding it," he said, and then after a few seconds added, "Of course, it'll provide more cover for our infiltration."

"How about cliff? Huh?" asked Gibbons softly, while he continued to scan the beach. "Cliff is a good word for a hill, but not precipice. For God's sake, Monkey, precipice sounds like an f'ing child asking to go to the toilet!"

"Precipice is an acceptable alternative to hill," said Monkey as he took a compass reading to the cliff to confirm their location. Monkey never trusted GPS, or anything more technical than an outboard motor. If he didn't understand it, then it couldn't be trusted. There were a lot of things he didn't trust. Radio was another one.

"What time is it?" Duncan asked.

"I've got zero one ten," H.J. replied. "Swimmer scouts should be ashore by now."

Ashore, the two swimmers pulled the boat with Beau and the chief onto the beach. Beau's squad broke off into two pairs, after a somewhat marginal effort at caching the boat. Peripheral vision was their best surveillance tool as they moved quickly from cover to cover, ambush-cautious.

Beau and McDonald ran west across the backshore along the base of the dunes. Ensign Bud Helliwell and Chief Judiah jogged east, taking the left flank. The two pairs ran about two hundred yards down the beach away from each other before disappearing into the tall dune grass that bordered the beach. Like well-oiled gears, the two pairs unknowingly complemented each other as they searched the landing site.

Once in the grass, both pairs waited a few seconds to see if their sprint along the beach had stirred unwanted notice. Two minutes later, satisfied, they began a stealthy climb toward the top of the hill above the beach. Beau dodged ahead for twenty to thirty feet until he found a suitable flanking position. Then he provided cover as McDonald rushed past. When McDonald went to ground, Beau sprinted ahead, past the petty officer, who cradled the lone MG-60 for his team. They continued in leapfrog fashion as they conducted the reconnaissance. In that manner, both pairs of SEALs circled the area where they expected to find President Alneuf and company. It took thirty minutes for the two pairs to startle each other near the top of the hill.

"Anything, Bud?" Beau asked Helliwell in a whisper.

"Negative. I didn't see any signs that anyone has been here lately."

"Me either. That must be the house," Beau said, pointing to a dark shadow that stood out against the stairs in the background.

"Yeah, think we should search it?"

Beau thought for a moment before shaking his head. "No, our job is reconnoiter the beach. Let's get the others before we go further."

Crouched, Beau started down the center of the search area toward the beach. He had taken only two steps when voices from above startled him. Without a word, the four SEALs split apart, taking cover behind nearby rocks.

The voices were in French and came from the direction of

the old house. A chuckle turned to loud bass laughter drowning out the normal murmur of conversation. Beau motioned to the members of the team and continued his trek down the hill. Bringing up the rear, McDonald followed, with Chief Judiah directly behind him. Helliwell covered their retreat from the house with his carbine. Near the beach, Beau removed his red-shaded flashlight. He flashed the dot-dash Morse code symbol for "Alpha" several times to ensure that Duncan's team received it. He expected and got no reply. Boats usually never flashed toward the shore.

"Bud," Beau said. "Take a position to the right above the landing. If those above decide to investigate the beach, don't fire unless you have to."

"Come on," Bud Helliwell said to Chief Judiah, and the two ran along the beach about fifty yards before disappearing into the dunes.

The sound of an outboard motor drifted in from the sea. "Turn that off," Beau said silently.

A hundred meters from the beach, as if Duncan read Beau's mind, he said, "Okay, cut the motor and grab the paddles."

Duncan lifted his carbine and removed the watertight sleeve from the barrel.

H.J. saw him do this and followed suit. Like Duncan, she shoved her "sleeve" into her front shirt pocket.

They paddled another ninety meters before the surf shoved them the last ten meters onto the beach. Beau and McDonald ran to the boat. The occupants hopped out and helped the two pull it over the sand and onto the dunes where the other boat rested. Beau wrapped the bowline around a nearby rock to secure it. Monkey and Gibbons hurriedly draped a cammie net over the hastily hidden boats.

They'd only be here a short time and gone by daylight, so Duncan answered in the negative Monkey's question about deflating and burying the boats in their bags. How the hell would they reinflate them?

"Anything?" Duncan asked Beau.

"Yeah, we've got visitors at the old house."

"How many?"

"At least three. Didn't try to find them or count them. I am presuming they are President Alneuf and his party. At least, I hope so."

"Okay," Duncan replied. He looked around, memorizing where the rafts were and the lay of the beach. He tried to visualize how the place would look if they had to run down from the top. It would be bloody embarrassing to achieve their mission only to find they had misplaced the boats. In the dark, the boats looked like an extension of the boulders leading down to the beach. In daylight, they'd be easily spotted.

"Where's Bud Helliwell and the chief?"

"They're in an enfilade position in case those above prove unfriendly," Beau answered, pointing to a spot about twenty yards above them and to the right.

H.J., Gibbons, and Monkey ran over and squatted near the two.

"Let's move out," Duncan ordered, looking at his watch. "We've got an hour and a half to find Alneuf and get back to *Albany*."

"Going to be cutting it close," Beau added, looking at his watch.

"Don't we always."

A minute later they came across McDonald at the base of the hill. The machine-gunner pointed upward.

"Come on," Duncan said.

Monkey and McDonald cradled their MG-60 machine guns as the other four held their Carbine 15s in position to bring them into play at the first sign of trouble. Monkey and McDonald had the heavy weapons and, in most SEAL teams, those assigned the MG-60s found the weight of the weapon slowed their pace. But, when the firefight erupted, those MG-60s were worth their weight in gold.

Gibbons shifted the radio manpack on his back and tightened the straps. Without the radio they'd have no backup communications, only their bricks. The bricks, MX-300 radios that every SEAL carried for local communications, were VHF and low-power. They lacked the broadcast range to replace the radio manpack. Duncan doubted that their signal would reach a mile, much less the range necessary to contact the *Albany*. That is, assuming the *Albany* was even monitoring the frequency of the MX-300s.

Cautiously, the six SEALs started up the hill, keeping their movement as quiet as possible. The wind continued to blow out to sea, and the slight sound of the rolling waves hitting the beach masked the few noises the rocky terrain produced as they threaded carefully uphill.

Bud Helliwell and Chief Judiah stepped out of the shadows and joined the others. Duncan nodded and pointed uphill.

Bud took a position near the point about twenty feet behind McDonald, whose finger had eased into the trigger guard of the cradled MG-60. Duncan and Beau followed. Gibbons, carrying the radio manpack, trailed a few feet behind Duncan, and spread out further behind was the rear security team of H.J., Chief Judiah, and Monkey. If they had to retreat, these three would provide the first covering fire.

Damn headache. Wish it would go away.

Above, voices escalated into numerous shouts followed by gunfire. The SEALs rolled apart, seeking the nearest cover. Duncan immediately thought they were firing at them. He looked for a target even as he moved.

Beau and Duncan rolled into each other, coming to rest back-to-back behind a natural fence of rocks about twelve inches high. Every gun pointed toward the sound of gunfire. Monkey scrambled further to the left, positioning the MG-60 to cover the left flank, while his counterpart, McDonald, did the same on the right.

The shouts, screams, and sporadic shooting continued. Duncan quickly realized they were not the targets of the gun-fight. He weighed the options of their next move.

"What you think?" Beau asked softly.

"I'm thinking, I'm thinking! Whatever is going on, they aren't firing at us," Duncan whispered. "Take your fire team and move out to the right. We'll take the left. Be careful. We came to rescue President Alneuf, not kill him, and whatever is going on up there may be his people fighting the Algerians. Beau, don't get involved. Stay back and let the situation clear itself. I have no intention of getting any of us killed over this operation."

"What'll we do if our objective has been captured? Or killed?"

"If killed, we abort the mission. If captured . . . Let's see how many there are before we decide. Be prepared to follow my lead. You've got five minutes to get in position."

"Duncan, how in the hell am I going to know what you decide if I'm over there and you're over here? I can't follow your lead if I can't see you."

"Beau, watch your brick. If the red receive light comes on, it means I'm moving in. But don't transmit unless you have to. I'm going to get as close as I can, and I don't want a radio voice spoiling our concealment. So, go. Take your squad and circle the house. Come in through the garden and assess the situation. Move from redneck to enlightened WASP for the next hour and we'll get out of this. Put McDonald where he can provide cover with that machine gun of his. I'll be coming through from the right side. Forty-five-degree overlapping fire for McDonald and Monkey. Okay?"

"Okay," Beau acknowledged. "Duncan, be careful."

"Naw, Beau. I'm going to get myself killed this close to mandatory retirement. Now, get your ass moving," he replied. He slapped Beau on the shoulder. "Be careful, shipmate. You still owe me twenty dollars."

"Rather owe it to you than cheat you out of it."

Beau got to his knees. Motioning to Chief Judiah, the fair-haired Georgian dodged to the left, tugging Helliwell's cammie shirt as he passed. The men followed as Duncan watched the night swallow them. McDonald was too far to the right for Duncan to see him join Beau. He wiped his sweaty palms on his pants. Damn. Bad enough coming in blind, but coming in blind to a combat situation!

"Come on," Duncan said, pointing to the left. At a crouch the four moved sideways, up the hill, toward the crumbling wall of the garden that surrounded the abandoned villa.

The shooting trickled off, to be followed by a renewed round of shouting. The noise of running feet above them sent Duncan and his squad diving for cover until the sound faded. Behind the convoluted noises of the battle above, the fading clamor of a vehicle engine mixed with grinding gears and spinning tires filled the night.

Someone was fleeing the firefight. Several shots rang out as a second vehicle took off, sending a shower of gravel raining against an out-of-sight wall. This was not going to be a good

night. Damn headache. He hoped his wife found the damn
dog. Duncan groaned as he remembered he still had her as
beneficiary of his Serviceman's Government Life Insurance.
Maybe she'd planned this. He moved forward. If so, her second old man was going to one rich mother.

At the waist-high wall the four SEALs lined up, keeping
their heads below it. Duncan motioned Monkey to cover. The
bulky petty officer waved a hairy hand in acknowledgment.
Duncan eased over the top.

The overgrown garden shielded him. Bushes, vines, and
stunted roses gone to seed had through the years flourished,
entangled themselves, died back, and repeated the cycle, creating a miniature jungle of undergrowth in the middle of the
arid country. Duncan crawled through the low clearance at the
base of the wild growth, careful to avoid disturbing the vege-
tation. They'd be nervous in the house, and probably shoot
first and ask questions later if they suspected someone of
being in the bushes. Twenty feet further, his hand touched the
graveled driveway leading to the villa.

Behind him H.J. and Gibbons followed. Duncan turned to
Gibbons. "Bring Monkey up."

Gibbons nodded and disappeared the way he came. The
two returned within a minute. Duncan motioned to the other
side of the road and the two SEALs darted across.

Around the bend of the road, leading to the house, four
people came running. The SEALs remained motionless as the
four strangers, three of whom wearing military uniforms, ran
by. The fourth appeared almost ghostlike as his Arab garb billowed behind him. The ancient rifle the Arab carried accented
the spectral moment. Duncan recognized the weapon as a
Kalashnikov rifle.

The SEALs creeped forward. Gibbons dodged ahead six
yards, passing Monkey, his thick finger resting lightly on the
trigger mechanism of the MG-60. If they encountered an ambush, those in front would hit the dirt as he blasted the area.

H.J. brought up the rear. Her eyes darted from shadow to
shadow as her finger rested light, but ready on the trigger. She
licked her lips, which caused her to realize how dry her mouth
was.

Twenty yards from where the curve broadened into a courtyard, Duncan stopped as he saw men standing in front of the weatherworn structure that had one time been a jewel of the Algerian coast. He counted seven bodies scattered in awkward positions around the piazza, with an eighth draped across the low wall surrounding an overgrown fountain. Death was always awkwardly met.

A large man in Arab dress laughed nervously as he talked to a military type who Duncan figured was the senior officer. Surrounding the two men, the majority of the mixed group of Arab-dressed and military-garbed individuals argued and gestured with each other. Some listened to the two men, while three others trained their guns on a group near the truck. Two of the military men stood warily near the front door of the villa. From inside the villa the flickering of a lantern bubbled across the opening.

The large truck was not military. It had wooden sides, and Duncan assessed it to be a commercial vehicle. The faces of the prisoners were easily seen in light of the small campfire burning nearby. Duncan motioned H.J. forward.

The three prisoners squatted with their hands behind the backs of their necks. They leaned against the rear right truck wheel. Duncan saw the fear in the men's faces. Two of the military-garbed men walked around the guards, grabbed a prisoner, and began to tie his hands behind him before roping the hands to the feet. Reminded Duncan of a pretzel. Finished, they shoved the prisoner onto his side, and moved to the next. They continued until all three were trussed up in the same fashion. Then several of the Arabs picked the prisoners up and tossed them, unceremoniously, into the old dry fountain in the center of the courtyard, to be rewarded with grunts and low moans as their captives hit the concrete bottom. Lucky for the prisoners it was only a couple of feet deep and dry.

An elderly individual emerged from the villa with a suit coat draped across his arm, his opened white shirt half-tucked into dark trousers. The man walked down the steps of the villa to where the huge Arab and the military leader talked. Duncan recognized the newcomer as President Alneuf from the photographs Commander Mulligan had shown him before they departed the *Nassau*.

Duncan waved Gibbons further left, knowing the petty officer would position himself to protect Duncan's flank while covering those whom they were observing. He tugged H.J.'s shirt. She scampered forward.

"Stay here and cover me," he whispered, holding his hand over his mouth to muffle the words.

"What are you going to do?" she asked.

"That's Alneuf. The gentleman we've been tasked to bring back. Can't think of a better way to find out if they're friendly or not than go introduce myself."

"I'd be careful, Captain. I don't think they're in any mood to take a chance. They may start shooting before you start talking."

"Yeah, that's my thoughts, too, but . . ."

Monkey gave a thumbs-up as he reached his position directly across the road from where Duncan and H.J. lay. Further left, past Monkey, Gibbons, in a prone position, trained his carbine on the crowd around the truck.

In this three-prong position, the SEAL squad had the entire group covered, able to deal out a deadly first fire if necessary. Without knowing for sure how the others were positioned, Duncan assumed that Beau and his squad had the left flank covered. The parked truck obscured their firing field, so it was up to Beau to take care of that vulnerability. Monkey's weapon would nullify anyone seeking shelter between the truck and the house. It would be up to Beau's squad to cover the blind side of the truck.

Duncan reached down and pressed the transmit button on his brick to activate the red light on Beau's MX-300. Duncan hoped Beau was in position and saw it. He released the button.

"Well, here goes nothing," Duncan whispered. He crawled forward another ten feet to distance himself from H.J. Her weapon pointed over Duncan's head at the Algerians.

He stood and stepped into the middle of the road. Duncan raised his hands, holding his carbine aloft gripped tightly in his right hand.

"Hello, the house!" he shouted.

The sound, like a thousand crickets, filled the night as safeties clicked off and they leveled their weapons at him.

Duncan had this quick, fleeting recognition that if they had been any less professional, they would have shot him.

The mustached leader shoved Alneuf behind him, where two of the Guardsmen moved in front of the Algerian president. Yosef brought his weapon to bear on Duncan.

"President Alneuf," Duncan announced in a loud voice. "I'm from the travel agent you phoned a couple nights ago."

Duncan took several steps forward. A couple of the Guardsmen ran from the sides toward him with the intention of taking his gun.

"No, I don't think that would be a good idea," Duncan said, holding the carbine aloft and out of reach of the shorter Guardsman, who reached for it.

"Leave him," Colonel Yosef said, waving his men back.

Two more Palace Guards walked casually behind Duncan. Duncan, his weapon still above his head, walked slowly toward Colonel Yosef.

"Tell your men not to get nervous with their weapons, as I'm going to bring my hands down. My weapon will point away from President Alneuf while I bring it down, and once down it will point at the ground. I would appreciate it if you could reassure your men, uh, General?"

"Colonel. Colonel Yosef."

"Roger, Colonel Yosef. If you would just reassure your men?"

Colonel Yosef nodded. "Most speak English. Just don't make any unusual moves, please. And you are American, I presume?"

"I am Captain Duncan James, United States Navy. And you, Colonel Yosef?" he asked as he lowered his weapon.

"Captain Duncan, welcome to Algeria. I am Colonel Daoud Yosef, commanding officer of the Algerian National Palace Guards."

"Colonel Yosef, my pleasure. I am here at the request of your president." Duncan pointed to Alneuf, who stood silent behind the colonel. "We are answering a diplomatic request from the president of Algeria to provide transportation to a safe haven out of your country." He licked his dry lips. His head still hurt, but he forced himself to ignore it.

Yosef cleared his throat and nodded. "Yes, I am aware of

President Alneuf's request. He told me of it last night when you failed to keep your appointment."

"I apologize for being late. As I am sure you are aware, we are having our own problems in Algiers."

"Yes, I know," Yosef replied, thinking of the truckload of Westerners he and his men had freed on their escape from the capital.

President Alneuf stepped around the two Guardsmen standing in front of him, and strolled forward to stand beside Yosef. He stuck his hand out to the tall U.S. Navy captain.

"Welcome to Algeria, Captain. We are pleased to see you," Alneuf said as they shook hands. A broad grin accented his statement.

"Mr. President, we have transportation on the beach below." Duncan looked at his watch. It showed two o'clock. "The primary transportation is due in an hour. We'll need to leave soon to make our rendezvous."

"Captain, where do you intend to take me?"

"Mr. President, my job is to get you out of the country. I have no idea where you go from there. I have been asked to relay from my government that the final destination is yours and to offer asylum in the United States if you so desire."

"I appreciate the offer of your government, but I think I would like to go to Tunisia," he said.

Duncan's eyebrows raised slightly. "I'm sorry, Mr. President. Algerian and Libyan forces invaded Tunisia two days ago. As of this morning it is under the occupation by those forces. If you are thinking of going to Morocco, I have to advise against that also as Morocco, like Algeria, is now in a state of rebellion. Let us get you out of the country and when aboard the *Nassau* . . ."

"*Nassau*? We are going to the Bahamas?" Yosef asked, interrupting Duncan.

"No, Colonel, not the Bahamas. The USS *Nassau* is the destination. The USS *Nassau* is an amphibious carrier off Algiers at this moment."

Alneuf nodded.

Duncan looked around the area. "What happened here, Colonel?"

Yosef followed Duncan's look around the area. "This was

our second night and I am afraid we relaxed our vigilance too soon. We were making coffee when a truckful of revolutionaries drove up to the front of the villa. It was only luck that the brakes on the truck squealed as it stopped. Otherwise, the story you are seeing could have been quite different."

"Yes, we heard the gunfire as we were coming up from the beach."

Yosef pointed to the fountain, where the three prisoners lay tied up like animals awaiting slaughter. Duncan wondered if the Algerians would shoot them before they left. He hoped he wouldn't have to face that moral dilemma. Above the prisoners, one of Bashir's relatives stood guard. Duncan saw the Arab grin as he poked the helpless prisoners with his Kalashnikov rifle. If they decided to execute those three prisoners, Duncan wanted to be far away when it happened.

"It seems that somehow the new government discovered we were at the old villa on the coast and sent a squad of their revolutionary guards to investigate," explained Yosef. "From what little the prisoners have said, they were surprised to find themselves fighting Algerian Guardsmen. They thought we were some upper-class citizens fleeing the carnage and chaos in Algiers. They figured to find a bunch of frightened civilians up here." He grinned. "Instead, much to their surprise, they stumbled on the only remaining Algerian soldiers in this area of the country. And those Algerian soldiers were the elite Palace Guard. Those eight won't bother anyone again, and those three we'll leave here and, if they're lucky, they'll be found before the insects drive them mad. Unfortunately, at least two escaped. We have two of Mr. Bashir's relatives"— he pointed to the large Arab standing near them, who grinned and nodded at Duncan—"and one of my Guardsmen in pursuit. We should know soon if they were successful. If they catch them, then we should be safe for a while. If not, then we can expect additional company soon. It will depend on how fast the new Algerian Army reacts," Yosef said, derision in his voice.

"I heard before we departed the USS *Nassau* that the rebels were mounting a big search east of Algiers, centered around a beached fishing boat that they believed President Alneuf had been on?"

"Yes, we were attacked by an aircraft. We were on our way to Tunisia when it surprised us. We barely beached the boat before it would have sunk. Mr. Bashir saw the battle, stopped along the highway, and thanks to his knowledge of the desert we avoided the rebels until tonight. For that, we owe him our lives."

"And I fed them, too," Bashir added as he walked up behind Colonel Yosef.

"Well, your adversaries were still searching that location twenty-four hours ago," Duncan said.

"You said, 'we,' Captain," Yosef continued. "How many are there of you and where are they, if I may ask?"

Duncan turned his head. "Come on out, Beau, H.J."

H.J. and Gibbons emerged from the bushes to stand behind the two Guardsmen who were standing behind Duncan. From the front of the truck, Beau, Chief Judiah, and Ensign Helliwell emerged.

"Very good, Captain," said Yosef. He snapped his fingers twice.

From behind H.J. two Guardsmen rose from the bushes, their weapons trained on her and Gibbons. Behind Beau another group of three appeared from the shadows.

"Very good, Colonel," said Duncan. He raised his hand. "Monkey! McDonald!"

Monkey and McDonald stepped out behind the five Guardsmen. Their machine guns pointed forward.

Yosef raised his hands and motioned the Guardsmen forward. They moved in front of the SEALs and joined their comrades.

"Touché, Captain," Yosef said admiringly. He grinned. "I guess it is true what they say about your Navy SEALs."

"I wouldn't know, Colonel. I never listen to rumors."

The two shook hands, satisfied they had earned each other's respect.

A cell phone rang, breaking the momentary silence. Bashir frantically patted the numerous pockets of his outfit. Finally, he grinned as his hand touched the telephone. Bashir turned his back to the group and walked away as he answered it. His deep bass voice, speaking a Bedouin dialect, carried through the compound.

"Captain, some of these people must leave with me," said Alneuf. "Colonel Yosef and his men must come. I cannot leave them behind. It would be unconscionable; a de facto condemnation to certain death. Mr. Bashir, who is on the phone, refuses to leave. He argues that his group will meld safely back into the population without anyone discovering their assistance to me. I pray that he is right."

"How many are we talking, Colonel?"

"I have eleven men, myself, and the President."

"Thirteen," Duncan said aloud.

Yosef's twelve and Duncan's eight made twenty for the two eight-man boats. President Alneuf made twenty-one. It would be tight, but they could do it. His team could hold onto the sides or swim independently as they moved out. They were only taking one civilian. The colonel's men were professionals like the SEALs. Unfortunately, they were soldiers. *Hope they can swim.*

Bashir flipped the phone closed. "Colonel, we have company coming. At least two trucks full of rebels. My nephews tried to catch the ones who escaped, but they must have had a radio or a telephone in their truck. My nephews are heading this way and coming fast. The soldiers are about two kilometers behind them, and my nephews are five kilometers from here. We have less than ten minutes before they arrive."

Duncan looked at his watch. "It's another hour before our transportation arrives."

"We have no choice, Captain," Colonel Yosef said urgently. "Two truckloads can be more than fifty men. I do not have the arms or the men to fight them, and even if we did, as soon as they suspect that President Alneuf is here, they'd have helicopters and aircraft overhead before first light. We have to go."

"Is there someplace we can hold up for thirty minutes until we get out to sea?"

"That won't help, Captain. What if we get out to sea and your transportation is not there? What then?"

"What do you suggest, Colonel?" Duncan asked as his mind quickly weighed the pros and cons of the situation. Suddenly, the insides of the USS *Albany* seemed very attractive.

"We leave," Yosef said.

Then the colonel shouted, "Quick, everyone into the truck. Hurry."

Turning to Duncan, he said, "We'll head west toward Bashir's village. There, we can get a boat and head out to sea. Can you make other transportation arrangements?" Yosef asked anxiously.

"Probably, but if we hurry we can get out to sea before they arrive," Duncan suggested again. "We have rubber boats on the beach and we can go wait offshore a couple of miles for the rendezvous. They'll be there."

"Captain, I appreciate what you are doing, but as I said, you can't be sure that your transportation will be there."

"You're a soldier, Colonel. The plan says they'll be there. If not, we'll just . . ." His voice trailed off.

"If they're not there, Captain, then we will be what you Americans call, shitting ducks!"

"Sitting ducks," Duncan corrected. "We may be sitting ducks, but I have strong confidence the submarine will be there."

OFFSHORE, THE USS *ALBANY* TURNED AWAY FROM THE coast. The Marconi radar detected earlier by the electronic warfare system had turned out to be an Algerian coastal patrol boat. Unknown to the American Navy, Algeria had been maintaining a nighttime maritime patrol along the coast to complement the helicopters flying the same surveillance during the day. The EW antenna on the periscope showed the Marconi loitering in the rendezvous area. USS *Albany* continued, reluctantly, to move away from the area even as Jewell developed a firing solution on the craft. At six thousand yards it'd be like shooting fish in a barrel. However, torpedoing the ship would alert everyone up and down the coast and endanger the SEALs ashore. It was also against the Rules of Engagement promulgated by Sixth Fleet. He lowered the periscope and ordered a new depth. The submarine descended as it headed further out to deeper waters to hunt Kilos until it returned for the second rendezvous at midnight, twenty-one hours away.

THE ALGERIAN COASTAL PATROL CRAFT LOADED ITS CANNON and fired. Ashore, Duncan continued his attempt to convince Colonel Yosef and President Alneuf to come with them. If they went east on the trucks, Duncan would take his teams back out to the rendezvous place. He did not intend to head out into Algeria with Yosef.

"But, Colonel," Duncan began, stopping in mid-sentence as the familiar whistle of an inbound artillery shell reached his ears.

"Take cover!" Duncan shouted. "Incoming!" He dove to the side, rolled once, and came up against the aged fountain. Looking back, he saw Colonel Yosef staring at him.

"Incoming!" he shouted again, pointing upward to the colonel, who gave Duncan a puzzled look that changed to recognition.

The intensity of the whistling grew. Colonel Yosef pushed Alneuf to the ground and threw himself over the president.

"Get down!" Yosef shouted.

The Algerians joined the Navy SEALs hugging the ground as the first shell hit the house, blowing the roof apart.

Pieces of red clay tile and dry stucco rained down on them, followed by a choking cloud of red dust.

Colonel Yosef jumped up, pulling President Alneuf with him. "Quick, into the trucks, everyone."

Duncan rose to his knees, his hand on the rim of the fountain. Well, there went his plan to head back out to sea and wait for the *Albany*. The roll against the fountain had slammed his right knee against the brick and porcelain fixture, bringing renewed waves of pain. He ran his hand searchingly down his leg, checking to make sure that nothing was broken. He limped to the truck. H.J. and Helliwell pulled him up onto the flatbed. Why did growing old have to be so painful?

Bashir hoisted his massive body into the driver's seat. His cellular telephone fell out of his pocket and landed beneath the front tire of the truck. Yosef shoved Alneuf into the cab and plunged in beside the Algerian president.

"Let's go, Bashir. Quick!" Yosef commanded.

The whistle of another shell drove out the sounds of the other men scrambling into the truck. It hit the rear of the old house as Bashir, with a jerky start, floored the gas. The truck bounced along the unkempt driveway that led out of the villa garden.

"Beau!" Duncan called.

"Here, Boss!"

"Take muster!"

"Have already and we've got a problem!"

"What is it?" Duncan asked, pulling himself upright on the wooden rungs of the truck siding.

"No passports."

The truck hit a deep hole as it pulled out of the entrance to the villa gardens, knocking Duncan and Beau off their haunches. Bud Helliwell leaned over the top of the cab. He pointed his carbine ahead. McDonald took a prone position along one side of the truck with the barrel of his MG-60 sticking through the lower rung of the wood siding. Monkey had the right side covered similarly. Duncan and H.J. guarded the rear of the truck. Alternating among the SEALs, the Algerians took their own defensive positions.

"Gibbons, come here," Duncan commanded.

The radioman crawled over to where Duncan sat.

"Yes, sir."

"Turn around. I need the radio."

Gibbons turned so that the captain had access to the radio.

"Shit," said Duncan.

"What is it, sir?"

"You can throw the radio away, Gibbons. And you can thank Motorola for your life."

Gibbons removed the manpack and twisted it around in front of him. A sliver of roof tile, like a foot-long icicle, stuck out of the center of the radio.

"So, that's what's been sticking me in the back."

"Can you fix it?" Duncan asked expectantly.

Gibbons shook his head. "I'm sorry, Captain. I don't think I can. I'm a gunner's mate trained to do first aid, not an electronics technician." Gibbons pulled the fragment out. A tangle of burnt wires and destroyed circuit cards filled the center of the radio where the audio-control system and antenna connections had once existed. "What'll we do, Captain?"

Duncan shook his head. "We'll do something, Gibbons.

Right now, looks like we're going on a dynamic tour of this North African country."

They were a hundred yards from the villa, bouncing across the weather-eroded drive, when the third shell hit the fountain killing the three prisoners.

"CAPTAIN, I'M PICKING UP NAVAL GUNFIRE," THE SONAR operator said to Jewell. "Look at the waterfall display on my CRT. See this blip across here?"

"Give me a headset," Jewell said, grabbing an extra pair hanging above the console. The muffled sound of the second round came through the underwater detection system.

He watched the slow waterfall of the CRT change its intensity as the sonar device recorded the Naval gunfire. The two sailors and Jewell looked at each other.

"It's definitely Naval gunfire," the chief sonar technician said confidently.

Jewell nodded in agreement. "Range and bearing?"

"Bearing one niner zero, Skipper. Range has to be under ten thousand yards because then you hit land."

The officer of the deck interrupted. "Captain, the sonar bearings cut through the rendezvous area and correlate with the EW bearing on the Marconi radar. The gunfire must be from that Algerian coastal patrol craft."

"Doesn't sound like large-caliber shells, Captain," the sonar operator volunteered.

Jewell hung the headset back up. "Can you hear the shells hitting?"

"No, sir. I would guess they're firing at a target or targets ashore," the chief replied.

"No splashes, Skipper," the sonar operator confirmed.

"Officer of the deck, clear baffles and prepare to come to periscope depth. I want a firing solution on that ship ASAP!" Jewell ordered as he hurried to the periscope.

Seeing the XO arriving through the forward hatch, Jewell stared intently for a second and then said calmly, "XO, man battle stations."

"Officer of the deck, man battle stations!" the XO shouted.

The OOD turned to the senior enlisted man in the control room. "Chief of the watch!"

"Aye, sir!"

"Man battle stations!"

"Aye, aye, sir!" The chief of the watch reached over and pushed the red lever on the ship's alarm system down. A soft bonging vibrated inside the sound-insulated hull to reach every nook and cranny in the attack submarine. Sailors tumbled out of their racks and left their night snacks scattered as they ran to their battle stations. Events began to roll off in sequence to turn the submarine into a deadly machine.

"Baffles clear," said the officer of the deck.

"This is the captain, I have the conn, make your depth six two feet."

"Up scope," Jewell said, more calmly than he felt.

"Steady on course one niner zero," the helmsman announced.

"Coming to six two feet," said the diving officer of the watch.

The periscope cleared the water. The running lights on the coastal patrol craft made it easy for Jewell to find the small boat. He pushed the button under his right hand, switching the periscope to infrared. The Algerian coastal patrol craft became instantly visible to the American submarine, the heat from its engine overpowering the coastal heat sources. On the bow several Algerian sailors were hand-loading the single-shot cannon.

"Captain, we have a firing solution," the XO announced from his battle station as the fire control coordinator.

"XO, the shore bombardment by this vessel is being directed against our Navy SEAL team. I see what I strongly believe to be them on the hillside," the captain said, knowing the infrared system was ineffective with a heat source like the patrol craft between *Albany* and the beach.

"XO, take a look and give me your assessment," Jewell continued, in a loud voice so everyone could hear.

The XO put his sound-powered phones down, and worked his way through the press of flesh jammed into the control room until he reached the periscope.

They exchanged a wink. Bending down, the husky executive officer viewed the craft through the periscope for nearly two seconds.

The XO looked up. Their eyes met. "Captain, I concur. I count a minimum of eight heat sources on the hill," the XO said in a loud voice.

Everyone in the control room would remember this exchange between the captain and his executive officer and, later, report it nearly verbatim to the investigating board.

"Captain, I recommend we take defensive actions to protect our forces ashore."

"Sir, he just fired again!" the sonar operator reported.

"Officer of the deck, note the XO's concurrence in the log. XO, return to your battle station." He touched the XO's shoulder as their eyes locked for a moment. Then the taller man wormed his way back through the mass of humanity.

"Make tubes one and two ready in all respects. Shallow-draft target, minimum enable. Tube one is the primary tube. Tube two is the backup," Jewell ordered.

"Roger, Captain," the weapons officer replied.

Across from the XO's battle station the weapons officer leaned over the firing panel operator. While the captain and XO had gone through their transparent charade, he'd used the time to confirm the torpedo room was ready.

"Firing point procedures," Jewell announced as his impatience grew to get a torpedo in the water.

"Ship ready, Captain," the officer of the deck reported.

"Weapons ready!" followed the weapons officer.

"Solution ready!" the XO reported, wrapping up the check-off sequence.

Jewell took a deep breath and let it out. "Final bearing and shoot. Up scope."

Jewell looked into the periscope. "Bearing . . . Mark," he said as he pressed the button on the periscope, electronically correcting the firing solution.

"Set," replied the XO.

"Shoot!" shouted the weapons officer into his mouthpiece.

The sailor on the weapons control panel turned the firing key. "Tube one fired electrically! Tube two ready!"

The submarine shuddered slightly as the torpedo exited the boat.

"Down scope," ordered Jewell.

Jewell shut his eyes and counted. This would be the first time since World War II that an American submarine had used a torpedo to sink a surface ship in an act of war.

"Weapon has enabled," said the weapons control coordinator.

"Conn, sonar, weapon speeding up!" announced the sonar operator. The torpedo had locked on target and was speeding for the kill.

Silence descended in the control room as every man willed the torpedo onto its target.

"He's just fired again, Captain," the sonar operator said, breaking the tense silence. Jewell watched. The sonar operator took off his headset as the display from the torpedo and the target merged.

Two seconds later the submarine shook as the torpedo blew up beneath the keel of the Algerian patrol craft. The explosion split the small boat into two halves. A shower of splinters and flesh skyrocketed into the air.

"Up periscope," Jewell commanded. He grabbed the eyepiece and handles before they were waist high. Directly ahead, the flaming remains of a bow and stern touched each other like a man bent backward until his spine cracks and his heels touch the back of his head. The small patrol boat sunk in seconds as Jewell watched.

A cheer erupted in the control room. Several looked away to hide wet eyes.

"That's enough," Jewell said. "We still have the SEALs out there. Down scope."

Jewell stepped away from the instrument as it slid belowdecks. "EW, keep a good lookout. Sonar, you, too. OOD, you have the conn, come to course zero one zero and keep her pointing that way in case we have to make a quick exit."

The XO left his position and joined the captain near the center of the control room. "What now, Captain?"

Jewell looked at his watch. "It's three ten. We'll wait thirty minutes and if they're not here, then we go to plan B."

"Plan B?"

"Yeah, we go look for Kilos until tomorrow midnight when

we'll return. That is, if the entire Algerian Navy isn't over-running this area by then."

"Sir," the XO said. "Good shooting."

"Yeah," Jewell replied. "Now comes the best part."

"What's that?"

"The second-guessing by Washington."

Jewell picked up the microphone for the ship's announcing system. "This is the captain. We have just sunk an unidentified ship that was firing on the SEALs we sent ashore earlier. Well done to all of you. We are going to remain at battle stations while we wait in this area to recover the returning SEAL team. Once again, well done."

He hung up the microphone. "XO, we need to let Sixth Fleet know what's happened. The rest of you keep a keen eye on your sensors.

"Up scope. Stand by with the infrared signal light on the scope." He wiped his sweaty palms on his khakis. There was an overriding urge to head for deeper water. His stomach felt queasy. He knew Duncan and his team wouldn't be waiting. By now, they had probably gone to ground. Regardless, in the fog of combat the SEALs' only alternative was for the *Albany* to follow the plan as closely as possible. Jewell had no way of knowing that his passengers were ten kilometers inland and heading deeper into Algeria as the *Albany* waited.

CHAPTER 7

⚓

THE PERISCOPE OF THE ALGERIAN KILO SUBMARINE AL *Nasser* slid into the well beneath the control room. Hydraulic fluid leakage around the mast dripped onto the deck, the sweet smell clashing with the unwashed scent of 120 sailors. Captain Ibn Al Jamal stared blankly at several sailors, who turned away, refusing to acknowledge his gaze. Eight thousand meters away the *Nassau* battle group steamed, as it had for the past twenty-four hours. Throughout that time the Algerian Kilo-class hunter-killer submarine had shadowed the Americans without even a tiny hint that they knew it was there—a credit to the Algerian crew's training.

His last futile attempt, two hours ago, to reach Algiers Naval Headquarters remained unanswered. He navigated at the edge of the American forces with no clear-cut orders, other than the ones issued seven days ago.

He wiped his palms. Out here, two American attack submarines patrolled. Submarines much more capable than the diesel he commanded. Despite his efforts, the two nuclear submarines remained unlocated. At least one of them had to be here. It would be a tactical failure to leave the American battle group undefended. But the captain was wrong. Neither of the American submarines was with the battle group. The USS *Miami* was en route to rescue the survivors of the USS *Gearing,* and the USS *Albany* loitered near the Algerian coast waiting for the second rendezvous attempt with the SEALs.

Captain Ibn Al Jamal walked to the plotting table, trying to appear more confident than he felt. On top, an outlined scheme of where their passive analyses and periscope sightings positioned the American warships was displayed. A penciled arrow shooting out from each symbol had the course and speed written along it for the American warship it represented.

He had selected the arsenal ship as the primary target, with the USS *Nassau* as number two. Without the arsenal ship, USS *King,* American firepower against Algeria would be limited to aircraft and the limited number of cruise missiles on the other ships.

The arsenal ship was an Admiral Boorda initiative, before his untimely death, to carry a reduced United States Navy into the twenty-first century. The USS *King* was unique; one of a kind. The arsenal program was canceled before the USS *King* was ever built, but Boorda supporters on the Hill voted funds for one to show the utility and tactical value of the concept. USS *King* was that one—kind of a memorial to Boorda.

Captain Jamal picked up a photograph taken earlier in the day through the Kilo's periscope. The arsenal ship was a modern-day monitor that looked similar to the historic Confederate warship CSS *Virginia*. A long, dark menace with a low waterline complemented topside by a triangular-shaped Aegis forecastle that ran from near the bow to about a third of the length of the ship. The rear two thirds was a flat deck covered with metal hatches, hiding the vertical-launched weapons ranging from Tomahawk cruise missiles to surface-to-air missiles. The ship could mix its missiles to fight an air, shore, and antisubmarine battle simultaneously, but it only provided the weapons. Other ships in the battle group did the targeting and the firing. The arsenal ship was a weapons platform for the battle group—surrounded by a half-inch-thick aluminum hull capable of stopping anything with less power than a .22 rifle. One good torpedo, properly placed, would sink her. He intended to put four into her.

Ibn Al Jamal checked his watch before he ran his finger down the navigational checklist taped to the plotting table. Sun set in thirty minutes. Add another thirty minutes for darkness, and then he would launch his attack. He looked at his watch. He would attack at twenty-two hundred hours, ten o'clock, when the Americans were announcing taps for the crew and their attention was distracted.

He gave orders to descend to one hundred meters. He'd wait fifty meters above the shallow sound layer until it was time.

Captain Jamal changed the course of the *Al Nasser* to parallel the heading of the *Nassau* battle group. He told the officer of the deck to maintain eight thousand meters distance from the Americans, and make appropriate course changes as necessary to maintain that separation. He wanted no accidental detection by the Americans. He'd close the battle group prior to firing.

Satisfied, Captain Jamal informed the officer of the deck that he was going to his cabin. He asked him to notify the steward to bring him tea. The captain strolled shakily out of the control room, turning sharply at the hatch as he remembered to tell the OOD to switch to red lighting. The next time the periscope went up it would be dark.

Crew members respectfully moved aside as he wormed his way down the narrow passageway. Each and every one murmured a greeting to the captain—none met his eyes.

He knew their reaction was to yesterday's execution of the three traitors who had attempted to sabotage the *Al Nasser*'s reduction gears. An unpleasant task, but a wartime necessity. The bodies joined six others in the galley's freezer, keeping the frozen food company on *Al Nasser*'s journey to greatness. He prayed that it wasn't to oblivion. He wondered how the rebel zealot was doing on the *Al Solomon,* waiting at the mouth of the Strait of Gibraltar. An involuntary shiver shook him as he thought of his counterpart on the other Kilo submarine.

The saboteurs had been seized quickly. A rapid inspection by the chief engineer had failed to find any obvious damage. But unknown to them, tiny flakes of hard metal had fallen into the gears. Millimeter by millimeter they had worked their way deeper into the gearbox, until hours later the spinning gears began to make a continuous clicking noise, which vibrated along the shaft and into the water. A soft noise anomaly, joining the myriad of sea sounds echoing through the water, inaudible to those inside the *Al Nasser*.

THE SONAR OPERATOR ON THE *SPRUANCE*-CLASS DEstroyer USS *Hayler* twisted the knob on the SQR as he finetuned the waterfall pattern. There was that blip again. He'd tried everything he knew to determine its source, with no luck. As much as he hated to do it, because of the ribbing he would take, he had no choice. He pressed the button on the ship's intercom for the chief.

"Chief, can you come up here a minute?" Sonar Technician Second Class Calhoun asked, and then grimaced as he waited for the snide comment. Herbert J. Calhoun was the son of a career deputy sheriff from a northern county in South Carolina. Career policemen seldom earned enough to pay for their children to go to college; deputy sheriffs earned even less. Herbert J. Calhoun knew his parents would have scratched, fought, and suffered to send him to college, but with two younger brothers and two even younger sisters, he knew they couldn't afford it. They couldn't even afford a community college. So he joined the Navy for the G.I. Bill, to discover, after four years, he was enjoying himself. He reenlisted. He had six more months to go on this second tour, and Calhoun intended to get out. His father's untimely death a year ago had a lot to do with the decision. The other was he had been accepted for the University of South Carolina to start in the spring quarter.

"What is it, Calhoun? I'm busy right now," Chief Boyce yelled back on the ship's intercom, leaning back as he threw his feet on the desk. With one shoe he pushed the enlisted fitness reports to one side. "Not doing anything I enjoy, but still busy," he mumbled to himself.

"Chief, I got a sound event on the SQR that I don't understand."

"So? Why should I be surprised about that?"

"Ah, come on, Chief. This is a real new one. I've never

heard anything like it before and I really need you to look at it."

"Like the whale with the cold in the Atlantic?"

"Ah, Chief. You can't expect us to be as good as you. I mean, look—you're a chief," Sonar Technician Second Class Calhoun said, patronizing the asshole. *Of course, I could always get my degree and come back in the Navy as an officer and fire your ass,* Herbert J. Calhoun thought.

"Okay, okay, okay. You win, I'm coming. Keep your shirt on, Calhoun, but if it's another whale I'm gonna be pissed," Boyce replied, clicking the intercom off. He shoved himself upright in the chair and tied his shoes. Chief Boyce leisurely shuffled the paperwork into a haphazard stack, and shoved it into his top desk drawer. Murmuring to himself about never having the time to do everything they expected him to do, he stood and stretched.

"Probably marine life," he grumbled as he walked out of the office, pulling the door shut behind him. A few minutes later he dashed through Combat to the ASW module, earning the lanky chief the attention of the watch-standers. His thin smoke-wrinkled face intentionally twisted into what he hoped showed a mask of professional concern. His brown eyes searched the compartment, pleased that Lieutenant Frank, the CICWO, noticed. Chief Boyce wiped his hook nose as he slowed near the ASW module. He knew he impressed everyone when they first met him.

What he didn't know was that it didn't take long for most to realize that Chief Boyce could "talk the talk" but couldn't "walk the walk."

"What is it, Calhoun?" Chief Boyce asked.

"Look at this, Chief," Calhoun said, pointing to a slight hiccup running up the graphic waterfall of the SQR. "See this blip here? It showed up on the last watch. Johnny told me, when he was going off watch, that he thought it was something in the system. But I've gone over the system, ran diagnostics twice, and can't find one damn thing wrong with it. When I switch to another frequency or try to get a reading on another bearing, the blip goes away." Calhoun paused as Boyce read the display.

"It's not us, Chief," he added with conviction, shaking his head.

"Has the sound event remained on this constant bearing even when we turn?" Boyce asked, his eyes shifting back and forth as he analyzed the display.

"I don't know, Chief. We haven't turned since I came on watch, and it's been on a constant bearing."

If the sound event remained on the same bearing when the USS *Hayler* turned, then most likely it was something in the system or resonating from the destroyer itself. If the waterfall showed the anomaly drifting off the bearing during a turn, then something was out there.

"If it's been there nearly two hours, then it'll be there later. Run another diagnostic, Calhoun, on the system and if that doesn't identify anything, then we'll see if the OOD will do a course change for us."

"Chief, trust me! Can we get him to do a turn now? I've run diagnostics twice and I'm telling you there ain't nothing wrong with the system. Besides, if it is something, then it may not be out there later, Chief," Calhoun said, gritting his teeth. He wondered if they had "dickheads" at the University of South Carolina. "I think we ought to report it."

"Calhoun, I've been in the Navy nearly twenty years. Twenty years I've been doing this job and while I know you've run diagnostics, sometimes a little experience, like mine, is just the thing to spot something you've probably missed." Chief Boyce patted Calhoun on the shoulder. "So, just run the diagnostics like I told you to."

Calhoun sighed. "All right, Chief, I'll do it. But, I'm telling you it's a waste of time. What if . . ."

"I know, Calhoun, what if it's a submarine out there," Chief Boyce finished. "'What ifs' bug the shit out of me. And you know why? Well, I'll tell you. 'What ifs' cause a lot of unnecessary work for everyone. Do you want to turn the crew out of their racks or jerk them away from the last ten minutes of the mess deck movie because we have a sound event, only to find out later that it's a loose wire or something? Do you know what shit I'll take in the goat locker when we finally do discover it and the old man secures from General Quarters?

'Hey, ASWipe,' they'll say, 'seen any subs lately?' And that would be the least of your worries."

"But, Chief, if we turn now and find we do have a submarine, then everyone is going to love the shit out of you and the captain's gonna pin a medal, right there, on you," Calhoun said, poking Boyce hard on the left side of his chest.

Calhoun wiped his jet-black hair off his forehead and threw his hands up in the air. "But, Chief Boyce, if we delay and it is a submarine, we may find ourselves floating in the middle of the Med like the *Gearing* sailors, and if that happens, then everyone will blame you."

"Calhoun, cut the crap and get the diagnostics ready," the chief said, rubbing his chin. What if Calhoun was right and he was wrong?

If it was a submarine and he missed it . . . he didn't want to think about what would happen. Calhoun was right about one thing, though. If it was a submarine then he'd be a hero. The chief paced back and forth behind the second class as Calhoun went about the mechanics of setting up the system to run a diagnostic program that Boyce knew would take ten to twelve minutes to run. Ten to twelve minutes if they didn't interfere or stop the testing to check out a reading.

Damn, he hated to make decisions; especially ones that had the great potential of reflecting adversely on him. September was less than seventy days away. Less than one hundred days until the Old Man ranked the chief petty officers for promotion to senior chief petty officer. Last time he was in the bottom half of the rankings with the "Promotable" block checked, with little chance this time of moving upward. He needed at least a "Must Promote," even if "Early Promote" was out of reach.

"'Bout ready, Chief," Calhoun said over his shoulder.

Of course, he hadn't really done anything eye-catching this marking period except coming back late from liberty in Naples two months ago. "Damn," he said. Boyce believed rankings were more a case of who kept their noses clean and "butt-snorkeled" the best rather than professional expertise. His performance was as good as, if not better than, the other chiefs in the goat locker. He couldn't do any worse than he already had, and all things considered, if Calhoun had a submarine, then he, the chief, would reap the benefits of the discovery. If not, he could always say how he had doubted it was a submarine, but felt the safety of the ship overrode any personal opinion. Yeah, it'd work. With a little luck, he could straddle that fence and shine with either outcome.

"Calhoun, you may be right," he said, patting the second class petty officer on the shoulder. Shoulders made hard and firm from a daily regimen of weight lifting. "Let's ask the watch officer if he'll have the OOD change course a few degrees for a couple of minutes."

"Thanks, Chief," Calhoun replied excitedly. Damn, vanity and fear had worked again with the chief. "That'll do it. Ten degrees will either cause the blip to move with us or change its line of bearing." Chief Boyce might not believe it was a submarine, but Calhoun knew it was. This was a real, live submarine and he had found it. Damn, nearly eight years in the Navy and his first submarine—exercise ones didn't count.

"Okay, keep tracking, Calhoun. I'm going to Combat and talk with the tactical action officer, Lieutenant Frank. He's an okay guy and if he tells the OOD to do it, then the OOD will alter course. Yeah, he's the one to talk to." He patted Calhoun again on the shoulder. "I'll be right back."

Boyce was gone only a minute before he returned. "It'll be a couple of minutes, Calhoun. Lieutenant Frank has to ask permission from the captain." Boyce thought Lieutenant Frank had the flexibility to maneuver the ship without asking the captain's permission. With the captain involved, the chance for Boyce to look bad increased. He had hoped to avoid the captain until they were sure of what they had. He wiped the sweat from his palms on his stained khaki trousers. Boyce regretted asking Lieutenant Frank to maneuver the ship. He was opening himself up to weeks—no, months—of ridicule if this proved bogus.

As they waited, Boyce and Calhoun scrutinized the display. Solid lines, millimeter-separated, flowed down the screen, displaying the underwater sound environment that surrounded the *Hayler*.

"Have you listened to this yet?" Chief Boyce asked.

"I tried to, Chief, but I can't hear anything. The only thing

I have is this steady blip that stays at two eight zero relative. Now if we turn ten degrees to starboard, then the blip—"

"Should be two seven zero relative. If we turn to port ten degrees, it will shift to two nine zero," the chief finished. "Calhoun, quit trying to be a smart ass."

"*Moi?* Not me, Chief, I wouldn't be trying that," Calhoun mocked, smiling, as he touched his chest in mock surprise. No way Chief Boyce was going to spoil this moment.

"That's all right. You're one good operator to catch that blip. Unless you're looking right for it you can't see it, and don't go tell anyone I said that. It'd ruin my reputation. I will see that you get full credit for it."

"Well, Chief, I really didn't catch it. Johnny saw it during his watch. He wasn't sure what it was."

"Did Smithy run a diagnostic?"

"No, I don't think so, Chief. He just pointed it out and said it was probably in the system."

"Then Petty Officer Smith didn't do his job. You did," the chief declared. Tomorrow he'd have a talk with Petty Officer John Smith about proper procedures in the ASW module. If they ran more ASW drills, he wouldn't have this problem of explaining what his sailors should know intuitively.

The captain walked through the hatch. Behind him stood Lieutenant Frank.

"What you got, Chief?"

Boyce jumped. "Captain," he replied hoarsely. "Calhoun has a sound anomaly that we are unable to equate to a systems glitch."

"Is it a possible sub?"

"I'm not sure, Skipper. What we would like to do, with your permission, sir, is change the ship's course about ten degrees to see if the blip follows us. If it does . . ."

"I know, Chief. I used to be the ASW officer on my first ship, USS *Caron.* Show me the blip." The captain moved to the SQR and stared intently at the waterfall.

"I don't see anything," the captain said.

"Right here, sir." Calhoun reached up with his pencil and pointed to the slight hiccup running down the waterfall.

"You sure that's a sound event and not just wishful thinking on a boring watch?" the captain asked, eyeing the young second class searchingly.

Sweat broke out on Calhoun's forehead. *Okay, Chief, you answer the Old Man,* Calhoun said to himself, but he knew Boyce well enough to know he wasn't going to answer. Damn. Oh, well, he only had six months to go.

Calhoun took a deep breath. "I don't think so, Captain," he said as confidently as possible. "I think something's out there." He crossed his fingers and hoped the Old Man agreed.

"Okay, let's find out. Let's see the history of the noise."

Calhoun reached up and twisted the knobs. Where before, the waterfall pattern was a series of slightly separated lines, it now displayed tightly packed lines running down the screen, covering a much longer time period. The periodic clicks now clearly showed a pattern.

"Okay, I see what you're talking about, Calhoun," said the captain as he reached up and touched the hiccup on the screen. He turned to Boyce. "Good work, Chief."

"Thank you, Captain," Boyce replied. "We thought you needed to know about this. Though, sir, it could be a system anomaly, but we've run diagnostics twice and they indicate a clear system." Stay astride of that fence, he thought.

"Okay, let's find out what we've got."

The captain reached over to the intercom box and pressed the button for the bridge. "Office of the deck, this is the captain. Come right ten degrees for ten minutes. Combat, notify the OTC that we are changing course to open up our baffle."

"Aye, aye, Captain."

The captain turned to the three men. "Don't want to alarm the battle group yet, do we?" The captain's face melted into a smile.

"Lieutenant Frank, go ahead and have Combat set the ASW team in the event we decide to call it a possible submarine."

"Aye, Captain," the lieutenant replied, and hurried out to get Combat ready.

That meant resetting the holographic table from surface to undersea. The holographic plot was a new analytical tool installed last year that allowed the *Hayler* to fight its battles from a three-dimensional display that showed range, bearing, altitude, and/or depth. Prior to holograph plotting, they depended on operators putting pencil markings on graph paper and connecting lines to show threat position and maneuvering. Most ships still depended on the manual method.

"Captain," the squawk box blared. "Officer of the deck; the OTC said five minutes, sir, and not to close the *Nassau* closer than six thousand yards. He said it's getting dark and he didn't want to have to start evasive maneuvering at this time of night."

"Roger, OOD. Go ahead and change course ten degrees to starboard. Then, I want to wait four minutes and change it back twenty degrees port. We'll stay there for another four minutes and then return to base course."

The OOD acknowledged the order and signed off.

"There!" the captain said to Boyce. "That gives you plenty of course changes to determine whether you're going to grab the brass ring or not."

Boyce stroked his chin. And he really needed that ring. Promotion to senior chief would be just enough to keep the wife and kids off welfare, if he could keep her off credit cards.

Lieutenant Frank reappeared. "We're nearly ready, Captain. It'll take a couple of minutes to reset the holograph plot."

The captain nodded, his attention riveted on the waterfall.

The USS *Hayler* heeled to the right as the ship turned to starboard. "Should have told him to use a five-degree rudder," the captain shared with those around him. "I think he's coming about a little too fast."

The tilt of the ship broke up the waterfall presentation and masked the reading. It would be a few seconds after the ship settled out before a valid reading could be obtained.

The ship came back on a level keel as the OOD brought the rudder amidships. SQR graphics began to etch their way from the top of the screen downward, millimeter by millimeter. The four men watched impatiently as the waterfall reached a quarter-inch thickness. The blip was still there, but on a new bearing of two seven zero.

They looked at the captain.

He nodded and flipped on the intercom. "OOD, this is the captain. I want a slow turn to port of twenty degrees. Minimum rudder. Got that?"

"Aye, aye, sir," the OOD repeated. "Twenty-degree port turn, minimum rudder, minimum roll."

"You got it, Lieutenant. Execute when ready."

"Lieutenant Frank, set the Gold TMA team," the captain ordered. "I want to start a target motion analysis against this anomaly."

"Do you want to call it poss sub, Captain?" Lieutenant Frank asked.

The captain bit his lower lip. "Not yet, Lieutenant. Not yet. I'm not completely sure it isn't something else. Let's do a bit of TMA. A little target motion analysis won't hurt anyone and it's good training. We don't get enough opportunities to do ASW training as it is."

"Yes, sir, Captain. Should I tell the OTC what we're doing?"

"No, not yet. I will, if I think we need to," he said, looking at his watch. "It's ten till now, so use the 1MC. I don't want to use it after taps, if we can avoid it. The crew is tired enough without disturbing what little rest they do manage."

"Yes, sir," Lieutenant Frank answered. He hurried out the hatch.

The USS *Hayler,* like other destroyers, had a minimum of two TMA teams of six to eight officers and sailors. The Gold team would begin a long, tedious computation by marking the bearings of the blip against the *Hayler*'s course changes. As ship's course changed, bearings to the blip would change and in fifteen to twenty minutes, the number-one TMA team, the Gold team, would have a rough course, speed, and range to the mysterious blip being tracked by ASW—if the target didn't change its course and speed. Depth would be the question mark.

"Captain, starting our turn to port," the squawk box announced from the bridge.

The turn was barely felt as the OOD eased the *Hayler*'s rudder to five degrees port. On the waterfall display the blip began to move slowly against the ship's direction. When the ship steadied on course three one nine, the sound event beared two eight nine.

"Chief, let's look at the history log on this blip," ordered the captain, barely able to keep the excitement out of his voice.

"Yes, sir. Calhoun, run the past three hours on the left screen."

On a side screen to the waterfall display, a rapid recap of the display for the previous two hours appeared. "Sorry, Chief, I only started recording it after I ran diagnostics. We only have about two hours of data."

"That's okay, son," said the skipper, putting his hand on Calhoun's shoulder. "You've done an outstanding job, regardless of what this may turn out to be. Don't you agree, Chief?"

"Yes, sir, Captain. Calhoun is one of the best operators I've trained." Damn. Calhoun was going to take this credit away from him.

"Darken the display and let's see what the blip shows."

On the increased background the sound anomaly ran down the screen until about 2130 hours, when it showed a slight turn to its present bearing.

The chief pointed to it. "Look here, Captain. This shows the blip turning."

"Maybe we turned?" Calhoun asked.

"Better not have turned without telling me," the captain said curtly. "We were put on a course of three three zero at eighteen hundred hours with orders to maintain that course until fifty miles out." He paused and then pensively added, "No, if we had changed course, the OTC would have been screaming at us."

He reached over and pressed the intercom button. "Bridge, this is the captain. Did we make any course changes or corrections between 2120 and 2140 hours?"

"Wait one, sir," the OOD responded. Several seconds later he replied. "Captain, we were on a course of three three zero, and I show no course corrections since twenty forty-five hours, and that was to correct for bearing drift."

"Okay, thanks, Bridge."

The captain cocked his head to one side, his bushy eyebrows nearly touching as he gave this problem his full attention. A minute later the captain looked at his watch. It was ten minutes after taps. Most of the crew would be drifting off to sleep now. He hated to do it, but the image of the USS *Gearing* loomed fresh in his mind.

"Chief, I'm beginning to have a bad feeling about this. Rather look a little foolish than take the chance. Upgrade this to possible sub," he commanded.

He patted Calhoun on the shoulder once again. "Good work, sailor. Now, let's see if you get the glory or I get egg on my face, but I'd be damned forever if we failed to do anything and it was a submarine."

The captain pressed the intercom to the bridge. "Officer of the deck, sound General Quarters."

Chill raising bongs rushed through the night. The captain stepped through the hatch leading into Combat to the sound of sailors hurrying to their battle stations. Boondockers pounding on the metal ladders mixed with audible curses as tired sailors hastened to their assigned stations.

The wind carried the GQ alarm to the sailors of the USS *King,* who were loitering topside on the fantail, enjoying their cigarettes in the night breeze. Several snide comments about nervous captains ran through the group. Then, their own General Quarters alarm sent cigarettes into the sea and them scrambling to their battle stations as, like dominoes falling, the battle group went to full alert.

"WHAT IS IT?" ASKED ADMIRAL CAMERON AS HE STEPPED into Flag Combat aboard the *Nassau.* He tossed the napkin, still in his hand, onto a nearby desk. The GQ alarm drowned out his voice. The clanging footsteps of the *Nassau* sailors running to their stations echoed through Combat.

"Sir, *Hayler* is prosecuting a possible submarine bearing two eight zero from her position," Captain Clive Bowen replied. He tapped the chart in front of him. "That'll be two two five from our position."

"What are they basing it on?"

"Admiral, they have a blip, a noise event, that is originating from outside the battle group. According to the captain, they've had it for at least two hours, but have just upgraded it to a possible submarine. They are unable to equate it to normal undersea noise or marine biologics."

"When this clears, Chief of Staff, find out why it took two hours. That's unsat. If the *Gearing* hasn't taught us to be wary, then I don't know what will. What orders have we given the battle group?"

Captain Bowen replied, "I've ordered everyone to battle stations as a precaution and we're already in a darken-ship status. Sir, if I may, I recommend a ninety-degree formation turn to starboard for *Nassau, Trenton, King,* and *Nashville* with an increase to max speed for ten minutes to open the distance to the possible submarine. Then commence a northeasterly zigzag at twelve knots. We have *Hayler* prosecuting, and I have ordered *Spruance* to join her. *Yorktown* is moving into defensive position between the four high-value units and the contact."

"Good work, Clive. Go ahead and issue the orders to take the amphibs and the arsenal ship out of the contact area," Admiral Cameron said. He looked around. "Where's the goddamn intelligence officer when I need him?"

"Right here, sir," Commander Mulligan answered, stepping out of the shadows in Combat.

"You're CTF Sixty-one's intell officer, Commander. No offense, but where's mine?"

"Sir, Captain Lederman fell down the ladder on the oh-two level. He broke his arm. Happened about an hour ago. He's sedated and in sick bay getting it set."

"Okay, then you're it, Commander."

Clive pressed the intercom and passed the admiral's orders to Commodore Ellison, who as the officer in tactical command was responsible for the maneuvering of the battle group.

CAPTAIN IBN AL JAMAL STEPPED INTO THE CONTROL room of the *Al Nasser,* careful to avoid bumping his head on the steel rim of the hatch. The vinegary smell of sweat seemed stronger than usual. The tea had been nice. Hot, steaming aroma with just the right amount of sugar. Some things in life must remain constant, if life was to be bearable. Birth and death were about the only two sure things in life. Most would add taxes, but too many avoided taxes for that to be a constant in his mind. Everything in between was determined by events, seldom by the person. But a good cup of tea was a constant. There was a small tea shop called Grosvenor's off Oxford Street in London that made an excellent cup, and from there, you could watch the American sailors going in and out of their European headquarters.

He looked at the navigational gauges over the shoulder of the helmsman. Twenty minutes spent updating his personal log in his stateroom with his thoughts and intentions had relaxed him somewhat. Still no word from Algiers. His last orders were to attack any ships within thirty nautical miles of the capital that posed a threat to the new nation. If he waited another hour, the Americans would be beyond that thirty-mile limit, but they'd return in the morning, and fighting a day battle against these incredible odds would severely diminish his survivability. No, the night was his. He brought *Al Nasser* up to periscope depth, where he easily found the arsenal ship. Ordering a spread of four torpedoes, he discussed softly the sequence of events he expected the *Al Nasser* to execute after firing the torpedoes. He wanted the officers and crew thinking about what they had to do, not waiting for him to tell them and then figuring how to do it.

Satisfied they understood, he turned to the periscope. The targeting officer informed him that the battle group appeared to be dispersing, with some of the ships, including the arsenal ship, changing course away from them. The captain looked up. "Then let's hurry," he told them, keeping his voice calm and professional. He twisted the focus knob on the periscope. The view sharpened in the starlight.

The arsenal ship's stern was swinging across the bow of the Algerian Kilo attack submarine. Less than six thousand meters separated the submarine *Al Nasser* from the most heavily armed and explosive-laden ship in the battle group. He ordered the Kilo's speed increased another four knots.

The speed increase added another minute to refine a firing solution. He paused in thought. When he fired the torpedoes, the Americans would try to sink the *Al Nasser.* For a split second he nearly ordered the periscope down with the frightened intent of running. But professionalism overrode the fear. This was his job. War was the profession he trained for. He no longer envied the other Algerian Kilo submarine *Al Solomon* on patrol near the Strait of Gibraltar. This was for the glory of Allah, the greatness of Islam, and the future of revolutionary Algeria.

He kept his eyes firmly against the periscope as he took several deep breaths to calm himself. Once he recovered, he turned, faced the crew, and ordered, "Down periscope. Fire torpedoes one, two, and three." The *Al Nasser* shuddered as the compressed air blew the three torpedoes clear of the tubes. He waited twenty seconds and fired the fourth. The fourth torpedo was aimed ten degrees to the left, off target. If the target turned to port to evade the main pattern of three torpedoes, it would turn into the fourth torpedo's path. Seventy-five seconds to impact. The tiny sonar in the nose of the torpedoes would home on the screws of the arsenal ship. If the passive side of the torpedoes lost the sound signature of its target, the tiny sonar would commence an active search, pinging until it acquired a target. Maybe he should have taken out the *Nassau*. It was the command ship. He shrugged his shoulders. Too late to change his mind. The torpedoes were in the water. The ballet of death in the next seventy-five seconds between the weapons and the target would determine the accuracy of his firing solution. He ordered the *Al Nasser* into a sharp turn away from the Americans. The wires, providing the initial guidance and connecting the torpedoes to the submarine, broke. But it didn't matter. The torpedoes were already activated and on their own sensors.

"I HAVE RAPID SCREW TURNS IN THE WATER!" SCREAMED Calhoun into the microphone in front of him. "Torpedoes, we got motherfucking torpedoes in the water!" he yelled. Tears sprang to his eyes as adrenaline rushed through his body. He tried to jump up, but the seat belt jerked him back hard. Over the loudspeaker in Combat the captain heard the warning.

"Activate NIXIE!" shouted the captain at the ASWOC officer.

Streaming from the stern of the *Hayler* was a NIXIE transducer that, when activated, sent sounds into the water to fool a torpedo's sensors and pull it away from the ship toward the transducer.

"Increase speed to flank three, left twenty-degree rudder," ordered the captain, and he immediately felt the ship heeling to starboard, creating a gigantic knuckle of water in its wake to further distract the torpedo sensors. "Bring her back down to twelve knots!"

"Chief, it's not us! It's not us!" screamed Calhoun, his breath short and rapid, holding on to the desk shelf as the ship rolled. "I have three torpedoes to our port side with a right-bearing drift, decreasing noise."

"Do we have a bearing, range from source?" yelled the chief, licking his dry lips. Boyce reached up, jerked the spare set of headphones down, and plugged them into the SQR.

"Bearing two eight two. Estimate range at six thousand yards," Calhoun replied, his voice shaking. "I've got the mother, Chief. I've got the mother!" Calhoun shook his head back and forth. "Yeah, I've got the mother," he muttered as he twisted the knobs on the SQR system refining the direction. The blip on the waterfall now had three distinct brothers separating from it.

Boyce put his hand on Calhoun's shoulders. "Stay calm," he said. His legs felt weak, almost as if they were going to give way. He leaned forward and rested his forehead against the warm electronics bay for a couple of seconds before straightening. His hand still rested on Calhoun's shoulder.

Boyce blinked a couple of times to clear his eyes, and then pushed the intercom button. "Captain, target bears two eight two. Estimate range six thousand yards." He surprised himself at the calmness in his voice, considering the butterflies in his stomach. He looked for a nearby trash can in case he threw up. The hell with what they might say.

"ASWOC, I want a Sealance, now! Target bears two eight two, range six thousand yards!" yelled the captain.

The Navy Tactical Data System operator plugged in the symbol for hostile submarine on the range and bearing echoed by the captain. The system immediately transmitted the symbol throughout the battle group, including the arsenal ship.

"Torpedoes on course zero four six, correction zero four

niner, been running for thirty seconds! Stand by mark. Five, four, three, two, one. Mark!"

The NTDS operator inputted the torpedoes into the system. Within seconds everyone in the battle group saw the target of the torpedoes as the arsenal ship, USS *King*.

"Time to impact?" the captain asked.

A yellow line shot out from the submarine on the holograph plot identifying the projected torpedo track. It ran directly to the stern of the arsenal ship.

"Forty-knot torpedo speed. Time—sixty-three seconds to target."

The TAO grabbed the handset in front of him. He heard the familiar beep of the radio cryptographic system, synchronizing the security keys. "*King,* this is *Hayler*; be advised three torpedoes inbound toward you. Estimated time to impact fifty-eight seconds."

"Roger, *Hayler,* we're aware and taking evasive and decoy actions!"

"Good luck, *King.*"

Familiar clicks of acknowledgment echoed from the speakers.

The captain moved to the right of the holographic plot for a different view of the situation. In the three-by-six-foot hovering display the ships of the battle group, in their relative positions, sailed northeast with a slight wake trailing behind each friendly vessel. West of the battle group a holographic submarine traveled at a depth of fifty meters with its bow pointed at the USS *King.* The holograph operator touched several heat-sensitive buttons, and from the nose of the submarine two additional yellow lines appeared, showing the torpedoes and their projected paths.

"What's the status of the SH-60?"

"Captain, airborne in thirty seconds, sir."

A speaker above the holograph plot came to life. "*Hayler,* this is *Yorktown.* Our ASW helicopter airborne in twenty seconds your way. Say when ready to assume control."

The ASWOC reported, "Sir, Sealance ready."

"Captain, ASW; we have a fourth torpedo in the water bearing two zero eight on projected course of zero zero seven."

On the holograph display a fourth torpedo appeared. This yellow line showed the torpedo passing harmlessly down the port side of the arsenal ship, unless the USS *King* turned into the torpedo's path.

"*Hayler,* this is *Spruance.* Ten minutes to position. You have the ball. Request instructions."

"*Spruance,* this is *Hayler.* Line-abreast attack formation. Request position yourself ten thousand yards to my starboard. I am in a twelve-knot turn toward contact bearing two eight two, estimated range six thousand yards."

"Roger, *Hayler.* We're on our way."

The captain lifted the handset for Battle Group Common. "*King,* this is *Hayler*; be advised fourth torpedo inbound your direction. Do not turn to port. I repeat, do not turn to port. Ambush torpedo launched to port."

"Roger, understand. We have NIXIE streamed and activated. Captain is steadying on course and intends to knuckle the water when torpedoes are twenty seconds away. One moment, *Hayler.*" A few seconds later the voice continued. "Captain asks you to send coordinates. We are armed and ready to fire, but need targeting data! We've got the weapons, you give us the targeting!"

"Roger," the captain of the *Hayler* replied. Turning from the handset, he said, "ASWOC, have you got a firing solution yet?"

"Sir, we have a proximity solution. Recommend we fire Sealance at four thousand yards along torpedo origination bearing, followed immediately with two others bracketing the area."

"Do it!"

"Sealance away!"

The ship shook slightly as the rocket-borne ASW weapon blasted out of the vertical-launch systems in the bow of the ship, immediately followed by two more, separated three seconds apart.

Aboard the enemy submarine, unless they heard the muffled sounds of the launches, they wouldn't know they were under attack until the airborne torpedoes hit the water and their rapid-turning props activated.

"Momma, this is Devil Six, ready to launch!"

"Captain, this is the bridge; coming right to course three three five for winds to launch the 60."

"Roger, after launch bring the *Hayler* back onto intercept course."

"Captain, ASW; we have lost contact with the submarine. I repeat, sir, we have lost contact."

The SH-60 helicopter was the most deadly ASW weapon that a surface ship possessed. It could fight a submarine miles from the mother ship without endangering the surface platform. In this case, the surface ships were in the middle of the battle, fighting an enemy who had attacked them. They had a general location from where the torpedoes were fired, but as the captain of the *Hayler* knew, the sea is a big shadow.

The captain of the USS *Hayler* speculated the enemy submarine had fired its torpedoes and then gone deep, changed direction, and altered speed to complicate ASW computations and to put as much distance as possible from its firing position. ASW was nothing but speculation. It was like playing chess blindfolded with the crowd only hinting as to what your opponent's moves were.

"Captain," said the lieutenant junior grade supervising the TMA plot. "We have a solution. Sir, the submarine is on a course of three three zero, speed twelve knots."

The captain knew the solution was wrong. The submarine had done something to cause them to lose it. Most likely, it had changed either speed or depth.

On the holograph plot in front of the officers, the virtual submarine shifted its nominal position to the TMA solution 2500 yards further north. Course and speed were added to the enemy symbol. On the NTDS console the same information was inputted and transmitted simultaneously to the fleet.

"Combat, ASW; still no contact with enemy submarine."

"Momma, this is Devil Six. We are airborne port side awaiting instructions."

"Devil Six, this is Momma; come to course three zero zero. Target is six thousand seven hundred yards. Depth unknown. Weapons loadout?"

"Momma, Devil Six; one Mark Forty-Six and sixteen sonobuoys. Course three zero zero. Six thousand seven hundred yards in the computer."

"Papa Oscar, this is Sugarloaf Eight; ready to switch control," called the SH-60 helicopter from the *Yorktown.*

"Sugarloaf Eight, I have you on radar. My position is to your port, bearing one two zero at a range of ten nautical miles. Devil Six is to your port also, eleven o'clock at six nautical miles. Descend to altitude two five zero for approach. Your engagement altitude will be seven five feet. Maintain fifty feet altitude separation from Devil Six. Ensure all navigation lights are on."

"Roger, navigational lights on. I have visual on Devil Six. Altitude is seven hundred fifty feet, descending to two five zero. Request vector to attack area."

"Devil Six, take altitude one hundred."

"Sugarloaf Eight, come to course two seven zero."

On the holograph plot the torpedoes showed twenty seconds to impact.

"OTC, this is *King,* making hard turn to starboard at flank speed. Trailing NIXIE. Decoys deployed in the water port side."

Two torpedoes on the holograph veered to the port decoyed by USS *King*'s acoustic NIXIE countermeasures system. One exploded, while the other passed through the decoy pattern and began an active search. The third torpedo plowed directly into the NIXIE system, blowing it to pieces in the wake of the arsenal ship. The explosion one hundred feet astern shook the warship, but did no damage.

"*King,* this is *Hayler.* We show misses. I repeat, we show all misses."

"*King,* this is OTC." Commodore Ellison's voice interrupted over the secure speakers. "At flank speed come to course zero five five. *Yorktown,* take defensive position between *King, Nassau,* and *Trenton. Nashville,* remain east of *Nassau.*"

"Sealances in the water, Captain!"

The Sealances, fired prior to the TMA solution, entered the choppy seas nearly two miles from the actual enemy submarine location. The *Hayler* captain knew they were misses and that they'd alert the enemy submarine it was under attack. Maybe the knowledge would cause the submarine to make a mistake. A mistake that would bring the wrath of ASW weapons raining down upon it.

"Captain, ASW here. We have the submarine again. The target is in a sharp port turn! Bearing two six five."

"Bingo!" said the captain softly.

The holograph plot showed the enemy submarine turning left, away from the main body of the battle group, which was now heading at max speed away from the battle scene. Between the main body of the American battle group and the fleeing submarine, the holograph reflected the USS *Hayler* with two SH-60 helicopters heading toward the datum.

The gas turbine engines of the USS *Spruance* sent spray over the bow of the oldest destroyer on active duty as it hurried to its assigned position abreast of the USS *Hayler.* Arriving, the two warships settled into an aligned formation at eight knots with a five-nautical-mile separation.

"*Spruance,* this is *Hayler*; report status of your 60."

"*Hayler,* 60 is down hard, awaiting engine parts. Request instructions."

"Roger, stand by."

"Sugarloaf Eight, request weapons loadout."

"Roger, Mother; Sugarloaf Eight with one Mark Forty-six and full sonobuoy complement."

"Sugarloaf Eight and Devil Six, this is Mother. Continue present heading. Devil Six, prepare for sonobuoy launches on my command. Sugarloaf Eight, prepare to launch torpedo at my command."

Two "rogers" blared from the ASW circuit.

"*Hayler,* this is *Yorktown.* Am in position astern of you fifteen thousand yards," the secure speaker announced.

"Roger, *Yorktown.* My intentions are to have Devil Six drop a zigzag row of sonobuoys to firm up target location, course, and speed. When target fixed, will have Devil Six drop its Mark Forty-six and then vector him ahead of target course for second sonobuoy pattern. Sugarloaf Eight will conduct a follow-on attack immediately after Devil Six."

"Roger, *Yorktown* standing by."

"*Spruance* standing by."

"Roger, *Spruance*; request you be prepared to launch subsequent attacks along threat course in the event helicopter attacks are unsuccessful. What I would like to do is have both of us launch Sealances and over-the-sides in a mass attack. You take the first hundred feet depth. *Hayler* will take from one hundred to four hundred feet depth. Report when ready."

"Roger, out."

"*Hayler, Spruance*; this is the OTC," Commodore Ellison broke in. "Be advised that with both of you traveling away from the main body, there is no, I repeat, no ASW protection with the exception of *Yorktown*. Request rejoin battle group soonest. How copy, over?"

"Roger, Commodore, this is Charlie Oscar *Hayler*. We expect resolution within ten minutes. Did you copy my intentions with *Spruance*?"

"That's affirmative, *Hayler*. You have the cog of the ASW group. You have twenty minutes and then we'll revisit the situation. Good hunting," Ellison said, and then in a hoarse voice that was probably not intended for transmission, "I hope they sink the bastard."

"Now, now, now!" shouted Devil Six as he commenced dropping an eight-sonobuoy zigzag pattern. Within a minute the saltwater-activated sonobuoys began transmitting passive noise data. The ASW teams of the three ships began analyzing the signals.

The zigzag sonobuoy field would reveal the course and speed of the submarine as it passed through the maze of sonobuoys. Like sinister miniature receivers, they silently collected the noise of the submarine as it tried to quietly evade the American ASW attack through the shadows of the undersea. The noise strength from the submarine, increasing in intensity as it approached the next sonobuoy, left a pattern of decreasing sound behind it. The *Hayler*'s captain wanted the attack to be perfect. He only had two torpedoes on board the helicopters. The SH-60s had the best chance of getting the sub. Realizing he was clenching and unclenching his hands, he wiped them on his khaki trousers to consciously stop the involuntary action. He also knew the submarine still had teeth. At any moment torpedoes could be coming out of the dark at them. As he waited for the developing information to refine the attack, he made decisions to himself on what evasive actions to take if the enemy submarine decided to fight.

He held back on the order to drop the active sonobuoy. He'd order it dropped just prior to the helicopter attacks. The active pinging of the sonobuoy would refine the targeting data, but it would also tell the submarine that it had been located. The submarine would attack then, if it was going to fight. If not, the submarine would run, executing a heavy series of evasive maneuvers to escape the sonar, including launching decoys. No, when he dropped the active sonar, the torpedo had to follow in seconds and he had to be ready for whatever happened next.

"Sealances are a miss, Captain," reported the ASWOC. "Too far away from the target."

Within one minute, the USS *Hayler* ASW team began entering the locating data from the eight sonobuoys into the NTDS. Other ships in the battle group watched the action on their consoles. Small pulsating red dots reflected the sonobuoy pattern on the holograph plot.

Thirty seconds later Petty Officer Calhoun pressed the button on his sound-powered phone. "Combat, this is ASW; I show submarine steadying on a course of one nine zero, speed twelve knots, depth estimated at one hundred twenty feet."

The submarine displayed on the holograph plot shifted as the system corrected for the new locating data. On the ocean top of the holograph plot, a tiny helicopter, representing Devil Six, flew five hundred yards to the south of the enemy submarine.

"Devil Six, come right to course one one zero."

"Report when in position for launch," the skipper said to the ATC.

"Aye, Captain," she replied.

"Sugarloaf Eight, do you have visual on Devil Six?"

"That's an affirmative. Still maintaining visual."

"Devil Six, I'm going to vector you ahead of the enemy," she said, trying to find the right word for the target. Enemy, probable submarine, definite submarine, possible submarine, adversary. So many to choose from. She chose "enemy" because of a scene from an old World War II movie on the mess deck the other night.

"Devil Six, turn right course one niner five. Sugarloaf Eight, come right course one niner five. Your separation is now one thousand yards from each other. Devil Six, descend to fifty feet altitude. Sugarloaf Eight, maintain one hundred feet."

The holograph plot reflected Devil Six ahead of the submarine. Sugarloaf Eight was abeam of Devil Six and to the left of the submarine.

"Devil Six, torp ready?"

"Torp armed and ready."

"Captain, we're ready to launch, sir."

The captain picked up the secure telephone in front of him. "OTC, all units, this is *Hayler*. We are commencing attack. I repeat, we are commencing attack at this time."

"Good hunting, *Hayler*," Ellison replied.

The captain hung the phone up.

"Okay, drop the active sonobuoy," he ordered.

"Aye, sir. Devil Six, drop active sonobuoy and be prepared for immediate torpedo attack."

"Roger, active sonobuoy away. Now, now, now!"

The lone sonobuoy hit the water, descended to fifty feet as its sensor device deployed beneath it. The capsule bobbed to the top and the antenna deployed. On board the ships the signals from the active sonobuoy began to arrive.

"Devil Six, turn right one hundred yards and launch."

"Roger, Mother; coming right." Several seconds passed. "At one hundred yards. Launching attack. Now, now, now! Torpedo away!" Devil Six cried.

In the starlight the crews of the two SH-60Bs watched the luminescence splatter as the Mark Forty-six torpedo entered the water. The Mark Forty-six possessed an active homing system backed up with nearly one hundred pounds of high explosives. A direct hit could sink a submarine.

"Depth setting?" asked the captain.

"No depth. Set to enable immediately and commence circular search pattern as it descends."

"Good," the captain of the *Hayler* mumbled to himself.

The torpedo launched by Devil Six activated as it hit the water, a series of active sonar beeps, searching for a target, emanating through the undersea environment. The torpedo continued five-hundred-yard circles on a downward spiral until one of its beeps returned an echo. The torpedo left its search pattern and began to follow the return toward the target.

"Combat, ASW!" shouted Calhoun. "We have lock-on! It's heading toward the target!"

The holograph showed the torpedo data point leaving its search pattern and heading toward the stern of the submarine. The silence in Combat was broken only by the ASWOC operator as she vectored Sugarloaf Eight into attack position directly over the enemy submarine. She sent Devil Six forward to lay another pattern.

"Time to impact twenty seconds!" Calhoun announced.

"Sugarloaf Eight, launch when in position."

"Roger, am launching now. Torpedo away."

"The target is turning port!" Calhoun shouted into the mouthpiece. "I think he's deployed a decoy."

The holograph display shifted to reflect the submarine's attempt to avoid the active seeking torpedo. A small data point in the holograph gave a virtual picture of the torpedo in search pattern. A blinking red blip represented a deployed decoy.

The echo returns were coming faster to Devil Six's torpedo when its logic head told it that the target was only yards away. Coming from the north, Sugarloaf Eight's torpedo arrived at the same time. The two torpedoes collided, exploding twenty yards from the propellers of the Kilo submarine.

"Underwater explosion!" shouted Calhoun. "Houston, we have contact!"

"Must promote," Boyce said aloud, thinking of the chiefs' rankings. Then he put his hand over his mouth as he realized what he had said.

"Thanks, Chief," Calhoun replied, proud Boyce thought this deserved a promotion. Maybe he would stay in the Navy if they promoted him to first class petty officer.

A cheer went up in Combat, with everyone patting each other on the shoulders and sharing congratulations.

"Devil Six, this is *Hayler.* Turn left to course one six zero and climb to one hundred fifty feet."

"Sugarloaf Eight, I am vectoring you to home plate."

"Roger, Mother. We have a problem."

"Say again, Sugarloaf Eight."

"We have a problem. Engine temperature is rising and we

are losing hydraulic pressure. Don't think we'll make it. Am steering toward you."

"Roger, Sugarloaf Eight. Turn right. Permission granted to land immediately on *Hayler.*"

A screeching noise from the speaker caused several to cover their ears with their hands.

"Mother, can't make it. Props have locked. We're going in. I repeat, we're going in!"

"Roger, Sugarloaf Eight. Break. Devil Six, come to course zero six five. Descend to twenty-five and prepare to rescue Sugarloaf Eight crew."

"Roger, Mother, we have visual on Sugarloaf Eight. She has impacted water. Wait one." Several seconds later, the speaker roared to life once again. "I count three lights in the water. Confirm souls on board?"

The ATC continued her vectoring and direction to the rescue effort as the remainder of Combat followed the ASW wrap-up.

"*Spruance,* this is *Hayler.* Let's go active and sweep the area."

Both destroyers activated their sonars and began active pinging of the area. Dangerous techniques because they also revealed the location of the destroyers to the enemy submarine making them vulnerable to a counterattack.

On the holograph plot a flashing "Man Overboard" symbol overlaid the Sugarloaf Eight symbol identifying the location where the helicopter had crashed. The NTDS operator entered the "Man Overboard" symbol on his system, transmitting the information to the other members of the battle group.

The underwater explosion appeared on the waterfall of the SQR system. The submarine was reflected as splitting in half on the holograph plot.

"Undersea explosion confirmed. I repeat, undersea explosion confirmed by SQR."

The captain grabbed the handset. "OTC, this is *Hayler*; we have sunk sub at location." And then he broadcast the geographic coordinates to the battle group.

On the NTDS system the enemy sub symbol blinked as the operator took course and speed to zero. The symbol would remain there for some time—a computerized monument to their success.

"ASW, this is the captain. You still have that little blip that gave away the submarine?"

Calhoun looked at the waterfall as it resumed its normal, boring run of the undersea noise environment. "No, sir, Captain, it's gone."

"Roger."

"OTC, this is *Hayler*. My intentions are to rescue Sugarloaf Eight and then rejoin battle group. We will lay additional sonobuoy patterns after rescue operations completed. For the time being, will continue at General Quarters."

"Roger, *Hayler*," Ellison replied. "Attack results?"

"Commodore, I would like to report detected sub; sank same." He knew the commodore had heard the earlier report, but suspected the man just wanted to hear it again. He grinned.

"Roger, *Hayler*. Well done to everyone. *Yorktown,* request you close battle group. *Spruance,* take point position and conduct sanitation evolution on your way."

"I'm going to the bridge," the captain of the *Hayler* announced. "Call me if anything appears that suggests he may have gotten away."

"Aye, Captain. Will do, sir," the TAO answered as the captain scrambled up the ladder to the bridge. "Captain out of Combat," the TAO said as the door shut behind the Old Man.

Probably, if Sugarloaf Eight had not crashed, the ASW formation would have done a more thorough scrub of the area to ensure the submarine was sunk. Everything pointed to the enemy sub being hit and sunk. No contact, no noise, no counterattack. Already the boatswain mates on the *Hayler* were cutting silhouettes to paint a submarine on the bridge wing.

TWO HUNDRED METERS DOWN THE ALGERIAN KILO drifted helplessly, its props bent and rudder gone. Several leaks were quickly stopped. The explosion had caused complete loss of steerage, and with the props bent, there was no way to move the ship.

Thirty minutes later the *Al Nasser*'s targeting module

showed the two American warships departing the area. Ibn Al Jamal would keep the *Al Nasser* drifting here, beneath the sound layer, until he was sure the Americans were gone. Then, he'd blow ballast, surface, and radio Algiers for help. He had completed his mission even if he had failed to sink anything. The Americans were pulling away from the Algerian coastline.

The emergency lights went out as the generator came back on-line. He grinned. It seemed to release the tension in the cramped compartment. Everyone started laughing.

They were alive.

Ten miles away, an undetected submarine slowly turned to a southwesterly course away from the scene of action. Its crew relaxed as the distance between the *Al Nasser* and the American battle group grew, but the skipper of the unidentified submarine remained at battle stations. His mission required avoidance, not confrontation. His mission waited ahead. The submarine steadied on a course toward the Algerian coast. He would surface later, when it was safer, for an update on the location of the signal guiding his mission. He only hoped the resupply ship would be at the rendezvous point when he started back.

CHAPTER 8

⚓

"**THE USS *ROOSEVELT* ENTERS THE RED SEA TODAY. THE**
Egyptian government has approved her northbound transit
through the Suez Canal for tomorrow. She should enter the
Mediterranean from the east about the same time the USS
Stennis enters it from the west," Roger Maddock said to Pres-
ident Crawford. "That'll put two aircraft carriers in the Med."

"I'm surprised," Franco Donelli, the national security advisor, said. "The Islamic Republic of Egypt isn't exactly pro-
American. In fact, they've been awful quiet during these
events."

"Our ambassador in Cairo reports that everyone of any im-
portance in the Government has suddenly become unavail-
able," Bob Gilfort, the secretary of state, said. "He is having
a tough time getting a pulse on what the Egyptians are thinking. The Egyptian newspapers call the Libyans heroes for
their military actions against us, and then, in the same article,
call them heroes for executing the ones who did it. Go figure."
Gilfort shook his head. "I have a hard time trying. Bottom
line, Mr. President, is we think Egypt will remain on the side-
lines until they see how events in Libya, Algeria, and Mo-

rocco unfold. But we need to keep a close eye on them; even a moderate religious republic is a radical one."

"Okay, I want an update tonight, as usual," said Crawford. "I would like to know when the two carrier battle groups have entered the Mediterranean. Roger," he said, pointing at the secretary of defense. "Schedule a video teleconference for me to address the Navy once they're together. It'll give me a chance to express my admiration for their position and let them know how much the American people are behind them. If our military is going to go into action, they deserve to hear the voice of their president. I want to assure them that the American people are one hundred and ten percent behind them."

"Yes, sir, we can do that."

"Roger," Franco added. "Let's work together in arranging the video teleconference so we can fold it into the president's schedule."

Roger nodded, picked up the cup of coffee in front of him, and glanced sideways at the diminutive man sitting on the couch with him. Franco would make sure the president said just the right thing in the right politically correct way. Christ, President Crawford could help his administration if he'd get rid of this sawed-off Napoleon he called a national security advisor. The only things Franco advised had Franco's health and welfare written all over them, and Franco was more concerned about his legacy after Crawford left this second term in office than the president's. Well, Franco wasn't the only one who could play that game. Roger sighed. Of course, Franco was a pro at it, and Roger was only an amateur. But sometimes, even amateurs win.

"This morning's intelligence brief reported Korean military elements have moved into position along the border," said President Crawford. "The question I need answered is, what are their intentions? Right now, no one knows and this mobilization makes me nervous." He took a bite of a Dunkin' Donut twirl before walking back to his desk.

"Yes, sir, Mr. President. U.S. and South Korean troops have reinforced the DMZ, and if the North Koreans cross, we should be able to contain them for the few days needed for additional troops to arrive," Roger Maddock answered. He glanced at Donelli, waiting for the diminutive asshole to rebut him again. Surprised when he didn't, Roger continued. "South Korea started calling up their reserves yesterday. We may have to consider mobilizing if another Korean War materializes." Roger saw Franco jerk his head up. *Here it comes,* he thought. *Donelli can't pass this one up.*

"Mobilizing? I think you're overreacting, Roger," Franco hurriedly added.

Of course, you would think I was overreacting, Roger thought. *Why? Because you didn't think of it, you little shit.*

President Crawford mumbled through the doughnut twirl he was chewing. He swallowed. "Franco's right, Roger. It'd be political suicide to go on television and tell the nation that we are mobilizing. No, wouldn't go down well at all. We need to put the proper spin on something like that, or we'll have the American public screaming and hollering. Find a better word than mobilizing—just in the event we have to do something." He laid the remainder of the twirl on the tabletop momentarily, then picked it up to spread a napkin under it.

"What do we have along the DMZ if the North Koreans decide to do something?" President Crawford asked.

"Not too much, Mr. President. We removed the land mines nearly five years ago in accordance with the international agreement signed by your predecessor. The only land mines along the DMZ are on the North Korean side, and those fields are miles thick. If they decide to cross in mass, then what we have are ditches, barbed wire, antitank weapons, and devices. Plus, we have clear fields of fire. If they cross, we stop them by outfighting them."

"We can do that," said the president. "An American is worth a Korean any day in battle, wouldn't you say?"

"That's a patriotic statement, Mr. President, and it'll play well, with some tactful tuning, to the American public," Franco said.

"Roger, where do we stand on our troop buildup in South Korea?"

"Mr. President, we have two carriers with complete air wings on board off the coast of the Koreas. The Air Force completed forward deployment of three squadrons of F-15s and two squadrons of F-16s yesterday. One squadron of A-10 tank killers arrives today to augment the two squadrons already in South Korea. The 82nd Airborne deployed yesterday and, after they complete unloading the maritime preposition ship that docked two days ago, they'll move toward the DMZ. We are flying the main infantry elements of the 101st Airborne to a point directly south of the DMZ to mount the largest paratroop drop since World War II. We want the North Koreans to see a major demonstration of our ability to respond rapidly anywhere in the world when necessary. Fort Stewart has completed loading its mechanized infantry brigade. They sailed yesterday for Korea. The Army chief of staff flew down to Savannah, Georgia, and gave them a rousing pep talk as they departed. He returned late last night and said that the morale of the troops was high and they were ready to fight on arrival. It will take about twenty-five days for them to arrive. The Seventh Fleet has moved an amphibious readiness group off the coast of South Korea to provide a flexible Marine Corps response. If the North crosses the DMZ, then plans call for the Marines to mount one of the largest amphibious landings since World War II."

"What are the Chinese saying about this muscle-flexing by their ally?"

"The Chinese are saying they have no influence over the North Koreans," Bob Gilfort replied.

"Well, we know that's bullshit!" Roger Maddock said.

"Roger, please," Franco Donelli said.

Roger opened his mouth to say something, thought better of it, and kept quiet. He gripped his knees. Just below his emotional gate was this primitive urge to reach over, grab Donelli by the throat, and pop his head like a pimple. Let's see how he'd spin that in the national newspapers! *SecDef Strangles National Security Advisor in Oval Office As President Crawford Pontificates and SecState Sips Coffee.* He grinned. Be a hell of way to resign and go back to the private sector.

"This isn't funny, Roger," Franco added, glancing at the president.

"Yes, sir, Mr. President," Bob Gilfort said from the leather winged armchair, watching his fellow cabinet member wrestle with his anger. In a way he sympathized with Roger. Franco could be an arrogant bastard sometimes. Maybe most times. Well, maybe all the time. "We know they have the influence to stop this, and they know we know. We can put economic pressure on them. Of course, it's never worked before on the Chinese, and I don't see it working this time. Didn't work with the EP-3E incident years ago. The United States has grown to be the biggest customer for the cheap goods that China produces. We may have more influence this time, though they could ride out any economic pressure in the time it takes for North Korea to invade. The Chinese economy has been rapidly growing since most-favored-nation trade status was awarded to them in the nineties. I don't see them risking this economy on the Korean Peninsula. United States forces have been in Korea since the Korean War. Additional U.S. forces should not bother them."

"Have we let the Chinese know that we know they can influence the North Koreans?"

"Yes, sir, in diplomatic terms we have, Mr. President."

"Well, tell them in less diplomatic terms that if the North Koreans attack, we will view it as an attack against the United States and will take appropriate actions to resolve the two-Koreas problem."

"We've been saying that for years, Mr. President. I think they are aware of our position, but I am not sure if they or the North Koreans believe it. The North Koreans still celebrate what they view as us losing the Vietnam War, and some in the north believe that if a North Korean offensive causes sufficient American casualties, the American people will demand a disengagement—that we will throw South Korea to the wolves."

Franco looked up from his computer notepad. "Mr. President, do we really want to flex our muscles in that tone with the Chinese?"

Bob rolled his eyes upward, and quickly pinched his nose to hide his expression of displeasure over Franco's interference. When he opened them, Roger winked at the elderly secretary of state. Their mutual distaste and distrust of the president's national security advisor was one of the few things they both agreed on. No one could ever accuse President Crawford of surrounding himself with yes-men.

"What do you suggest, Franco? I can't let this situation

continue to deteriorate. Did you see the *Washington Post* polls this morning?"

"I recommend a quiet, tactful comment to the Chinese that we believe they have more influence than they suggest and would hate to see a large Western military presence on the Korean Peninsula because of the propensity for a misunderstanding between our nations. Then within twenty-four hours of passing that quiet diplomatic démarche to them, we flood the Korean Peninsula with American military presence."

"Franco, we're flooding Korea now with American military presence, and you want the president to threaten war against the Chinese? I don't have that much more military capability to flood Korea with," Roger Maddock added testily.

"Quite true," added Gilfort, nodding in agreement.

"I am not threatening war against the Chinese, Roger," Franco said. "Give me credit for some intelligence. We are constrained by the situation in the Mediterranean and that ties our hands somewhat." He turned to the president. "I propose, Mr. President, we divert the aircraft carrier *Roosevelt* from the Red Sea and send her to the Sea of Japan. Let the USS *Stennis* continue into the Mediterranean and we tell General Sutherland, as commander in chief European Command, to handle the situation with theater forces. What we need to do, I believe, is—first and foremost—stop a second Korean War. We can do that only by putting enough presence and force in the region so the North Koreans will go home and starve quietly."

"How much military experience do you have, Franco?" Roger asked.

"As much as everyone else in this room. None. But this isn't about military experience and knowledge. It's politics, and we've got more experience and knowledge here than anyone else in the country."

"Some of us do," mumbled the secretary of state.

"That may be, Franco," Roger said, fighting hard to keep anger from his voice. Then, turning to President Crawford, he appealed, "Mr. President, politicians don't put their lives on the line. The military does. Before you decide to follow Franco's expert military advice, I strongly recommend that we involve the Joint Chief of Staffs to weigh the pros and cons. We lack the military strength we had during the Cold

War. Our military is less than a third of what it was when we fought Desert Storm in '91. Look at the problems we had tackling Kosovo and keeping Iraq in line at the same time. I think, Mr. President, if you choose to commit our military fully to Korea, then we will be unable to hold the crisis in the Mediterranean. In fact, I would submit that we will have to vacate the Med."

The president pulled his chair out and sat down. Everyone watched while he tapped his pencil on the desk and thought. He ran his free hand through his graying brown hair. This was where the rubber meets the road. Everything he'd read about previous presidents revealed that sometime during their time in office a major crisis required them to make a decision that had a long-term effect on America and its people. This was his Rubicon, and all of the advice provided didn't change that fact. A week before the events in the Mediterranean and Korea, the American people had seen him as a strong leader who displayed a steady confidence in his decisions. Even he knew that the majority of those decisions were national ones, along with international decisions of significantly less magnitude than this one. Today, the polls showed a different story. Korea might be the most volatile, and it was. It was also ironic that the majority of America's military might was in the Pacific, while sixty-five percent of its gross national product depended on trade with Europe. Trade that depended on stability in a region that historically had been unstable. Instability quickly turned to war. He knew that whatever decision he made, good or bad, history would place the responsibility on him. What he wanted to do and what was strategically the right thing to do were sometimes two different things. Someday historians would use their Monday-morning quarterbacking to tell how his foresight was wrong, but the cards were shuffled and dealt and he had to play them. He had two areas of gross instability. Both had the potential to cost American lives. One already had. His decision must be based on a logical outgrowth of that reasoning. Which one would save more American lives?

After several minutes President Crawford put the pencil down, gave a quick nod, and said, "Thank you, Roger. You too, Franco and Bob. But in weighing what is facing us, I have to agree with Franco on this. Korea is the powder keg with the most potential of igniting a world war. Events in the Mediterranean are the more emotional. They cause every red-blooded American to want to grab a weapon and kick ass. But I think we're going to have to continue with a holding situation in the Mediterranean. I agree with Franco. We will divert the USS *Roosevelt*. Roger, tell General Sutherland to hold the Mediterranean crisis with the forces he has in Europe. I don't want to do this, but we have to. We are going to show Libya the consequence of attacking American forces. I promise you that. But Korea must come first. I suspect the newspapers will have a field day with this decision, Franco. But you're right. It's the right decision. As for passing on our thoughts to the Chinese, Bob, work with Franco to develop a thoughtful, but firm and private, démarche for the Chinese on our intentions if they do not rein in North Korea."

The president paused and took a deep breath. Roger Maddock inched forward on his seat to speak. The last thing Crawford wanted was dissent. Before the secretary of defense could speak, President Crawford asked him, "What's the latest on our missing SEALs in Algeria?"

"Won't know until tonight, Mr. President, when the USS *Albany* tries another pickup," Roger responded. If the president depended so much on Franco for his military advice, then why in the hell did he need a secretary of defense? But, in the end, Roger Maddock kept this thought to himself.

"Keep me informed and let me know when they've been recovered. The last thing we need is for the radical regime in Algiers to have a bunch of Americans marching through the streets. How about the USS *Gearing* survivors?"

"As you know, Mr. President, they were picked up late yesterday by the USS *Miami*. The submarine is en route to Naples and is expected to arrive sometime tomorrow. The report from the *Miami* showed sixty-two survivors rescued, including the captain of the *Gearing*. Four sailors are in critical, but stable, condition. A medical team from the *Nassau* is on *Miami* and treating them. All have suffered some degree of exposure. We'll have a team of intelligence specialists, led by the N2 from CINCUSNAVEUR in Naples, to interview the crew, and Bethesda Naval Hospital has sent a team of psychi atrists to help."

"Okay. Keep me informed. Franco, get Allison and send her to Naples to represent me with the crew of the *Gearing* Have her see me and I'll give her a handwritten letter to read to the crew members. Roger, keep the press away from them Let's give those brave American boys and girls some breath ing room to recover."

"Yes, sir, Mr. President."

"Maybe we should give the commanding officer a medal?"

Roger Maddock answered, "Yes, sir. We are considering it but we need to know all of the events before we do, It i known that the USS *Gearing* shot down at least one aircraft is believed to have sunk a submarine—that'd be one of th old Libyan Foxtrot subs—and the reconnaissance aircraft tha recorded the action confirms the sinking of one missile patro boat by the destroyer. On paper, it shows a hell of a fight, bu the Navy wants to finish its investigation before considering any awards for the captain and the crew."

"Okay, but right now, America needs some heroes. So tel the Navy to work this one fast. From what I've read in th paper, we should consider the Medal of Honor for Captai Heath Cafferty."

"Yes, sir," Roger acknowledged, expecting Franco to say something, and surprised when the national security adviso did not. "The Navy is working this one fast. Chief of Nava Operations has sent the vice chief of Naval Operations t meet the crew when it docks in Naples. His team will start th investigative wheels rolling. We wouldn't want to inadver tently award the Medal of Honor erroneously."

"Okay. Keep me advised, Roger. We need a hero, so tell th Navy to expedite its review process." President Crawfor stood up and walked toward the door. "I have to go. I'll se all of you tonight. Think about it, and if you see other issue we need to address, I want to know about them as soon a possible. Roger, I want a Medal of Honor winner somewher in this mess. The nation needs it; we need it."

He stuck his hand out as he walked by his national securit advisor. "Franco, let me have the book. Let's see if your poll are better to me than the *Washington Post*'s." *And I need bet-ter polls,* President Crawford thought as he left the room.

THE LIBYAN-REGISTERED RO-RO SHIP WAITED UNTIL THE USS *Roosevelt* sailed through the Bab El Mandeb Strait and into the Red Sea. Once the *Roosevelt* was out of sight over the horizon, the Libyan ship turned north, too. The white merchant vessel passed through the narrow body of water that connected the southern end of the Red Sea to the Gulf of Aden. The red sun waved hazily through the African heat rising off Ethiopia as it moved lower in the sky. The fine desert sands blown off the Arabian deserts to the east obscured the vision in that di-rection. No other ships were visible. The Libyan RO-RO sur-face radar was useless as Miserah Island, in the middle of the strait, and the close land masses on both sides created land smear across the radar face to blank out the scope. The ship's crew laughed at the half-naked African natives who, with their fishing lines out, dotted the beaches along the Ethiopian shore. The natives were a minimal risk, easily ignored as the ship conducted its mission. Natives never communicated anything past their village, and what would they say anyway? *"Big ship circle Miserah Island."*

Satisfied he had the best operational security available in this well-traveled funnel of water, the captain of the RO-RO gave the go-ahead. The rear ramp lowered halfway to reveal a metal contraption. Hydraulic gears rolled the ramp past the gate to hang over the stern by ten meters. The crewmen began pushing pins through the various joints of the arrangement to make sure it wouldn't fold up on itself. Then they placed a barrel-shaped mine on it, and watched it roll down to drop off past the stern into the water. The sowing continued at regular intervals, giving the mines tactical separation. The mines sank until they reached a preset depth of fifty meters, where a small sea anchor deployed to hold the undersea weapon in position. The logic sensor in the head of each mine would activate an hour after hitting seawater. The program told each weapon the strength of magnetic field and the acoustic signal-to-noise ratio needed to coincide for it to activate. The sea anchor would de-tach, whereupon, like a small torpedo, the weapon would home against the nearest magnetic source to explode on contact. With one hundred kilos of explosives in each warhead, one torpedo mine could sink a fishing vessel or cause serious damage to a destroyer or cruiser. Enough successful torpedo mine hits would either sink the American aircraft carrier or cause sufficient damage to send it into repair. It would not take too many hits on the American carrier to limit its capability to launch or recover aircraft.

The Libyan captain was well aware that it would take numerous hits to sink a carrier, but if the plan worked, there would be an American aircraft carrier sitting on the bottom of the Red Sea within the next forty-eight hours.

The RO-RO ship continued its slow 360-degree transit around the island. Crewmen wrestled each of the heavy mines to the stern of the ship, grunted as they hoisted them manually onto the deploying ramp, and then took a two-minute break as each mine rolled into the sea. When the ship finished the southern transit of the Bab El Mandeb on the western side, it turned north again and sowed its deadly cargo through the narrower eastern waters. By midnight, the lethal work had effectively sealed the southern end of the Red Sea. The only safe passage out of the Red Sea for the USS *Roosevelt* was the Suez Canal, and the Egyptians would seal that tomorrow.

THE FRENCH *ATLANTIQUE* TURNED BACK TOWARD DJI-bouti, the small African country located at the western end of the Gulf of Aden, to reach the military airport before nightfall. Its highly accurate electro-optic surveillance cameras recorded the suspicious Libyan RO-RO ship to its north and caught the mine-laying contraption as it deployed. The highly focused computer-enhanced cameras corrected for distance, and refined the focus for the French airmen to discern that the RO-RO was dumping barrels into the strategic strait. Their "end of mission" report, transmitted while airborne was en route to their base, caught the attention of the Foreign Legion colonel who controlled the French military presence in the former French colony. His orders from headquarters were very explicit. They required him to forward anything having to do with Libyan or Chinese activity in his area. He didn't know why, but those were his orders. Automatically, he turned the report around to headquarters in Paris, adding the distribution code identified in his instructions.

An hour later when the reconnaissance aircraft touched down, Paris had already replied to the colonel, directing him to send a wooden-hull ship with French special forces embarked to conduct an underwater reconnaissance of the strait at first light. In Paris, someone already had an idea what the Libyan merchant vessel was doing, but this initial analysis remained within French channels, pending confirmation. Twenty hours later, this intelligence analyst would be patting herself on the back as French divers confirmed her analysis, and wondering why her superiors decided not to share this information with France's allies.

THE USS _ROOSEVELT_ BATTLE GROUP CONTINUED SAILING north toward the Suez Canal for its early morning transit, unaware of the threat astern of it.

At the Libyan operations room south of Tripoli, the soldier marked events zero two two and zero two three as "in progress" on the chart. Colonel Alqahiray smiled as he read the new notation. He casually flicked ashes to the left. When these two events were completed, event zero two four would be initiated. The event that would catapult Jihad Wahid— Holy War One—into the history books. He reached for the phone. Walid stood nearby, waiting for orders the colonel might give, but also in position to overhear anything said.

"Mintab," Colonel Alqahiray said when the phone was answered. "Time to go. Good luck and we'll be watching. I envy you this great moment in history."

Colonel Alqahiray listened for a minute, and then with an angry scowl replied, "Yes, as planned, my friend! Everything is on schedule. We have done our part; it is up to you to finish it. May Allah be with you as he has been with us." Colonel Alqahiray slammed the receiver down and butt-lit another cigarette. "Too many people worry needlessly," he said aloud to himself.

Walid's eyebrows raised slightly as he wondered what Mintab had said.

CHAPTER 9

⚓

"I HAVE HIGH-SPEED TURNS, I MEAN CAVITATION IN THE water!" shouted the USS *John Rodgers* ASW operator over the intercom.

The warning blared from the bridge speakers of the destroyer, bringing immediate silence to Combat.

Captain Warren Lee Spangle dashed from the starboard bridge wing, where he had been enjoying the Spanish sun during their approach to the Strait of Gibraltar. He slammed his hand down on the intercom button. "What have you got, sonar?"

"Sir, I have multiple high-speed props in the water bearing one zero five with a slow left-bearing drift. Captain, I'm sorry, sir, but I think they're torpedoes. They sound like tor—"

"Sonar, keep the data coming," Spangle told him.

Spangle turned to the boatswain mate of the watch. "Sound General Quarters, Boats." He pressed a second button on the intercom. "Tactical action officer, this is the captain. I have the conn and the bridge." Adrenaline rushed through his veins. The young sonar technician was probably wrong. At least, Spangle hoped so. It'd be at least three minutes before the chief and the ASW officer got to their stations and confirmed it.

From the bridge and Combat, the OOD and TAO acknowledged Captain Spangle's control of the ship. The numbing bongs of the GQ alarm sent chills up Spangle's back. Even during drills, the call to General Quarters sent adrenaline soaring. No sailor remained calm with sounds of imminent combat rattling the bulkheads. The metallic clicking of metal-toed boondockers pounded the ladders between decks as sailors raced to their battle stations. The slams of watertight doors echoed through the ship as metal handles were rammed down to set Condition Zebra. Spangle heard the ship-wide ventilation system winding down. Seconds later the ship was at battle stations, effectively sealed internally into small isolated airtight pockets designed to sustain damage, stay afloat, and continue fighting.

The BMOW, buckling his life vest, moved to shut the wing hatches to the bridge.

"Leave them open, Boats," Spangle ordered. "I may need access to the wings and I don't want to have to open them."

The BMOW acknowledged the order as he pulled the chin strap tight on his helmet.

Captain Spangle lifted the red secure phone. "*Stennis* battle group, this is *John Rodgers*. We have torpedoes, starboard to our position, inbound toward the battle group!" He surprised himself by how calm his voice sounded. It was true what they said about "you fight like you train." He saw the fear in the eyes of everyone on the bridge, like the deer he hit two years ago, trapped in his oncoming headlights. The only thing keeping fear from turning into runaway terror was confidence earned from constant training, drills, and what their fellow shipmates would think if they showed how fucking scared they felt. He felt it himself.

"Captain, this is TAO, NIXIE streamed and activated."

"Bridge and Combat, this is ASW. Bearing drift increasing slightly, torpedoes bearing one zero zero. Target is not *Rodgers*. I repeat, target is not *Rodgers*."

A bearing drift meant the torpedoes were targeted against another unit in the battle group. With the left-bearing drift, it meant the torpedoes would pass across the bow of the *John*

Rodgers. Spangle knew, without asking, that the carrier was the target. It was the highest-valued unit in the battle group. With over a hundred aircraft and six thousand sailors, the carrier was central to a Navy battle group projecting its power. Without it, discounting cruise missiles, Naval power was limited to sea and coastal operations. With the carrier, they not only controlled the sea, but could project Naval power thousands of miles inland. Naval aviation gave a battle group a multitude of choices on how that power was projected.

"Probable target?" Spangle asked, proud in a command way at how the anxiety in his voice was hidden. How he conducted himself impacted the performance of the ship. If he remained calm, then the crew, for the most part, would function similarly. If he lost it, then the fear, held back inside every person on the ship, would burst free and wreck vengeance on the *John Rodgers.*

"Sir, if the torpedoes continue this track," the ASW petty officer replied, stuttering slightly, "they'll hit the *Stennis,* sir. I say again, probable target is *Stennis.* I count six torpedoes, Captain."

"Range to torpedoes?"

"Estimate ten thousand yards, Captain."

Ten thousand yards—five nautical miles. Modern torpedoes could be fired from over twenty miles away. He knew that trailing from the rear of the forty-knot weapons were thin electronic wires, connected to the submarine and being used to guide them into the target. Survival of the aircraft carrier was paramount to the mission, even over the survival of USS *John Rodgers.* If he could cause the enemy submarine—and he thought of the boat out there as an enemy—to maneuver sharply, the thin wires would break. The torpedoes would continue, but they'd be dependent on their own logic heads in the nose. Decoying them would be easier.

"*Stennis,* this is Charlie Oscar *John Rodgers.* Minimum six torpedoes inbound your way. Target is *Stennis.*"

"Roger, *Rodgers.* All units battle group, *Stennis* is in hard left turn. Take appropriate evasive actions."

Surface warfare officers manning the ships in battle groups watched carrier maneuvers as closely as they would watch an enemy warship. A maneuvering carrier has as much capability to change course, or avoid anything in its path, as changing the direction of an avalanche or stopping a charging rhino. A carrier maneuvered. Others avoided.

The USS *Stennis* turned to port, swinging its stern toward the torpedoes. Unfortunate, Captain Spangle thought. He shook his head. The *Stennis* had turned the wrong way, helping the torpedoes' acoustic homing system as the props of the USS *Stennis* churned the ocean. He would have turned in another direction—maybe even toward the torpedoes in the hopes that the huge bow would block out the acoustics of the props. It wasn't up to him to second-guess the battle group commander. Every captain had his own tactical opinions, and as good as Captain Holman was, he was still an airdale.

"Captain," the OOD interrupted. "General Quarters is set, sir. Time, two minutes fourteen seconds."

"Captain, ASW. Sir, this is Chief Johns. Confirm sonar contact as torpedoes."

Spangle nodded. The lieutenant on the bridge acknowledged Chief Johns. "Thanks, Chief."

When they joined the *Stennis* battle group in its dash across the Atlantic from their Caribbean deployment, the best time he had been able to muster from the crew was three and a half minutes. It was amazing what inspiration a war at sea provided. He wished he had read closer the events of last night when the *Nassau* amphibious task force had been attacked.

"Bridge, Combat; torpedo noise increasing. Estimate six minutes until they pass our nose. Closest point of approach at current speed and course is two miles."

Spangle turned to the officer of the deck. "Lieutenant, give me a maneuvering-board solution to intercept those torpedoes. And hurry, Lieutenant!"

"Captain, this is ASW. Torpedoes have changed course to match *Stennis*. Torpedoes still headed toward the carrier."

"Roger, ASW. Combat, this is the captain. Put a couple of torpedoes over the side toward where you think the submarine may be based on his torpedo tracks."

"Aye, Captain. We don't know yet where it's at. TMA just started!"

"TAO, fire a couple in that direction!" Then he remembered the USS *Seawolf*. "Make sure it's not into the *Seawolf*'s operating area," he warned. This was one time he wished the American submarine community were more forthcoming with their locations.

"Captain, *Seawolf* operating area is clear of the target zone. Safe shot, but it'll be luck if we get it."

"TAO, fire the damn torpedoes!"

"Roger, sir." A tense twenty seconds passed. "Torpedoes launched, sir."

Spangle heard the whoosh of compressed air. From the next level below the main deck, two torpedoes shot out from the starboard side of the USS *John Rodgers*. Spangle rushed onto the starboard bridge wing in time to see the two splash into the water. He had little expectation that the torpedoes would score on the submarine. It'd be a "Hail Mary" if one hit. But he knew the sonar operators on the enemy sub would detect the incoming torpedoes. They would hear the cavitation of the props. The submarine would scurry to put as much distance as possible from the searching torpedoes, and that turn to evade would break the wires.

The OOD ran to the plot table, and as the quartermaster punched in the data on the navigation computer, the OOD waited, vocally impatient, watching over the sailor's shoulder. Occasionally the officer of the deck glanced at Spangle, hoping the captain wasn't going to shout for the data before they finished running the program.

"Left full rudder, steady on course zero one zero!" ordered Spangle. The direction was a ballpark guess for an intercept course while he waited for the results of the maneuvering board. A guess based on years of maneuvering at sea as a surface warfare officer.

The quartermaster mumbled a few obscenities as she erased the results and began again with the new course in the equation. She was already perspiring from the hot summer temperatures, and tension and fear sent new beads of sweat rolling into the dampness of her armpits, creating growing wet half-moon-shaped patches on her dungaree shirt that were visible whenever she lifted her arms.

"Captain, TAO here, sir. We have a targeting solution on the submarine based on backtracking the torpedoes' course and speed."

"TAO, go active with the sonar. He knows we're here. Let's find out exactly where he is." Spangle paused and looked at the wind meter. "TAO, launch the SH-60 when it's ready."

"Roger, Captain. Estimated time to launch is five minutes."

"Not good enough, Commander. Have them airborne in three minutes. Weapons loadout?"

"One Mark Forty-six torpedo and full complement of twenty-five sonobuoys."

"I thought I told them to load two when we reached the Mediterranean!" Spangle snapped.

"Yes, sir. I've checked, and they had intended to load the second Mark Forty-six later this afternoon as we entered the Strait of Gibraltar."

"Captain, TAO. The two 'over the sides' have gone into circular search mode. No contact."

The ping of the *Spruance*-class destroyer's sonar rose through the skin of the ship like a muffled pistol smothered deep within a pile of pillows. Ten pings later, the ASW voice returned. "Submarine located twenty-six thousand yards on a bearing of one one zero. Its speed is twelve knots and target is steering a course of zero six zero heading for the entrance to the Strait of Gibraltar, Captain."

"Good job, ASW. Turn that sonar up until it hurts. I want a slow increase to full power. Make him think we're bearing down on him. Scare the shit out of him!" The enemy submarine had turned east. It no longer had wire control of the torpedoes. It was running. The inbound torpedoes would be functioning on their passive and active logic programs only. The quick torpedo shots, though they hadn't scored, had accomplished what Spangle wanted.

"Captain, intercept course to torpedoes at flank speed is one minute on course zero eight five!" yelled the navigator.

"Roger, right full rudder, steady on course zero eight five," Spangle ordered.

The ship tilted slightly to the right as the helmsman acknowledged the command and brought the destroyer onto the new course.

"Have targeting solution for Sealance launch!" shouted the TAO on the intercom.

"Launch!" shouted the captain. He turned back to the helmsman. "All ahead flank."

"Captain!" the navigator, who was buttoning his life vest, shouted. "Current course and speed will bring us in front of the torpedoes, sir!" He leaned over the quartermaster and ran his finger along the chart. "Recommend new course zero nine zero. That'll take us behind the torpedoes as they pass."

"Maintain current course and speed," the captain reiterated.

The whine from the four LM-2500 gas turbines of the USS *John Rodgers* climbed to a spine-chilling screech as the nose of the warship leapt out of the water on a collision course with the torpedoes. Spangle felt the acceleration as the destroyer knifed through the water, leaving its normal twelve-knots cruising speed behind as the same engines that powered a Boeing 747 surged the USS *John Rodgers* to a flank speed of twenty-nine knots.

Spangle grabbed the 1MC. "This is the captain. We have minimum of six torpedoes fired from long range heading toward the *Stennis*. My intentions are to put the *Rodgers* between the torpedoes and the *Stennis*." He wiped the sweat from his palms on his pants leg. "Engineering, give me all the power you can and be prepared to evacuate the spaces if necessary. Damage control parties stand by for action."

He replaced the 1MC and moved to the center of the bridge. Fear beat inside him, screaming to be released. He took a couple of deep breaths. This was his first time in combat, and he suddenly realized intellectually—it surprised him to think that he was able to reason at that level—that fear must be a constant companion to warriors. And without arrogance or conceit, Spangle placed himself on the same level as great military leaders of the past, to include Spruance, Halsey, Patton, and his favorite, Robert E. Lee. He felt a calm he'd never envisioned possible for him.

Some would have called it heroic—bravery. But neither of those romantic images resonated in Spangle's thoughts. It was years of training and acceptance of duty that guided the destroyer's captain now as, knowingly, he sent *Rodgers* into harm's way. In the back of his mind was a forlorn hope, an unreasonable belief, that the ship would survive the torpedoes. He accepted the fact that sailors under his command were going to die as he accepted the fact that he might be one of the dead. All he had to do was steer the ship, according to figures provided, and ignore the consequences. Too many near-heroes in the past had given in to fear. Failure to conquer fear caused retreat, and with retreat, defeat followed. Retreat was not a word they taught in the United States Navy. It was not something they taught at the Academy. So Captain Spangle stood, looking out over the bow of the destroyer, knowing the ultimate sacrifice for him and his crew was less than a nautical mile ahead. His knees felt weak. He put a hand against the narrow shelf that ran along the front of the bridge. Going knowingly to one's death shouldn't be like this. What was it about "not going quietly into the night"? But here he stood doing just that.

"ASW, this is the skipper. Status of inbound torpedoes?"

"Captain, our calculations show they're still heading toward the carrier. No change, sir."

The only thing left to do was pass the word to the battle group.

Captain Spangle lifted the secure phone. His mouth dry, he took a sip of water from a bottle sitting in the cup-holder on his bridge chair. The water eased the lump in his throat. "*Stennis,* this is *Rodgers.* Torpedoes remain on course, inbound your way. Our calculations show your maneuvers ineffective in losing contact. I am steaming into a defensive position between you and them. Recommend you reverse course westward and deploy ASW decoys. Submarine located, Sealances fired. NTDS data entered. SH-60s launching even as we speak."

There were other things he wanted to say. *Tell my wife and kids I love them. Tell them what we did and try to convince them why we had to, even when my soul cried for me to run.* But he put the red phone down, vaguely noticing a tingling sensation in his palm. He forgot that no reply came from the *Stennis.*

A half minute later the secure speaker came to life.

"Warren, this is Dick Holman," the commanding officer of the *Stennis* transmitted. "May God be with you and your brave crew at this time. Our prayers are with you, and regardless of what happens, our weapons will avenge your actions. I am launching helos to your position."

"Thank you, Captain," Spangle said softly into the handset. He took a deep breath. "I think you know what each crew member here would like to tell their loved ones. Please convey those thoughts, if necessary."

The SH-60 helicopter from the USS *John Rodgers* roared by the starboard side of the bridge.

"*Rodgers,* this is USS *Hue City.* Our 60 airborne at this time, heading your way."

"*Rodgers,* this is USS *Ramage.* We are four miles to your starboard quarter and closing at flank speed. Request orders."

"USS *Ramage,*" Captain Holman broadcast before *Rodgers* could reply. The *Ramage* was an *Arleigh Burke*–class destroyer capable of waging an antiair, antisurface, and antisubmarine battle simultaneously, much like the DD-21 class.

"Aye, *Stennis,* this is *Ramage.* Go ahead."

"Request you assume OTC ASW and go sink the bastard."

"Roger, sir, but *Rodgers* had initial contact and in better position to control the attack."

"I know that, *Ramage*! But *Rodgers* is defending *Stennis.* Just do it!" Holman shouted, and then in a softer voice added, "And sink the son of a bitch."

"Roger, sir. *Ramage* going in for the kill."

"Captain, this is ASW," the sonar technician on USS *John Rodgers* said into his mouthpiece. "The torpedoes are on a constant bearing, decreasing range, sir. They're heading into us, Captain! Recommend a course change at this time."

"ASW, this is Captain Spangle. You've done a good job, son. How soon to impact if we maintain this course?"

"Captain, I would give us less than a minute. At this range, Captain, even if we turned now, they could lock on our props. Sir, we really need to do something," the petty officer replied, his voice shaking.

"TAO, this is the Captain. Is NIXIE activated?"

"Yes, sir. It's activated and transmitting, but Captain, at this course and speed, the torpedoes would have to go through us to get to it. I recommend come left to course"—the TAO drew out the word "course" as he did a quick calculation—"zero five zero. That would open up the NIXIE to the torpedoes."

"If I do that, Commander, what are the chances that all six will lock up on the decoy?" He knew the answer, but wanted confirmation.

"Captain, if we turn now, at least two to three of them may be decoyed to our NIXIE and even miss us. If we don't turn immediately, we're going to be hit by all six."

"Captain, this is ASW. Time to impact forty seconds! We need to do something, sir," the sonar technician cried.

"Thank you, sonar." Captain Spangle reached in his back pocket, pulled out his wallet, and flipped open the photo section. He took a quick look at his wife, who had stopped her own career in marketing to support him in his, raising their two daughters and one son, while he spent the years at sea defending the nation. He smiled. His son was so proud of batting over .300 in this year's Little League. One daughter was a cheerleader at Norfolk Catholic High School, and the other was the star point guard on the school's basketball team. The next time he saw them he was going to make sure they understood how proud he was of them and how much he loved them. He folded the wallet and put it back in his pocket—yes, the next time. He had missed too many "next times" because of the sea. He hoped the Navy got to his family before the press did.

"Thirty seconds to impact!"

"Boats," he said as he looked at the bridge chronometer. "Broadcast torpedoes starboard side, impact thirty seconds."

The boatswain mate of the watch lifted the 1MC and passed the word.

Tears leaked down Captain Warren Lee Spangle's cheeks in the final seconds of his life. Standing silently in the center of the bridge, he faced the bow so the bridge team wouldn't see the tears. It wasn't fear that caused his emotion. A great sadness descended and enveloped him. He thought about so many of life's future moments that he'd planned and wanted to enjoy and share and now would never see.

CAPTAIN HOLMAN HURRIED ONTO THE BRIDGE WING OF the carrier, his helmet straps swung unfastened alongside his huge neck. He lifted his binoculars and focused them on the

USS *John Rodgers,* now less than two thousand yards, one nautical mile, from the giant carrier and closing USS *Stennis* at an oblique angle. "XO, are the helicopters ready?" Holman asked.

"Yes, sir. We have two Sea Kings airborne astern of us. Two more are launching, and we are prepping a fifth SH-3. We should have liftoff of the next two any second and overhead *Rodgers* within a minute."

"Okay, but not before the . . ." His voice faded before he finished the sentence. He was going to say not before the hits. He and everyone, in unnatural silence on the bridge and in Combat, recognized the imminent sacrifice of the USS *John Rodgers.* The carrier would survive, but at a cost that civilians would never understand, in an act they could never appreciate or comprehend—an act of honor and courage.

Holman jumped as the first explosion hit the bow of the *Rodgers,* followed quickly by a second. The bull-nose portion of the *Rodgers* disappeared in a cloud of smoke and debris as the forty-kilogram warhead exploded. Three more explosions followed one after the other along the length of the destroyer. An explosion far to the stern of the destroyer sent ocean waters racing a hundred feet into the air. Holman figured a torpedo had been decoyed into the NIXIE.

The concussion from the blasts knocked Holman and the XO off their feet. The gigantic black master chief, standing behind Holman, reached out and stopped the heavy bridge door from slamming shut and crushing Captain Holman's midsection. Then the master chief reached down, grabbed Holman by the arm, and with one tug, pulled the overweight captain to his feet as effortlessly as he would pick up a suitcase. The taller XO, gasping, pulled himself up hand-over-hand to the bridge wing.

A huge pall of smoke boiled upon itself where the USS *John Rodgers* had been. It was already stretching hundreds of feet into the air when a burst of flame broke through the spreading black cloud. Secondary explosions erupted along the length of the *John Rodgers,* causing the three men to involuntarily duck below the bulkhead.

When they stood, Holman stared at the conflagration. "Hold the helicopters until the smoke clears," Holman said with awe in his voice. He had never seen anything like this—never—in twenty-eight years of service.

The wind blew the smoke northward, rolling toward the *Stennis*. "Increase speed, port ten-degree rudder, steady up on course two seven zero," Holman shouted through the open hatch.

The carrier lurched to port, the deck tilted slightly as the high-value unit eased out of the smoke.

Pieces of ship and debris rained down on the ocean surface and the USS *Stennis* flight deck. Where the USS *John Rodgers* had been, it was as if nothing had existed. No ship, just a vacant expanse of ocean littered with debris where less than a minute ago 330 officers and sailors had manned a 563-foot warship. Sucked into the storm of war, vanquished with honor, but gone, as if they never existed, to become a footnote in Naval history.

Holman looked at the XO and pulled his handkerchief out of his back pocket. He wiped his eyes and then handed it to the XO. "Get the smoke out of your eyes, XO. We've got a calling card to deliver. When this is over, I think you know what medal I am going to recommend Captain Warren Lee Spangle for."

"Captain," the OOD said, sticking his head out onto the bridge wing. "*Ramage* has the submarine pinpointed. *Hue City* has joined *Ramage,* and the two are running abreast, using active sonars to herd the submarine into the Strait of Gibraltar. SH-60s are being vectored onto the location. *Ramage* reports she expects to commence attack within one minute."

"Thanks, Commander," he said to the young lieutenant commander who was the officer of the deck. "Keep me appraised."

He turned to his executive officer. "XO, it appears that we will be attacking the submarine within the Strait of Gibraltar. Radio the Spanish and British garrisons at Gibraltar and Algeciras and tell them what has happened and our intentions. Ask them to clear the strait of all shipping as we are engaged in battle. Ensure the HMS *Invincible* battle group behind us is aware of what is happening."

"Sir, Admiral Sir Ledderman-Thompson has been monitor-

ing our communications. He is aware and has dispatched
forces toward our area."

Overhead above the USS *Stennis,* the gigantic battle flag of
the United States whipped in the westerly winds as sailors
hurriedly cleared debris of the USS *John Rodgers* from the
flight deck.

The phone on the bridge wing rang. The executive officer
picked it up, and after several exchanges put his hand over the
mouthpiece. "Captain, the ASW S-3 Vikings are ready for
launch, sir, but we need to turn east again to bring the wind
across the bow."

"Go ahead, XO. Make it so." Not many of the S-3 aircraft
remained in the Navy inventory, and all of them belonged to
the reserves.

The executive officer lifted the phone and gave the go-
ahead. After hanging up, he stuck his head into the bridge and
gave the necessary orders to reverse the course of the *Stennis.*
The OOD looked at the captain, who nodded in approval of
the XO's orders.

The XO lifted the bridge phone and relayed instructions to
Combat concerning the warnings to the British and Spanish
authorities ashore. Simultaneously, on secure communications, Combat updated the British admiral and the Royal
Navy battle group, forty-five nautical miles behind them and
closing. The United States Navy in the twentieth century had
never gone into conflict without being able to look over its
shoulder and find the Royal Navy steaming proudly beside it.
When fighting together, the two Navies had never been defeated. It gave Holman a warm feeling to know the twenty-
first century had started no different.

The USS *Stennis* turned starboard toward the Spanish
coastline, leaving the destruction of USS *John Rodgers* behind. Six Sea King helicopters methodically searched the explosion area for signs of survivors—even a lone survivor. The
ocean was carpeted with pieces of the *Spruance*-class destroyer, but the human body is a frail instrument. The crew
had vaporized along with the second United States warship to
be sunk in battle in a week.

"How long until the S-3s can launch?" Holman asked.

The master chief released the sound-powered phone button. "Sir, Flight Deck says as soon as we steady up, we can launch the two S-3s. The Vikings are idling on the catapult, waiting for the signal to launch."

"Captain," the officer of deck relayed. "Admiral Ledderman-Thompson sends his respects and offers the services of the Royal Navy. He has detached the HMS *Boxer,* at flank speed, to join us, and has launched three ASW Sea King helicopters our way. He says they are yours and he requests you assume control at your convenience."

Captain Holman stepped into the hatchway. "Give me the phone." He took the phone connecting the bridge with Combat. "Combat, this is Holman. Tell Admiral Ledderman-Thompson I accept his offer of assistance. Have His Majesty's Ship *Boxer* contact *Ramage* for instructions. Ensure *Ramage* has positive control over those Royal Navy bubbas before sending them forward." He handed the phone back to the OOD.

Holman turned to his XO. "I knew the Royal Navy couldn't stay out of the fight long; too near Trafalgar."

The Battle of Trafalgar was the greatest sea battle in Royal Navy history. Off the coast of Morocco in the late 1790s Lord Nelson outnumbered, attacked, and defeated a combined French and Spanish fleet, ensuring British dominance of the seas for another hundred years. In the course of the battle Lord Nelson was shot and killed.

Holman moved to the far side of the bridge wing and stared at the fading area behind them where the *Rodgers* had disappeared into history. Two minutes later, the turn of the carrier hid the site. No matter how much someone is dedicated to the Navy, they never expect to make the ultimate sacrifice. He had wondered about that in his early years in the Navy. It wasn't until he hit his forties before he began to believe in his own mortality. Even now, when he was so sure they were heading to war, he doubted that he himself would suffer the ultimate sacrifice. But then, he thought, so did Warren Lee Spangle.

"Sir," the master chief said, glaring fiercely in the same direction the captain stared. "*Ramage* says the submarine has submerged beneath the layer and they've lost him on sonar.

Last course was a direct path to the strait." He pushed his button on the sound-powered circuit. "Wait one, Captain."

Holman waited as the master chief acknowledged the speaker on the other end. The tall, black master chief looked up. "Captain, *Ramage* has ordered the *Rodgers* Mark III to launch its torpedo. The *Hue City*'s SH-60 is launching one mile ahead of last reported course. *Ramage*'s SH-60 is laying a below-layer sonobuoy pattern between the attacking helicopters. *Ramage* further reports positive control of three British Sea King helicopters, in the area in five minutes. British helicopters are outfitted with one torpedo each. After the two U.S. SH-60s make their attack, the British will move forward and replace them."

He had forgotten about the *Rodgers* SH-60 helicopter out there. There was a possibility that the helicopter did not know about its mother ship. He looked at the master chief, who like most master chiefs read minds also.

The master chief nodded. "Yes, sir. They know."

"XO, tell *Ramage* that *Rodgers'* helicopter will bingo to *Stennis* once this is over," Holman replied.

"Yes, sir. Will do." He picked up the phone and passed the information to Combat for further relay to USS *Ramage*. A minute passed as he traded conversation with Combat.

"Captain," the XO said as he hung up the phone. "*Ramage* and *Hue City* request the status of *Rodgers*. They are seventeen miles ahead and saw the explosion. They have no radar return on the *Rodgers,* and NTDS shows her symbol DIW. They want to know the situation. What should we tell them, sir?"

He paused for a moment as he weighed the pros and cons before reaching a decision. "Tell them *Rodgers* has suffered torpedo hits and we are assessing the damage."

"Sir, the bastard sunk her. With all due respect, Captain, they should know that *Rodgers* is gone!" the XO said.

"No, XO. You're wrong. The *Rodgers* isn't gone. The Navy is full of USS *John Rodgers,*" replied Holman softly as he stared out to sea. "We've had captains like Spangle and ships like *Rodgers* throughout our history, and we'll have captains like him and crews like the *Rodgers* in the future, and when our enemies want to defeat us, they won't be able to. For you can never defeat the courage of those like Captain Spangle and the USS *John Rodgers* who make our Navy what it is. XO, they need to know the courage of that ship, in that you are right. But for the time being, I want *Hue City, Ramage,* and those SH-60s' attentions on that submarine. I don't want them grieving for *Rodgers*. I don't want emotions overshadowing their duty. There will be time to wake the *Rodgers* memory when this is over. Right now, I want that submarine!" Holman slammed his palms down on the hard rail of the bridge wing and faced the two men. "And I want to know who in the hell was responsible, because I may not want the crew to be emotional, but by God, there's no goddamn reason why I can't be!"

"May I recommend then, Captain, we tell them *Rodgers* has been hit and we will fully brief them following battle stations."

Holman nodded. "Okay, XO. Tell them that. It's what I said anyway."

The master chief interrupted. "Captain, the S-3s are ready for launch."

"What course are we on?"

"We are steadying up on course zero niner zero, Captain." So we, too, are heading into the Strait of Gibraltar.

"Tell them to launch when ready."

Several seconds later the roar of engines, seeking full power, roared through the bridge, followed almost immediately with the blast as the cherries broke and the catapult shot the aircraft from zero to two hundred knots in three seconds. The S-3s shot off the end of the flight deck, dipped slightly beneath the bow before their two engines pulled the antisubmarine jets upward.

The Viking aircraft turned right, away from the Spanish mainland. The aircraft immediately changed channels and contacted USS *Ramage*'s ASW control.

The master chief looked down at the captain. "*Ramage* reports both torpedoes a miss. He is moving one of the Royal Navy helicopters eastward into the Strait to lay a sonobuoy pattern along with the two SH-60s from *Hue City* and *Ramage*. The other two Royal Navy helicopters are positioning themselves for attack. *Ramage* estimates that the submarine, if it continues east, will enter the strait in five minutes. The *Rodgers* helicopter is headed our way. *Ramage* has passed control to *Stennis* to direct a sanitation sonobuoy barrier ahead of the carrier. *Ramage* wants to ensure that we only have one submarine out there."

The captain nodded. "Good idea. XO, we should have thought of that. I'm glad the *Ramage*'s captain is thinking about the whole battle group with the workload he has swamping him. Make it so."

"Captain, recommend we change our course and slow our speed until we know for sure the submarine has either left the area or been sunk," the XO suggested.

"No, the hell with them. Why do you think we were attacked? That's what they want. It doesn't matter whether they sink us or not. What they're trying to do is keep the United States Navy out of the Mediterranean. To hell with them. In this narrow body of water I'll run over the son of a bitch and send him to the bottom, if I have to. This is a carrier. It ain't no destroyer. It'd take more than one submarine with torpedoes to stop *Stennis*, and I'm not going to let them tell a United States warship when and where it can go." He paused and pulled a cigar out of his vest pocket. "I just wish I knew who 'they' were," he mumbled.

"May be a Kilo submarine, Captain. Those are the only missing submarines within five hundred miles."

"Could be, XO. But, I don't know for sure yet, and neither does Ellison on *Nassau*. But I will, and when I do, I'm going to blow hell out of them and every swinging-dick warship they've got," he said, his eyes moist, flashing with anger.

"What if we don't find out?"

"Then we'll bomb Libya. At least, bombing Libya has always made us feel better."

The master chief interrupted. "Captain, Combat reports USS *Seawolf* has joined the ASW attack." He held up his hand as he listened. "And *Ramage* has halted further air attacks while *Seawolf* is in the battle zone. *Ramage* is securing active sonar at this time and turning the ASW prosecution over to *Seawolf*."

"If we're sending the submarine *Seawolf* in, make sure

Ramage maintains firm and positive control over those helicopters, including those Royal Navy bubbas."

"Yes, sir," the XO replied. "*Seawolf* can go below the layer
and find the enemy submarine, hopefully before it escapes."

"Okay, make it so. Tell *Ramage* to continue sonobuoy and
passive prosecution, but not to conduct any further attacks
until cleared by me. I know I am overemphasizing, but I do
not want a 'blue on blue' misunderstanding sinking the *Seawolf.* Tell *Ramage* to keep firm control on those itchy airdale
trigger fingers," Holman said, his Texas drawl pulling the
"blue on blue" out.

"Let's move to the forward bridge wing where we can have
a better view ahead of us," Holman added. An unlit cigar
hung from his lips. "Damn!" Holman exclaimed as his helmet
bumped the top of the hatch, jarring his head as he entered the
bridge.

The XO shook his head and followed.

The master chief unplugged his sound-powered phone and
followed the two officers off the starboard bridge wing into
the bridge, turning sideways so his massive chest could get
through the hatch. A minute later the three stood on the forward bridge wing directly below the windows of the bridge.
The hatch behind them remained open so the OOD could talk
directly with the captain.

"Sir," the master chief reported. "*Ramage* has broken off
attacks and reports contact with *Seawolf* on its passive sensors."

"Roger, warn them once again not to initiate any attacks
without my permission, and even then, not until they are sure
that *Seawolf* is out of harm's way." Holman had a bad feeling
about this. Too many things go wrong in the heat and fog of
battle. Eventually war boils down to the human level.

"*Seawolf* has disappeared beneath the layer. *Ramage* estimates put enemy submarine inside the Strait."

ABOARD THE ALGERIAN KILO, FLEEING THE AMERICAN
battle group, the captain, sweat running off his forehead and
into his eyes, had ignored the orders to remain on station for
thirty days prior to returning. He wiped the sweat from his

eyes, momentarily clearing his vision. The captain of the *Al Solomon* screamed and shouted at the crew as the Algerian submarine fled to perceived safety on the other side of the strait.

Terrified, he increased the speed of the *Al Solomon* as it entered the main transit channel of the Strait of Gibraltar. The pinging of the American sonars and active torpedoes had sent waves of panic through the crew, who added to the confusion by their own screams and shouts at each other as the submarine maneuvered to evade contact. The quiet associated with a professional crew was never evident as the Algerian submarine crew shattered into frenzied chaos. Twenty-five frozen bodies rested in the refrigerators of the mess decks—among them their best tactician and their best helmsman. Revolutionary zeal combined with political intolerance never failed to claim a lot of lives.

The chaos diminished with the fading sounds of American sonars and torpedoes, herding the Kilo eastward.

When the sound of active pinging disappeared, a small cheer burst forth as the crew congratulated themselves on losing the American force. Five kilometers behind them, the dark cigar-shaped American hunter-killer attack submarine USS *Seawolf* silently eased beneath the layer.

By chance, *Al Solomon* avoided the first two mines, sowed by its sister ship, *Al Nasser,* by entering the strait four miles south of their location.

Five hundred meters further on, the third mine's logic head weighed the magnetic contact of the *Al Solomon* and the noise ratio of its props before it activated. The sea anchor cut loose. The mini-torpedo turned east and quickly reached forty knots. The homing device in the head of the mine changed its trajectory minutely as the explosive underwater device headed directly for the spinning props of the Algerian submarine.

The ASW operator on the *Al Solomon* heard the high-speed prop cavitation in his earphones, but the celebrations within the control room drowned out his warning shouts. The propeller-driven mine was two hundred meters from the submarine when the next mine picked up the magnetic and noise signature of the *Al Solomon*. Its sea anchor detached and it started on its deadly path toward the Algerian submarine just as the captain of the *Al Solomon* increased speed again, this time to fourteen knots to hurry their transit through the strait. The increased speed aided the torpedo mines in their targeting.

The USS *Seawolf* detected the high-speed turns of the mines-turned-torpedoes, and immediately executed a sharp left turn and cut all engines to barely making way. The maneuver saved the *Seawolf,* the world's quietest nuclear submarine. Unknowingly, it had turned away from the first mine, where the logic head had already locked on the magnetic signature of the *Seawolf* and was only milliseconds away from a valid acoustic detection.

Failing to get the two factors it needed, the mine's program reset and it resumed its lethal wait for the next opportunity. The mines were programmed to deactivate in another twenty-six days. Until then, they guarded the strait against ships the size of carriers and supertankers and against any submarines trying to sneak through submerged.

"CAPTAIN," THE MASTER CHIEF SAID. "RAMAGE REPORTS underwater explosions dead ahead in the strait at a range of ten nautical miles."

"Looks like *Seawolf* bagged a submarine," the XO said, a smile breaking across his rugged features.

"Let's hope *Seawolf* did and that it wasn't the other way," Holman replied. He took his lighter from his trouser pocket.

"*Ramage* reports they have a target above the layer. Looks as if it's surfacing, Captain."

"Tell *Ramage* and *Hue City* to take it under gunfire if it surfaces and refuses to surrender. The submarine either hoists the white flag immediately or it's sunk. Tell the bridge that I want channel sixteen, bridge-to-bridge common, down here. I want to tell that bastard myself." He lit the saliva-soaked cigar despite seeing the grimace on the XO's face. "By the way, XO. The *Stennis* is no longer a smoke-free ship."

"Captain, *Ramage* says another underwater explosion detected! They have regained *Seawolf* on their sonar and report her safe. It's the enemy submarine taking hits, Captain!"

"Outstanding! Tell *Seawolf* well done!" Holman yelled.

A minute passed as *Stennis* continued her approach toward the Strait of Gibraltar. The afternoon sun baked the ship and those topside. Holman could see several cases of sunburn already. The strong smell of fuel exhaust enveloped the carrier as the summer sun created miragelike heat waves over the top of the flight deck.

"Captain, *Seawolf* is at periscope depth and in comms with *Ramage*. She reports she broke off her attack against the submarine because of torpedoes in the water. She did not fire at the enemy submarine. *Seawolf* recommends against entering the strait. Charlie Oscar believes torpedo mines attacked the enemy submarine."

"XO, bring us down to six knots!"

"Yes, sir, Captain." He stuck his head inside the bridge and relayed the orders to the OOD. It would take the *Stennis* two miles to slow. The strait was ten miles away.

The master chief continued. "*Seawolf* says they were three miles from enemy submarine with firing solution when the first explosion hit the target. It appears the target either tried to surface, or the first explosion sent it upward and the second explosion down. *Seawolf* showed no enemy target when it passed the layer. They are leaving the immediate area and await further instructions."

"One instruction is make sure everyone knows the *Seawolf* is coming back out and not to attack it." Holman knew that USS *Ramage* and USS *Hue City* would be paying close attention to the American submarine's presence. His order was unnecessary, but not without value.

The carrier's forward momentum eventually slowed to six knots. Throughout the next hour the USS *Stennis* maneuvered outside the strait to recover its aircraft. The ASW surface action group continued to lay sonobuoy barriers and scan the undersea environment. The Royal Navy helicopters hovered as they refueled in flight from the three surface ships: USS *Ramage,* USS *Hue City,* and the HMS *Boxer.* Then, they turned toward the western horizon and the HMS *Invincible* and its small battle group, the remnant Navy of a once-great maritime power.

"Captain, we've recovered the Vikings and *John Rodgers'* helicopter. Combat requests to recover the Sea Kings before nightfall and secure from the SAR operations of the USS *John Rodgers*. HMS *Invincible* reports ready to recovery the Royal Navy helicopters. Admiral Sir Ledderman-Thompson sends his compliments and says they are taking station twenty-five miles behind us. He asks to be kept informed of our intentions and offers any assistance that the Royal Navy can provide."

"Roger, send my personal respects and thanks to the admiral for his assistance, and tell Combat to keep the Royal Navy up to date on our status. Call *Ramage* and tell it to detach the Sea Kings for return to home plate before nightfall." Captain Holman took the stub of the Cuban cigar and tossed the butt overboard. Best thing America ever did was lifting the embargo with Cuba once Castro died.

"Well, XO, it's time to figure out how to get through the Strait of Gibraltar since it's mined."

"I don't see how we can, sir."

"Have you been watching the merchant traffic?"

"Not really, sir, except for those who were coming too close and we ordered them away."

"Well, XO, seems they're still going through the strait, and not a single one of them has been attacked, or hit a mine."

"Yes, sir, but now that we know it's mined, it explains what happened to that supertanker a few days ago."

"Could be, XO. I don't think so, but it's a good point to consider."

"So, what do we do, Captain?"

"Glad you asked, XO," Holman replied, pulling another Cuban cigar from his shirt pocket. "We're going to take the old girl through a minefield and we're going to do it without hitting any of them." He pulled another cigar from his shirt pocket. "Secure from General Quarters. Give the crew a chance to stretch their legs. Later I'll go on fleet television and explain today's events. I know a lot of questions are out there."

"Yes, sir, will do. As for the mines, Captain, how do you intend to get us through the strait?"

"Watch and learn, XO. Look at those transiting unharmed and you have your answer. Round up the department heads and have them meet me in the operations conference room in ten minutes. No one is going to stop the United States Navy from sailing any goddamn place it wants to sail."

He stepped inside the bridge and stopped abruptly. The XO bumped into him. "XO, have *Ramage* and *Hue City* rejoin. We'll need *Ramage*'s power for what we're going to do. Also, call USNS *Concord* and tell her to quit lollygagging back there and get her tail up here with us. I want the ships topped off before morning, so *Concord* has a busy night ahead of her. That means, XO, *Concord* needs to start refueling operations now."

CHAPTER 10

⚓

THE RIFLE BUTT HIT THE CHARGING ALGERIAN REBEL ON
the underside of the chin. The impact of the CAR-15 broke
the jaw, teeth rocketing out to bounce off Duncan's shirt. The
attacker's feet folded neatly to a momentary kneeling position
before he fell forward. His head bounced off Duncan's boots.
Eyes glazed and face bloody, he lay motionless at Duncan's
feet.

"I told you I've got a headache!" Duncan growled through
clenched teeth.

"Shit, Boss! If it's a migraine, they don't stand a chance,"
Beau said, breathing heavily. He glanced at the unconscious
Arab before he picked himself up off the ground and brushed
the dirt from his cammies.

Shouts came from around the building. Beau leaned around
the corner. "Shit!" He fired a burst down the street and
jumped back. An avalanche of return fire tore off parts of the
white-walled house. Stinging fragments of plaster peppered
them.

A "whoosh" sound filled the air. A quick, wide-eyed, knowing look at each other, and the two men dove away just as a
rocket-propelled grenade shattered the side of the house. De-

bris showered them, followed by a rolling cloud of choking dust.

"Damn, Beau. I guess you showed them," Duncan said, wiping his eyes.

"Look, you told me to go! Ergo, I went. Next time don't send me."

"Next time, don't bring back half the insurgent devils in the world with you." He touched Beau on the shoulder. "Let's get out of here!"

They ran down the narrow street, Duncan several feet in front of Beau. Duncan scanned the windows and doors ahead, while Beau tried to watch the intersection behind them.

"Faster, Duncan," said Beau. "Must go faster."

"I'm going as fast as I can. I ain't the Flash, you know."

A figure stepped from a doorway ahead. Without slowing, Duncan raised his gun even as he recognized Colonel Yosef. He relaxed the pressure of his trigger finger and lowered the carbine slightly as he veered toward the Algerian officer. All along the street Algerian Palace Guards pressed against doorways or crouched behind abandoned cars and furniture.

Duncan and Beau shoved themselves into the wide doorway with Yosef. "We've got company, Colonel," Duncan said.

"Yes, I heard," Yosef replied. "The others are still at the petrol station, Captain. Go down this alley." He pointed to a narrower passage a few yards further down. "We'll try to hold them for ten minutes and then fight a retreat. Have the truck ready, okay?"

"Good luck, Colonel. They have an RPG launcher."

"I know. I saw it hit. You were very lucky, Captain."

Duncan peeked around the corner. "Come on, Beau. Good luck, Colonel."

"Captain." Yosef grabbed Duncan's arm. "Did you find any food or water?"

"No, just a bunch of pissed-off Arabs. See you at the truck. Don't be late, Colonel."

"We won't, but don't leave us," Yosef said, a hint of menace in his voice.

Duncan touched Yosef's shoulder. "SEALs don't leave anyone, Colonel."

Duncan and Beau dodged into the street, keeping close to the front of the nearby houses as they ran. Once in the alley, they straightened and began a wild dash down the four-foot-wide passage.

A minute later they reached the end. Sounds of shooting and a minor explosion told them Yosef and the Guardsmen had engaged the rebels. "Let's hope they hold them long enough," Duncan said.

The two men leaned against the walls. They peered around the corners.

Dead bodies swayed from each lamppost to disturb the stillness of the empty street. The hot sun created shifting heat waves above the rough pavement.

The two men dashed across the street. Disturbed from their feeding, hundreds of crows rose from the day-old bodies, filling the afternoon sky with their displeasure. The ripe, sweet smell of sun-rotted flesh assaulted the two men as they ran past more streetlights—a decaying body swinging from each created a macabre gauntlet along their path.

The sound of combat from Yosef's direction increased in intensity as they crested the hill. Below, the truck was parked under the small green awning of a deserted petrol station.

"Captain!" Lieutenant H.J. McDaniels shouted, startling the two. She crouched behind a small garden wall.

Ensign Bud Helliwell waved from the next garden. Across the street from H.J. and Bud, Chief Judiah and Gibbons held a cross-fire position.

Duncan and Beau jumped the low stucco and rock fence to land in a crouch beside H.J.

"What's going on, Captain?" she asked.

"I think we stumbled on the people who did this slaughter. Colonel Yosef intends to hold them for at least ten minutes, then they'll be coming the same way we did. We've got major problems and need to get the hell out of here. How much longer until they've got the truck refueled?"

"I don't know, sir. I followed your instructions and deployed the team as soon as we heard the firing. Colonel Yosef and his men raced ahead. Monkey and McDonald are down the hill in position with their MGs, guarding each end of the street."

"Good thinking, H.J. We're going down and try to hurry everything along. Colonel Yosef and his Guardsmen should be the next bunch to come this way. Don't shoot them. Give them cover.

"Come on, Beau," Duncan said, then shouted to the two men across the street. "Chief, you and Gibbons hightail it down to the truck and warn them!" In his haste to get everyone out of the village and escape the rebels coming their way, Duncan failed to consider that without the Chief and Gibbons, H.J. and Bud were left with no immediate backup and in an untenable position if the enemy attacked.

"H.J., Bud," Duncan said to the two. "As soon as Colonel Yosef and his men pass, give them one minute and follow. We'll provide cover from below."

"Aye, aye, Captain," the two replied simultaneously.

H.J.'s hands tightened on the CAR-15.

Duncan and Beau leaped over the four-foot wall and ran down the hill to where the truck was parked. Chief Judiah and Gibbons followed. They swung their weapons to point down an empty side street that separated the petrol station from H.J. and Bud. The narrow street ran toward a small residential area leading to the outskirts of the village. A hundred feet further on, the SEALs passed Monkey at the base of the hill, his MG-60 pointed toward the crest where H.J. and Bud waited nervously on point.

H.J. wiped her palm on her cammie pants.

"Sweaty palms?" Bud asked.

"Better than hairy ones." She grinned.

The Volvo truck was a scene of scurrying activity. The metal cover of the petrol tank lay to one side. A hose snaked into the gasoline. The other end of the hose ran to a small five-gallon can. A Bashir relative, with a second red five-gallon container at the truck, poured the contents into the fuel tank. Bashir milled around the area, shouting directions and encouragement as the obedient relatives ran between the truck and the fuel tank.

McDonald squatted on his haunches at the opposite side of the petrol station, barely visible from behind a garden wall, watching the street from that direction.

Gibbons joined two Guardsmen near President Alneuf. Alneuf had his handkerchief to his nose in a futile gesture to block the sickening smell of decomposing bodies that permeated the atmosphere of this small Algerian village. The lack of wind trapped the stench within the village. A small park across from the petrol station had been used as an execution field. About sixty bodies lay haphazardly on top of each other against a ten-foot-high white wall. The wall was pockmarked with gray holes where shots had hit and ricocheted.

Petrol, food, and the necessity of leaving the highway before dawn had driven them into the interior of the country. They'd stumbled on this small village in the afternoon. The scope of the carnage had only become apparent when they were several blocks inside it. If fuel and provisions had been less critical, they would have continued their journey without stopping, but the silence of the village had given a false sense of abandonment.

Duncan and Beau ran up to Bashir.

"There are no young women," Bashir said, an ominous tone in his deep bass voice. His triple chin bounced to the rhythm of his words.

"What do you mean?" Duncan asked, catching his breath. He rubbed his knee. His hand could barely feel the kneecap through the swollen joint. Water around the knee.

"The young women. All the dead that you see"—he waved his hand at the park across the road—"are men, old women, and children. The rebels take the young women for *temporary marriages*," Bashir said caustically. "And after they have raped and shared them, they cut their throats. Sometimes, for entertainment, they cut this way"—he made a slashing gesture along each side of his neck—"so that they are not killed outright. Then they are hung by their heels to bleed slowly to death. Sometimes they are mated with dogs and donkeys for the men's entertainment. When they become bored, they kill them."

"That's disgusting!" Beau said.

"No, that's the new Algeria, *mon capitaine*," Bashir said angrily. "It is the Algeria that President Alneuf fought against. I doubt the new government will allow this conduct to continue, but until stability returns to Algeria, this will be one of the hazards of the people."

"How much longer until the truck is fueled, Mr. Bashir?" Duncan asked. They'd come here to rescue Alneuf, and instead found themselves fighting for their lives in the middle of revolutionary massacres.

Bashir shrugged. "Ten, maybe fifteen minutes. We have put five cans into the truck. We need another five to top off."

"You have five minutes. Colonel Yosef is outnumbered and fighting a holding position against the Algerian rebels, so do what you can. We don't have much time. Fill extra cans, but start getting everyone on board. You're not going to have time to top off."

The sound of an automotive engine drew their attention. A military truck careened out of the side street that separated them from H.J. and Helliwell. Monkey opened fire. The front tires exploded. Out of control, the truck crossed the street and crashed through the low wall, coming to an abrupt stop as it rammed the house a few feet beyond. Rebels jumped from the back, firing as they ran uphill toward H.J. and Helliwell. The driver lay slumped over the steering wheel.

"Keep filling the truck, Bashir!" Duncan yelled as he and Beau raced up the hill toward the enemy vehicle.

H.J. and Helliwell surprised the rebels by opening fire. The return fire sent both of them diving for cover. Protected by the low garden wall, H.J. and Bud scurried along the wall, shifting their position to open up a better field of fire, but the volume of rebel return fire kept driving them down. They were pinned. The attackers split into two groups. One focused its attack against H.J. and Bud, while the other forced their way into the house across the street. Automatic fire tore up the street, narrowly missing Duncan and the others as they ran uphill.

Several rebels crouched behind the smoking truck, shooting at those in the petrol station. A volley of shots bracketed Monkey, sending his language back into the "streets of Newark" vernacular. He stood quickly with the MG-60 braced on his hip and raked the vehicle from bumper to bumper. Four rebels hiding in the bed jerked as bullets riddled them.

McDonald raced from his position at the other end of the petrol station to the opposite side of the street from Monkey.

He opened fire as he ran, blowing the dead driver off the steering wheel and hitting two attackers who were attempting to escape up the near side of the street. The remaining Algerian rebels kept the truck between them and the machine-gunners as they fled uphill to where their comrades were attacking the two trapped SEALs.

H.J. and Bud fought a mismatched battle as the attackers reached the top of the hill. Rebels screamed as they assaulted the low garden fence.

Several Guardsmen from the petrol station joined Duncan and Beau. In leapfrog action they fought their way up the hill toward the battle surrounding H.J. and Helliwell. A barrage of gunfire from the occupied house across the street from H.J. and Bud sent Duncan and his group rolling for cover. Monkey and McDonald peppered the house with return fire, effectively stopping the rebels.

Duncan ran his hand through his close-cropped hair. *So close, but so far away. If H.J. and Bud can hold out for another minute . . .*

Shit! Algerian rebels dove over the wall where H.J. and Bud were hiding. H.J. shot two of the rebels as they came over the top. Duncan and Beau stood simultaneously. Two rebels at the rear jerked as the duo's bullets sent them, like maladroit puppets with tangled strings, dancing backward before they fell in the street. Duncan started running, ignoring the excruciating pain in his right knee. He could always get an artificial knee. Bullets kicked up the pavement around him, the shards stinging his legs. A fierce battle raged out of sight behind the wall. Duncan dove behind a nearby garden wall as a sniper bullet barely missed him. He waited a few seconds before sprinting toward the empty rebel truck, about fifty feet away.

He looked up in time to see a rebel hit H.J. from behind with his rifle butt as another grabbed her rifle. She spun and kneed the man behind her in the crotch, with as much force as possible. Duncan grimaced. The Algerian rebel fell forward, his weapon hitting the ground as both hands flew in protection over his nuts. H.J. whipped out her knife from its leg scabbard and slit his throat, shoving him to one side. A rebel fired point-blank at the female SEAL. H.J. grabbed her shoulder.

The force of the impact spun her around before she disappeared behind the wall with rebels jumping on top of her. Duncan leaped up and, in a quick sprint, made it to the wrecked truck.

Bud Helliwell was in his own battle and unable to help his partner. A rebel ran toward the mustang officer and tossed a grenade. Helliwell blew him into paradise. The grenade landed a few feet from him.

Bud dove over the wall as the grenade exploded. He hit the road hard, rolling left downhill. Shrapnel caught him in the left arm.

Beau snapped his gun to his shoulder and shot a rebel who had swung his gun toward the wounded SEAL, expecting an easy kill. He shot two others who had stood to shoot Helliwell. Bud began to crawl as fast as he could downhill, dragging his left arm beside him. Blood from the wounds made a red streak along the paved road. Shots from the rebels disturbed the ground around the wounded officer. Bits of gravel and dirt ricocheted over Bud, but miraculously failed to score.

Enemy fire from across the street sent Duncan ducking back behind the smoking rebel truck. Beau crouched across the street opposite Duncan. Duncan waved at Beau and motioned toward Helliwell. Beau gave a curt nod. Gibbons rolled into the area behind the truck, crowding Duncan from behind.

Suddenly McDonald sprinted past Duncan and Beau, heading uphill. Duncan whistled and waved for McDonald to stop and take position where he was. McDonald rolled behind a nearby fence.

Duncan motioned Monkey to move across the street, and with the two machine-gunners on opposite sides of the street, he had them in overlapping fire position.

Small bursts of pavement erupted as Chief Judiah ran up the middle of the road toward the wounded SEAL.

"Give him cover!" Duncan shouted.

"Yeah, give me cover!" the chief yelled as he bobbed and weaved, trying to make himself a harder target.

Beau leaned around the corner and fired several short, rapid bursts at the enemy. Monkey released a tattoo of MG-60 bullets along the doorways of the buildings, while McDonald blew out the remaining windows on both sides of the street.

Duncan and Gibbons gave the roofs their full attention. The SEALs effectively silenced the enemy fire long enough for Chief Judiah to reach Helliwell.

The chief jerked Helliwell to his feet and threw him over his shoulder. He half-dragged, half-carried the wounded ensign to a nearby wall, where they took cover.

"You okay?" Judiah asked.

"Sure," Bud replied, his right hand under his left armpit pressing against a pressure point. "It's only a scratch."

Chief Judiah pulled his belt off and handed it to the wounded officer. "Here, let's put a tourniquet on that scratch before you bleed to death."

"It ain't as bad as it looks, Chief. Give me a few minutes and the bleeding will stop." Bud grimaced as Judiah slipped the makeshift tourniquet up the arm. No, it wasn't the wound that hurt. Bud could tell the arm was broken, but it was easier to set a break than shove blood back into the body. The blood just made the wound look worse than it truly was.

"Go, Chief. I'll be fine here. Hand me my piece."

As the SEAL fire slacked, four rebels jumped up and ran across the street toward H.J.'s position. Two rolled over the wall. Machine-gun fire from Monkey sent the last two pitching forward, hands outspread, to land motionless on the street. Their weapons bounced off the cobblestones.

Duncan waved at Beau and pointed to himself. Beau pointed uphill. Duncan nodded. Duncan crawled around the tail of the truck. Above him a frightened Algerian leaned over the tailgate with his rifle aimed at the back of Duncan's head. Gibbons shot him. The attacker fell, landing on top of the startled Duncan, who pushed the body off him and under the truck.

Taking a deep breath, Duncan jumped up and began a zigzag run uphill for thirty feet. He hurled himself over the garden wall of a nearby house. Gunfire from the house stitched a neat series of holes along the wall above him. Bits of plaster peppered his back, bringing up small stinging blisters.

Beau's return fire silenced the guns from across the street. Duncan crawled several feet forward and peered around the corner of a cast-iron gate. Chief Judiah tumbled over the wall

and, crouching, ran toward Duncan's position. The chief un-
limbered a stun grenade and tossed it over a wall two houses
up before he dove for cover one house down from Duncan.
Duncan drew back as the explosion went off.

Dust from the explosion obscured the area. Duncan jumped
up, rolled over the wall, and came up running as he crossed
the street to where H.J. had gone down. As he passed, Chief
Judiah joined him.

Covering fire against the rebels in the house across the
street pinned them as he and Chief Judiah leaped the wall
where the chief's grenade had exploded. Chief Judiah hit the
other side, his CAR-15 blasting away to dispatch a stunned
fundamentalist to whatever paradise fanatics rush to go to.

"How's Ensign Helliwell?" Duncan asked. The two
crouched side by side, their eyes searching the area.

"He'll live, Captain."

"Serious wound?"

"Another Purple Heart, but he'll be standing to get it."

"I saw you carrying him."

"Yes, sir, and he bitched the entire time."

"Good. Sounds as if he'll live."

Duncan had counted at least six rebels where H.J. had been
shot, but no return fire came from that direction, much to the
surprise of the two SEALs. Why would a woman want to do
this line of work? Didn't they realize what happened when
they were captured? But his was not to reason why. That was
the province of the politicians who had—

Duncan stood up slowly behind a wide telephone pole. The
enemy fire had slacked for some unknown reason. He motioned Beau and Gibbons forward. McDonald repositioned to
provide better cross fire.

Duncan and Chief Judiah watched the hill, firing once at a
sniper who had reached the second floor of the house across
the street and recklessly leaned out the window to take aim at
Beau and Gibbons. Their bullets hit the sniper simultaneously, catapulting the dying rebel head over heels off the bal-
cony to land with a sickening thump on the road below. His
screams stopped when he hit. The rifle clanked several times
as it bounced on the pavement.

Chief Judiah crawled over the end of the wall. Duncan followed. Moving quickly, they eased over the next wall into another walled garden. The one after this was H.J.'s.

Surprised, but thankful that no return fire came from the garden, Duncan and Judiah still approached carefully.

Across the street Beau and Gibbons cautiously worked their way to where they were directly opposite Duncan and Chief Judiah. Their eyes scanned constantly, working their way along the doorways and windows and roofs. Watching for a warning when the next attack would start.

"We're going in," Duncan mouthed as he motioned to the next building.

Beau nodded.

Duncan and Chief Judiah crouched against the wall. On the other side should be more Algerian rebels. Duncan moved to the far side, while Chief Judiah braced his back against the side of the house. Chief Judiah pulled another grenade. Duncan nodded.

He eased up to peer into the next yard, ready to drop if spotted. Gunfire erupted from the building, hitting the wall, sending a shower of dust and pieces of brick into the air. Duncan and the chief stuck their carbines over the top and fired a random burst toward the house. Judiah lobbed a grenade up and over the wall. It exploded. The two men rolled over the wall into the yard next door, the smoke from the grenade screening their presence. The door to the house was open.

Duncan's eyes scrunched as he weighed the situation, trying to see through the cloud of dust. He looked at Chief Judiah and waved the grenade down. Then, he motioned the chief to the right and forward. Judiah put the grenade away. Crouching, he ran along the side of the house. Gunfire erupted from the top window; the shooter, failing to see them, was firing over their heads at a target in the street. Duncan stood, took two steps back to the left, and shot the rebel in the top window. The rebel tumbled out of the window, screaming in pain until the ground stopped his fall.

Duncan looked at Chief Judiah, lifted his right fist, and began to uncurl his fingers one at a time. When the third finger flipped up, Duncan nodded sharply. The two rushed the doorway. Duncan came up short on the left side, while Judiah braced his back against the front of the house on the right side.

Beau and Gibbons dashed across the street and rolled into the garden behind them. Judiah pulled the stun grenade off his belt again. Duncan shook his head, and with a downward wave of his hand motioned the chief to hold the grenade. Judiah was determined to use that grenade. But Duncan didn't want to take the chance of injuring H.J.—if she was still alive.

A pause in the gunfire allowed the noise of a fight inside the house to reach them. Then the sound of enemy gunfire from around the far side of the house told Duncan that more rebels were using the downstairs as their position. The SEALs had taken out the rebels in the front, but how long before the others inside realized their flank had been broken?

"Cover me," he said.

Chief Judiah nodded.

Beau and Gibbons moved forward to join the two.

Duncan drove through the doorway, his trigger finger tense on the carbine. A rebel fired at him from the top of the stairs. Beau shot him from the doorway and rolled to Duncan's right. The rebel fell over the banister, hitting the floor with a loud clump. Judiah dashed into the house, glanced in the room to the right, and fired a quick burst. A short cry followed Judiah's shots. Duncan rose and dashed down the hallway. Beau and the others followed. From outside a renewed round of fighting increased in intensity.

TWO REBELS HAD H.J. PINNED ON THE FLOOR. HER SHIRT was ripped and shredded. Her bra hung by a single strap down her side, exposing both breasts. She twisted to the right, dislodging the rebel holding her feet long enough for her left leg to come around and catch him upside the head, knocking him senseless against a nearby couch. A gaping right shoulder wound bled profusely as H.J. spat at the man holding her arms. Blood ran out of her mouth from bleeding gums where someone had beaten her severely. She pulled her legs up and caught the remaining rebel's head between her calves. She rolled to the left, pulling him away from her wounded shoulder.

Behind the couch, two other rebels were firing out of the window, ignoring the commotion behind them. They were overconfident in their satisfaction that they had subdued the American female. Their attention was so focused on the battle outside that they failed to notice H.J. had gotten the upper hand. The rebel who H.J. had kicked with her foot shook his head, and looked up. Duncan appeared in the doorway. Seeing Duncan, he dove for his gun.

The burst from Duncan's CAR-15 catapulted the rebel across the room, the bullets rippling up the torso, blowing away his manhood, abdomen, and chest. The last bullet left a single, well-defined hole in the forehead. Chief Judiah burst into the room, two steps to the left of Duncan. The two rebels at the windows whipped around at the gunfire, one of them shooting as he turned. Judiah and Beau fired, killing the two. A stray shot from one of the rebels at the window hit the rebel who was fighting to free himself from H.J.'s murderous leg grip.

H.J. released the dying man, pushed herself up with her left arm, and struggled to her feet. She stood there, weaving back and forth, like a half-naked goddess. Gibbons ran forward to help, unsure of what to touch or grab. Finally, he took her arm.

"You okay, Lieutenant?" Duncan asked, his gun trained on the bodies of two rebels near the windows. Even though he knew the answer was, "No, I'm not okay."

She nodded. Her face was bleeding and there was a vacant, moist look in her eyes. Shock, Duncan thought.

Beau stripped a shirt off one of the rebels and handed it to her. She reached up and tore the remaining strap of the bra, letting the useless undergarment drop to the floor.

She took the offered shirt and pulled it halfway over the good shoulder, but was unable to cover the wounded one. Gibbons stopped her. She shifted the survival knife on her belt to one side.

"Ma'am, excuse me," Gibbons said, "but I need to dress this shoulder and wipe away some of this blood before we put on the shirt."

H.J. nodded, a slight twitch evident in her right cheek. Gibbons ripped open a medical-dressing package and began to wipe the blood away. Blood trickled downward from a shallow stab wound on the side of H.J.'s left breast. Her vacant face betrayed no emotion when Gibbons finished a couple of minutes later and then helped her button the shirt. She had yet to speak, but Duncan noticed her hands did not shake.

"Gibbons, make it quick," Duncan said.

She looked at the dead rebels. A growl, like a cornered mountain lion, erupted from her throat, startling the four men. She pulled the knife from Gibbons's scabbard, turned, and with a movement too quick for Duncan to stop, slashed the throats of the two dead Algerians nearest her.

From outside came the sound of running feet.

"H.J., let's go," Duncan said.

Gibbons reached up and gingerly took his knife back, wiping it on one of the dead men's shirts before he slid it back into the scabbard.

"Let's go, aye, Captain," she said, her voice a monotonous slur.

Beau led the way as he ran out of the house and turned downhill.

Ahead, two rebels were in a hand-to-hand fight with Monkey. The gorillalike SEAL held one by the neck with his massive right hand. He backhanded the other rebel as the man charged. Monkey freed his knife. The other rebel regained his feet and leaped onto Monkey's back. Beau rushed forward and with his butt of his rifle knocked the man off Monkey's back. The rebel in Monkey's grip kicked the SEAL. Monkey shoved the razor-sharp weapon, blade up, into the rebel's stomach and jerked upward. Beau dispatched the other with one shot. Monkey jerked his knife to the right before he pulled it out. He held the man's face close to his so he could look directly into the man's eyes as he died. The glazed shroud of death creeped across the eyes. Monkey, expressionless, pushed the dead rebel off the knife.

"I wonder where they go," Monkey said.

H.J. walked unsteadily outside behind Duncan and Judiah.

"Down, ma'am!" Gibbons shouted as another attacker appeared on the other side of the wall. He roughly shoved her aside.

A single bullet seemed to miss H.J. as she catapulted off the side of the house from the force of Gibbons's push. Duncan shot the rebel. Gibbons put two more bullets into the body.

"Let's move. There's more rebels here than was in that truck," Duncan said. Fighting from where he had left Colonel Yosef reached his ears. At least the colonel and his Guardsmen were still alive.

H.J. slid down the white wall, leaving a trail of blood against it as she came to a sitting position. "You know, Captain, this is not making a good impression for my first time out as a SEAL," she said weakly before she passed out.

"Beau, you and Chief Judiah bring the lieutenant." He gestured to Gibbons. "Stay here and guard the road. As soon as Colonel Yosef and his men come through, you follow them down. We're going to load the truck!"

"Aye, aye, Captain!" Gibbons shouted.

They moved down the hill. Beau and Judiah held H.J. between them, trying not to further aggravate the bullet wound. Beau pulled the shirt up and over the wounded right shoulder, covering H.J.'s breast, exposed again when she passed out.

"Yo mama!" shouted Gibbons as he shot a rebel coming out of a side street further up.

McDonald rolled to the left as a hand grenade landed near him. It exploded harmlessly as the machine-gunner raked the building from where it came.

A single sniper from a window nearer Gibbons's position began firing at the petrol station. Gibbons scrambled six steps further to the right to line up for a clear shot. He licked his finger, touched the far sight of the carbine, and fired. The rebel's hands flew up. The gun went twirling out of the window and into the brush below as Gibbons's bullet tore through the man's chest. The sniper fell backward into the building.

Duncan leaped the wall and helped Helliwell to his feet.

"Come on, Bud. Enough rest time."

"Damn, Captain, I was just getting comfortable. I'm okay. I can walk." He stood, weaved slightly, and pulled himself over the wall.

"McDonald!" Duncan shouted. "Help Ensign Helliwell to the truck!"

Helliwell fell.

"Hurry!"

"I've got him, Captain," McDonald said. He slung his MG-60 across his back and pulled the ensign up.

Draping the good arm around his shoulders, McDonald more pulled than helped Helliwell to the truck. Sounds of combat near the crest of the hill reached them.

Duncan began a stiff-legged run back up the hill just as Colonel Yosef and his men poured over the top. He passed Beau and Chief Judiah carrying H.J. between them.

At the crest, Colonel Yosef and his Palace Guard fanned out to fight a rear-guard action as they retreated toward the truck.

Duncan crouched beside Yosef. "I see you brought them with you."

"Is Bashir ready?" Yosef shouted between gasps for breath.

"They're loading now. What have we got?"

"At least two companies of revolutionaries. They were enjoying the fruits of temporary marriages when you disturbed them. We have to go before they bring up the armored car."

"Armored car?"

"Yes, armored car—a Russian BTR-60. It attacked our position on the other side. It can't get through the narrow alley, so they'll have to back it out to turn it around. I give us five, maybe seven minutes before we have more company than we can handle."

"Cannon?"

"No, only a machine gun in a front-mounted turret. Has to turn to fire anywhere other than the front one hundred twenty degrees. Eight wheels for all-terrain."

"Oh, that's good," said Duncan, rolling his eyes. "Probably eight-wheel drive, too."

Yosef gave Duncan a quizzical look. "Good? I don't think so, Captain!" *These SEALs are crazy!*

Shots interrupted before Duncan could explain. Yosef rose and fired several bursts at a group of Algerian rebels, who ran back into the alley. Yosef yelled for his men to fall back.

The rapid beeping of Bashir's truck horn sounded behind them. The truck pointed away from the conflagration. Everyone on board yelled and made rapid motions for the men to hurry. McDonald and Monkey crouched at the tail of the truck with their MGs pointed uphill.

Yosef waved frantically to his men. "Hurry!"

"Come on, Gibbons! Let's haul ass!"

The remaining SEALs and Guardsmen ran down the hill. They leaped at the tailgate of the truck, and Bashir's relatives pulled them aboard. Monkey and McDonald blanketed the crest with machine-gun fire as a wave of rebels poured down it. With the machine-gun fire, they poured back up it.

Duncan shoved his way to the front. "Let's go!" he shouted, slapping his hand repeatedly on the cab of the truck.

The truck lurched as Bashir gave it gas, slowly picking up downhill speed away from the attacking force chasing them. Duncan worked his way along the bouncing truck bed to the back. Guardsmen and SEALs fired at the rebel force. The truck wheeled around a corner and headed out of town.

Five minutes later they were bouncing along a dirt road that led into the desert.

"You know, Colonel Yosef, we are driving further and further from the coast and our transportation is out there." Duncan pointed north toward the ocean. "And unless we get President Alneuf out to sea soon, none of us may leave this place."

"I know, Captain. Survival sometimes means taking whatever opportunity is available at the time and hope the next choice improves your chances."

"Well, this one definitely didn't," he replied, rubbing his temples. August, less than forty-five days to retirement, and here he was fighting for his life instead of preparing for a new one. He hoped he lived long enough to enjoy some of the fruits of a military retirement. And he would prefer not the medical ones.

Duncan worked his way to where H.J. and Bud Helliwell lay side by side. Gibbons was bent over Ensign Helliwell, redressing his wounds. H.J.'s shoulder wound had been bandaged. Her cammie shirt, partially unbuttoned, exposed a bloody cleavage. Part of the shirt had one side taped up.

Gibbons finished swabbing an antibiotic solution on Ensign Helliwell's arm wounds. He ripped open a wide-gauge bandage pack and began to wrap it around the shoulder in such a way as to cover the cleansed wound. H.J.'s eyes were shut. Bud watched Gibbons closely as he finished the bandaging.

"How you doing, Bud?" Duncan asked Helliwell.

"I am getting fed up, Captain. Every time I go on a mission I wind up shot. I don't like it. It's beginning to piss me off. I was shot when I was a first class in the Middle East. I was shot as a senior chief in Liberia during the African Wars. And now that I'm an officer, I'm shot again. Shit, Captain, I thought officers didn't get shot. Guess I should have read your medals better." Bud raised his right arm. "One good thing, at least I'm right-handed."

Duncan smiled.

"How's the lieutenant?" Duncan asked Gibbons.

"Could be a serious wound, Captain. Biggest challenge is to keep it from becoming infected. Other than that, she should pull through. Bullet went clean through and, from where it hit, I'd say she may have a broken collarbone, but with the swelling, I can't tell. Luckily, the bullet missed her arteries."

"Okay," Duncan said. "Button up her shirt when you finish."

The truck hit a series of holes, tossing everyone around the bed of the truck. H.J. moaned and her eyes opened.

"H.J., how do you feel?"

"Like shit," she said softly, her eyes half-open. "So this is combat? It's almost as bad as a sale day at Macy's."

"It isn't pleasant, but Bud is a better authority on that than me. You need to rest." They hit another pothole. "As much as possible. I don't know how long it'll be before we're far enough away so we can slow down. I'll talk with you later."

"And I don't have a broken collarbone. At least, I don't think so."

"Good."

Duncan made his way to where Colonel Yosef squatted on his haunches.

H.J. turned her head toward her wounded companion. "What's the matter, Ensign. Can't let a woman get wounded without you copying her?" The truck bounced. She grimaced as a wave of pain sent dots of light dancing across her vision.

"There, sir. That should hold you," Gibbons said.

The bandage ran from Bud's shoulder past the elbow to where Gibbons had taped it down by tying it around the wrist. The slight wounds on the back of the hand had stopped bleeding, so Gibbons left them uncovered. "Don't let the flies settle," Gibbons warned Helliwell, pointing to the arm. "Are you sure it's not broken?"

"Thanks, Gibbons. I'm okay," Bud said. Yeah, it was broken, but they had more important things to worry about than a simple fracture. The bandages would hold the arm steady, and besides, he'd been around long enough to know that since he could still move his fingers, the break wasn't a serious one.

Gibbons grinned. "No sweat, sir. Just in a day's work."

When he finished buttoning up H.J.'s shirt and adjusting it so it wouldn't dislodge the bandages, Gibbons stood and fought the movement of the truck to where Monkey stood watch.

"How many bullets you take?" H.J. asked Helliwell weakly.

"None. I didn't roll far enough away from a damn grenade."

"Shit, John. You could have been killed."

"Yeah. And I would have been, too, if the manager of Kmart hadn't come out and unplugged that thing."

She grinned.

Helliwell smiled. "That's what makes being a SEAL so much fun. You never know when you're going to leave a lot of creditors upset. Just think, Lieutenant, many SEALs go their entire career without getting shot. You manage it in your first mission. There's going to be a lot of jealous shipmates when we get back, ma'am."

"*If* we get back," she corrected.

"Never 'if,' ma'am. It's always 'when.'"

"Quit calling me ma'am, I'm not your mom, John. Call me, H.J. I think that being wounded together gives us something in common."

Helliwell reached over and squeezed her hand. She weakly returned the gesture. "Don't think this means we're engaged or anything," he said, smiling.

"Not even a casual relationship?" she asked, her voice trailing off. H.J.'s eyelids fluttered and then closed.

"Not yet, and besides, only my parents call me John. Call me Bud, like everyone else," he said. Several seconds passed.

"Get some rest, H.J. You did an excellent job. I'm proud to call you a Navy SEAL."

"That's not what you said aboard ship," she slurred, her eyes closed.

Bud started to apologize, but saw her shut eyes, and watched quietly as her breathing slowed and she slid into unconsciousness. The truck hit another series of rough spots, bouncing everyone around. She slept through the tumble. Bud hoped they got back soon. He'd seen what wounds like hers could become without proper treatment—blood poisoning, gangrene, and a slow, painful death.

Beau slid in beside Duncan as Yosef moved off to check on his men. "Where to now, Boss?" Beau asked.

"We've got to get out of this country."

"No argument from me on that score. Do you have a plan?"

Duncan nodded. "I've discussed it with Colonel Yosef and he agrees. We are going to have to return to the coast. Our only chance lies in getting out to sea where Sixth Fleet can pick us up."

Beau nodded, and then leaned close to Duncan and whispered, "I don't understand why they didn't kill her."

"Think about it, Beau. The fight wouldn't have lasted forever."

THE ARMORED CAR SCREECHED TO A HALT AT THE PETROL station. Algerian rebels pushed and shoved as they crowded into the cramped spaces of the military vehicle.

Ten minutes later the armored car took off in pursuit. The rebel captain, confident they would soon overtake the old truck, screamed into the radio, trying to establish contact with Algiers. He threw the microphone against the dashboard in frustration when no answer came immediately. President Alneuf had been recognized.

CHAPTER 11

⚓

"**MR. PRESIDENT,**" **FRANCO DONELLI SAID.** "**IF YOU WANT** to talk with Ambassador Cannets while the Algerian ambassador is giving his address, we have a direct phone line at the United Nations up and running." He pointed to the red phone between them. "It's a secure line."

"Thanks, Franco," Crawford replied as he picked up the phone. "Alex, you there?"

A voice on the other end answered.

"Can you put him on, please," the president replied. He put his hand over the mouthpiece. "Franco, are we watching C-SPAN or CNN on the wide screen?"

"It's the State Department's camera, Mr. President."

The president uncovered the mouthpiece. "Alex, old friend, this is President Crawford. Has there been a prerelease of his speech yet?"

"No, sir, Mr. President. But I did speak with the new ambassador late last night, as you directed. A debrief was sent via classified e-mail to Washington earlier today. I was very adamant, nearly to the point of threatening, when I demanded the safe conduct of American and Western citizens out of the black hole of Algiers. I was surprised by his reaction. He seemed almost apologetic; very receptive, but he never actually apologized. He promised to personally expedite their departure. Further, he assured me of their safety and security. We were interrupted several times by others, but he said that our concerns were being blown out of proportion to events in Algiers. Even so, he promised to resolve our concerns."

President Crawford heard the American ambassador to the United Nations sigh. "What he didn't say was *when.* I am speculating, Mr. President, but I think if we keep the political pressure on, Algeria will release our citizens soon."

"Alex, I hope you're right, but I do not intend to wait much longer. The press is comparing Algiers to Tehran under Jimmy Carter. According to Bob Gilfort, Westerners are still being forced into the compound. The ambassador there is rationing food and water, and attributes six deaths since yesterday to cholera." President Crawford sighed in return. "Alex, the newspapers are crucifying the administration. I may have to send in the military to take the pressure off us."

Franco touched President Crawford on his arm and shook his head.

President Crawford scowled, shifted the phone to his left hand, and continued. "What are your thoughts on this new Algerian ambassador? Why does he want to address the General Assembly? Will he honor his word on the plight of our citizens?"

"I don't know the answer to any of those questions yet, Mr. President. This unusual request to address the full body, plus the world attention on the situation at the American embassy in Algiers, gives him an opportunity to show a humanitarian side to the chaos in that country," Ambassador Cannets added.

"Alex, I hope you're right. For your information, this morning I gave orders to prepare to evacuate our citizens regardless of whether we have permission to go in or not. I am holding off the execute order to see what Ambassador Mintab has to say. It is the only thing holding me back."

"I take it then, Mr. President, our forces are already in the area. This morning on CNN they said that mines in the Red Sea sank the USS *Roosevelt* and that the USS *Stennis* was blockaded west of the Strait of Gibraltar because the strait is mined. What's going on, sir? Is there anything you can tell me before the speech begins? I have already had the British and Canadian ambassadors asking me questions about the newscast. Australia and New Zealand will also support our position, but they're half a world away."

The president glanced down at the STE telephone to confirm the digital readout. Seeing "TOP SECRET CODE WORD" displayed, he continued. "Alex, CNN, for once, is wrong. This is top secret, so it's close hold, though I suspect the news agencies will know soon enough. The aircraft carrier *Roosevelt* was not sunk. As you know, the Egyptians closed the Suez Canal based on some story about it being mined. But Farbros told me that the CIA believes it's a fabricated story to keep the *Roosevelt* battle group from entering the Med.

"We didn't force the issue because by then we had redirected the USS *Roosevelt* to reverse course and join the Seventh Fleet off Korea. When the *Roosevelt* battle group hit that narrow strip of water, linking the Red Sea with the Gulf of Aden, the lead destroyer hit a mine." President Crawford stopped and covered the mouthpiece.

"Franco, what's that area called?"

"The Bab El Mandeb, sir," the director of the CIA, Farbros Digby-Jones, answered before Franco could respond.

President Crawford removed his hand. "Yeah, that's it. The Bab El Mandeb, Alex. The destroyer suffered considerable damage. The battle group turned north after saving the destroyer, and about five miles later several torpedo mines hit the *Roosevelt*. She is damaged, but still under her own power. You can't sink a major ship of the line like a carrier without a lot of effort. Commander United States Naval Forces Central Command in Bahrain reports that the United States Fifth Fleet has dispatched three minesweepers from the Persian Gulf to the area, and we expect them to arrive day after tomorrow. I'm told it'll take two days to clear a path through the mines. Even so, the *Roosevelt* cannot continue to Korea. The Navy is ordering her to Singapore for repairs."

As for the USS *Stennis . . .*" Crawford chuckled. "A piece of good news through all of these misfortunes. You'll love this story, Alex, being a former Naval officer. Captain Holman, the commanding officer of the USS *Stennis,* had a destroyer tow the carrier through the strait while the battle group hugged the Moroccan coast."

"What did the Moroccans do, Mr. President?"

"They didn't do a damn thing, Alex. Holman had F-14s and F-18s swarming overhead the battle group like angry hornets. He made the submarine do the transit on the surface. The message sent to Sixth Fleet and to JCS indicates that Captain Holman believes the mines are keyed to magnetic-field size and sound-level intensity, whatever that means. He says that's why the submarine that attacked them was sunk. Oh, Alex, you can share that information about the evacuation and the minefields with the British, Canadians, Australians, and New Zealand. But don't do it until after five o'clock this afternoon. The Royal Navy carrier was towed through the same way after Holman shared the information with them."

"So, the *Nassau* battle group, full of Marines, and the *Stennis* battle group, with its air wing, are together?"

"Hold on a minute, Alex, I am going to put you on speaker phone." Crawford hit the speaker so Alex could hear. "Franco, are the two battle groups together yet?"

"Not physically together, sir." Franco turned to General Eaglefield, who was sitting in the second row. "General, what is the status of the two battle groups in the Mediterranean?"

General Eaglefield nodded to the chief of Naval Operations sitting beside him.

"Mr. President," Admiral Farmer answered. "They're close enough to conduct operations. *Stennis* sailed past the southeastern tip of Spain two hours ago, and *Nassau,* forty nautical miles north of Algiers, is closing the city."

General Eaglefield added, "Kenneth Sutherland, Commander European Command, has designated Admiral Cameron as the Commander Joint Task Force, Mr. President. Feedback from Stuttgart estimates that the Navy and Air Force assets will be in position by this afternoon to commence an evacuation when ordered. We will receive word when preparations are completed. At that time, Mr. President, when you give the go-ahead, they'll go."

"Not when," Franco interjected. "Not when, General, but if."

"Alex," the president continued. "Did you hear all that?"

"Yes, sir, Mr. President. Do you want me to say anything to the Algerian ambassador? A warning or anything?"

Admiral Farmer, sitting to the left of General Eaglefield, touched Franco's shoulder and shook his head vehemently. Franco nodded, touched President Crawford, and mouthed "No."

"No, Alex," the president replied, watching Franco's lips. "Let's see what he has to say. How much longer before he begins?"

"Five minutes, Mr. President. His name is Ahmid Tawali Mintab. He arrived at the General Assembly about twenty minutes ago, and has been engaged in animated conversation with the other new ambassadors from Morocco and Tunisia and with the acting Libyan ambassador. I asked the CIA for a bio on him, but have yet to receive a reply."

The president leaned back in his chair and turned around to Farbros Digby-Jones. "Farbros, you have anything on this new ambassador?"

"No, sir, Mr. President. Our databases do not have an Algerian politician or revolutionary by that name. The only person we can find by that name is a minor functionary in the Libyan foreign service, but nothing that ties him to Algeria. The Army provided that information, and I don't know where they got it."

"Okay, Alex," Crawford continued, speaking firmly. "We're going to watch the speech from the White House. This phone patch will be kept open and you can talk directly to Bob Gilfort, Franco, or me. Do not let anyone know that I am on the other end. But if we don't like what we hear, then the next phone call will be from General Eaglefield to the European Command. We are bringing out our citizens, with or without the help of the Algerian government." He glanced over at Roger Maddock, who nodded once in quick agreement. "Okay, Alex, I'll talk with you later."

The phone clicked as it was put on hold on both ends.

"General Eaglefield," the president said pensively. "We're waiting for everyone to move into position to rescue our citi-

zens. What if we had to go right now, before all our forces
were in place?"

"Mr. President, we have always had the Marines offshore.
One word and they'll own Algiers before nightfall."

"I think sometimes, Roger, you are too melodramatic,"
Franco said.

COLONEL ALQAHIRAY SAT IN THE CENTER SEAT OF THE
operations theater, absentmindedly brushing cigarette ash off
his tunic. Overhead, the live transmission from the United
Nations General Assembly filled the large screen.

He turned to those sitting in the row behind him. "Colonel
Walid, I am thankful you are behind me, protecting me from
these ill-bred intelligence officers," he said, smiling, as he
pointed to Major Samir and the two officers who always shadowed the morning intelligence briefer. "Why are they here
anyway? Haven't I told you, Walid, that Intelligence Officers
are supposed to be making intelligence, not watching it so
they can come to me a few hours later, rearrange the events,
and then tell me what I've just seen?"

Colonel Alqahiray smiled at the discomfort his remarks
caused. He laughed. "Don't shake like cowards, Major. We
have proven that Libyan warriors are anything but cowards."
Alqahiray had little idea the shaking was anger waiting for its
time.

The silence dragged out. Finally, Alqahiray stood and faced
the small crowd. To his right sat the cousin who had led the
execution of the junta. The remaining seats in the first row
contained the other two operations officers from the command post. In the second row Colonel Walid, Major Samir,
alongside the two other intelligence officers, sat with two individuals Colonel Alqahiray recognized as senior security
guards of the compound. Why were they here? He was on the
verge of ordering them out, but in the exuberance of the moment he decided they could stay. The more witnesses to his
victory, the quicker the word would spread.

He cleared his throat. "This is a glorious moment in history,
my fellow Islamic warriors. In ten days we have shook the
world as no Moslem has since the eleventh century. Tomor-

row, we will no longer be a Third World country to be ridiculed, ignored, and scorned by the West. No, we'll be in a position to control the world economically, defend ourselves militarily, and wield world influence unparalleled for a Moslem country. We will control the lifelines of the world. We'll own the Mediterranean. We'll have power. We will inspire every Arab in the world as we lead Islam once again into greatness. For that, you will be remembered as architects of the rise of Islamic greatness in what the Westerners call the twenty-first century. The great years are yet to come as Allah ordains our victory."

On the screen the new Algerian ambassador began his walk down the aisle toward the podium, where the huge lectern gave the speaker a grand view of the enormous hall and the gallery above it.

Walid coughed slightly. "Colonel, it has begun."

The colonel's eyes gleaned with a flash of anger over being interrupted. He hated to be interrupted. Alqahiray buried the fiery emotion quickly, and reluctantly sat down to yield the attention to the screen in front. No applause. No adulation. It was Walid's fault. Who was more important? Him or his mouthpiece at the U.N.? Walid needed to be reminded of his place. That would come with time.

Walid wiped the sweat from his forehead. So much to do in the next hour, and even though he was committed to doing it, Colonel Alqahiray still frightened him.

Colonel Alqahiray was Jihad Wahid. Without his insight and cunning, without his forethought and plans, without his leadership and political tempering of tribal diversities—without him making the covert arrangement with the Chinese, they would not be here today. It brought tears of respect to Walid's eyes. And tears of sadness, too.

THE CHINESE GENERAL WALKED SLOWLY AROUND THE room, shaking hands and exchanging small talk with the others. The air-conditioning was cool on his skin after the brisk walk uphill in the hot morning sun. Sharing the thrill of a plan coming to fruition, he basked in the admiration and the congratulatory comments. Several attentive minutes later he sat down at one end of the long, well-polished table to join the high-ranking Chinese ministers. He took a deep breath when he realized he was the only military person present. He wiped the sweat from his palms. A great honor, if nothing goes wrong.

The ancient gentleman in the dark suit at the other end pushed himself up from his seat. "General Xing, congratulations on your accomplishment. We honor you for the brilliant execution of a scheme that furthers the world influence of the People's Republic of China. Few could have taken a concept such as this and achieved the secrecy and applied the tact necessary to bring it to a successful conclusion—a conclusion without tainting our hands. One that will enhance Chinese influence throughout the world with little, if any, political fallout." He lifted his wineglass. "Gentlemen, please stand with me in drinking a toast to General Xing, without whose foresight and clarity our government would not have achieved this success. To paraphrase the English despot Churchill, 'Never have so many owed so much for so little.'" Dao Chu Shai smiled, knowing everyone in the room attributed the success to his foresightedness.

General Xing remained seated. He nodded deeply, and forced the smile from his lips as he paid respect to the wispy gray-haired Chairman Dao Chu Shai. Everyone stood, lifted their glasses to him, and sipped the French wine. They would have been drinking champagne if the chairman hadn't preferred wine. A round of polite fingertips-in-palms applause followed. Every one of them envied the chairman's power, but his knowledge of their weaknesses and their interwoven intrigues kept them pitted against each other.

One of the two assistants who were always with him pulled the chairman's chair further out. The chairman put his hand on the arm of the shorter assistant as he turned and began his shuffle toward General Xing. The old man balanced his movement with a hand on the back of the chairs along the way. Why did the body always go before the intellect? He waved the assistant back. The others remained standing, but no one offered to help the frail leader of the People's Republic of China. They remembered, too well, the last time. Each nodded respectfully as Dao passed. And when he passed, each finished off the remnants of wine in his glass and nervously poured a refill. They should be worried, Dao gloated to himself.

The general stood as the chairman reached him.

"General, on behalf of a grateful nation, I award you the Red Order of Mao." he said, his voice vibrating from age. "You have done well, and we of the People's Republic of China are proud of our patriots. Your initiative highlights the increased decline of American supremacy and relegates both Americans and their lackeys to a secondary status. And the funny thing is, General, they don't even know it! They will never realize our success or how this marks the turning point in world dominion."

The chairman put his hand out to brace himself on the walnut table. "I am hopeful that I may live to witness Communism spread in its true form as hand-in-hand we lead the lesser nations into the future. World dominion cannot be accomplished militarily. No, world dominion is like a good game of chess. One must be patient to the point of even allowing your opponent the initial onslaught on the board. Let him expend his forces against a strong defense while you look several moves beyond for the ultimate victory. Never confront him head-on when you can enter his garden from the rear. And when the time is right, you strike with everything and send him reeling back until he cries in defeat. We could have accomplished the same things by military force. But military conflict drains a country. It destroys a nation and changes its destiny. It opens the opportunity for instability, and wherever you have instability you have forces that jump into adventurism. We are achieving world dominion by a combination of economic might and political stealth and without a single loss of a Chinese life." He chuckled. The others around the table laughed with him.

The chairman, a smile on his face, waved his hand for quiet. Silence descended like a dropped curtain. "The Americans did it to the old Soviet Union, and ironically, they fail to recognize their own method turned against them. I ask you, when was the last time someone in America brought something that did not bear the imprint 'Made in China'? Remember the EP-3 incident years ago when their reconnaissance aircraft collided with our fighter? When the families of the crew members circled their trees and houses with yellow ribbons, what did they discover when they reached the end of the roll? 'Made in China' was what they found."

Applause erupted as the withered Dao Chu Shai draped the bright red ribbon around General Xing's neck. An oval gold medal with the profile of Mao Tse-Tung hung from the ribbon. Xing bowed with genuine modesty to the crowd, who smiled broadly at the chairman. The portly general bowed several more times in appreciation to hide his apprehension. When adulation focused on one in China, there were only two ways to go.

As the applause dampened, Dao waved everyone to be seated. He waited for the noise of scraping chairs and rustling clothes to stop before he asked, "And now, General, have we pulled our lackeys, the dog-eating Koreans, back into their hole? Have we tightened their chains?" He curled his withered gargoylelike hands into shaking fists, the long four-inch fingernails on both thumbs clicking against the other nails like caged crickets.

Dao deliberately turned his back to the general and began his unaided journey back to his seat at the other end. Hopefully, this would put a stop to rumors about his ill health.

"I am honored, Mr. Chairman," General Xing replied to the chairman's back. "This morning I issued orders to the Koreans, thanking them for their cooperation and confirming delivery on our promise. I have personally passed my thanks to the Korean General Staff, and asked them to notify me immediately when they have commenced moving away from the border area. This will defuse the crisis with the southern puppets of the United States. Normality will return to the Korean Peninsula. Our brothers in the north will demobilize and send their reserves home. When this has happened, our trains and truckloads of food will cross the border and the loans promised to support their agriculture programs will be deposited in appropriate bank accounts in Hong Kong."

"General Xing, this, too, will be used to our advantage," the chairman said as he continued his trip to his seat, his breathing noticeably heavier. "I have instructed our foreign

ministry to immediately inform the American government
when the Koreans begin demobilizing. We will deliver the
news quietly, without much fanfare, but in such a venue that
the Americans can hardly fail to recognize that it was our direct intervention that defused the Korean crisis. In the balance
sheet of geopolitics they will owe us. The Americans will give
credit to the People's Republic. America will be honor-bound
to continue their most-favored-nation trade status with us. It
is unfortunate that our success cannot be told to the world, but
someday, when we assume our rightful role as the true world
leader and only superpower, it will be."

He reached the end of the table. The two assistants helped
the chairman to sit down. "Give us ten more years."

Everyone waited quietly while Chairman Dao Chu Shai re-
filled his glass and caught his breath. Several minutes passed
before he raised his head. "Of course, the food and agriculture
support offered to the North Koreans to pull back must not be
borne solely by the People's Republic. We will ask America
to provide the financing to pay for such a humanitarian gesture and, I daresay, they will jump at the chance. It's in their
genes to be overhelpful." He laughed, and the others joined.
"They are so naive."

When the laughter ceased, General Xing replied, "You
have great insight, Mr. Chairman. I would also add that we
must be thankful that when Hong Kong rightfully rejoined the
rest of China, its treasure of Western computers and information technology remained in place. Without Western technology combined with Eastern wisdom and integrated into our
military operations, we would have never achieved this pin-
nacle of success."

Everyone in the room nodded in agreement.

"And we must thank the Americans for their freedom of
sharing information. The Internet has provided so much help
in our transformation and progress."

On the wide-screen television to the left of the chairman,
the Algerian ambassador began his walk down the aisle of the
United Nations.

"Now to enjoy the fruits of your efforts, General," Dao Chu
Shai said. He patted his pocket several times. An assistant
leaned forward and extracted a nitroglycerin tablet from a

small pharmaceutical bottle. Chairman Dao weakly grabbed the tablet and placed it shakily beneath his tongue.

"MY FELLOW MEMBERS, THE AMBASSADOR FROM THE Is-lamic Republic of Algeria, Mr. Ahmid Tawali Mintab," the presiding officer announced. To polite applause he stepped down and nodded to the balding, middle-aged man waiting nearby. The Spanish presiding officer shook the offered hand politely as he walked past.

Ahmid stepped up to the stand, reached up, and bent the microphone lower. He cleared his throat, the sound echoing in the chambers to simultaneously silence the audience. He waited several seconds for various ambassadors to position their earphones. He wanted to ensure they received the near-instantaneous translations of his remarks, which were to be given in modern standard Arabic—the language of the Koran.

When the wave of motion, caused by the movements of the audience, eased, he began. "My fellow ambassadors to the United Nations. Today, I announce a most glorious moment in the history of the Arab people and the Islamic world—the for-mation of a new country, a new government, a new beginning. This new government that I represent intends to fight in pro-moting freedom from fear and hunger. It intends to give everyone the right and access to the resources needed to live a fruitful life under the benevolent protection of Islamic laws as prescribed by the Holy Prophet Mohammed in the most holy of books, the Koran."

He paused to take a sip of water from the glass in front of him. "I, Ahmid Tawali Mintab, have the honor to explain the events of the past days and reassure those who view with con-cern what is happening in North Africa.

"To address the most important issue, I direct my com-ments to the great Western powers of the United States, En-gland, France, Italy, and the other countries who worry over their citizens' well-being in Algiers. Even as I speak, your cit-izens, who voluntarily sought refuge in the American Em-bassy in Algiers, will be offered free access to the harbor area—"

"**SOUGHT, HELL,**" **BOB GILFORT SAID.** "**THEY WERE** rounded up and shoved into the Algerian version of the Black Hole of Calcutta."

"**—WHERE THEY CAN BE PICKED UP BY YOUR GOVERN-** ments. We will provide the necessary security and protection to those who wish to avail themselves of this opportunity. For those who wish to stay, they may petition the new government. Friends of the Islamic Republic will be welcomed with opened arms. Enemies will be crushed."

"**CRUSHED! TORTURED TO DEATH, MORE LIKELY,**" **ROGER** Maddock added.

AMBASSADOR MINTAB PAUSED TO ALLOW THE MURMUR that buzzed through the crowd to fade.

Satisfied, he continued. "The Arab countries of North Africa and the Middle East have been treated as Third World nations in the eyes of the West. And have been since the collapse of the corrupt Ottoman Empire. For many reasons our economic growth has been slow in comparison with the industrialized nations of the West. We have had little influence on Western culture and world events. Even though the Islamic religion is larger than Christianity, it has always been misrepresented as a militant religion of intolerance with radical, inflexible ideas."

He looked up from his notes to find that he held the attention of his audience. Good.

"The Jewish stranglehold on the financial capitals of the world coupled with their adept manipulation of political opinions and policies must be admired. The Arab world, with so much more economic clout, has never been able to match the astute wiliness of our Semitic brothers in controlling the West. The Jews have kept moderate Arab views from being objectively considered in every venue and in every forum.

Never has the Arab world been permitted to have a moderate voice in politics on the world stage.

"Today, the Arab world stands on the threshold of renewed greatness. A threshold to where the Jewish problem that threatens a free world can be met. A threshold where moderate perspectives can be expressed objectively and considered with thoughtful analysis before unilateral decisions are made that adversely affect over one quarter of the world's population."

Ambassador Mintab's spirit bubbled when he noticed the Israeli ambassador engaged in a hand-waving, dynamic conference with his assistants at the Israeli cubicle. He paused unintentionally. Realizing he was staring, he looked down momentarily to force his eyes away from the Israelis and to give himself a couple of seconds to regain his momentum. He shuffled the notes in front of him for a moment. This address was more important than enjoying their discomfort.

Mintab looked up. "Because of the intransigence by the Israelis, there are more Arabs today as refugees than any other ethnic group in the history of mankind. We have Islamic babies and children living in squalor while their parents beg and dig through garbage to keep their families alive. The Arab and Islamic world have a refugee problem that is now generations old because no humanitarian country has stepped forward and said, 'We'll take them.' Even our own Arab countries have refused to step forward.

"We are committed to changing that. The Arab world has been remiss in meeting its Islamic duty of charity by failing to give these refugees an opportunity for a full life. Just as we have failed to help them regain their homeland, so have we failed to resolve their misery. The children of Allah must have the opportunity to grow and mature in a stable environment. An environment where they may study the lessons of Mohammed and strive toward their righteous destiny.

"The Arab and Islamic nations have a duty to continuously review their moral obligations as well as their laws and politics to ensure that as the world changes, their governments evolve accordingly. For that reason, we are forming an Islamic Republic to meet those moral obligations. This new Islamic Republic will be built on an architecture that guarantees individual freedoms within a framework of religious and traditional social precepts.

"That is our responsibility, just as it is the responsibility of every true Moslem. Today, I have the honor of presenting to you, the nations of the world, a decision taken by Arab and Islamic leaders that will have far-reaching impact on Moslems everywhere. It will impact the world, as you will see," Mintab emphasized. He paused, wanting the anticipation to grow.

He was pleasantly surprised to discover that he had captivated the audience. He knew he was not a skillful speaker. Only a few quiet conversations continued in the audience, with the Israelis being the most noticeable.

Another sip of water, a deep breath, and he continued. "I ask for the ambassador from Morocco, the ambassador from Tunisia, the ambassador from Libya, and the ambassador from Egypt to join me on the podium."

The low background murmur increased in intensity as those named turned the nameplates of their countries facedown and marched proudly to the podium.

The phone on Alex Cannets's desk blinked. He picked it up. What did the turning down of the nameplates mean? He racked his mind, trying to determine the reason.

"Alex, what's going on?" President Crawford asked.

"I don't know, sir, probably Arab posturing. We'll have to wait and see."

"When they're done, I want your opinion."

"Yes, sir," he replied as the phone clicked off.

When the four other representatives reached the podium, Ambassador Mintab shook hands with each. They stood side by side behind the lectern as the Algerian ambassador returned to the microphone.

He tapped the microphone lightly. The noise in the gallery tapered off and stopped as he cleared his throat. Now the finale—the crowd-pleaser.

"My fellow United Nations brothers and sisters. As of this time today, the countries of Morocco, Algeria, Tunisia, Libya, and Egypt cease to exist as independent countries. As of today we are the Islamic Republic of North Africa and Barbary." He paused to permit the import of his words to sink in.

The noise level in the chambers rose to a crescendo before Mintab raised his hands for quiet. He felt his eyes watering. A minute later the hubbub subdued sufficiently.

He cleared his throat and continued. "We have asked Sudan to join our republic, and expect it to accept within the next two weeks, and there is a strong probability that Somalia may follow."

At the Sudanese table the ambassador stood and shouted, "Never! Sudan is independent and will remain so." But without the speakers to carry his voice, only the nearby representatives heard him. The Somalia cubicle was empty, as it had been for years.

"For the near term," Mintab replied. Sudan had little support from the West; therefore it had little choice in what its neighbors decided. "I will be turning over my role as the United Nations ambassador for our new nation in the next few days. Those behind me will serve as deputies to whomever we desinate as my relief. We will build a capital for our new nation near the ancient site of Carthage in what was Tunisia. As we consolidate our position to firm up a central government necessary to support this New World Order, we ask for your indulgence and patience. As the United States discovered over two centuries ago after its revolution, a new birth requires patience and wisdom. Many will find this incredulous, but we intend to model our new nation along the lines of the United States of America. I will address this later."

Isolated applause, mixed with shouts from Third World representatives, greeted his comments. He held his hands up. Several seconds passed before the cheering stopped.

"Let me tell you some of the things we will do now. Effective immediately, the Islamic Republic of North Africa and Barbary will accept any Arab refugee as a citizen, wherever they may be or however they may come. The way to greatness is through Islam. Our country will accept all true followers of the Islamic religion. The Islamic Republic of North Africa and Barbary will be an Arab home where any Moslem or Arab can come and live as citizens in search of their own destiny. It will be a bright beacon of righteousness for the world. This new nation will assume its rightful place in the community of nations as the true representative of the

Islamic faith and Arab world. We intend to work politically and faithfully to achieve that aim as we build an Islamic empire."

The four deputies behind Mintab applauded, bringing additional shouts and cheers from the majority of the Third World countries that made up the General Assembly. The roar drowned out Mintab's words, forcing him to stop until it tapered off.

"We will establish a government much like the United States, but with necessary modifications to reflect the Islam religion. The Lower House to be determined much like the Lower House of Congress in the United States. This should make the people of America happy."

A few chuckles, followed by applause, came from the gallery. Mintab nodded toward the American delegation, who sat expressionless with their arms folded.

"Population will determine the number of representatives. The difference will be in the Upper House of our Congress. The Upper House will consist of Islamic holy men from throughout the Barbary nation. They will provide judgment on the government to ensure that the new nation adheres to the true religion. In this Dar Al Hikma—House of Wisdom— these senior religious leaders will elect one hundred religious senators to interpret and approve the laws proposed by the Lower House.

"We see a moral country growing from this small seed. A country where religion guides the day-to-day lives of its people as they enjoy the fruits of their freedom."

Mintab stopped, opened his mouth to say more, and then decided against it. The next step was up to Walid. If he accomplished his part, then the new country had a chance.

He bowed to the audience. "My fellow ambassadors, that concludes my remarks. Thank you for the honor to address the General Assembly."

He stepped down from the lectern as a multitude of indecipherable conversations and discussions erupted on the floor of the chamber.

A runner handed a note to Ambassador Mintab, who read it. He hurried back to the lectern. He tapped the microphone, and when some semblance of order returned, spoke. "My apologies, my fellow ambassadors. But I would like to take this quick moment to say thanks to the People's Republic of China." He held aloft the slip of paper. "Which has become the first country to formally recognize the Islamic Republic of North Africa and Barbary."

He stepped down once again. Mintab and his deputies hugged and kissed each other on the cheeks before he led them to the Libyan table. There, Mintab removed the sign with "Libya" on it, and from beneath the table, brought out a bright bronze plaque bearing the name of the new country engraved in Arabic, English, and French in deep, black script against a green enameled background.

PRESIDENT CRAWFORD TURNED TO FRANCO. "WHAT DOES this mean?"

"I'll tell you what it means, Mr. President," General Eaglefield replied angrily. "It means that, if this new country survives its genesis, it'll have a stranglehold on the economy of Europe. It'll be in a position to control the Mediterranean."

"Go ahead, General, tell me your concerns in a nutshell. Heaven knows I can use it."

"Well, Mr. President, history shows that the nation that controls the Mediterranean controls the economy of the world. Militarily, this new country will be in position to contest the control of the maritime choke points of the Strait of Gibraltar and the Suez Canal. If they bring Sudan into the fold, this new country will control the coastline from the Atlantic Ocean to the Red Sea. If they take Somalia, nearly fifty percent of the African coast will be theirs."

"The general is right, Mr. President," Franco added. "If they are able to meld those North African Arab countries into this new nation, then that country is going to be a direct threat to the United States and its allies. Our economy and quality of life depend on free access to the Mediterranean. We fought the Barbary Coast wars in the late eighteenth century— against the forefather of this new nation. If it succeeds in its founding against the myriad of tribal and ethnic conflicts in this region, then our influence will pale in the remainder of the Arab world compared to theirs. And on top of that, Europe is going to be influenced politically and economically by them. That will in turn affect our politics and world influence." He shook his head. "No, Mr. President, we have a big problem here. Even bigger, if this new Islamic country ends up like Iran and Egypt."

The red phone blinked. President Crawford picked it up. "Go ahead, Alex."

"Mr. President, the People's Republic of China has been the first to recognize the new Islamic Republic of North Africa and Barbary. What do you want me to do? Should we take the bull by the horns and become the second?"

"Nothing, Alex. I don't want you to do anything until we have had time to sort out our position. Let Bob handle any recognition that we decide. What I do want you to do is to walk over to the Israeli delegation—be visible about it—and speak with them. I don't care what you say, but I want the members of that assembly to see that America remains firmly behind Israel. Your presence at the Israeli desk will help send that message. If we think this will affect our politics, then you can bet your bottom dollar that the Israelis will see this as a threat to their survival."

"Yes, sir, Mr. President. I'll have a summary of the reactions here on your desk in the next couple of hours."

"Alex, let us discuss the issues here and determine how we want to play this new hand that has been dealt."

"And the evacuation operation?"

Franco leaned over. "Mr. President, Ambassador Mintab said that the Algerians would escort our citizens to the harbor for pickup, and that they should be doing it now."

General Eaglefield spoke up from behind the president. "Mr. President, I propose a flash message to Admiral Cameron, identifying some options, depending on the situation there. He is the on-scene commander, and I am sure that they saw the CNN broadcast of this speech. They will be waiting for directions."

"Roger, take care of that," the president ordered.

President Crawford stood. The television showed various members of the General Assembly leaving their desks to mill about in small groups. Already future politics were being decided at the United Nations level, and here he was without a clear idea on how this was going to affect the United States. Why didn't he have any foreknowledge of this? Whatever happened, it would affect America, and it was not going to be to America's advantage. Most of the Third World representatives from Africa and the Middle East were shaking hands with Mintab and the new deputies.

President Crawford looked away from the screen. "Bob, I want a worst-case assessment of what this means to America, our economy, and how this new political entity will influence our foreign policy. Got it?"

Franco hurriedly scratched notes on a three-by-five card from several that he carried in his shirt pocket.

"Also, I want a series of options and recommendations on what our reaction should be depending on what scenarios unfold, and I want it tonight."

"Yes, sir, Mr. President."

"Give me the book, Franco, and I want to know what the new polls say about this as soon as possible. I want to compare it with what's in there now."

He reached over, took the black three-ring binder from Franco, and opened it as he left the small theater. Head down, he scanned the poll results from last night. He passed a military courier hurrying into the theater, who stopped, snapped to attention, and rendered a snappy salute.

"Oh, hi," the president mumbled without looking up.

As soon as the leader of the Free World passed, the courier walked briskly over to General Eaglefield.

"General Eaglefield," the courier said breathlessly. "It's North Korea, sir. You'd better come."

COLONEL ALQAHIRAY APPLAUDED AS HE JUMPED TO HIS feet. The audience rose quickly.

"Bravo, bravo. We have done it, my fellow warriors. Today we have changed the world and we have done it without destroying ours to do it." He clenched his fist.

"Go, and spread the news to everyone. As of now, this headquarters is the supreme military headquarters for the Islamic Republic of North Africa and Barbary. I am the

supreme military commander for every military unit, Air
Force element, and Navy ship between Morocco and Egypt.
By this time next week, Sudan will have joined our new coun-
try. Well done!"

He reached across the seats and grabbed Walid. Pulling the
man to him, the colonel hugged him and planted a kiss on his
forehead and both cheeks before releasing him. "Can you feel
the excitement in the air, Walid? The electricity? Can you
feel the call of destiny to our people?" Alqahiray's eyes
sparkled with emotion, looking to Walid like small pools at
the bottom of a dark canyon.

When Walid failed to reply, Colonel Alqahiray continued.
"Well, I can. I feel it in every fiber of my being. This is a glorious moment for us—a most glorious event!"

"Yes, Colonel," Walid answered, his voice low. "Our new
country is something that must be treated as a mother would
care for her newborn infant. With tender care we must nurture
it to adulthood." His voice grew in strength. "We may spill
some of the nourishment as we feed it, and we will clean the
waste from its mistakes as we grow. It is time for politicians
and not for the military to lead the way. It is a time for us to
show the world that we are a civilized military responsible to
a civilian authority. We must be an instrument to guard the
government so they may determine in peace how we will be
governed!"

The colonel stepped back and grinned. "Ah, Walid. Foolish
words—profound, but foolish. Politicians are shit. They only
argue and seek material gains for themselves. It is we, the new
military, who will guide the politicians in how they form the
new government. We will take a lesson from the Turkish General Staff. As they guide their government behind the scenes,
so shall we."

Colonel Alqahiray raised his arms, his hands outstretched.
"Did you hear what Mintab said? That's camel dung for the
Western press! Do you think we can sit idly by and let such a
radical government germinate? A government where the people are manipulated to whatever designs that a good orator de-
sires? People need discipline. Discipline that only we can
give. We will tell the world what they want to hear, but we
will do what is right for us. Do you think I intend to let the

Palestinian trash into our country? That is more foolish political talk. Wherever Palestinian refugees have been accepted,
there has been trouble. Look at Lebanon and Jordan." He spat
on the carpet. "That is what I think of that idea."

Walid and Samir walked to the end of the row and approached the colonel. The other two intelligence officers
stepped apart. The colonel's cousin moved beside Alqahiray.

"Ah, Colonel," said Walid. "I think I understand. What you
intend is a military dynasty to drive the Arab world and build
an empire. Unfortunately, the majority of us believe this is an
opportunity to build an Islamic nation dedicated to Mohammed and the Moslem faith. Are you not a Moslem, my
colonel?" Walid stood directly in front of the Colonel.

Colonel Alqahiray's eyes blazed in anger. Walid imagined
the canyon pools bubbling with heat, and quickly looked
away.

The colonel pushed Walid backward. Walid stumbled a
couple of steps. "What's the matter with you?" Alqahiray
demanded. "How dare you speak to me like this! I am your
superior. I promoted you and I can disgrace you, like this."
He snapped his fingers at Walid. "Everything you are is because of me and don't forget it. I could have you shot, as
quick as this." He snapped his fingers again. This time six
inches from Walid's face. His anger grew, fueled by his arrogance.

The cousin reached for his pistol. Samir pulled his first and
shot the man. The pistol clattered as it hit the floor and rolled
across the tiles. The shot echoed in the small theater. The two
operations officers reached for their pistols, but stopped and
quickly raised their hands when the two Intelligence Officers
swung their guns on them. Smoke curled from the barrel of
Samir's pistol, and the smell of cordite quickly filled the
room. To one side, the two senior security guards trained their
weapons on the two operations officers.

"Keep your hands raised, please," Walid said firmly. "Don't
try anything and no one will get hurt." His hands shook.

"Help me! I've been shot!" cried the cousin, holding both
hands over a spurting stomach wound. Blood flowed between
the man's fingers, forming a spreading pool around him.

Colonel Alqahiray looked down at his cousin. "Sorry, Mahmud. It's a stomach wound, and a bad one, it seems. I think you should pray to Allah." He turned back to Walid, ignoring the weapon pointed at him by Major Samir. He focused on Walid, oblivious to the continuing entreaties from his dying cousin for help.

The security guards herded the two operations officers against the far wall.

"Walid, what is the meaning of this?" the colonel asked in a dejected voice, hoping the change of tactic would work. "Why have you betrayed me? It was I who pulled you along with me wherever I have gone. Have you not been taken care of? Where is your loyalty?"

"Colonel, you have never taken me along with you!" Walid yelled. "You kept me with you because you needed someone to fawn over your every whim and desire. I met those qualifications. I foamed at the mouth like a panting dog. When we started on this path two years ago, your dedication to the cause and the sterling principles of Islam inspired me. They inspired all who followed you. Months ago some of us began to suspect that your dedication was rhetoric and little else. This realization was like the disappointment you feel when you first discover that your father is not omniscient, but has faults. You were that father to us. So, no, this was not an easy decision that brought us to this point."

Walid leaned forward and removed the colonel's pistol. "We cannot allow personal ambition to override the true purpose of the revolution. You yourself two years ago would have agreed. Not so today. As our new nation tries to escape the pains of birth, it is time for you to step down. You will retire to the countryside as a founding father of the new nation. In short, my colonel, you are being retired."

Walid thought he detected a slight sag in the colonel's shoulders.

"Colonel Alqahiray, you will be retired as a hero—to a position of honor. A position that requires twenty-four-hour protection against the enemies who would see your death as a strike against the Islamic Republic. Your advice will be asked and your thoughts will be promulgated to provide guidance and encouragement to our people. You will be seen as a fountainhead of Islamic thought. To help you with this effort,

Samir will author those thoughts for you so that you will truly be seen as the father of this new nation."

The colonel's head snapped up, anger overriding his attempt to twist the moment. "You camel-dung beetle! Who else could have accomplished this? Tell me who, you piece of desert shit!" the colonel shouted, his face beet-red. "I'll tell you who . . . no one! I am the only one in the Arab world who could have forged this magnificent creation. I am the father of the Islamic Republic of North Africa and Barbary. I am the designer of every event that led to this creation! And you stand there and tell me that now, when the country is born, that my services are no longer needed? Who the hell do you think you are?"

Moaning came from the figure lying on the floor. "Can't you die in quiet, Mahmud?" Colonel Alqahiray yelled. He kicked his cousin in the side, drawing a weak scream from the man. His combat boot came away spotted with blood. The cousin's head fell to the side as he exhaled and died.

"To hell with you, Walid. What if I refuse to retire? What if I refuse to go to the countryside and, as you say, become a shrine for the people to worship as a founding father of the new republic?" he asked, derision dripping like hot fat from his lips. "Who is going to run this diverse military? You?" He laughed. "You can't even run the computers without someone sitting there punching the keys for you. You've never been in charge of anything larger than a platoon on a field exercise. No, Walid, you can't do it. This new country needs me and you know it." He paused. Then, sticking his hand out, and in a voice disturbingly calm, he said, "Surrender those guns and return to your positions and we will forget this ever happened." He reached for Samir's gun.

Samir stepped back out of reach; the gun never wavered from Alqahiray's direction.

"Colonel, unless you accept our offer of early retirement then we will be forced to go to plan B," said Walid.

"And what, pray tell, is plan B, camel shit?" The calm tone disappeared.

Samir pulled the slide back on his pistol, glanced to make sure a bullet was loaded, and then let it go.

"Plan B is that you become a martyr, sir. Your cousin killed you and we killed your cousin."

"I have had it with playing around with you three low-caste dogs." Colonel Alqahiray leaped for Walid.

Samir shot the colonel in the arm, knocking the man backward into the wall.

Though the operations theater was soundproof, Walid still glanced at the locked door as if expecting a security team to burst in at any moment.

Colonel Alqahiray moaned and put his hand over the bullet wound.

"Congratulations, Colonel," said Walid. "You have been wounded in the battle. It will add to your mystique. What more could a hero ask for? A new nation needs heroes to rally a diverse populace. You are that hero. Dead or alive, we accomplish the same results. The Islamic Republic of North Africa and Barbary will need respected public figures to represent the will of the people. Respected figures to present on parades and give guidance. Colonel, please accept our offer," Walid begged. "It is your one way to live in greatness. We do not want to kill you."

The colonel continued to press his left hand over the wound as he stared past Walid at the far wall. "You shot me."

Walid sighed. "It is truly the only offer we are prepared to make."

Colonel Alqahiray looked down at the bullet wound. "You shot me?" His eyes were wide in astonishment. He had made the plans for this victorious day. "I can't believe it. You shot me. Me, Colonel Alqahiray," he mumbled, disbelieving what was happening.

"It was with reluctance that Major Samir shot you, Colonel. It was truly an accident."

"Yes, with true reluctance," Samir added, smiling. He lifted the pistol to his lips and blew across the barrel. "True reluctance."

"Samir, no!" Walid cried. Then he turned to Colonel Alqahiray. "The story we will tell is that your cousin shot you. A cousin who worked for the satanic CIA. In self-defense you killed him, but not without receiving a wound yourself. You will be a hero, Colonel. The people will worship you as no other Arab leader has been worshipped, including Gamal Abdel Nasser, Muammar Qaddafi, Anwar El Sadat, or the aging Saddam Hussein. Only Mohammed will be better known than you. All you have to do is cooperate."

The colonel slid down the wall to a sitting position. His hand compressed the wound to slow the bleeding. He opened his mouth to say something, but words failed. How could this be happening? This entire scheme had been his idea—his genesis. He'd personally convinced the Chinese it would work. He shook his head in disbelief.

"Colonel, though you are shaking your head no, I believe what you are trying to say is that you accept our offer?"

After a few seconds the colonel raised his head, looked at Walid, and nodded.

Walid smiled, a breath of gratitude escaped. "Thank you, Colonel. As a retired hero you must not try to regain your position or plot against the republic, and will not try to escape from your retirement home. Agreed?"

The colonel nodded again. How could this be happening to him? He was Colonel Alqahiray—Al Madi. "I can't believe you shot me," he whispered. "I can't believe it. I am the father of this new nation."

"Yes, my colonel, you are. But even fathers someday must step aside for their sons."

Walid motioned to the two intelligence officers standing nearby. One of the security guards walked to the door and opened it. Additional security personnel rushed inside.

"Lieutenant, the colonel is wounded. His cousin, working for the American CIA, shot him, and the colonel was forced to kill the traitor. Please take him to medical for treatment. Major Samir and his team will accompany you, and escort the colonel to a safe haven afterwards."

The security guards saluted Colonel Walid. They reached down and pulled Colonel Alqahiray up from the floor. They lifted the hero of the republic between them.

"Colonel," Walid said, touching the founding father affectionately on the good shoulder. "It has been a pleasure to serve with you. The republic owes you its birth." Walid turned to the audience. "Three cheers for Colonel Alqahiray."

Walid whispered in the colonel's ear, "Go with Allah, sir."

The security guards carried the wounded colonel out of the room to enthusiastic cheers led by Colonel Walid.

"Samir, call me when you arrive at the villa," said Walid. "I will call Mintab and tell him that event alpha has been accepted. This afternoon we will release the first of the press releases attributed to Colonel Alqahiray. Little does he know how famous we intend to make him."

Then Walid added as Samir reached the door, "Samir, be careful. He is still dangerous, but don't do anything foolish. Okay? He is more valuable alive right now."

Samir nodded as he departed, hurrying to catch up with the security force he had personally selected.

"SO, GENERAL XING, WHAT DO YOU THINK?" DAO ASKED as the operator muted the sound on the screen. The crowd on the floor of the United Nations milled about in discussion.

"I think, Mr. Chairman, that Ambassador Mintab said the right words to appease the West and encourage the East. Whether he meant them remains to be seen."

"You are right, General. Words are what the West want. Seldom do they weigh the actions that back them. But what do we care as long as the Arabs remember who supported them in their genesis endeavor. The People's Republic is the first to recognize the new power in the Mediterranean. They will remember that, and we will ensure that they do. With this new power, our influence will wield an economic might that the world has not seen since the Ming Dynasty."

Dao's wrinkled face broke into a thin smile. "Sixty-five percent of America's trade is with Europe, the majority of which goes through the Mediterranean. But America fails to learn from history. Unlike us, in the East, who study and learn from the ways of our ancestors." He laughed. "You know what will happen? America will divert even more of its trade to us."

The laughter turned to coughs and the coughs to a racking fit. His lips turned blue from the exertion before the attack eased and his breath returned to normal. No one moved to help him.

Several minutes passed before he continued. "The Islamic

Republic possesses more economic potential than any two countries in the Western alliances, with the exception of the United States and Germany. Of course, it will be the Islamic Republic's challenge to develop that potential. We will benefit while this happens, and we will be careful that they do not turn and bite their masters." He pensively tapped his lips with his forefinger. "No, we must ensure that this new potential is never directed against the People's Republic.

"The other issue is control of the Mediterranean Sea. When you control the Mediterranean, you control the West. I sometimes wonder if America knows this. Eventually, we can expect them to try to wrest back that control. Separately, those Arab countries have little influence in the Mediterranean, not even sufficient to control events along their own coasts. In the past few minutes, that whole picture has changed. History has shown that the country that controls the Mediterranean wields exponential world influence and power. When the Americans drew back to their own shores at the turn of this century, they left a vacuum in the Mediterranean. So goes the control of the Mediterranean, so goes world influence, and I state here that influence will go to the new republic and that we, the People's Republic, will enjoy the fruits of their labor. We showed the new nation that you don't need a strong military to control a sea. All you need are mines, stealth, information technology, and the balls to do it." He reached under the table and weakly grabbed his crotch.

Everyone clapped as the chairman finished. Just as the chairman appeared to be dozing off, he raised his head and added, "The Americans are checkmated and don't even know it. They have no reason to go after the Libyans, because the country that attacked them no longer exists. Those responsible for the attacks have been executed; at least, the ones the Americans believe ordered the attacks are dead. And finally, the American citizens in Algiers are being evacuated. When that is finished, they will have no reason for military action, and only military action can stop this new country from rising like a phoenix from the ashes of Arab history. No, the West will pontificate—talk—wring their hands in an attempt to try to stop it, but they will keep their military caged."

He leaned forward. "We will obtain significant prestige in the eyes of the world as Korea stands down. At the end of the day on the world stage, we will be the winners."

The chairman turned to the four stewards who stood at attention near the cart. "Please," he said to them, waving his hand at the members around the table.

The stewards hurried to break out the French wine, providing each member with his own bottle.

The general forced himself to look pleased. He hated the drinking binges the chairman enjoyed, but when the chairman drank, everyone drank. And when the chairman eventually napped, everyone waited.

The door opened. A colonel flanked by two soldiers entered.

The chairman raised his eyebrows at the intrusion, his aged lips pressed thinly together. Patience was not a virtue that ripened with old age and power. His bodyguards placed their hands on the weapons beneath their coats.

The colonel bowed to the chairman. "My apologies, Mr. Chairman. It is urgent that I speak to the general."

The chairman reluctantly gave a curt nod.

General Xing rose and walked to the door, where the taller colonel bent down to whisper in the general's ear. Their muted conversation took several minutes. Minutes in which the chairman waited impatiently for the intruders to depart so the celebration could start. General Xing gave the colonel his orders and dismissed him. Sweat broke out on the general's forehead. After several nods from the colonel to ensure he understood his directions, General Xing marched to where the chairman sat. The door shut behind the messenger.

"Mr. Chairman, I have grave news to report and then I must leave," he said, his face pale.

"What is it?" Dao asked impatiently. He knew the general never enjoyed his celebrations, but had never expected him to employ a ruse to avoid one.

General Xing took a deep breath. "Mr. Chairman, the North Koreans have refused to stand down. In fact, about thirty minutes ago, they crossed the border at three different points. They are about five miles into South Korean territory."

He paused, his face growing whiter. "And, sir, they have overrun the American positions. There have been heavy American casualties." He bowed his head.

The chairman's reaction belied his frail health. He stood and slapped the general. "You said they were drawing back! You said that they would demobilize! You said that they would do all of this for food! For food, damn you! Why didn't the Americans stop them? Where were the South Korean allies? You have failed China, General!" His eyes blazed with anger. Even with bad arteries, both of the chairman's cheeks turned red.

General Xing stood with his head bowed, fury boiling inside over the public humiliation under the hands of this pompous and senile old man.

"Request to be excused, Mr. Chairman, to try to turn them back before it is too late?" General Xing asked in a whisper.

"Too late! You don't know the Americans, General Xing," the chairman said sarcastically. "What is winging its way east is a wave of fury that will wash over the American public like a monsoon storm. A tidal wave of hate and determination will erupt. They will rise to the attack as they have always risen through history. They may never pay attention to the lessons that history offers, but one thing that history shows is that if you provoke the Americans' ire, they fight to win."

The chairman sat back down, and one of his guards helped him place another nitroglycerin tablet under his tongue. "You have little time to convince your 'lackeys' in Korea to return to the border before the Americans bring every facet of their economic and military might against this unprovoked attack. When that happens, China will be in an untenable situation. Stupid! Why make war when patience, economic moves, and political power can achieve world domination and influence. Let America sleep as it is doing, and it will follow the Soviet Union into oblivion. The Koreans have once again woken the sleeping giant. Go! Get out of my sight!" He reached up, ripped the medal from around General Xing's neck, and slung it across the room, where it bounced against the wall. "Get out!"

General Xing, his cheeks red and eyes moist from anger, strolled briskly to the door and departed. He wiped the sweat from his forehead as he left.

Chairman Dao downed the first glass of wine and collapsed against the chair. The doctor in the back of the room hurried forward, taking his stethoscope out of his pocket. The steward immediately filled the glass again as everyone silently watched.

The doctor put the stethoscope against the aged chairman's chest. The chairman pushed him away. The doctor moved aside as Dao Chu Shai pulled himself upright.

"Gentlemen, while we contemplate this unforeseen event, let's celebrate our new comrade in the West, the Islamic Republic of North Africa and Barbary."

Then he mumbled, "And let's contemplate General Xing's future."

CHAPTER 12

⚓

"WHAT THE HELL IS TAKING THEM SO LONG?" DUNCAN
asked. A bullet whistled by his ear. He instinctively crouched
lower. "Damn, that was close!"

The wall of flour bags behind Duncan and Beau absorbed a
torrent of shots. Flour rained on them. Every time a bullet hit
the flour bags, the sound reminded Duncan of a baseball
player slamming his fist in his glove. So many bullets had
been fired that a metallic tang filled the air, overriding the
harsh fish smell of the surrounding harbor. How could Beau
look so calm?

"Shit! I hope it's not much longer." Beau leaned around the
edge of the flour bags and fired a short burst at the warehouses
across the road from the pier.

Well, maybe not too calm.

The fierce cross fire sent Duncan and Beau diving to the
wooden pier. They leaned into the flour bags in front of them.

"Damn, Beau," Duncan said as the shooting tapered off.
"We can't stay here. We'll be killed if we do! We've got to
move. Follow me."

"The hell you say?" Beau mumbled, grabbing his carbine
by the stock as he took off after Duncan. He wiped the sweat

from around his eyes, smearing dirt across his sunburned face.

The two men scrambled around and behind more pallets, putting several thousand pounds of flour between them and the Algerian rebels who had them pinned. They looked at each other, amazed neither was wounded.

Grinning, Duncan said, "See! God still loves us. Let's go."

Dodging from pallet to pallet, they were fifty feet from where they started when an explosion sent them rolling down the pier. Duncan grabbed his right knee as a thin trickle of blood stained his cammies. Star bursts danced across his vision.

"Splinter," he blurted through clinched teeth to Beau's unasked question. Duncan grabbed the three-inch piece of wood and jerked it out.

At least it was his bad knee, he thought as he rubbed the swollen, arthritic, now bleeding, joint. Small flesh wound, he told himself.

Smoke and flames engulfed the front of the pier.

"Armored car?" asked Beau.

"No! Rocket-propelled grenade. The armored car is out there. If it's the one from the village, it doesn't have a cannon," Duncan replied. "At least, Colonel Yosef said it didn't."

"Well, that gives me a warm fuzzy. We'll just ignore its machine gun."

From the other side of the pier Monkey fired a long burst from his MG-60. Several rebels running down a side alley achieved martyrdom. The others turned back to the warehouse from whence they came.

"*Allah Alakbar* that, assholes!" Monkey yelled.

Rapid tooting of a whistle from the end of the pier drew the attention of the SEALs on the pier. The SEALs on the boat waved for them to hurry. The whistle signaled the diesel engine on the old coastal water carrier had finally been started.

"Maybe we should have stayed with Bashir," Beau remarked.

"If I'd known those assholes were this tenacious we would have. How the hell they found us is beyond me."

"Think he'll be all right?"

"Who?"

"Bashir."

"Of course. Bashir is a product of the desert. Who else could have found a doctor in the middle of the night, in the middle of nowhere, like he did?"

"Good thing, too. H.J.'s shoulder wound would have been septic by now. I was amazed. Amazed doctors existed in Algeria and amazed he had penicillin."

A series of shots dug small holes in the pier near them.

Screams in Arabic interrupted from the other side of the barrier. Machine-gun fire rippled over their heads.

Duncan peeked over the top of the bags. He raised his carbine and fired at several attackers who had decided to make a dash across the top of the warehouse. One of them grabbed his stomach as he tumbled off. The abandoned cargo blocked their view of the rebel hitting the road.

Movement across a warehouse window caught Beau's attention. He fired a burst, shattering the window.

"How the hell did they followed us, is what I want to know," Duncan said, more to himself than to Beau.

Another explosion rocked the flour bags to the left, knocking Monkey back into a nearby pallet.

"Doesn't matter. They have and . . ." Beau stopped as the sound of a revving engine reached their ears. "Shit! They're working up nerve to try the armored car."

"Monkey!" Duncan shouted. "You okay?"

Monkey sat up, shook his head to clear it, and then gave Duncan a thumbs-up.

"Let's hope they have that boat ready. If they don't, then we're going to have one hell of a problem. Let's go!"

The SEAL machine-gunner only needed to be told once. Monkey looked like a hunchbacked Neanderthal dragging a club as ran down the pier, his backpack and MG-60 gripped tightly in each hand. Bullets peppered his footsteps as he zigzagged toward them.

"Damn, that hurts!" he shouted as wood splinters hit his ankles and calves.

Beau rolled from cover, fired several bursts from a horizontal position in the direction of the rebels. He was rewarded with a cry as one of his random shots hit.

"That makes twenty-two."

"Twenty-two what?" Duncan asked as Monkey tumbled into the small space behind the sacks of flour. Beau rolled to the right, following Monkey behind the barrier.

"Twenty-two kills."

"You keep count?" Duncan asked incredulously.

"Well, not exactly, but I like to round things off to a good statistic."

Monkey tossed his pack aside and threw himself prone with his MG-60 ready to fire.

Duncan looked at Monkey's legs. "Monkey, you're bleeding."

Monkey looked down at his legs. Small pinpoints of blood flowed from where several inch-long splinters stuck out from his calves. He reached down and began to pick them out like bothersome thorns from a walk in the woods. "It's nothing, Captain. More blood from where that came from."

From the direction of the water carrier, Colonel Yosef and Chief Judiah ran up the pier, dodging from cover to cover as snipers on the warehouse roof tried to shoot them.

Monkey raised the angle of his MG-60 and sent a deadly blast along the roof. A rebel screamed as a bullet in the chest sent him tumbling off the edge to his death below.

"That's two roadkill now," Beau added.

"Twenty-three," Monkey said, grinning at Beau. "You're behind, Commander."

Yosef and Chief Judiah shoved themselves into the crowded space. "Captain, you look as if you could use some help," Colonel Yosef said.

"You remember that armored car that chased us out of the village yesterday?"

Yosef nodded.

"We didn't lose it. It's up ahead somewhere. It'll come through these sacks of flour any minute, like grease through a goose. The wood pallets and metal containers crisscrossing the head of the pier are the only things stopping it. That, and they're probably still trying to figure out what they're up against. When they figure out we don't have anything to stop it, then they'll come."

Colonel Yosef reached into his pack and pulled out several square packages. He tossed one to Duncan.

"Semtex?"

"Semtex. I brought it with me when we fled the palace. Semtex can be a great tonic when applied properly."

"And how do you propose to apply it?"

Yosef rapped his knuckles on the pier. "The pier, it is only wood. We will blow it. Then the armored car will be trapped on one side while we are on the other."

"And then we're stranded with only the sea behind us," Beau added.

"That's true, but we're already trapped with only the sea behind us. Besides, the boat engine works and it is a water carrier. And there's tinned food on board."

Turning to Duncan, the Algerian Palace Guard commander continued. "Captain, I am trained in explosives. Chief Judiah tells me he is your explosive expert?"

"That's true. Though it's a skill we didn't expect to use."

"In fact," Beau added, "we didn't expect to spend three exciting, fun-filled days in an Algerian shooting gallery as targets."

The firing from the rebels increased in tempo.

"I don't think we have much longer."

"I think you are right, Captain. I suggest that you, Commander Pettigrew, and your machine-gunner Monkey retreat to the boat. Chief Judiah and I will lay the explosives."

"I'll stay here," Duncan said.

"Captain, you need to hightail it with the commander," said Judiah. "Colonel Yosef and I can set the plastique. All we need is for Monkey and McDonald to lay a screen of protective fire from the boat. Once that starts, we'll plant the explosives and get the hell out of here ourselves."

"True, but I'll stay and provide—"

"Captain, your knee is bigger than a house right now. You can see it through your cammies. If we have to run for the boat, you couldn't make it without me throwing you over my shoulder," Beau added.

"I could," Duncan replied curtly. "And the only reason you'd throw me over your shoulder is to use me as a bullet sump."

"Captain, you need to go, sir," Chief Judiah added.

A tattoo of bullets laced the top of the flour bags, sending another white shower floating down on the men.

"I'll stay, Captain," Beau said. "You go back."

"No, Commander," Yosef corrected. "All three of you go back. Cover can be provided from the boat. The boat is ready. Everyone but the two Guardsmen watching the prisoners is on board. Have my men shove the prisoners into the harbor and cast off. We don't want to take them with us, and I do not kill captives. We'll set the explosives, run to the end of the pier, and jump toward the boat. You haul us in and, *voilà,* we're gone."

"But I can stay and give protective cover," Beau objected.

"Yes, you can stay, and then there would be three of us who could get shot."

"He's right, Commander," Chief Judiah added. "We'll be fine. There's enough plastique here to blow up the whole city if we need to."

Reluctantly Beau nodded as he accepted the chief's judgment. He pushed himself up from his haunches. "Be careful, Colonel; Chief."

Duncan pulled himself up. "Yeah, be careful, and we'll be waiting at the end of the pier. Just don't get yourselves shot."

"We won't," Yosef replied.

"Come on, Duncan. Let's get you on that ugly boat. You've always wanted to sail the Mediterranean, and here's your chance. Monkey, I'll help the captain. You bring up the rear."

Beau reached toward Duncan, who jerked away. "Beau, my knee may be gone, but I am still a United States Navy SEAL. I still have one leg and two arms."

"So what'd you want? Twenty-five-percent disability?"

Without a word, Duncan turned and began an ambling run toward the boat. Beau and Monkey deliberately slowed their pace to stay with Duncan. The three SEALs weaved along the pier, keeping pallets of merchandise between them and the rebels. Fifty feet later, Colonel Yosef and Chief Judiah disappeared from their sight.

"OKAY, THEY'VE GONE," CHIEF JUDIAH SAID TO COLONEL Yosef.

"Be careful, Judiah, there's a twenty-meter clearing to cross. This close to going home—"

"Call them, Colonel. They're are out of sight now. No one around, but us."

Colonel Yosef pulled a small transmitter from his pocket. Flicking it open, he pressed the prominent red button near the top three times, waited a couple of seconds, then pressed it five times.

"You think that was how they were able to follow us?" Chief Judiah asked, pointing to the transmitter.

"Could have been. But President Alneuf had a cellular telephone and he used it twice last night."

"Who'd he call?"

"I am not sure. He has never called when I have been within hearing. Neither have I been successful in seeing what phone numbers he dialed. Our people would have liked to have had the numbers he used."

"I thought the only phone was the one Bashir lost at the villa."

"He found another and gave it to him last night while we were at the doctor's," Yosef replied, shrugging his shoulders. "I know he spoke English with whoever he called."

Chief Judiah handed Colonel Yosef one of the explosive squares with the fuse already pushed in it.

"Okay, I'll set the charges here. You be careful and do it on the other side."

Chief Judiah touched Yosef's shoulder. "It was good to see you again, Daoud."

"And me, you, Zackeriah. Different roads since '93, but it's amazing how many times paths cross in our field. I can't tell you how hard it was to pretend not to recognize you when you shocked me by appearing out of the darkness at the villa."

"You would think they'd give us a heads-up. Small field; large world."

"Sometimes not as large as we would like it."

The two men pulled the pins simultaneously on the grenades. They tossed the grenades behind them. A chemical smoke curtain spewed forth, screening Judiah and Yosef from Duncan and the others on the boat.

Judiah pulled two more grenades from his satchel and handed one to Yosef.

They looked at each other, grinned, shook hands, and

pulled the pins. Standing quickly, they hurled the smoke grenades forward of their position. A minute later the smoke, forward and behind, isolated them visually from both the Algerian rebels and their former comrades.

Three frogmen crawled over the side of the pier behind them. Their black wet suits glistened in the sunlight. Surprised, Yosef swung his gun toward the figures. The lead frogman raised his arms as he pulled his face mask off.

"*Shalom,* my friends."

"And you are?" Yosef asked. His eyes narrowed. Yosef's finger tightened on the trigger in the event of the wrong password. They could still make the water carrier if they had to.

"Three dits, pause, five dits, Colonel. We are your passport out of here."

Yosef lowered his gun, unaware until then how tight his finger had been on the trigger. The three frogmen took cover with them.

"Here is the situation." And Yosef briefed them on the attacking force and how the Americans and the remainder of the Algerian Palace Guards intended to spirit President Alneuf out of the country.

"We need to blow the pier before the rebels attack in their armored car. If they do, and are successful, then President Alneuf may be captured. Headquarters wants him safely away," Yosef explained as he held out the plastique toward the Israelis. "All we've got is this."

"Don't need it, Colonel," the leader of the Israeli Special Forces replied. "We wired the pier to explode when the firefight started." He grinned and slapped Yosef's shoulder. "Sometimes, great minds think alike. If the armored car had attacked, we would have blown it."

"Good," Yosef replied, knowing if they had blown the pier, the explosion would have killed Duncan, Beau, and Monkey. "How is this going to work? How are we going to blow the pier and disappear?"

The frogmen unpacked a waterproof bag hauled up from beneath the pier. "Put on these suits. They'll protect your body heat. Here's the plan. . . ."

Yosef and Judiah pulled on the diving suits as the Israeli talked. Beneath the pier, two sets of aqualungs waited for the

American and Algerian Israeli agents. Outfitted, they followed the commandos over the side of the pier. The frogmen activated the explosions to give them three minutes to clear the area. Three minutes was ample time. Leading the two agents, the Israeli commandos swam toward the underwater shuttle. The leader estimated less than an hour to the Israeli diesel submarine submerged outside the harbor.

"CAST OFF, MCDONALD," BEAU SHOUTED FROM THE controls of the boat. He bent slightly to check the gauges below the helm.

The water carrier was a small hundred-foot-long boat used to carry fresh water from the reservoirs to the coastal villages that lacked a natural water supply. From the condition of the boat, it looked as if the water carrier had seen many years of service. The bridge, crammed near the bow, gave the boat a fallen-water-tower appearance, with an engine on one end and a control station on the other. Basically, that was exactly what she was. The full load of water drove the waterline to within two feet of the surface. Duncan doubted the craft had much maneuverability, and it definitely had no sustainability in anything but calm seas.

Unfortunately, she was the only craft of the twelve tied along the pier that was seaworthy. The others had been vandalized and looted, even to the rubber lining around the hatches. The ugliness of the water carrier and its dilapidated condition must have fooled the looters into believing there was nothing of value on board. Beau guessed that the rebels had stopped the looters before they could take the flour and other things on the pier.

A Palace Guard emerged topside, a can opener in one hand and an unopened tin of beans in the other. Beau's mouth watered with the sight.

Near the stern, Gibbons's head popped up from the engine room. He gave Beau a thumbs-up. "I'm ready when you are, Commander Pettigrew," he shouted, jerking Beau's attention reluctantly away from the beans and back to the matter at hand.

"Captain, I can't see them!" Monkey shouted from the

stern, his MG-60 pointed toward the front of the pier. "There's smoke all over the place."

The sound of intense gunfire came from the direction of the smoke.

Duncan hobbled to the stern and stood beside Monkey and McDonald. "Damn! Can't see a thing through that soup. Keep a good eye out. First two people through the smoke will be the colonel and the chief. Don't shoot them." At least, they should be Colonel Yosef and Chief Judiah. He mentally crossed his fingers.

Monkey and McDonald gave the captain an irritated look as if to say, "Captain, we know what they look like and we're professionals. We don't go around shooting our own guys." But they kept quiet. McDonald licked his cracked lips. Those beans looked appetizing.

Across the pier from the boat, the Guardsmen prodded the rebel sentries off the pier and into the polluted harbor waters below. Then, they turned and ran to the water carrier. The boat rocked slightly as they jumped aboard.

The engine increased in tempo as Beau gave it power. "Cast off all lines!" he shouted. "Damn! I sound just like a surface warfare officer. Whatever you do, don't tell my parents!"

Awkwardly, the water carrier wallowed away from its berth and gradually began to move forward. The distance from the pier slowly opened from inches to a foot to several feet.

A gigantic explosion sent a shower of debris a hundred feet into the air. Some fell on the water carrier as the dark cloud from the explosion spread. When the smoke cleared, a twenty-foot section of the pier had disappeared.

Duncan gripped a line that ran from the deck edge to the top of the aft mast, keeping his balance as he scanned the pier for Judiah and Yosef. A minute later the boat reached the end of the pier, turned right, and put-putted at two knots across the end of it. A small trail of dirty gray smoke from the diesel engine marked their passage. There was no sign of the two men.

"Here, Captain," McDonald shouted as he tossed his MG-60 to Duncan.

Duncan caught the machine gun. McDonald scrambled up the twenty-five-foot-high aft mast.

"Do you see them?" Duncan shouted.

McDonald reached the top. "Sir, they're not there."

"What do you mean they're not there? Is the smoke too thick?"

"No, sir, the smoke is nearly gone. And so is the pier from where you were fighting to the harbor road. Colonel Yosef and Chief Judiah aren't there."

Lost? A cold wave of nausea and guilt rushed over Duncan. He should have stayed with the chief and the colonel. To come so far, with escape this close, and to lose them. He wondered briefly if Chief Judiah had family back in Norfolk. It depressed him further to realize how little he knew about the sailors with him.

Beau glanced over his shoulder. He knew what was going through Duncan's mind. He shouted to draw Duncan's attention. "Captain, what now?"

Duncan nodded. Good professional training overrode his emotions. His gut reaction was to turn and search for the two, but he knew he couldn't. His mission was to rescue President Alneuf, and he still had the lives of those on the boat to consider. He pushed the thoughts of Judiah and Yosef to a recess in his mind, to pull forward later when he had the time.

"Get us out to sea, Commander," he finally said reluctantly.

"Aye, aye, sir," Beau acknowledged, knowing that if the two weren't dead, then they were leaving them both to a fate worse than death. He recalled the tortured victims of the village where they had fought yesterday. Hopefully, the two were dead. He pushed the power to full.

Dark smoke spewed from the small stack at the rear of the boat as the diesel engine strained toward its full power of ten knots.

Duncan ran his hand across the top of his head. Once through the harbor entrance, they should be safe.

President Alneuf climbed up from below.

Leaning on the water tank along the centerline of the boat, Duncan hobbled across the deck to where the Algerian president stood, a lost look on his face. President Alneuf searched the faces of the SEALs and the remaining Palace Guards.

"Captain, where is Colonel Yosef?"

"Mr. President, Colonel Yosef, along with one of my men,

Chief Judiah, are missing. They blew up the pier to allow us to escape. I am sorry, sir." Seeing the shocked and sad expression on President Alneuf's face, Duncan added, "If they're alive, they're resourceful and will escape."

"Do you believe that, Captain?" President Alneuf asked hopefully.

"Yes, sir, I do. I truly do," Duncan said with as much conviction in the lie as possible. There was no way to escape from the pier.

President Alneuf nodded, recognizing the doubt in Duncan's words.

President Alneuf looked back at the battle scene, slowly receding, as the boat sailed through the entrance of the small harbor. "It is so sad, Captain. There have been so many deaths in the past few days that death has replaced the Algerian way of saying, 'Peace be upon you.'"

Duncan opened his mouth to reply, then stopped. He didn't know what to say, so he touched the Algerian president on the shoulder and left the man to his thoughts. Duncan's mission was nearly complete. Algeria was not his worry. He went below to check on H.J. and Helliwell.

The two lay across from each other on the bottom of a pair of bunks crowded into a closet-size space.

"How we doing?" he asked.

"Great accommodations, Captain. Sleeps four comfortably, eight intimately," H.J. replied.

H.J.'s shoulder was tightly bandaged, with her arm wrapped against her side. A red damp spot, where the doctor had sewed the incision shut, identified the location of the wound. The doctor had discovered and removed a bullet. He'd told them that Allah had been with her. The doctor had said two bullets had hit her. Both hits had been at an oblique angle that, luckily, deflected the full force of the impact. One bullet had passed clean through, missing bone and major blood vessels. The other hadn't, and it had fractured her collarbone before coming to rest beside the bone. Now H.J. had the bullet in her cammie shirt pocket.

Helliwell's arm was broken. Duncan guessed Bud had known it was broken ever since the encounter yesterday, but had kept the injury to himself until Bashir produced the doctor. A cast ran from his left wrist to his shoulder.

"Why didn't you tell me your arm was broken?"

"Wasn't broken that bad, Captain. Just slightly cracked in two places—clean cracks that will heal in a couple of weeks. Besides, couldn't have our lieutenant thinking us mustangs were wusses."

Duncan looked at Heather J. McDaniels. "H.J., where's your medicine?"

"Here, Captain," she replied, patting the small bottle in her shirt pocket.

The doctor had given them fifty penicillin tablets each with instructions to take two every four hours. Bud kept his meager supply hidden in his pants pocket, knowing his wounds were superficial in comparison to H.J.'s.

Bud Helliwell raised himself slightly. "Captain, I'm fine. I'd like to rejoin the group on deck. I can handle a weapon and you can prop me up somewhere."

"If he's going to be a hero, then I want to be one also, Captain," H.J. said. She threw her legs off the bunk and sat up. Her face turned white. She weaved slightly on the edge of the bunk. "Damn altitude," she said softly.

Duncan shook his head as she fought to stay upright on the edge of the bunk. The muted sound of gunfire coming from the head of the pier could be heard here belowdecks. "Right, Lieutenant. I can see you're ready to go into combat." He pushed her gently, and she fell back onto the bunk. "You just came out of an operation less than twelve hours ago for two bullet wounds. There's nothing to prove, and if we need you, you'll hear the screams and bloodcurdling yells from above. Meanwhile, you two rest while you can. We're under way out of the harbor and, with any luck, we'll be safely at sea soon."

Duncan took a deep breath. "H.J., well done. You've handled this mission like any Navy SEAL I've served with. You've fought. Been in combat. Got yourself at least two Purple Hearts, and I don't think there's a one of us who don't think of you as anything but a Navy SEAL."

Duncan leaned close, feeling embarrassed, and in a low voice said, "I want to say that I'm sorry about what happened. Being captured and tortured—"

H.J. interrupted, with a fierceness that caused Duncan to jump back and Bud to examine the bulkhead. "Captain, don't say it. What happened is something I will deal with. Not you. Me! Okay? There's not a woman in the military that doesn't know what might happen if she's captured. Men can't protect us from it and they shouldn't carry guilt about it. I know what would have happened if you hadn't rescued me. Women have known this since Desert Storm when the Iraqis sexually assaulted American women they captured. It's something each of us has to come to terms with in our own unique way. This is something I can, and I will, handle."

Duncan blushed. "Sorry. I didn't mean to sound patronizing, nor for you to think I was insulting you."

"You weren't, Captain, and you aren't. You were just being a man." She touched him on the arm and squeezed. "You don't know how happy I was to see you rush through that door. I figured at any moment they would kill me rather than hold me for . . ." She stuttered to a stop. Then, after a couple of deep breaths, she continued. "This is something a man cannot understand and never will, as much as they may wish to," she finished softly.

"I know, but . . ."

"There are no buts, Captain. You think it was your fault. It wasn't. It is part of the game of war in regards to women who want to play it. It's a part, if we want to play, we have to come to terms with, and you men can't blame yourselves for it. I won't be the last woman to be captured. And women are going to be raped and tortured when captured. I was lucky being a SEAL. I knew you would come after me."

Duncan detected a slight waiver in H.J.'s voice as she mumbled the last sentence.

"OK, H.J. Just the same, you're one of my SEALs and I refuse to ignore the concern I feel." He started to pat her good shoulder, but then thought better of it.

H.J. shut her eyes and nodded. "Thanks, Captain."

Duncan turned to Helliwell to change the subject. "You were wounded in Liberia, weren't you, Bud?"

"Yes, sir," he replied, looking back at the two.

"What happened?"

"Small-caliber fire, similar to one that Lieutenant

McDaniels got; only mine was in the back and I only had one wound." Then, smiling, he continued. "Unlike her, I learned fast and dodged the second bullet. Unfortunately, it seems I have to relearn this lesson every time I go on an operation."

"Asshole," she said, opening her eyes and grinning at Helliwell.

"Did you get back into battle?" Duncan asked.

"Hell, no. I don't even remember being hit. The next thing I remember was being back on the USS *Guam,* coming out of surgery and spending the next two weeks in sick bay until they evacuated me to Germany."

"Well, one thing about this. Neither of you have to prove yourselves in combat. Lieutenant, this was your baptism under fire. For you, Bud—Ensign Helliwell—it's one more combat action for your record. In today's Navy, there are not many who can say they've been in combat. Combat-experienced veterans are going to be hard to come by in the next few months, and I think the United States is going to need all it can find. Both of you stay here and rest. We don't know how long we'll be at sea before rescue arrives. If something happens and we have to abandon this old tub, you're going to need all the strength you can muster."

"Sir, I think this is cruel and unusual punishment," H.J. replied with an audible sigh.

With a bemused look, Duncan asked, "How is that?"

"Leaving me in a room this small with Ensign Helliwell. He is a junior officer, you know." She grinned weakly. "Any chance of separate staterooms?"

"Captain!" came a shout from topside. He recognized the voice as Beau's.

"See you two later." Duncan pulled himself away to head up the ladder to topside.

"Captain," H.J. said.

Duncan turned, one foot on the ladder leading up.

"Thanks," she said. "I'm sorry if I sounded angry."

"Don't worry about it, H.J. Good luck. You, too, mustang."

Helliwell turned to H.J. when the captain disappeared. "You were rough on the Old Man, don't you think?"

"I know, I didn't mean to be, but . . ." Her voice trailed off. "You wouldn't understand."

"You'd be surprised what we understand. Sometimes you women don't give us a chance before you pull a holier-than-thou act on us."

Duncan hobbled up the few steps to topside. President Alneuf stood where Duncan had left him. In the distance, about two miles, the small port city blended with the unbroken, sandy coastline.

"What is it, Beau?" he asked, looking up at the Navy lieutenant commander who was steering the boat.

"We've got visitors," Beau said, pointing left.

Duncan took two steps to the port side of the water carrier. On the western horizon a gray speck, spewing white smoke from her stack, was speeding toward them.

"What's her bearing?" Duncan shouted.

"She's on a constant bearing decreasing range, Skipper!"

Duncan studied the approaching craft. The amount of white smoke increased. She was pouring on speed. A constant bearing with a decreasing range meant the ship was on an intercept course with the water carrier.

Duncan turned and pulled himself up to the bridge area. "This thing have a radio, Beau?"

"Yes, sir. Right here."

The bridge-to-bridge radio was mounted awkwardly beneath the panel. Duncan lowered himself to the deck, reached under, and flipped the radio on. The frequency band digital display lit up, showing 156.8 megahertz. Channel sixteen, the frequency where commercial vessels and harbor control conducted routine business. He looked for the search-and-rescue frequencies, and it took him several seconds of fiddling with the knobs and switches before 240 megahertz appeared on the digital display.

Duncan took the microphone and pressed the transmit button on the side.

"Any United States Navy unit this station, this is Special Unit Two in emergency need of assistance." He clicked off and waited for a reply. Only static came across the channel.

"Special Unit Two? Who's that?"

"Got to tell them something, Beau. The code word is 'Big Apple,' so we got to call ourselves something until we make contact."

Beau looked at the craft speeding toward them. "Better make contact quickly because I would say in about ten minutes we're going to be in hot shit!"

Duncan pressed the button again. "Any United States Navy unit this station, this is Special Unit Two in emergency need of assistance." Static echoed from the receiver.

"Not looking good, Duncan," Beau said. He bit his upper lip. "I hope they put a plaque up with my name on it in the Fort Myers officers club."

Duncan pressed the transmit button and, twice, sent the same message again. U.S. Navy units continuously monitored the international emergency frequencies. Why weren't they answering?

"You're right. Not looking good, Beau." He hung the microphone back on the side of the unit. "I'll get the men spread out. Let's hope he has orders to take us alive and we can lure him in as close as possible. It's our only chance for a fair fight." Fair fight! The approaching warship would blow them out of the water before it came within rifle range, but he'd be damned if they didn't go down fighting.

A boom drew their attention, causing everyone to turn. A small cloud of smoke rose from the bow of the closing warship. A spray of water two miles away shot up as the cannon shell hit.

"I would say, Duncan, their orders do not include having to take us alive," Beau remarked. "What kind of patrol craft is it?"

"Don't know. It's still too far away. I don't think it's one of their OSAs."

"Why not?"

"If it was, we'd have a missile up our ass by now. I think it's a Kebir-class fast-attack craft."

"Missiles?"

Duncan shook his head. "Guns only. Maybe we can hope for a boarding party."

"Keep hoping, Skipper. If they were going to send a boarding party, they wouldn't be shooting at us. But keep hoping. Nothing would surprise those Algerian sailors more than to leap aboard a vessel filled with pissed-off SEALs." Beau laughed. "Scared, pissed-off SEALs at that."

Suddenly the speaker on the radio blared. "Special Unit Two, this is a friendly Ranger. Please provide identification."

Duncan grabbed the microphone, only to drop it and see it bounce off the deck a couple of times before he recovered it. He pressed the transmit button. "Friendly Ranger, this is Big Apple. I repeat, Big Apple."

Nearly half a minute passed before the voice answered.

"Roger, we copy, Big Apple. Welcome back. The Navy is here. We have a bearing on you at this time. Can you confirm your coordinates?"

Duncan looked at Beau, who shook his head. "All we can confirm, Captain, is we are about five miles off the coast of Algeria, west of Algiers, and fixing to have hostile company."

"Roger, Big Apple. Can you provide coordinates?"

"Friendly Ranger, this is Big Apple. We do not have our co-ordinates. We need assistance ASAP. We have bad news in-bound and no way to defend. Looks like a Kebir-class fast-attack craft. Can you help? We are under fire!"

"Big Apple, stand by one. Keep your transmitter keyed so we can track you."

Another half minute passed. It seemed like an hour.

"What's wrong with them! Are these radio waves slower nearer the Sahara?" Beau asked. He lifted his cap and wiped his forehead.

"No, I think they're relaying our request to higher author-ity. Or probably checking with someone—"

Another cannon boom interrupted Duncan. This time the shell was a mile and a half shy of the lumbering boat.

"Not too good on that gun, are they?"

"As they get closer, they'll get better," Duncan said.

"Killjoy."

"Friendly Ranger," Duncan transmitted. "It's getting real unfriendly here, so if you'd like to show up we'd appreciate it."

"Big Apple, Friendly Ranger; how will we identify you? Interrogative your vessel?"

"Ranger, we are embarked on a low-riding water carrier and are the only one being shot at. And if you don't hurry, we'll be the only one sinking."

"Are you lower in the water than the approaching enemy vessel?"

"That's an affirmative, Friendly Ranger."

"Help is on its way, Big Apple. ETA five minutes."

"Thanks, Friendly Ranger, but five minutes is too long. We need assistance now! Request—"

A high tonal transmission blanked out Duncan as someone on the net began a constant keying of their mike. He tried several more times to transmit, only to find the steady keying jammed the frequency.

"I think they've discovered who we are," Duncan added. He hung up the microphone, leaving the speaker on.

TWENTY-FIVE MILES OFF THE COAST RANGER TWO NINER, the EP-3E Orion reconnaissance aircraft of fleet air reconnaissance Squadron Two, relayed the information to Commander Sixth Fleet, who passed tasking to the USS *Stennis* located seventy-five miles northwest of the water carrier. Four F/A-18s assigned combat air patrol duties to the east of the USS *Stennis* began receiving vectoring instructions from the E-2C air-surveillance platform orbiting overhead the carrier. A data link between the E-2C and the *Stennis* relayed the radar picture. The data links between *Stennis* and the entire American fleet provided them with the same digital layout. With the information provided by the spooks on board the EP-3E and relayed by the E-2C, the carrier fighters went to afterburners. Armed and ready, the deadly Hornets commenced a high-speed run directly toward the water carrier. S-3 tankers trailed the fighters to provide the refueling these gas hogs would need. Ranger Two Nine informed Sixth Fleet that for the duration of the operation their call sign was now Friendly Ranger. They'd explain later.

The USS *Stennis* turned into the wind and launched the ready "cat." Two additional F/A-18s of the United States Marine Corps Moonlighter squadron shot off the cat dipped slightly below the flight deck before reappearing at a forty-five-degree angle, afterburners on, heading for altitude. The bongs of General Quarters sent the ship's company running to battle stations. The lone American carrier was entering combat.

Captain Holman smiled. The sight of the gigantic battle flag of the United States of America flying overhead brought moisture to his eyes. The battle group was closing the action area. Another pair of fighters moved into launch position. The hot, oily smell of idling jet engines stung his eyes. The deck crew hurriedly connected the two F/A-18 Hornets to the catapult. A mile ahead, the two alert F/A-18s broke to the right, having reached two thousand feet altitude. One minute later, the F/A-18s merged with the two Hornets on combat air patrol.

"Algeria, you're up shit creek. I have more firepower idling on my deck than you're got in your entire Air Force," Holman said to himself. He pulled a Dutch Masters Panatela cigar from his shirt pocket and lit it. He leaned back in the captain's chair and took a deep drag. Cuban cigars were okay, but too expensive and too strong. Of course, he had smoked his last Havana Monte Cristo last night.

Stomping ass and taking names was what carriers did best. Naval air at its finest. He looked again at the flag overhead. He wished he had the flag from his living room in Norfolk. The one from his collection with a hissing snake entwined across the field of red and white stripes, with the notation "Don't Tread on Me" hand-stitched in gold thread across the bottom. John Rodgers, *here comes another payback. Life doesn't get much better than this,* he thought as he took a deep drag on his cigar. Then started coughing—wasn't supposed to inhale. He grinned, thinking about the expression on the faces of his officers as the *Ramage* had towed the carrier safely through the Strait of Gibraltar. He'd told them not to worry. He was glad it worked. He had kept his fingers crossed the entire transit, unsure himself if his guess was right.

"THEY'RE GETTING CLOSER. THAT ONE WAS ABOUT A thousand yards. Life doesn't get more exciting than this, Duncan."

"Or last much longer if help doesn't arrive soon."

A burst of machine-gun fire from their stern caught their attention.

"Hold your fire!" Duncan shouted. "They're too far out for small arms yet."

"Beau, put the son of a bitch off our port stern. It'll reduce our cross section. It's taking him about a minute between firings, so we'll stay this course until we're within range of his guns. Then, every time he fires, we'll give him a chance to reload and then change course."

"I'm willing to try anything. I can't stand to think of the wailing and crying at the Fort Myers officers club if I got myself killed." Beau reached down and twisted the volume knob on the radio. The loud screeching of the jammed frequency filled the air. He shook his head as he spun the wheel to starboard.

"Shout if they quit jamming!" Duncan yelled.

"Sure! You'll be able to hear me all the way to Washington," Beau replied, then added in a whisper, "Which is where I wish we were."

Duncan climbed down from the open bridge.

"President Alneuf, would you go below and watch the wounded? It looks as if things are going to get hotter out here. And you and them put on life vests!"

The Algerian president nodded, and climbed down the narrow ladder to the cramped kitchen area below the bridge.

"McDonald, Monkey! Come here!" Duncan shouted.

"Sergeant Boutrous," he added. "Space your men around the ship and try to pick off anyone topside on the craft. Our only chance is to keep them at a distance and hope their aim fails to improve."

"*Oui, mon capitaine,*" the Algerian replied with a snappy salute. He hurried off to brief the remaining Guardsmen.

The two machine-gunners stopped in front of Duncan.

"Listen up," Duncan said to the two men. "We're turning tail to the patrol craft. You keep that forward deck where their gun is clear. If they can't stay topside, then they can't fire that peashooter of theirs. Rake the bridge, too. Convince the captain of that Kebir to stay away from us and we have a chance. Keeping them at a distance is the key. Too close and they won't need accuracy to sink us."

He knew they wanted more. They wanted assurance they were going to survive. But there were few assurances in life, and even less in the SEALs. "Help is on its way," Duncan added. "All we have to do is stay afloat until it arrives."

"We'll keep that deck clear, Captain. Just leave it to McDonald and me."

"You know, if they hit this old tub it'll break apart," McDonald said.

"Then, let's make sure we keep them far enough away they don't hit it," Duncan told him. "Good shooting and good luck, men."

"No sweat, Captain," McDonald said.

The two SEALs hurried aft. Monkey stopped at the engine compartment and yelled for Gibbons to get his butt topside. The African-American crawled out. The two put their heads together for a quick conversation. Gibbons turned, reached into the compartment, and retrieved his carbine. Monkey pointed to the approaching patrol craft, easily visible about five miles from them. Gibbons nodded twice, strapped his carbine to his back, and scrambled up the aft mast.

Duncan looked up at Beau. "Beau, be careful. You're awful exposed up there."

"Duncan, if they hit me, they get the entire boat."

"Good luck, shipmate," Duncan said earnestly.

Duncan limped aft, moving carefully as he watched his footing along the narrow one-foot-wide walkway between the curve of the water tank and the deck edge.

Behind him, Ensign Bud Helliwell crawled up, his face scrunched in pain and bathed in sweat. Lieutenant H.J. Mc-Daniels held his belt to help her up the small ladder. Tears eased down her cheeks from the pain she was fighting to make the short trip topside. Bud let his satchel fall to the deck.

Seeing the captain moving aft, they turned to Beau. "Where do you want us?" H.J. asked, her breathing short and rapid.

"Washington, D.C., is where I want us, but you might as well sit down right where you're at. See how many times you can send the sailors on that patrol craft scurrying belowdecks. Three points for each sailor, four for an officer, and you get five points if they fall overboard. Six if a shark gets them. Winner to be determined later."

"H.J., you ever get a straight answer from Commander Pettigrew?" Bud asked.

She used Bud's good arm to ease herself down against the starboard side of the cabin. Sweat-matted hair stuck to the side of her head.

"I've known him about a week. I think a straight answer from him is like truth out of a politician. Of course, it could be he had a troubled childhood." She shut her eyes and took several deep breaths.

Helliwell coughed as he sat down. "Damn, Lieutenant, just when I was beginning to think you might be an 'all-right Joe,' you turn into a psychoanalyst like other women."

"Sorry," she fired back, grinning. "Just when I was thinking of you like a sister, you act like every other man I've known."

"How are you feeling?"

"How do you think? My hair's a mess and I've lost two nails."

They both laughed.

H.J. raised the butt of the carbine against her good shoulder and took aim at the approaching warship. She fired. Her shoulder bounced off the bulkhead, drawing a painful grunt and sending stars dancing across her vision. Her face appeared pasty for a few seconds as pain racked her.

"Watch those carbines. They kick when you least expect it. Take several deep breaths."

"I know. It must be hard to remember I'm a woman," she muttered through the pain. "It's easy to do when your nails are broken, two side teeth are missing, and you're having a bad-hair day. But the good news for us and the bad news for them," she lied, "is that I'm in the middle of PMS."

H.J. lifted her carbine again and sighted it carefully. Her tongue showed partially through her lips as she concentrated on her aim. Squinting her right eye, she leaned forward slightly, aligning the left eye with the barrel and the two sights. She braced herself for the kick this time. Gently squeezing the trigger, she fired another round.

Helliwell watched the patrol craft, and saw the tiny figure to the left of the bridge wing throw his hands into the air and tumble backward out of sight.

"Damn, H.J.! No one can do that! It's too far."

"I'm not a no one, Helliwell. I was number two at the all-military rifle championships two years ago, and the Navy Academy's leading marksman for my last three years there."

"Wish we had the winner here."

"You don't. You're stuck with me."

The patrol craft eased left, away from the water carrier. It seemed to Duncan the rifle fire had been effective. The Kebir had stopped closing the water carrier. It began maneuvering about a mile away. Zigzagging close enough for the odd rifle round, but more than close enough for their cannon.

The next shell sailed over the water carrier to impact seventy feet off the starboard bow. Water from the geyser rained over the small craft.

"Mon capitaine," Palace Guard Sergeant Boutrous said. "My men have discovered two barrels of petroleum products in the engine room. Maybe at such a time as this we should consider smoking our departure."

"Smoke screen?"

"Oui, a smoke screen," Sergeant Boutrous replied, nodding his head as if he understood the term.

"Monkey, give the Guards a hand pulling those barrels on deck."

Monkey handed his MG to McDonald and with three of the Algerians, wrestled the two barrels of kerosene onto the deck and to the stern. They shoved one to the port side and the other to starboard. Sergeant Boutrous pried the tops off both of them.

Duncan scratched his head. Good idea, if they could get it lit and build some smoke before the Algerians blew them out of the water. What he needed was time. Time for rescue and reinforcements to arrive.

"Mais oui, Mon Capitaine. C'est tres bien pour le smoke screen."

"Right! Whatever you say, Sergeant Boutrous." Duncan wet his finger and held it up. The wind was coming from aft, blowing across the boat. "Don't light it yet. If you do it'll blind us."

Duncan hurried, as fast as his injured leg allowed, to the front of the boat. He frowned when he saw H.J. and Bud. "What's wrong with you two? Can't obey orders?"

"And let you have all the fun, Captain?" Bud asked.

Duncan looked up at the exposed bridge. "Beau, bring the boat around so the wind is off the starboard bow. We're going to lay a smoke screen and hope the Algerians don't know how to fire with radar."

Bud reached in his satchel and pulled out a flag. "Captain, I've always carried this with me and we may want to fly it now."

Another shell whistled overhead, exploding twenty yards to port. McDonald and Monkey raked the fast-attack craft that had maneuvered to within five hundred yards of the boat. The Kebir rolled to port as its powerful engines moved the patrol craft out of range.

"Beau," Duncan said. "Take this and run it up the mast in front of you."

Beau reached down and took the flag from Duncan. Steering to starboard with one hand, he unwrapped the mast line with the other. A quick release of the wheel, and Beau ran the American flag up the mast. The shifting wind to starboard quickly caught the fabric. The yard-long flag snapped like a whip in the wind. Duncan glanced at the flag. A cheer from the stern of the boat erupted from the SEALs at the sight of Old Glory challenging the Algerians. They might die in the coming minutes, but the Algerians were going to know whom they were fighting.

Duncan cupped his hands to his mouth and shouted, "Light the barrels!"

The Palace Guards patted their pockets. The sergeant tugged on McDonald's shirt, making a flicking motion with his fingers. McDonald shook his head as he patted his pockets. He didn't smoke.

The Guardsmen looked at Duncan and shrugged their shoulders. Sergeant Boutros made a flicking motion to Duncan.

"Beau, we need a light!" Duncan yelled, and then added excitedly, "Flares! Beau, are flares up there somewhere?"

Keeping one hand on the helm, Beau reached down and ripped open the small doors to a storage cabinet on his left. He pulled the junk inside onto the deck.

"Here they are!" he cried. He held up a square metal tin

with a fading picture of a flare on the top of it. He pitched it down to Duncan.

Duncan caught the box and hurried aft. A cannon boom announced another inbound shell. This one exploded about thirty yards astern, sending sea spray raining down on the water carrier.

He pulled two magnesium flares from the box and tossed the residue on the deck. Duncan ambled aft, holding the magnesium flares in his left hand. He handed them to Sergeant Boutros, who popped the trigger and tossed them, one after the other, into the kerosene. Flames shot ten feet into the air before quickly disappearing. Dark black smoke billowed out as the conflagration sent waves of smoke flowing at sea level off the port side. Within seconds an impenetrable barrier hid the water carrier from the Algerian patrol craft.

A shell whistled by, splitting the aft mast in half, before it impacted off the starboard quarter. Gibbons was hurled forward off the mast like a shot from a catapult. He landed in the water twenty yards off the port bow. Beau whirled the wheel to port, aiming the bow toward Gibbons.

Gibbons floated facedown, unmoving. Thirty seconds passed before the water carrier closed the distance. Gibbons bounced off the side of the port bow of the low-riding boat, and continued to bounce along the side of the water carrier as the boat moved past. Two Guardsmen and Monkey grabbed him and pulled him aboard.

Monkey rolled his friend onto his back, touched his neck for a pulse. Feeling nothing, he tilted Gibbons's head back and began CPR. Duncan moved as fast as possible past the Guardsmen who had helped rescue Gibbons.

"Don't give up, Monkey," Duncan said. He picked up the MG-60 from the deck.

Beau estimated the direction of the smoke barrier, and changed course slightly so the water carrier paralleled the smoke screen. The engines of the Kebir could be heard oscillating wildly from the other side of the smoke as it maneuvered in its search for the water carrier. A shell exploded nearly a hundred feet off their port side. The gunners on the Algerian warship were firing blind.

Beau steered, watching the burning diesel fuel and keeping the water carrier near the smoke screen.

Duncan expected the patrol craft to appear through the smoke at any moment. Dreaded anticipation drove his anxiety. But when several minutes passed and no Kebir appeared, Duncan began to suspect that their small-arms fire had achieved its purpose and made the Algerians overcautious. So overcautious that he knew the Algerians weren't going to come charging through the smoke screen until they knew where the water carrier was. They had surface radar, so they had to have some idea where the water carrier was. Then he noticed the shoreline, and recalled that surface radar became ineffective this close to land—land smear they called it.

Gibbons coughed twice, vomited up a lungful of water, some of which went in Monkey's mouth.

Monkey spat several times. He rubbed his mouth briskly. "Hey, man, just because I saved your life don't mean you have to spew up in my mouth."

Monkey rolled Gibbons onto his side to make it easier for the SEAL petty officer to cough up the remainder of the seawater.

"That wasn't a spew, Monkey. I was kissing your ugly puss," Gibbons mumbled.

Beau turned the water carrier north and began another smoke screen at an oblique angle to the first one.

Duncan rubbed his knee, trying to ease the ache, as he watched the smoke rising from the stern. This second smoke barrier Beau was building would let the water carrier zigzag from one to the other, playing a deadly game of hide-and-seek with the Algerian patrol craft. What would they do once the kerosene burned itself out?

Another shell landed further right than the last one.

Suddenly, less than one hundred yards off their stern, the Algerian patrol craft ripped through the smoke screen. A scurry of activity broke out on its bow near the cannon with excited pointing and shouting by those on its bridge. They were as surprised as the SEALs. Algerian sailors hurried to turn the cannon toward the water carrier.

Duncan and McDonald raked the deck of the ship with

their machine guns. Two sailors fell. Duncan raised his sights and peppered the bridge. The people on the bridge of the Kebir disappeared behind the armored sides. The gunners on the forward deck twisted the cannon toward the water carrier.

No way they can miss at this distance, thought Duncan.

Beau whirled the wheel to the right, and the tiny water carrier slowly turned to port and eased into the smoke screen.

An Algerian sailor, near the cannon, grabbed his chest and tumbled backward onto the deck. The patrol craft tilted sharply to the right as the warship increased its speed just as the cannon fired.

The unexpected hard-right rudder of the Kebir threw the Algerian shot off target. The shell sailed over the water carrier and exploded directly astern, knocking Duncan, McDonald, and the Palace Guards off their feet. Monkey was hurled outward. He grabbed a line, once connected to the destroyed aft mast, and as his momentum carried him toward the edge of the deck, his firm grip brought him up short of being thrown into the sea.

Below the waterline, the explosion ruptured the caulk sealing the propeller shaft. Mediterranean seawater rushed through the crack, widening it as the pressure carved away the aged sealant. White smoke began to pour from the engine compartment as seawater flooded the engine room.

"We're losing speed!" Beau shouted. He whirled the wheel to port. The water carrier, with its waning momentum, sailed out of the smoke barrier. The slowing boat was once again separated by the smoke screen from the Algerian patrol craft.

Duncan knew they only had a few minutes before the wind dissipated the protective barriers. Without forward momentum, the smoke from the kerosene was at the whim of the light wind coming from the south. It would curl upward and mark their location rather than hide them. So much for changing his life-insurance policy.

The engine coughed, sputtered to life again for a few seconds, coughed twice more, and died. The water carrier coasted another thirty yards before it stopped.

"We're DIW, Captain!" shouted Beau. He left the wheel and scrambled down the ladder. The boat began to wallow from side to side as low waves hit it. The squeech of the radio sounded louder without the competing noise of the diesel.

Fifty yards to starboard, the first smoke screen was fading. Duncan was surprised to see the crossing southern wind carry the smoke from the burning kerosene to feed the last barrier Beau had started. But the stern was sinking, and it was only a matter of minutes before the barrels would tumble into the sea. Already seawater lapped at the bottoms of the barrels.

Ahead of them and to starboard, clear visibility reigned.

"Monkey!" Beau shouted. "Get below and hand out the life jackets!"

On the starboard side of the boat, Duncan hurried forward to where Beau stood beside H.J. and Bud.

"Well, I have to say, Duncan. This is another fine mess that you've gotten us into," Beau said, imitating the voice of the chubby member of the old Laurel and Hardy comedy team.

"I think you're right. The radio?"

Beau pointed to the bridge. From the speaker came the same steady jamming signal. "Hasn't let up. They knew we were on it and I don't expect them to give us an opportunity to get back on the air."

President Alneuf emerged from below, a bright yellow life jacket tied on him.

"Your man, Captain Duncan, does he ever take no for an answer?" President Alneuf asked as he pulled the straps on his life jacket tighter.

"Mr. President, I'm sorry, but it's only a matter of minutes before the patrol craft comes through the screen. Our engine's gone. We're taking water and we're sinking."

Overhead, a sonic boom broke the conversation as two jets roared by.

"Damn!" said Beau. "MiG-29s. Not enough the Algerian Navy is trying to blow us out of the water. Now the Algerian Air Force wants some of our ass."

"Captain!" shouted McDonald. "Look!"

From the east, at low level, another four aircraft could be seen headed inbound toward the water carrier.

"Shit! Just send their entire gawldamn Air Force at us, why don't they," griped Beau.

The two MiG-29s turned right in attack formation, and came out of the turn to line up on the water carrier.

"Well, look's who's back," Beau said, pointing to the Algerian patrol craft as it rounded the edge of the smoke screen two miles away. "At least we made them take the long way around."

A puff of smoke rose from the bow-mounted gun. The shell passed overhead and exploded harmlessly inside the fading, older smoke screen.

The stern of the water carrier entered the sea. The burning barrels of kerosene tumbled off. The smoke abruptly stopped as the barrels disappeared beneath the waves.

The MiG-29s roared in with cannons firing. Three-foot-high sea sprays marked the path as the shells rushed toward the water carrier. Two thirty-millimeter shells hit the small boat amidships, rupturing the water tank. Fresh water poured onto the deck and ran overboard. When Duncan looked up, two Guardsmen were gone. The loss of ballast caused the water carrier to rise slightly, but seawater continued to flow into the boat belowdecks.

The noise of the Kebir, as it increased speed, came across the water. The next shell missed the water carrier by less than twenty yards. Water showered the deck.

"I'd give them one more miss before that piss-poor bunch of gunners have our range," Beau said.

"Here they come again!" shouted Monkey, pointing to the two MiG-29s in another tight right turn.

A massive concussion rocked the water carrier as the Algerian patrol craft exploded. Algerian sailors jumped from its smoking hulk into burning oil that was spreading quickly across the top of the sea. Their dying screams reached the water carrier.

"What happened?"

"I don't know, but I like it. God!" Beau shouted, looking up. "Do the same with those aircraft."

The lead MiG-29 finished his turn, his wingman lined up perfectly to the right with a thirty-meter altitude separation.

With cannons firing, they bored down on the unarmed water carrier. Navy SEALs filled the air with small-arms fire.

Behind the two MiG-29s, four F/A-18 Hornets appeared over the smoke screen. Four Sidewinder missiles, already in the air, led the attack. Three of the air-to-air missiles traveled up the tailpipes of two MiG-29s. The airburst of the lead MiG sent burning debris raining into the sea and onto the water carrier. The SEALs and Palace Guards threw themselves to the deck, hands over their heads. The disintegrating wingman passed over the water carrier, spinning end over end. Duncan felt the heat as it passed overhead, barely missing the forward mast on its downward spiral. A burning cartwheel, the Algerian fighter jet slammed into the water near the Algerian Kebir, killing the few survivors who had swum clear of the burning oil.

Beau looked back up at the sky. "God, good job. Next time, could you get here a little sooner?"

The F/A-18s, gray blurs, roared past the water carrier. Duncan pulled himself up to the bridge and grabbed the microphone. The jamming signal had disappeared with the destruction of the patrol craft.

"This is Big Apple. Do you read?"

"Big Apple, this is Friendly Ranger. Nice reception committee you had for us."

"Are you the F/A 18 pilots above us?"

"No, we're the four-engine-jobber that took out that ship. We're just a little old EP-3E four-engine turboprop, trying to make do in a jet-engine world. We're heading in now. What is your situation?"

"We're dead in the water. Sinking slowly. I estimate about ten minutes before we're treading water."

"That's not too good. We're about seven minutes out."

The Hornets flew by wiggling their wings.

"I forgive them for Tailhook," H.J. said, crossing herself.

"Tailhook hell! I may kiss my first man when I see them," Beau added.

"Never can tell, Commander. Some of those pilots may be women."

"They can have head-of-the-line privilege."

"Big Apple, we'll drop a life raft, water, and food. Rescue

is on its way. Two Royal Navy helicopters are inbound to provide transport back to the bird farm. Should have you out of there within the hour and back on board, sipping hot soup."

"Hey, Duncan! Ask them if we can go to a British ship. I feel like something stronger than Navy coffee."

Duncan grinned at Beau. "We won't be on the ship long enough to have a cup of coffee before they have us out and headed toward some recovery site ashore."

Beau reached in his back pocket and handed Duncan his handkerchief.

"What's this for?"

"Your cheek."

"My cheek?" He touched the right side of his face, bringing away a hand bathed in blood. "How did that happen?"

"I have no idea, Captain. It's not like we've been doing anything dangerous."

Duncan pressed the gray handkerchief against the wound. Just what he needed, another scar on his face. He looked down at Beau's legs and pointed.

Beau didn't look. "Flesh wound, Captain. Just a damn flesh wound."

"If it's a flesh wound, then why the tourniquet?"

"Latest fashion."

"What happened?"

"I think I stopped some shrapnel from that first MiG run. We were lucky. My leg stopped it before it could damage the boat. I've looked. It sliced the pants and the leg, but I'd say the pants look worse than the leg."

"Sit down here with H.J. and Bud until the helicopters arrive."

"Sure thing, Captain. Where do you want to sit?"

"I can't."

"Then don't ask me to. Besides, if everyone wounded sat down, there wouldn't be room for anyone to stand."

Duncan shaded his eyes as he looked to the north. A silhouette of an EP-3E grew against the clear sky. The black bulbous radar dome beneath its fuselage made it easy to identify. "I think I have a visual on you, Friendly Ranger," Duncan said into the microphone.

"Roger, Big Apple, stand by for your drop. You can rest a

little. Those F/A-18 fighter jocks are your personal combat air patrol until the helicopters arrive. They are taking requests—barrel rolls, combat turns, and formation aerobatics—whatever you need and there are more on their way. One moment, Big Apple."

A minute passed before the EP-3E aircraft returned to the emergency frequency. "Big Apple, Sixth Fleet wants to know if you have the package you were sent to retrieve."

Duncan looked at President Alneuf, who stood with the remainder of the Palace Guards. "Yeah, we have it," he said slowly. "And it's in good condition and ready for pickup."

"Roger, stand by, here we come, but no barrel rolls with this bird."

The EP-3E roared overhead, its four turboprops vibrating the water carrier. A single Harpoon missile remained under the port wing. Friendly Ranger had sunk the patrol craft from over the horizon without ever seeing the target. Sneaky bastards—thank God.

Duncan pushed the transmitter. "Friendly Ranger, how did you know which one was the target when you fired?"

"Didn't, Big Apple, but figured we had a fifty-percent chance of hitting the right one and you said they had the higher profile. Plus, with you sinking, we knew your cross section would be even smaller."

"Yeah, but what if you had missed and hit us?"

"Well, Big Apple, as you probably noticed, we had a second Harpoon if we had missed."

The bright orange number-three life raft tumbled from the rear door of the aircraft, inflating as it fell. It hit the sea fifty feet from the water carrier.

"Big Apple, be careful with the life raft. That's the second one the squadron's given up in a week and AirLant is looking for someone to pay for them."

"Tell them to send the bill to me."

"Don't say that too loud, Big Apple. One of their budget weenies will hear you and do just that."

McDonald handed his MG to the recovering Gibbons and dove into the water. A half minute later he pulled himself into the orange life raft.

McDonald pulled an oar from beneath a panel and paddled

the large life raft to the boat. The stern of the water carrier was awash now.

Duncan decided the water carrier would go down quickly when it went and it could go any second. Not the minutes he'd thought they had.

As the life raft bumped the water carrier amidships, Duncan yelled, "Come on, everyone! We're going home."

He hung up the microphone and worked his way to where Beau was helping H.J. and Helliwell pull themselves up.

"I guess the Fort Myers officer club will breathe easier now."

CHAPTER 13

⚓

ONE HOUR AFTER DUNCAN AND HIS TEAM WERE RESCUED, the evacuation of Algiers began.

"Afternoon, Clive. How's Captain James and his team?" Admiral Cameron asked his chief of staff as he walked up to the plotting table. Captain Jacobs, the fleet surgeon, had quit shadowing the admiral sometime during the past two days as the Iron Leader rapidly recovered from his wounds.

The low murmur of the officers and sailors manning the blue-lighted staff combat information center filled the background. The intelligence officer, Commander Mulligan, moved around the table to give the two superior officers room to stand beside each other.

"Afternoon, Admiral," Clive Bowen replied. "Captain James and his team are safely on board USS *Stennis* confined to medical. The surgeon says everyone has a wound of some sort. Lieutenant McDaniels, the woman SEAL, is the most serious, but none of them are critical. That being said, they'll be in sick bay for a while for their wounds and exhaustion. The N2 on board *Stennis* is going to start debriefing the team members as soon as the doctors finish their work. It'll take a couple of hours for the initial story, so I have asked Intell to focus on what happened to Chief Judiah and events surrounding President Alneuf. What we know is that Chief Judiah was killed when he and an Algerian officer blew up a pier to keep attacking rebels from overrunning them."

"Clive, I want to read the report when it's done and before it's transmitted out of theater. Are they going to remain on board the aircraft carrier for the time being?"

"*Stennis* intends to medevac them to Naples sometime tomorrow."

"What's the arrangements?"

"Helo to Sigonella and ASCOMED to Naples. Ambulance will meet them."

"Good. They're lucky to be alive. On the subject of President Alneuf, I talked with Admiral Sir Ledderman-Thompson about twenty minutes ago and asked that the Algerian president and party be transferred to the *Stennis*. He refused. I still fail to see how they could have done what they did. It's not like the British. As far back as I can remember, it's the first time we kept secrets from each other." He paused. "Well, maybe not the first time, but this is our Navies we're talking about!"

Captain Bowen agreed. "Admiral, I'm as perplexed as you are. The British split the group apart—SEALs in one helicopter and Algerians in the other. The helicopter with our SEALs airlifted Captain James and team to *Stennis*; the British flew President Alneuf and his party direct to the HMS *Invincible*. I followed up your conversation with Admiral Sir Ledderman-Thompson with his chief of staff, a Captain Battleton, a few minutes ago. He told me, in a syrupy posh accent that made me think he was looking down his nose at me, that they were honoring a request from President Alneuf for asylum. I told him we also promised Alneuf asylum at his request and we were the ones who sent a rescue team in country."

Clive ran his hand through his short, wiry gray hair. "Bottom line, Admiral Cameron, is we're not going to solve this. It's way above our heads. Our governments will have to iron it out. Captain Battleton concurs. Their hands are tied without further guidance from CinCFleet."

"That's bullshit! President Alneuf contacted us for rescue. That weasel played us and the British against each other. Now

that Alneuf is safely out of his gone-to-shit country, he's
telling us he wants to go to Britain?" Admiral Cameron asked
incredulously. "Who the hell does Alneuf think he is?"

"Yes, sir, I feel the same way, but the CIA agreement was
that he could go anywhere he wanted after we got him out. I
guess he either took us at our word or wanted to test if we
would honor it. Captain Battleton says that MI-5 contacted
them and that their instructions came from the highest levels
of government. He assures me that the Royal Navy is only
acting on orders from their ministry of defense. I believe
him."

"But how do we know for sure that the British didn't take
him against his wishes? Has anyone talked with Alneuf?"

Clive Bowen shook his head. "No, sir. I haven't, but this is
the Royal Navy, not the British government, and if they tell us
Alneuf asked them for asylum, I would say they're telling the
truth. Or the truth as they know it." Clive shook his head.
"Christ, sir, it's the Royal Navy."

Admiral Cameron sighed. "Yeah, you're right, Clive. These
last ten days have made me more than a little paranoid. Regardless, we need to hear it from President Alneuf's own lips.
Ask the British for permission to send someone over to interview President Alneuf. Let me know if you need me to talk
personally with Admiral Sir Ledderman-Thompson."

"Aye, aye, Admiral. I don't foresee any problems if we do
it before Washington and Whitehall get involved. I've already
asked Captain Battleton, and he is discussing the issue with
Admiral Sir Ledderman-Thompson. He thinks there should
be no problem with us interviewing President Alneuf."

"Good. At least when Washington starts raining on our pa-
rade, we'll be in a position to report exactly what the president of Algeria wants, or at least says. Take one of those
voice-actuated recorders I've seen in the ship's store. That
way we can truthfully tell them, verbatim, why he prefers
London to Washington. We may trust the Royal Navy, but our
government won't. Clive, tell me how can he prefer London
over Washington," Admiral Cameron said earnestly. Then, realizing what he'd said, he grinned.

"You're right. We have to phrase that question a little differently. Once we've talked directly with Alneuf, it'll help keep Washington off our backs."

"Yes, sir, I'll take care of that ASAP. Meanwhile, Admiral, the two LCACs arrived in Algiers harbor about thirty minutes ago. They are prepared to load the evacuees upon arrival. Colonel Stewart, commander of the amphibious landing force, has four Cobra gunships orbiting just outside the harbor, but in visual sight of the armed Algerians who have surrounded the pier."

"What's the situation in the harbor?"

"According to Bulldog . . ."

"Bulldog?"

"Sorry, Admiral. They call Colonel Stewart 'Bulldog.'"

"Why doesn't that surprise me—a Marine Corps colonel called Bulldog."

"According to Colonel Stewart the Algerians refuse to discuss the evacuation. What we have is a standoff where everyone knows why we are there, but refuses to admit it. On the positive side, the Algerians aren't firing at us, nor have they tried to obstruct Colonel Stewart securing the harbor. I think they want the same thing we do—for us to load our people and leave Algiers as soon as possible."

"Then we both have the same objective. When are the evacuees leaving the embassy?"

"The Algerian transport trucks arrived a few minutes ago and the evacuees are climbing into them now. Should be heading toward the harbor within the next few minutes. Ambassador Becroft will ride in her armored sedan at the front of the convoy. There is a Marine radioman with her and he has a direct link with Colonel Stewart. The Marine security force and the added fire teams are dispersed throughout the twenty-five military trucks, carrying the six-hundred-plus evacuees. That's about two Marines per truck. Not really enough. If anything happens, then we're—"

The speaker in Combat rattled to life. "Sixth Fleet, this is LCAC One with relay from commander, amphibious landing force. The Algerians have informed us that the convoy has departed the embassy en route to the harbor. Colonel Stewart has informed them that we will be sending helicopters to assist as LCACs alone will be unable to complete the evacuation by nightfall. The Algerians told him to wait until they get permission. Colonel Stewart has informed them that this was not a request and that permission was not required."

The red telephone near Admiral Cameron and Captain Bowen rang. Commander Mulligan leaned over and picked it up. "Commander Mulligan here."

He listened, acknowledged the voice on the other end, and hung up. "Admiral," Mulligan said. "Ambassador Becroft has notified Colonel Stewart that the convoy is en route. That confirms what the Algerians told him."

"Thanks," the admiral replied, almost absentmindedly. He ran his hand through his hair. He looked up, biting his lower lip.

Clive recognized the pensiveness. He had seen it too many times in too many exercises and operations. Something was bothering the three-star admiral. Clive believed that he and Admiral Cameron made a good team. He knew he handled the immediate tasks at hand and handled them well. Unlike a lot of chiefs of staff, he tried not to wear his master's rank to an extreme.

Admiral Cameron was like a master chess player whose thoughts were always several events ahead of the action. He continuously rolled things around in his mind, looking for those crucial moves to ensure victory, or moves that toss a monkey wrench into an operation.

Clive would be surprised if they hadn't overlooked something. Navy-Marine Corps operations were complex, convoluted, and evolved at a rapid pace. Most revolved around a "get in quick, get out fast" type of strategy. But no matter how well they planned or how many times they exercised, Murphy's Law still lived. Beanballs were waiting to be thrown. Rakes were waiting to be stepped on. Monkey wrenches were waiting to trip. All hurt when they hit. It was what, Clive thought, made Navy and Marine Corps officers a cut above the rest; being able to handle the unexpected.

Clive leaned over and put both hands on the plotting table as he surveyed the order of deployed forces. He kept quiet. The admiral would tell him when he thought of anything. And *he* would tell the admiral if *he* did.

He looked around Combat. His mind filtered the myriad of

operational orders and information flowing through the battle staff. Clive soaked in the data, allowing it to create a mental image of ongoing events ashore. The air tactical net had four Harriers in a low-level combat air patrol just over the horizon out of view of the Algerians. All were armed with air-to-surface missiles and free-fall bombs. The Cobra attack helicopters orbited at varied altitudes, their weapons trained on the Algerians. Marines surrounding the LCACs had their safeties on, but ready to engage at a moment's notice, and wandering, ramrod straight, in the immediate vicinity of the LCACs, was Bulldog Stewart.

The Marine Corps colonel was probably more intimidating to the Algerians than all the firepower directed against them.

Twenty nautical miles northwest of the evacuation zone, F/A-18 Hornets wove an angry pattern, waiting impatiently for when they were needed. There was little the ships could do at this juncture. Everything rested with the Marines and airpower. Ground forces won wars. All military leaders knew that. All the airpower could do was influence the outcome.

Clive recognized the voice of Admiral Pete Devlin, Commander Fleet Air Mediterranean, on the tactical surface net. Admiral Devlin had arrived on USS *Stennis* yesterday to assume command of the carrier battle group. The admiral's prominent Alabama accent informed Sixth Fleet that eight F/A-18 Hornets were joining the TacAir picture of Sixth Fleet. That put twelve of them in the air. The operation called for the Hornets to take out the Algerian Air Force by destroying the bases around Algiers if anything happened during the evacuation. Pete Devlin had been a close friend and Academy classmate of Admiral Prang. It had been Admiral Devlin who had identified the bodies and handled the car bombing in Naples days ago when the senior U.S. Navy admiral in Europe was killed. It was the same day terrorists attacked Admiral Cameron and his staff during a social gathering at a local bistro in Gaeta, Italy, killing the admiral's wife.

The Algerians could expect no mercy from Admiral Devlin if Cameron gave him permission to unleash his Naval air. There would be no Algerian Air Force within two hours from the time "execute" was given.

The United States Air Force RC-135 Rivet Joint fed another sitrep to Sixth Fleet. Clive leaned forward and ran his finger over the chart taped down to the plotting table. Orbiting near the RC-135 were six United States Air Force F-16 Fighting Falcons and a KC-135 tanker. If airpower had to be employed, it would be a joint Navy–Air Force action. The Falcons had chopped to Sixth Fleet twenty minutes ago after topping off from the tanker, and were on their way to a combat action station east of Algiers. He now had the Algerian capital bracketed by United States fighter aircraft.

The near-empty CH-46s and CH-53s from the amphibious task force were en route to the harbor area. The helicopters would be within visual range of the Marines any second.

So far, everything had been tense, but textbook-perfect. Even so, like the contemplating admiral, something nagged at the back of Clive's mind. Something they should be considering. The fog of battle, which Clausewitz had so eloquently defined, always grew thicker with every passing minute of an operation. Time increased the confusion factor. It definitely increased anxiety.

"Clive," the admiral said, interrupting his chief of staff's thoughts. "Do the Algerians know about our fight a couple of hours ago with their Navy and MiGs?"

That was it—the monkey wrench. A cold shiver ran up his spine. "I don't see how they couldn't, Admiral. We shot down two MiGs and sunk a Kebir patrol craft. Someone ashore has to know."

"I know that, Clive. But what I'm saying is, has this information reached Algiers? We know their command, control, and communications C3 system is in disarray. If this information hasn't reached Algiers, what will happen when the Algerian military commanders are informed? Especially if they find out before those evacuees reach the staging area where we can protect them? Will the Algerians react negatively? Are we getting any national intelligence help? Is NSA giving us any data on this?"

"No, sir," Commander Mulligan replied. "All of their resources are focused in support of the Korean situation. We don't meet their threshold of concern. But even if we did, they aren't geared to this type of action. Any tactical support we have to produce ourselves."

"What are the cryppies getting up in their spaces?"

As if hearing his name, the Sixth Fleet cryptologic officer burst into Combat. "Admiral, we've got problems."

The chill spread across Clive's shoulders. This was not good. Whenever a cryptologic officer showed up from "behind the green door," like Joe Rochefort of Midway fame, then something was up and that something was usually bad. Clive shut his eyes momentarily and shook his head. He saw the sweat pouring down the commander's face and recognized the emotion in the voice. *Wonder if Joe Rochefort acted the same way when he told Nimitz about Midway?*

"What is it?" Admiral Cameron asked, a slight tremble in his voice.

The admiral already knew, Clive realized.

"Algerian troops have been given orders to stop the convoy. They are already en route to turn the evacuees back and to force our troops out."

"To hell with them," Admiral Cameron replied. Even in the darkened Combat spaces, Clive saw the red of anger shoot up the admiral's face. "Clive, call Colonel Stewart and the ambassador. Give them a heads-up, but tell them they are to continue forward. Let's hope it's a bluff. Either way we continue."

"Admiral," the cryptologic officer said. "The Algerians are authorized to use force if we refuse to follow their orders. They have permission to open fire. I don't think it is a bluff. These are fanatics we are dealing with, sir. Admiral, with all due respect, in about ten minutes you can expect the convoy to come under fire."

"Admiral," Clive added softly. "We have over six hundred unarmed civilians protected by fifty-six Marines. They have another five miles to the harbor. If the Algerians attack the convoy, then it'll be a massacre. We don't have the forces ashore to protect them."

The admiral looked at his cryptologic officer. "How sure are you of this information?"

"I'd give it high credibility, Admiral. There's no reason for the Algerians to spoof us on this. I estimate ten minutes maximum, sir, and then you're going to have dead Americans on your hands."

"I'd say thirty minutes, Admiral," Commander Mulligan, the intelligence officer, said. "The nearest Algerian garrison is less than five miles from the embassy. If the troops are bivouacked there, they are probably in alert status, which I am sure they are with American Marines at the harbor. Thirty minutes is a more reasonable time for them to hit the convoy."

"And the minimum time?"

"Minimum time is any minute now."

The cryptologic officer nodded in agreement. "Unfortunately, Admiral, not all of the Algerian troops are bivouacked in their garrisons. Most are already deployed."

The intelligence officer gave his cryptologic counterpart a fierce look.

Admiral Cameron turned to his chief of staff. "Clive, get more Marines in there. I'm not going to abandon those people. If the Algerians want a fight, then they've come to the right place."

"Yes, sir. The USS *Nassau* prepositioned their 46s and 53s as soon as the Harriers launched. Marines are already on board, in hot standby. We have another hundred in battle gear for a second wave, if we need them."

"Then launch them. Tell Colonel Stewart to expect additional forces. How many Marines do we have ashore at the staging area?"

"About eighty, sir."

"Good, tell him to expand the corridor. The Algerians at the harbor may be unaware of the orders about the convoy. If they are, then we had better find out on our terms and not theirs. Tell the Marines to lock and load. Colonel Stewart has permission to use force as he sees fit."

He turned to the cryptologic officer. "I hope you're right, Commander."

"Yes, sir," the cryptologic officer replied. "I hope I'm not," he mumbled to himself.

"Commander, what is the situation in the harbor?" the admiral continued.

"Best we have on the harbor situation, Admiral, is that the Algerians there are regulars and the group heading toward the convoy are rebel fundamentalists. Those at the harbor have been ordered to neither hinder nor cooperate with the Americans. If that is, in fact, their orders and we try to move out, they should stand aside and allow it." The cryptologic officer crossed his fingers and said a prayer to Joe Rochefort, the saint of cryppies.

"Good! Let's find out. Clive, tell Colonel Stewart to inform the Algerians that we are sending a force forward to meet the convoy and escort them through the lines to the LCAC. Keep the Algerian regulars in the dark as long as possible. Jam their radios. Tell Bulldog to do it even if it involves hostile engagement."

"Aye, aye, Admiral," Clive responded.

The anxiety of imminent hostilities settled over the darkened spaces of Combat like a widow's cowl. The noise level decreased further as professionalism drove the watch-standers to an increased level of concentration.

"Clive, I want Devlin's F/A-18s to overfly our forces in the harbor and the convoy. Tell them to expect a hostile reception. Tell the Cobras to close the convoy and take up a defensive protective corridor around the trucks, and if attacked, they are to respond accordingly. Direct the Harriers to the harbor to provide protection there. If necessary, we'll send them in to support the convoy."

"With your permission, Admiral, I would like to return to the cryptologic spaces."

"Permission granted, Commander. Keep me up to date. And, Commander, good job. Go ahead and notify Washington of what's happening."

"Already done, sir," the cryptologic officer replied as he saluted. He then hurried out of Combat, leaving Commander Mulligan behind to support the intelligence needs of the admiral. Intelligence needs hindered by national resources targeted half a world away, leaving the European command blind except for its own tactical cryptologic and intelligence resources. Mulligan grimaced at the thought of the cryptologic officer's teasing comment a month ago that the Naval intelligence triangle was "CNN, *USA Today,* and cryptology." Why can't those cryppies stay in their box? Cryptologists' job was to bring the information to him. He'd decide whether to pass it on or not. But, no, they wanted credit for every damn thing they did.

PAUL MCMILLAN, THE CIA AGENT, PULLED HIMSELF aboard the third truck in the convoy as it moved slowly past. He patted the shoulder of a young Marine he recognized from the embassy security force. He couldn't recall the Marine's name, though he should know it as many times as they had chatted.

"Glad to be out of there, Corporal?" he asked, jerking his thumb back toward the abandoned embassy.

"You know it, Mr. McMillan. I can think of many other places to be, and every one of them is better than Algiers." The Marine's eyes searched the area as he spoke.

Paul sat down on the wooden bench that paralleled the side of the green Algerian Army vehicle.

"Just think, you'll have one hell of a story to tell your grandkids someday."

"Just hope that I've reached the end of the tale. I've had all the sickness, frustration, anxiety, and fear I care to add to any story I would ever tell."

Paul laughed. "You're still young, plenty of time to add some colorful sides to the story. Try to relax a little. Another thirty minutes and we'll be at the harbor." He pushed his graying hair out of his eyes.

"Aren't you scared?" the young Marine asked softly.

"Scared? I'm petrified," Paul replied, nodding his head. "And I'll stay that way until I'm on board one of our Navy ships. Funny, isn't it, how much we forget about you guys until something like this happens."

The truck jerked as its revved-up engine engaged the second gear, and the speed increased to five miles an hour. Only six miles to the rendezvous point.

"Whoa," Paul said, grabbing the Marine by the belt to keep the young man from falling off the rear. "Grab hold of the side or sit down, Corporal. Won't do to have you fall out this close to rescue." Paul nodded at the Algerian driver in the truck following. "Don't think he'd stop if you fell out."

The Marine corporal eased himself onto the edge of the wooden bench. Paul knew the Marine couldn't be comfortable sitting like that. Made his butt hurt just thinking about it.

Paul studied the corporal's face. Marines made you feel

safe. The corporal's eyes never ceased searching the surrounding area. Where would America be without them?

The convoy moved from the open area in front of the embassy into the city street, where dark, silent buildings on both sides closed like a haunted forest in a fairy tale filled with ghosts and goblins. The corporal's fingers twitched nervously on the M-16 as he scanned the quiet buildings and grayshrouded streets.

Paul pinched his nose to stifle a sneeze. *So this is how a cornered rabbit feels.* He recalled the hunts in North Carolina with his dogs, and the rabbits he brought home time after time. He didn't think he'd ever hunt again after this. He opened and shut his mouth several times, trying to assuage the dryness. He wished he'd remembered to bring his bottle of water. Thirty more minutes; forty-five at this rate.

Fifteen minutes later the last truck in the convoy entered the maze of buildings as they inched their way toward the harbor. The grinding of gears, the noise of racing diesel engines, and the smell of bad exhausts filled the air.

The Marine looked at Paul and smiled. Paul was a station CIA agent who masqueraded as a State Department political analyst; not that it fooled anyone inside or outside the embassy. The corporal knew Paul was armed. Fifty-six Marines to guard six hundred plus people! What were they thinking?

Along the route, shops and darkened apartments hid behind boarded windows and pulled shades. Little chinks of missing plaster and bricks decorated the walls of the buildings where bullets and shells left evidence of how violent the revolution had been. "Looks like a city with smallpox," Paul said to the corporal as the noisy trucks continued their trek through the otherwise silent city.

Paul looked at his watch. Another twenty minutes and they would be at the harbor area. He'd feel a hell of lot better when they arrived. Another eighty jarheads waited there. He watched the Marine wipe his sweating palms on his pants leg, and did the same.

"How you doing, Corporal?"

"I'm okay. Mr. McMillan, when I get to that harbor where the other Marines are, I'm gonna kiss every one of them—

unless it's a gunny sergeant. No one kisses gunny sergeants and lives." He grinned.

Paul laughed. "Know how you feel. I may join you."

The *"whump-whump-whump"* of helicopters caused the corporal to point his M-16 skyward. The light-green silhouette of two Marine Cobra gunships passed overhead. Paul touched him on the shoulder as they watched. "What a beautiful sight!"

The helmet deflected the bullet, causing it to ricochet downward into the corporal's temple and out the right eye. Brain and bone parts splattered Paul and several of the other evacuees. Two mothers reflexively threw themselves over their children. The crowded truck hampered movement, causing everyone to knock each other around as they fought for the bed of the truck. Ignoring the screams, Paul instinctively drew his pistol and fired several shots at a window on the third floor where he thought he saw movement. He pushed the young Marine corporal to the floor.

"Oh, son, so sorry. So sorry," Paul mumbled, his hand touching the dead Marine, but his eyes remained fixed on the building. He had seen death enough to recognize it. It affected him more as he grew older and recognized his own mortality.

Firing erupted simultaneously from the buildings, raking the convoy. Ahead, a light armored car pulled across the street and blocked the convoy's route. Snipers fired into the mass of unarmed humanity, scoring hit after hit. The Marines returned fire at the unseen enemy. Many jumped from the trucks and took cover near the rear of each.

Paul holstered his pistol and grabbed the dead corporal's M-16. Along with two other Marines in the truck, Paul sent a burst at the surrounding buildings that stood like silent sentinels of death hanging over the stalled convoy. New pockets of missing plaster and brick joined the earlier ones.

A Cobra helicopter whirled around at the top of the buildings; stopping directly over Paul's truck, the downdraft blew dirt and debris into the air, causing everyone to shut their eyes. A missile blasted forward from the helicopter, its heat felt by the occupants beneath it. Ahead of the convoy the missile hit the armored car. The vehicle exploded, sending a shower of burning metal raining down around it. The Cobra roared up and over the buildings.

The Algerian drivers jumped from the trucks and ran, leaving the occupants to their fate.

Paul grabbed a Marine near him. "Get in the truck and drive!"

A spray of sniper fire hit the center of the truck bed, killing a woman and wounding the two children under her. Cries and screams rose from every truck to join the chaos of combat. Two men in the back of Paul's truck tried to jump down.

"Stay!" Paul yelled. "You get out now and you're dead! Your only chance is to stay put."

They looked at Paul and each other. The older man sat back onto the floor of the truck while the other jumped down, dodged around the side of the vehicle, and ran several steps before bullets riddled him. The body hit the side of the truck and rolled into the street.

The Marine ran to the opened driver's door. A bullet hit him in the arm as he hoisted himself into the seat. The impact knocked the Marine into the cab.

"You okay?" Paul shouted.

The other Marine fired a burst at the window where the sniper hid. A cry came from inside.

"Sure, I'm okay!" the Marine driver shouted through gritted teeth. "It's only a fucking arm wound. I've got two arms. Who the hell needs two!" The truck was idling, the motor left running by the fleeing driver.

At every truck, Marines fought their way to the driver's seats. Out of sight of the convoy, Paul heard the sounds of Cobra gunships and Algerian forces exchanging fire. He wasn't a soldier or a Marine, but he knew if they stayed there they'd die, or worse. He had seen enough atrocities by Algerian rebels to know what waited for those who survived. The choice for Paul was easy—the harbor or death.

"We can't move until they move in front of us!" the Marine shouted from the cab as he wrapped a tourniquet around his arm.

Paul jumped up and ran forward toward the steel-sided car where the ambassador and several of her staff rode.

The front two wheels were gone, probably shot away by the

armored car when it blocked the street. Two vehicles blocked the convoy's path—the ambassador's car and the burning hulk of the Algerian armored vehicle. At the first truck, directly behind the ambassador's car, Paul leaned into the bed.

"Marines!" he shouted. "I need one of you to help me with the ambassador. You!" He pointed at the one nearest the cab. "Keep us covered!"

The Marine near the rear jumped out. It was Captain Edgar Banks, the Marine security force officer in charge. "Let's go, Paul."

As they ran by the door of the cab, Paul leaned in. "Driver, when I give the signal, you gun the engine and push the car out of the road and keep going as fast as you can toward the harbor. Don't stop for anyone until you get there."

The driver looked at Captain Banks, who nodded. "Do it, Private."

"Yes, sir!" the Marine shouted.

Captain Banks ran ahead of Paul. He was helping the disheveled ambassador out by the time Paul ran up.

"Come on, ma'am. We've got to get you to the truck," Captain Banks said.

She nodded, said thank you, and passed out.

Paul, breathing heavily, asked, "How is she?"

"No wounds. I think she's just stunned." Captain Banks picked her up and threw her over his shoulder. Paul helped the other three members of her staff out of the car. They seemed slightly dazed, but alive. Paul hurried them to the truck, where those in back pulled them on board. Someone lightly slapped the ambassador, trying to bring her around.

The Marine guard in the car pulled himself out. Dazed, he walked shakily back to the truck as bullets tore up the road around him, miraculously missing. He shook his head to clear it.

"Sergeant!" Captain Banks shouted to the Marine as he jerked him out of the road and behind the truck. "Get in back with the ambassador. Keep your head down and stay with her."

The career Marine nodded and crawled silently into the truck.

Captain Banks gave a thumbs-up to Paul, who waved the

truck forward. A bullet whizzed by Paul's ear, so close he felt the breeze and the heat as it passed. He threw himself to the street, rolled to the right, and fired. A fresh pain in his shoulder told him the impact had been harder than he expected. He had no target, but firing made him feel better.

Thinking Paul was shot, Captain Banks rushed to the prone CIA agent. He touched Paul on the shoulder, saw he was unharmed, and commenced scanning the windows overhead.

Captain Banks said, "Won't ever kill anyone that way, Paul. Don't waste your bullets if you don't know what you're shooting at." He gripped the CIA agent by the sport coat and pulled, more than helped, him up.

The two rushed to a nearby doorway as the truck eased forward, gears grinding to push the disabled car. The car slid off to one side as the truck eased forward. The metal ground against the surface of the road as the truck pushed it into a nearby alleyway. Twenty feet ahead, the armored car blocked the road.

The truck moved forward; its bumper made contact with the burning Algerian armored car, and stopped. The Marine driver raised his hand to shield his face from the flames. He gave the truck gas, the engine revved, and the burning hulk began to move ever so slowly. The people in the back shifted to the right side to put as much room as possible between them and the flames of the burning vehicle. Then, suddenly, the armored car was out of the way and the truck was past. Clear of the obstructions, the engine revved up as the truck sped off at nearly seven miles an hour down the road toward the harbor.

"Come on, Paul," Captain Banks said. "Let's practice our running and grab a lift. I don't relish the idea of spending another night in Algeria, and definitely not out here."

"Run?" Paul asked with short, breathless pants. "I'm State Department. We don't run."

"Yeah, and I'm FBI and we do. Let's go!" He grabbed Paul by the pants and with a quick tug, the muscular Marine jerked him up.

The two ran the twenty feet to the nearest truck, rolling slowly past, where two Marines hoisted them aboard. Several wounded and dead evacuees lay about the bed. Captain Banks and Paul fell into the back of the truck as the Marines returned the gunfire from the buildings.

"There, Paul, we made—" Captain Banks said. A bullet hit him in the chest, sending the Marine flying across the truck to land on top of several cowering civilians.

A Marine near the front let loose a tattoo of automatic fire at the window where the shot originated. A body crashed through the remaining glass to fall ignominiously on the street and roll under the front wheel of the truck behind them.

Paul bent down and touched the neck of the Marine captain. His heart was still beating, but Edgar was unconscious.

Paul turned his attention to the surrounding buildings. What would America do now? Korea in flames and now Algeria. He knew what would happen. It happened in World War II. It happened in Korea years ago. So many times in history countries had underestimated America. We'd respond. Hell, yes, we'd respond, but Paul knew it wouldn't happen overnight. F/A-18s roared by overhead, followed by four Harriers that hovered over the convoy firing their cannons at unseen targets to the left. America would come armed for vengeance. But with the size of the military today, it would take time.

An explosion ahead knocked Paul to the bed of the truck. The lead truck burned. Those still alive jumped from the back, their clothes aflame. Their screams carried the length of the convoy. The convoy stopped once again.

Overhead two CH-46s roared in. Ropes cascaded out of the helicopters. United States Marines followed as they hot-roped into the battle and onto tops of the surrounding buildings. Paul saw a couple of the Marines, during their quick journey down the ropes, toss hand grenades through nearby windows. Within minutes another thirty-six Marines were on the street. The two Ch-46s disappeared, to be replaced by a CH-53. Along the sides of the streets leading toward the convoy, Paul saw shadowy figures coming around the edge of the burning convoy truck. Sweat broke out anew on his forehead and he wiped it off. Then he breathed a sigh of relief when he saw they were Marines, not Algerians. The Marines came out of the smoke like specters, their guns blazing as building by building they drove the rebels back. He looked behind him, trying to see the end of the convoy that was lost in the smoke, twists, and turns of the street. The gunfire from back there told him some sort of battle was going on.

He never heard the bullet. One moment he was watching the approaching Marines, the next he was against the cab of the truck on top of a woman crouching there. She eased him off her, ripped her dress, and pressed the simple compress against the shoulder wound.

"Don't move," she whispered.

He put his hand over hers and relaxed. "Your powers of persuasion have convinced me, miss."

All along the convoy, United States Marines hurried the evacuees out of the trucks. Sporadic fire from the buildings tapered off as the Marines did what Marines do best. Dead and wounded enemy soon outnumbered the casualties of the evacuation. Marine fire teams rushed from one building to the next, lobbing grenades into each, and then following the explosions inside with rifles on semiautomatic fire. Prisoners were not being taken.

The evacuees, most with vacant stares, followed the Marines as they fought through the smoke and smell of battle toward the harbor. Two embassy men helped Paul out of the truck.

Paul looked back to where two Marines crowded around Captain Banks. One shouted for a corpsman, who ran by Paul to jump into the truck. Paul wanted to find out Banks's condition, but the two men pulled him forward. Paul leaned on them as they started north. He hoped the brave Marine lived. Paul looked up as another formation of helicopters filled with Marines roared past. *Well, Algeria, you've done it. You've unleashed the Pandora's box of America's might.*

Those were not frightened faces on the Marines hurrying by him toward the sounds of battle at the rear of the convoy. They were angry faces. Determined faces. Faces of America's youth.

Paul fell forward. The two men grabbed him before he hit the pavement. As Paul faded into unconsciousness, the thought came to him that America had arrived and it was angry.

SOMETHING EXPLODED IN THE SKY...

...something metallic, something swirling, something from hell. Four dark beasts filled the southeastern horizon like the lions of the Apocalypse. The reflection of morning light off the sand splayed like blood across their wings...

HOGS: GOING DEEP
by James Ferro

__0-425-16856-5/$5.99

Also Available:

__*Hogs #2: Hog Down*   0-425-17039-X/$5.99

__*Hogs #3: Fort Apache* 0-425-17306-2/$5.99

__*Hogs #4: Snake Eaters* 0-425-17815-3/$5.99

PATRICK A. DAVIS
THE GENERAL

ONE MAN STANDS BETWEEN CONSPIRACY AND TRUTH—IF HE CAN LIVE LONG ENOUGH TO SOLVE A MURDER....

❏ 0-425-16804-2/$6.99

"DAVIS IS THE REAL THING." —W.E.B. Griffin

"A hard-hitting, no-holds-barred novel of mystery, suspense, and betrayal." —Nelson DeMille

"A gung-ho military thriller...lots of action."
—*Kirkus Reviews*

"The mystery is puzzling, the action is intense, and I could not stop turning the pages."
—Phillip Margolin

MARINE SNIPER

Charles Henderson

The incredible story of the remarkable Marine, Carlos
Hathcock, continues—with harrowing new stories of a man
who rose to greatness not for personal gain or glory, but
for duty and honor. This is a rare inside look at the U.S.
Marine's most challenging missions—and the man who
made military history.

☐ 0-425-18172-3/$14.00